SEVEN SEAS ENTERTAINMENT PRESENTS

SERVAMP

story and art by TANAKASTRIKE

VOLUME 17

TRANSLATION
Wesley Bridges

LETTERING
Courtney Williams

COVER DESIGN
Nicky Lim

PROOFREADER
Krista Grandy

SENIOR EDITOR
Shanti Whitesides

PRODUCTION DESIGNER
Christa Miesner

PRODUCTION MANAGER
Lissa Pattillo

EDITOR-IN-CHIEF
Julie Davis

ASSOCIATE PUBLISHER
Adam Arnold

PUBLISHER
Jason DeAngelis

SERVAMP Vol.17
©TanakaStrike 2021
First published in Japan in 2021 by KADOKAWA CORPORATION, Tokyo.
English translation rights arranged with KADOKAWA CORPORATION, Tokyo

Seven Seas press and purchase enquiries can be sent to Marketing Manager Lianne Sentar at press@gomanga.com. Information regarding the distribution and purchase of digital editions is available from Digital Manager CK Russell at digital@gomanga.com.

Seven Seas and the Seven Seas logo are trademarks of Seven Seas Entertainment. All rights reserved.

ISBN: 978-1-63858-615-9

Printed in Canada

First Printing: October 2022

10 9 8 7 6 5 4 3 2 1

W9-BIT-405

FOLLOW US ONLINE: *www.sevenseasentertainment.com*

READING DIRECTIONS

This book reads from *right to left*, Japanese style. If this is your first time reading manga, you start reading from the top right panel on each page and take it from there. If you get lost, just follow the numbered diagram here. It may seem backwards at first, but you'll get the hang of it! Have fun!!

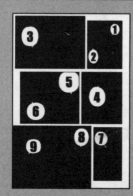

SERVAMP ACADEMY ⑪

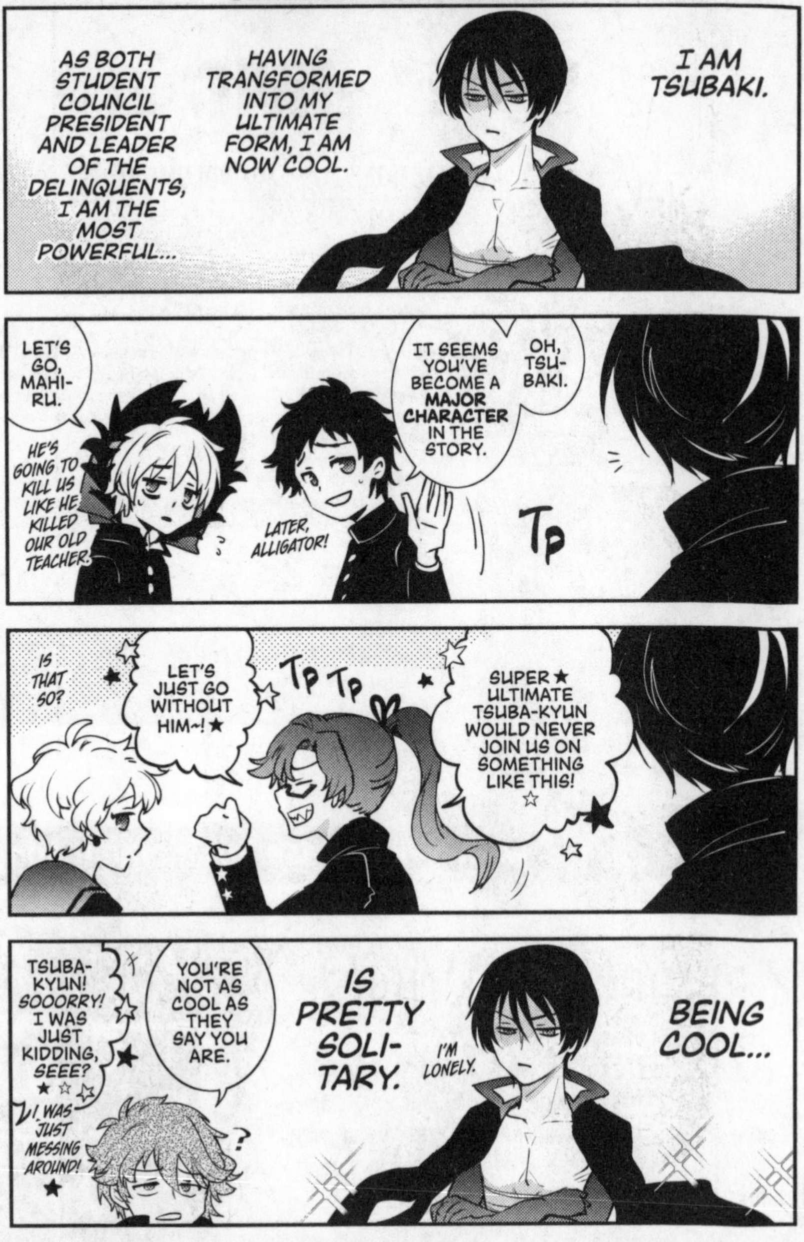
I AM TSUBAKI.
HAVING TRANSFORMED INTO MY ULTIMATE FORM, I AM NOW COOL.
AS BOTH STUDENT COUNCIL PRESIDENT AND LEADER OF THE DELINQUENTS, I AM THE MOST POWERFUL...
Tp
OH, TSUBAKI.
IT SEEMS YOU'VE BECOME A MAJOR CHARACTER IN THE STORY.
LATER, ALLIGATOR!
LET'S GO, MAHIRU.
HE'S GOING TO KILL US LIKE HE KILLED OUR OLD TEACHER.
SUPER★ULTIMATE TSUBA-KYUN WOULD NEVER JOIN US ON SOMETHING LIKE THIS! ☆
Tp Tp
LET'S JUST GO WITHOUT HIM~!★
IS THAT SO?
BEING COOL...
IS PRETTY SOLITARY.
I'M LONELY.
YOU'RE NOT AS COOL AS THEY SAY YOU ARE.
TSUBA-KYUN! SOOORRY! I WAS JUST KIDDING, SEEE? ★☆
I WAS JUST MESSING AROUND! ★

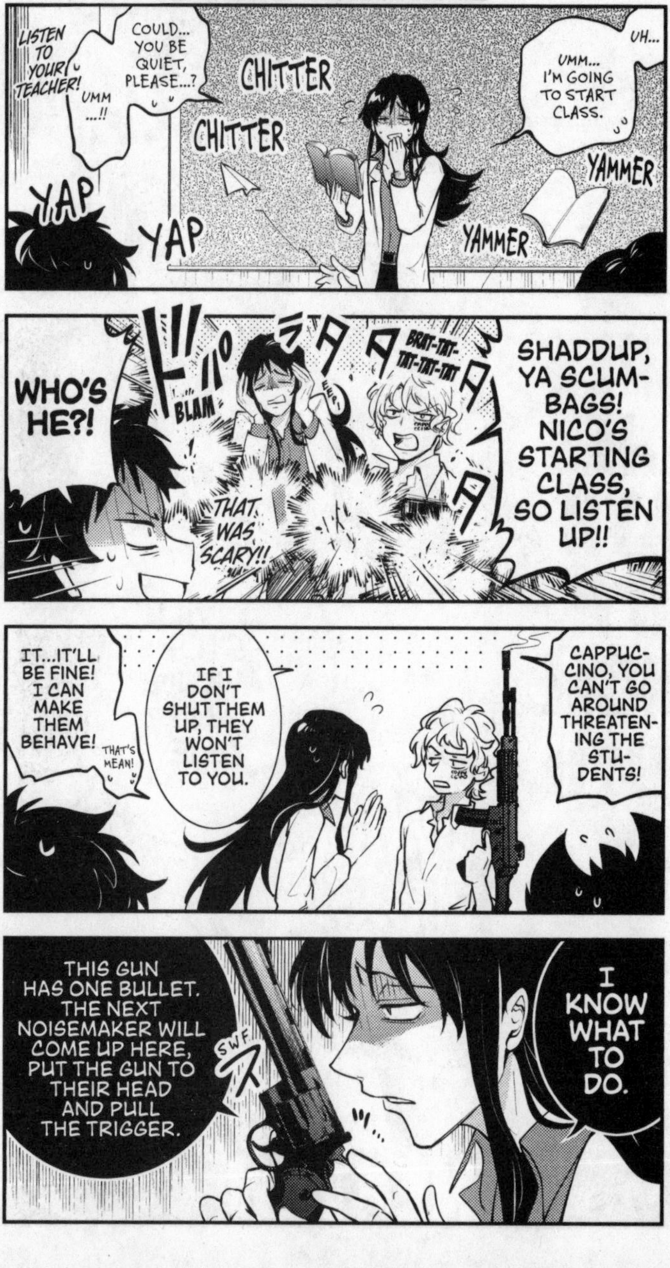
UH...
UMM... I'M GOING TO START CLASS.
YAMMER
CHITTER
CHITTER
COULD... YOU BE QUIET, PLEASE...?
LISTEN TO YOUR TEACHER!
UMM ...!!
YAMMER
YAP
YAP
SHADDUP, YA SCUM-BAGS! NICO'S STARTING CLASS, SO LISTEN UP!!
BRAT-TAT-TAT-TAT-TAT
BLAM
WHO'S HE?!
THAT WAS SCARY!!
CAPPUC-CINO, YOU CAN'T GO AROUND THREATEN-ING THE STU-DENTS!
IF I DON'T SHUT THEM UP, THEY WON'T LISTEN TO YOU.
IT...IT'LL BE FINE! I CAN MAKE THEM BEHAVE!
THAT'S MEAN!
I KNOW WHAT TO DO.
THIS GUN HAS ONE BULLET. THE NEXT NOISEMAKER WILL COME UP HERE, PUT THE GUN TO THEIR HEAD AND PULL THE TRIGGER.
SWF

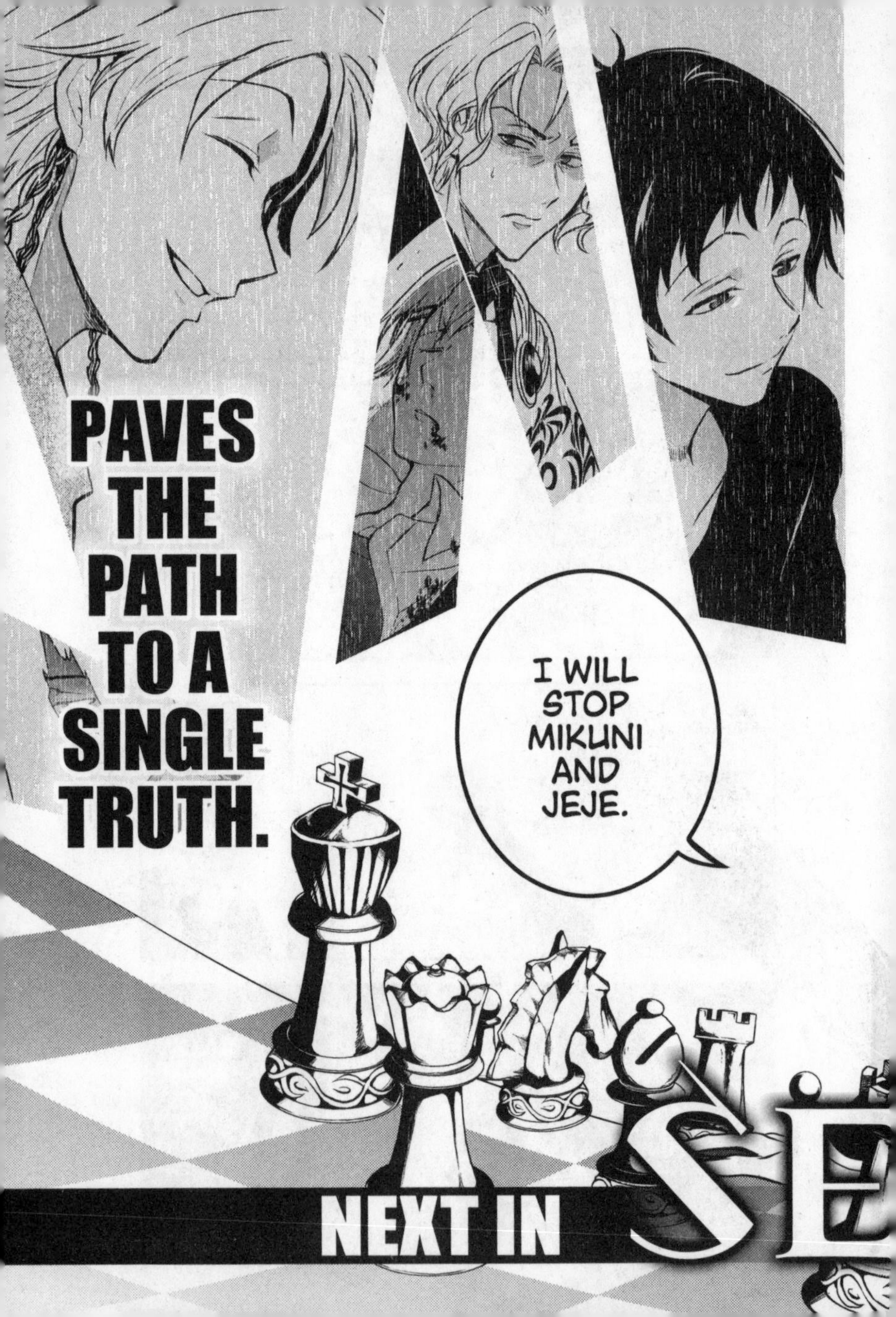
PAVES THE PATH TO A SINGLE TRUTH.
I WILL STOP MIKUNI AND JEJE.
NEXT IN

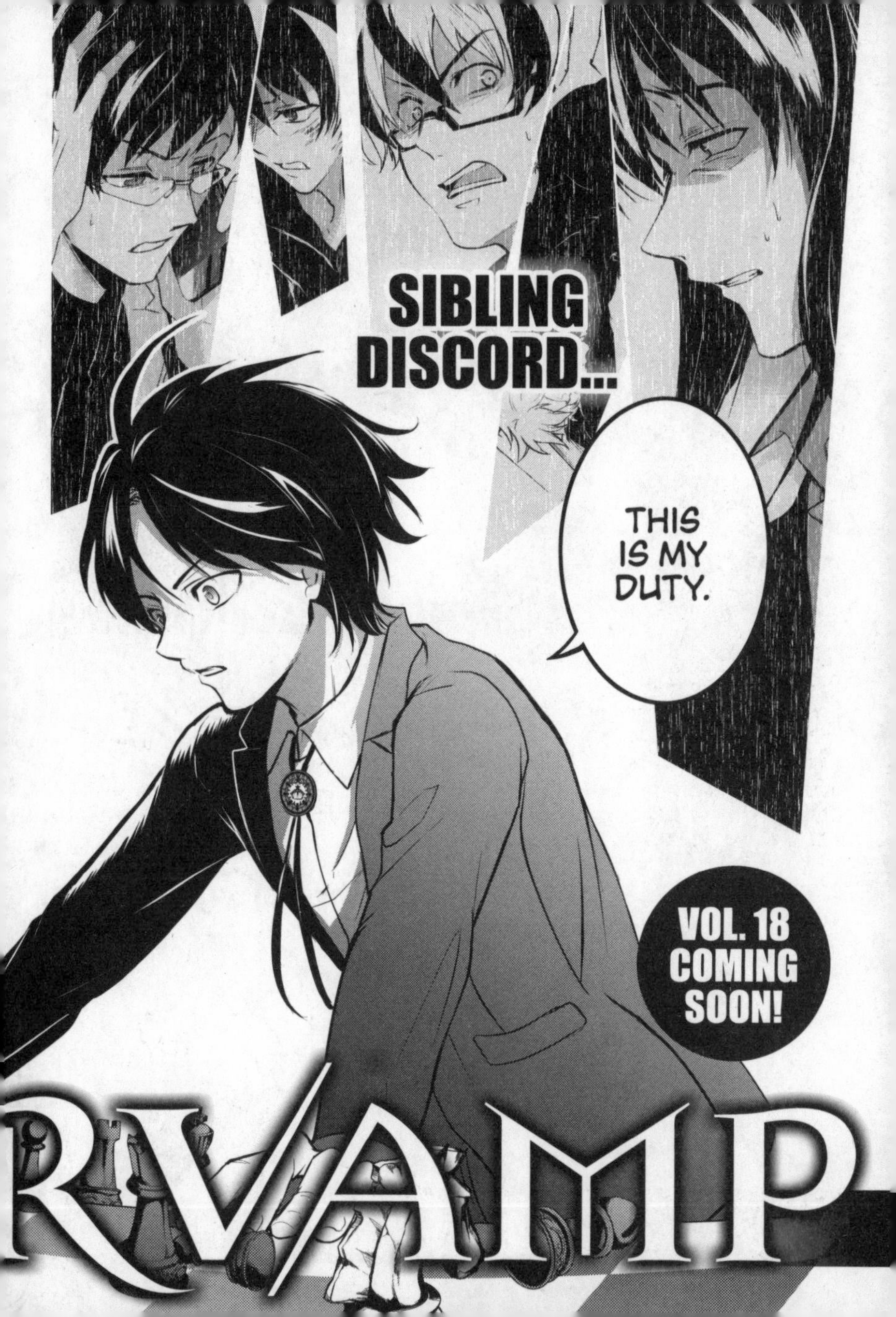
SIBLING DISCORD...
THIS IS MY DUTY.
VOL. 18 COMING SOON!
RVAMP

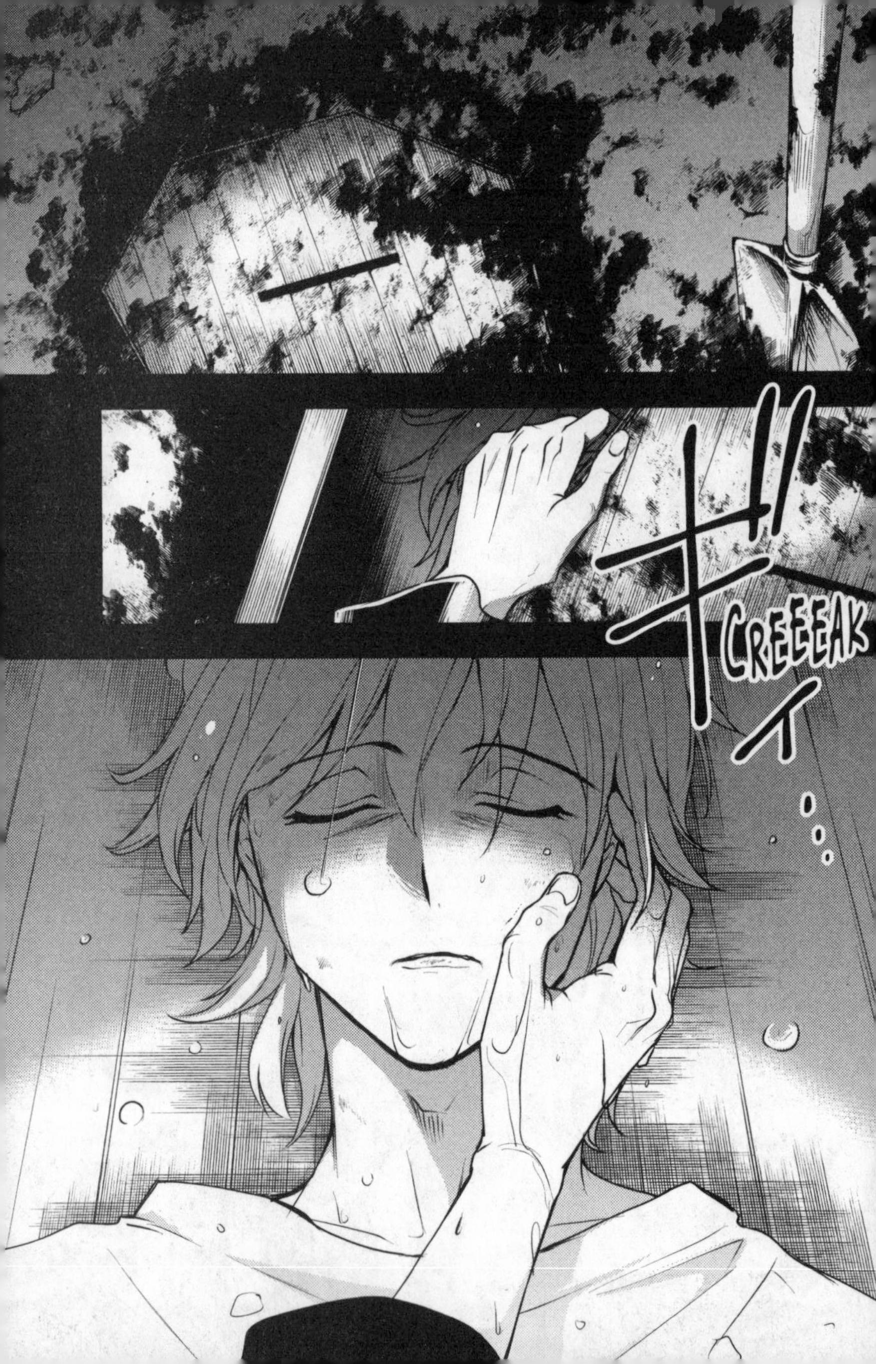
CREEEAK

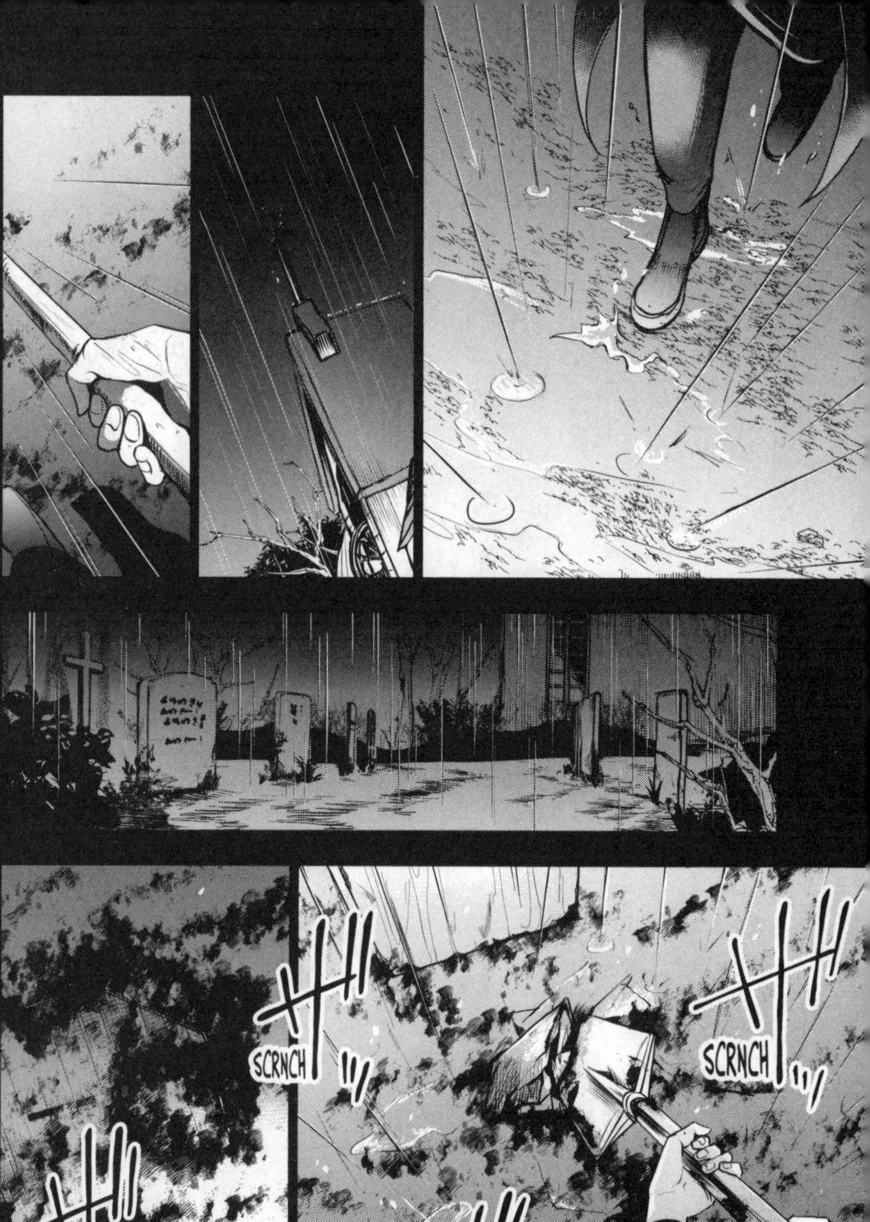
SCRNCH
SCRNCH
SCRNCH
SCRNCH

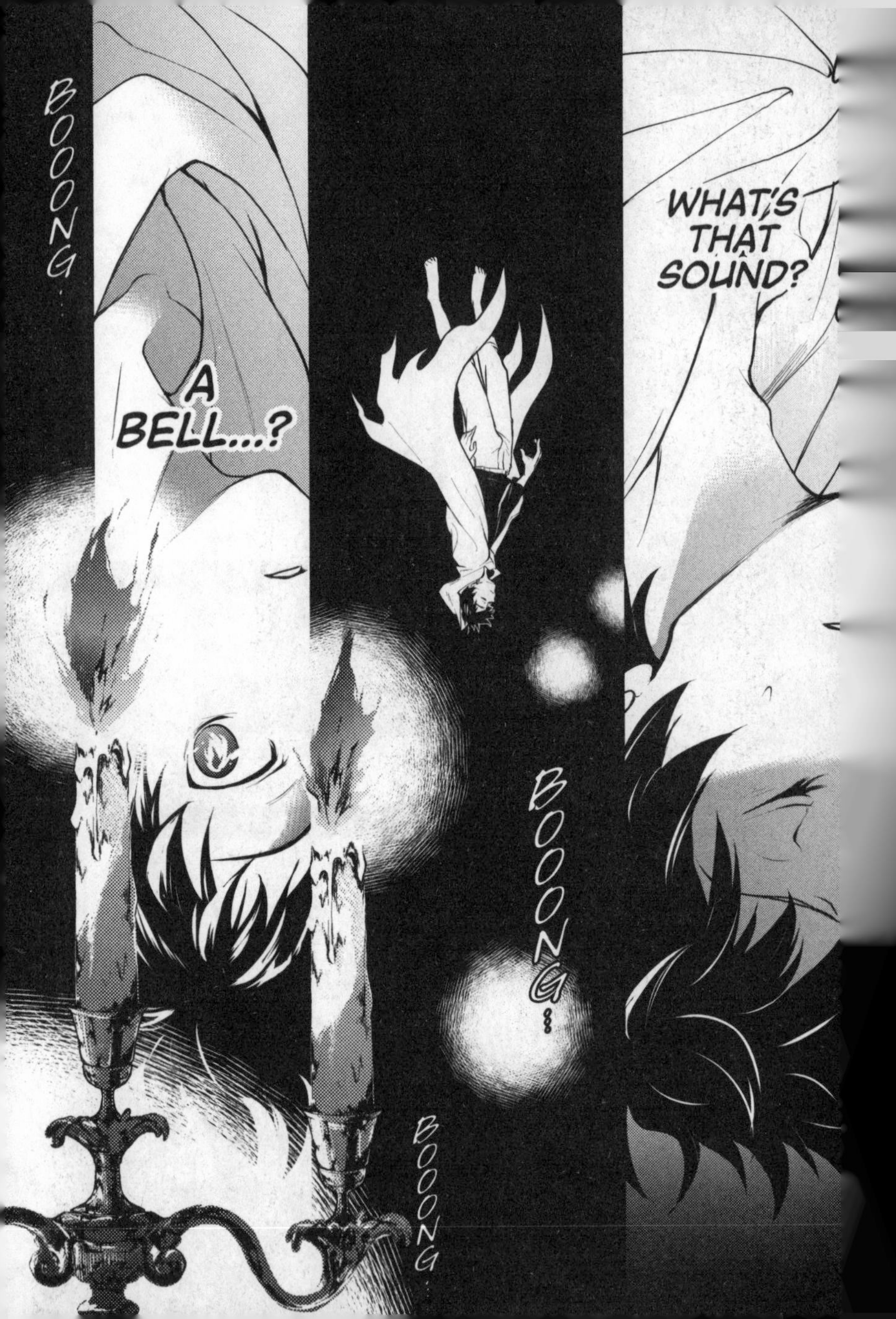
WHAT'S THAT SOUND?
BOOOONG..
BOOOONG..
A BELL...?
BOOOONG..

BOOOONG...
BOOOONG...

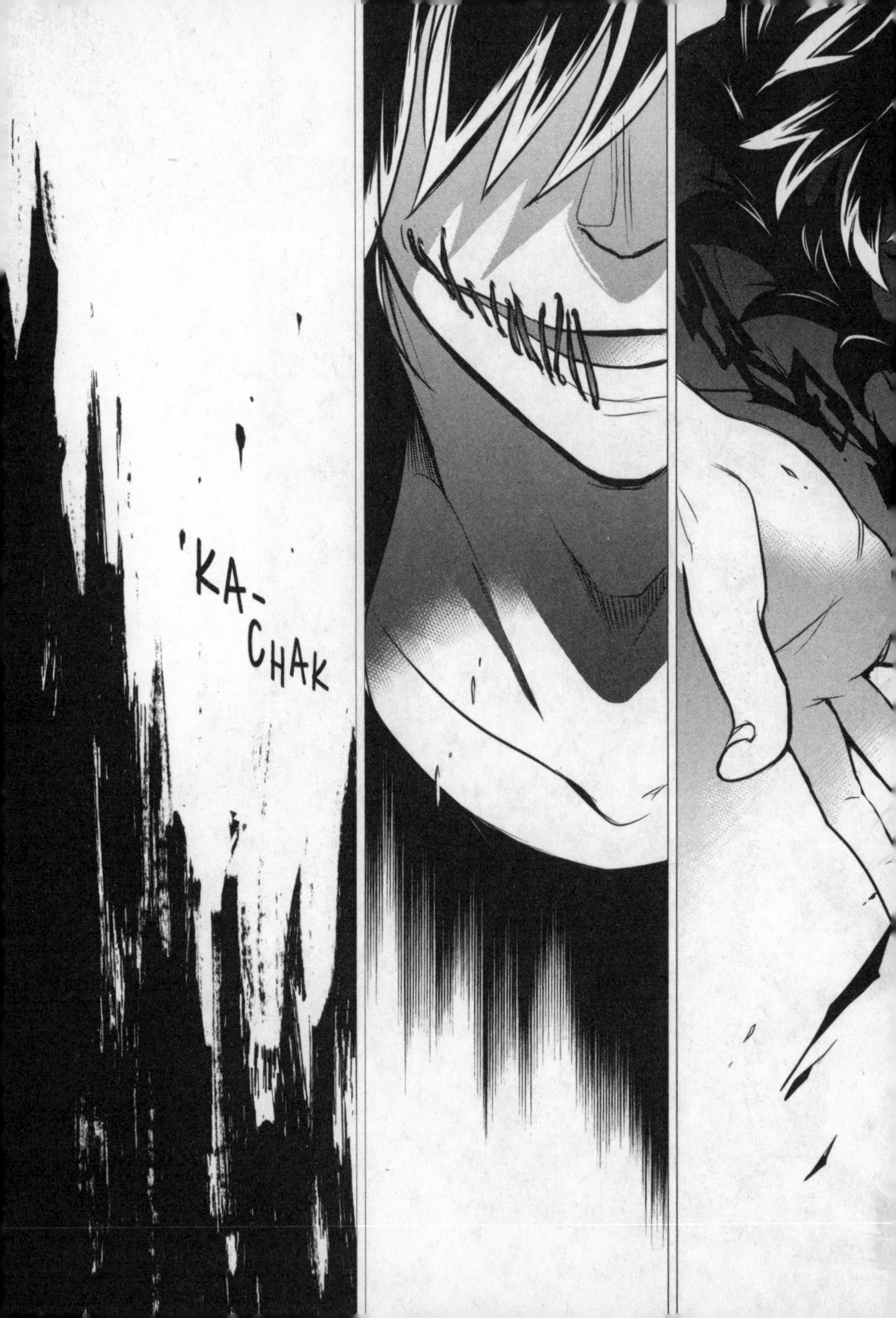
KA-CHAK

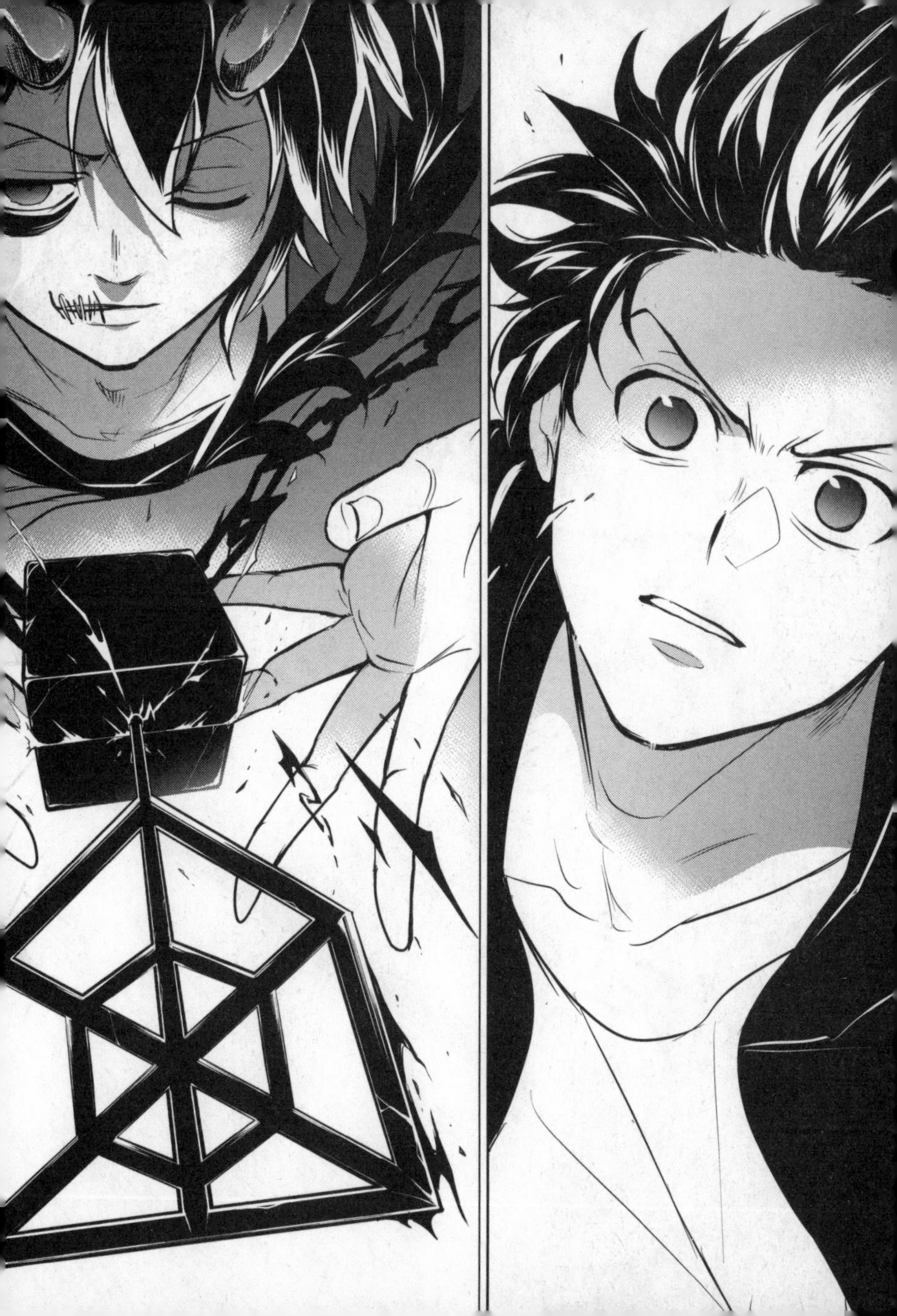

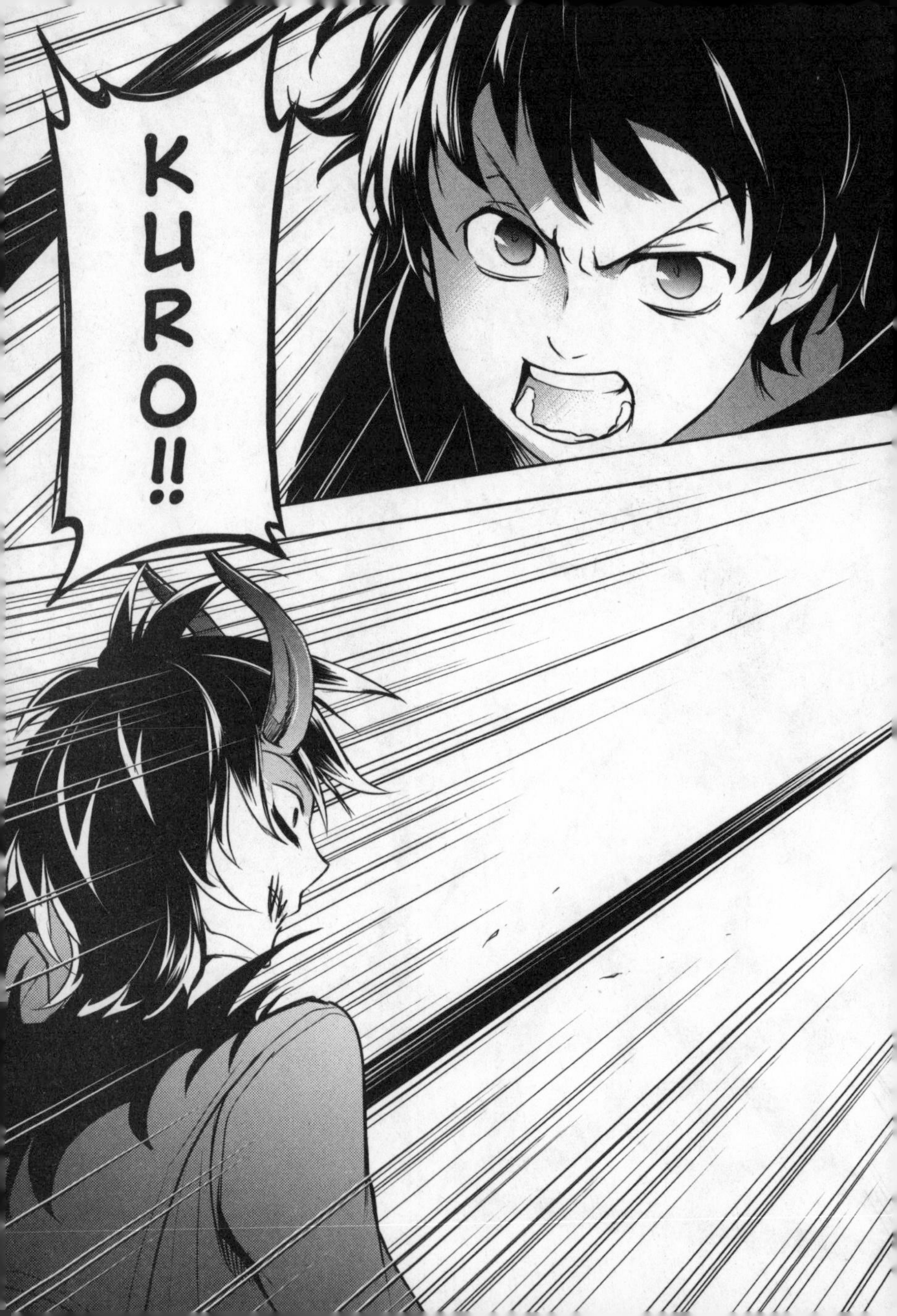
KURO!!

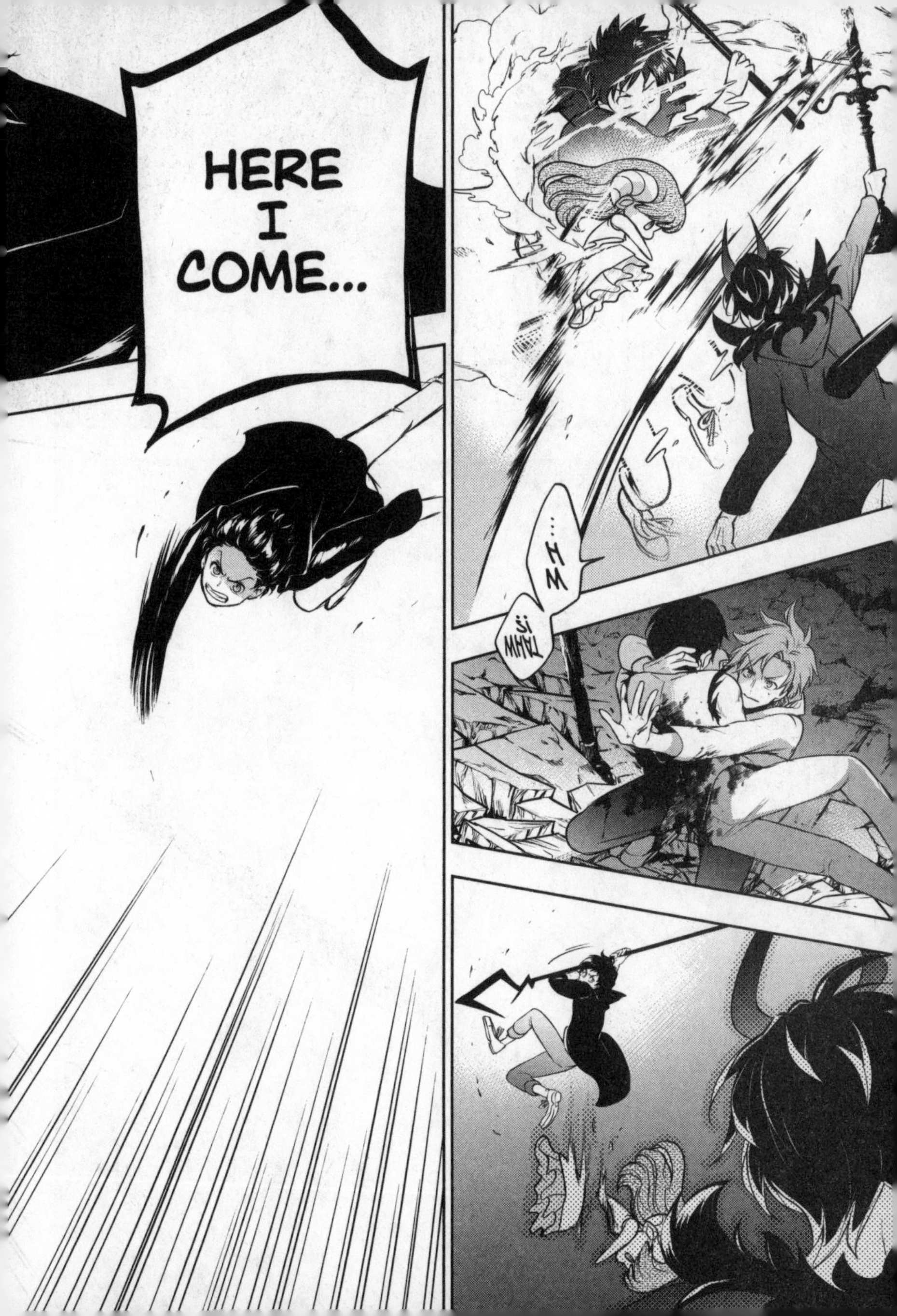
WH...
WHAT is?
HERE I COME...

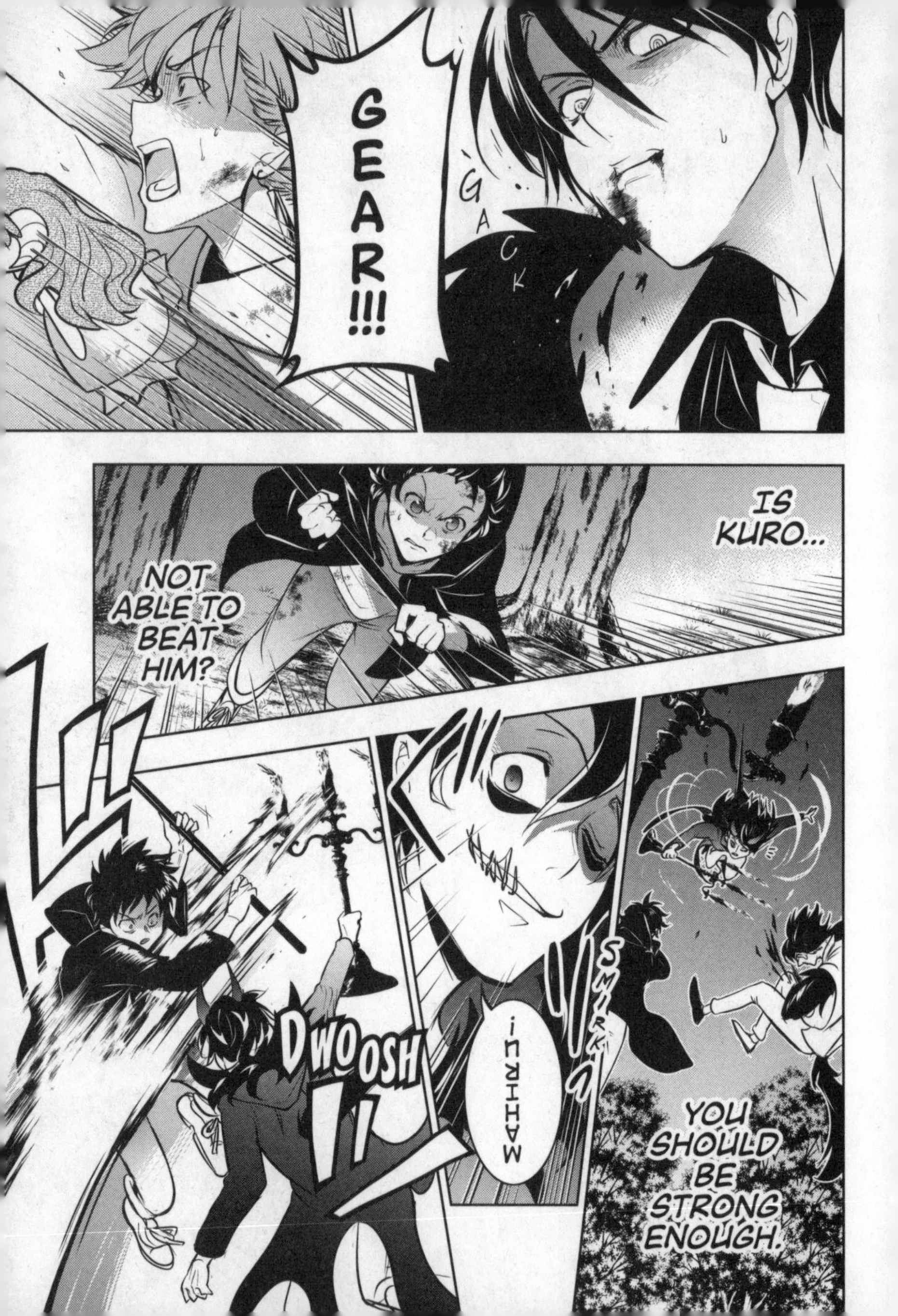
GEAR!!!
GACK
IS KURO...
NOT ABLE TO BEAT HIM?
YOU SHOULD BE STRONG ENOUGH.
SMIRK
MAHIRU!
DWOOSH

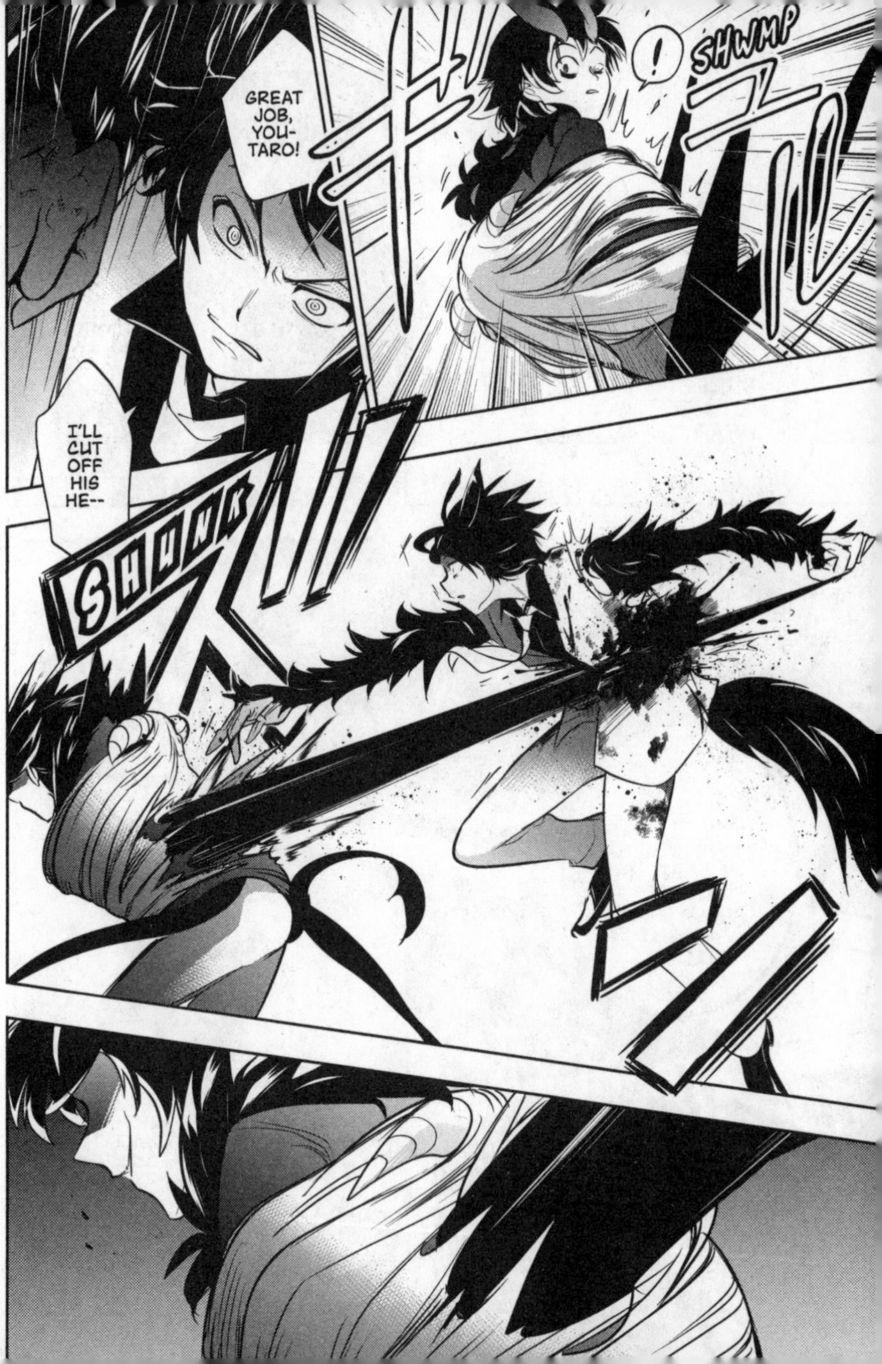
!
SHWMP
GREAT JOB, YOU-TARO!
I'LL CUT OFF HIS HE--
SHUNK

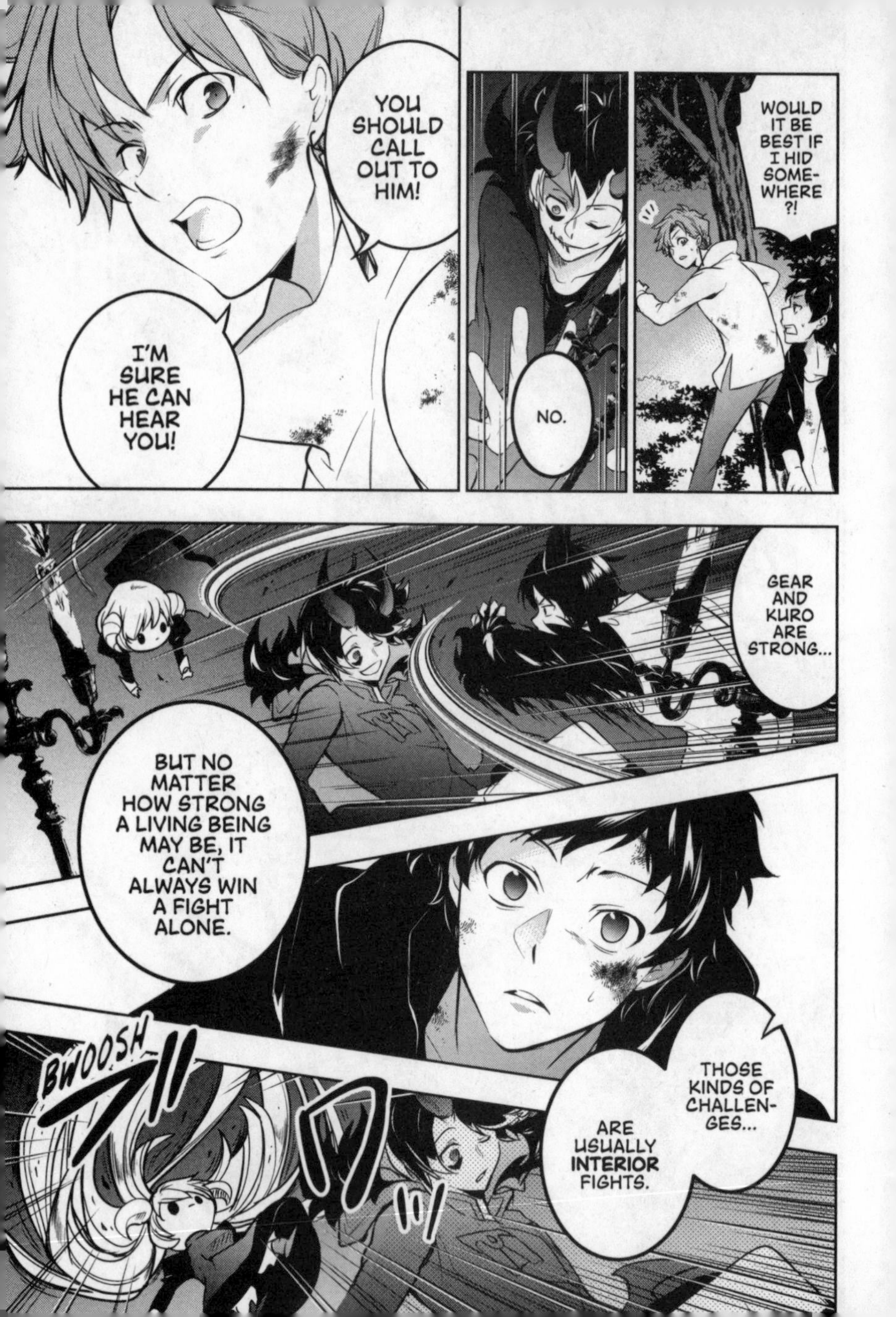
WOULD IT BE BEST IF I HID SOME-WHERE?!
NO.
YOU SHOULD CALL OUT TO HIM!
I'M SURE HE CAN HEAR YOU!
GEAR AND KURO ARE STRONG...
BUT NO MATTER HOW STRONG A LIVING BEING MAY BE, IT CAN'T ALWAYS WIN A FIGHT ALONE.
THOSE KINDS OF CHALLEN-GES...
ARE USUALLY **INTERIOR** FIGHTS.
BWOOSH

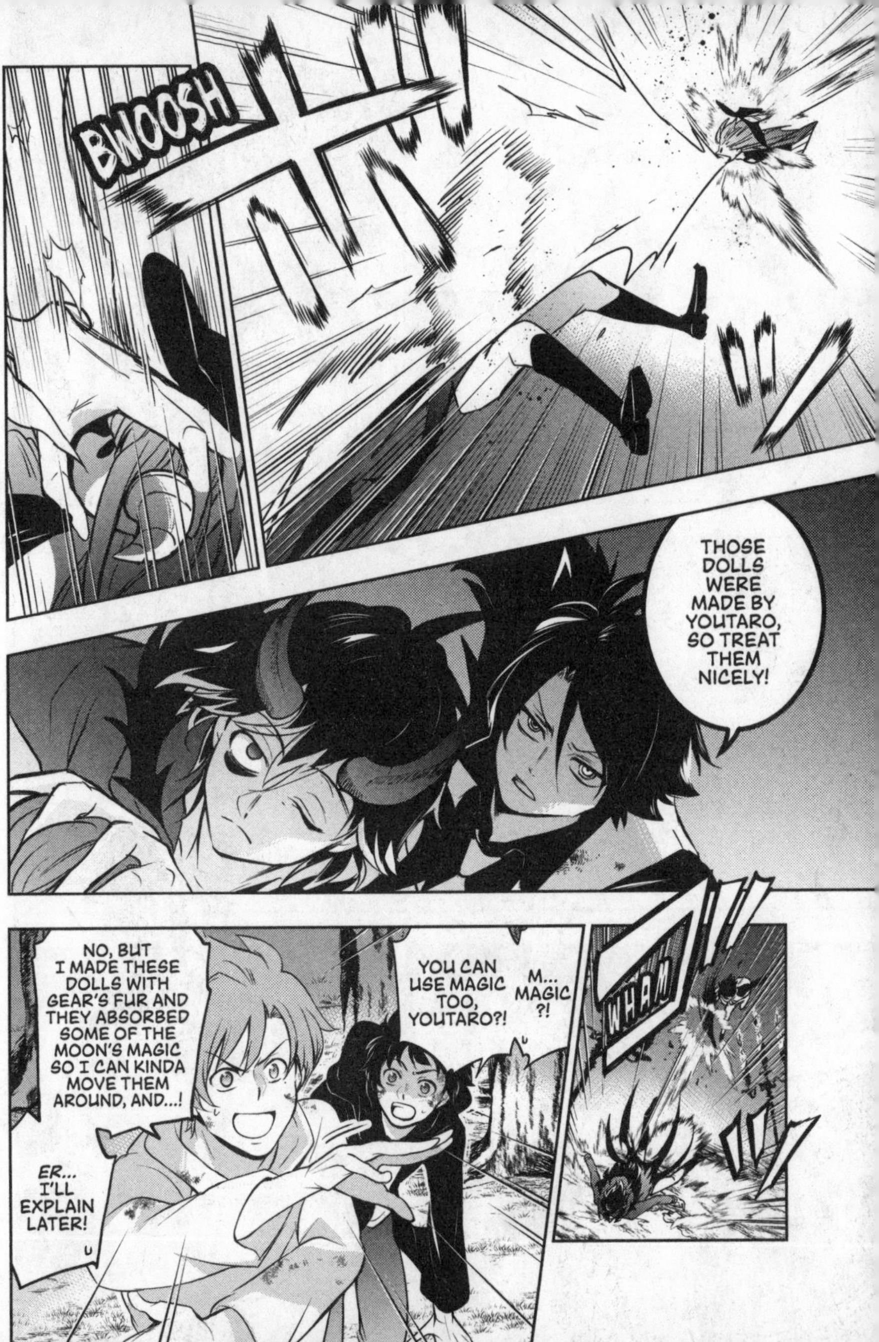
BWOOSH
THOSE DOLLS WERE MADE BY YOUTARO, SO TREAT THEM NICELY!
WHAM
M... MAGIC?!
YOU CAN USE MAGIC TOO, YOUTARO?!
NO, BUT I MADE THESE DOLLS WITH GEAR'S FUR AND THEY ABSORBED SOME OF THE MOON'S MAGIC SO I CAN KINDA MOVE THEM AROUND, AND...!
ER... I'LL EXPLAIN LATER!

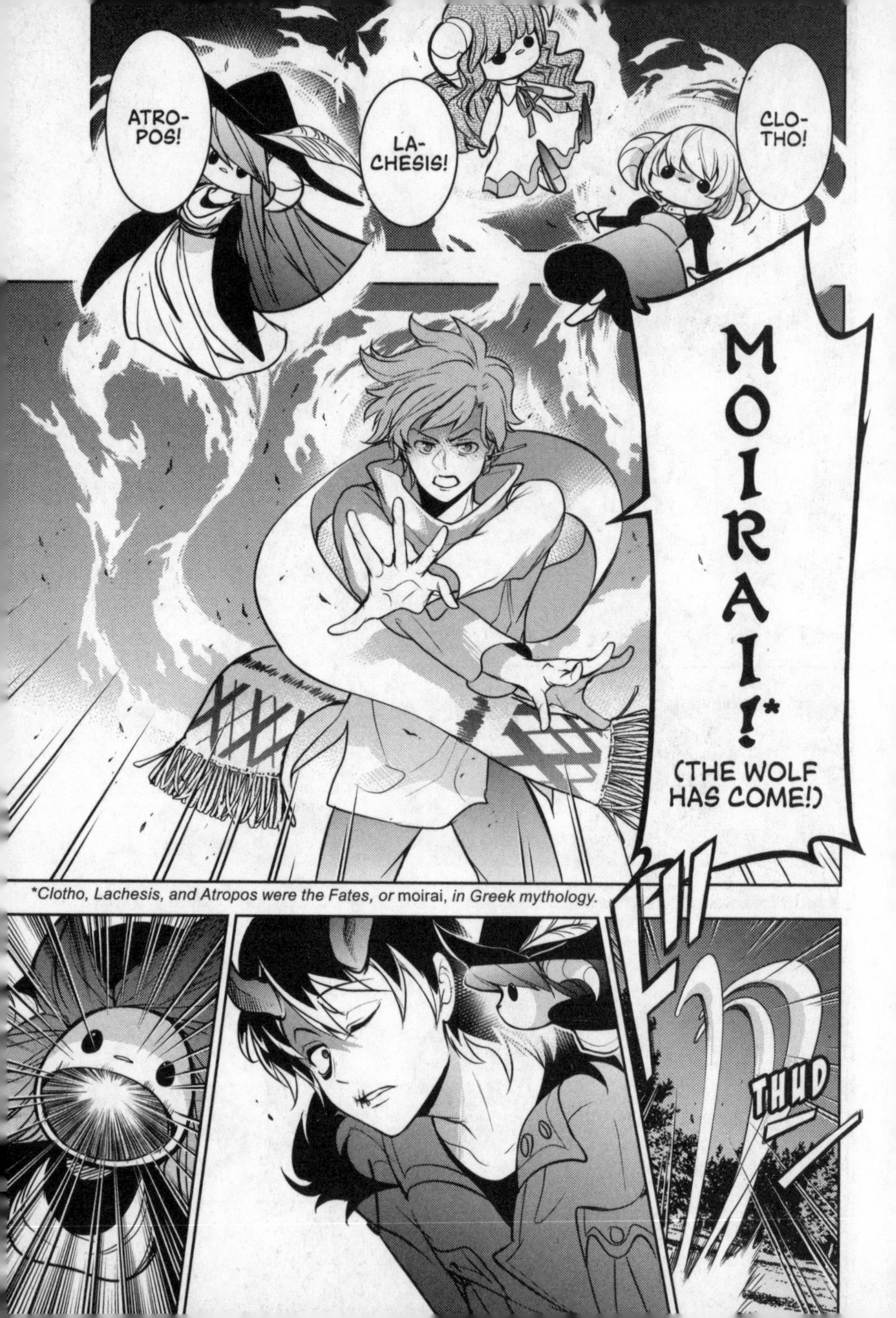
CLO-THO!
LA-CHESIS!
ATRO-POS!
MOIRAI!*
(THE WOLF HAS COME!)
THUD

*Clotho, Lachesis, and Atropos were the Fates, or moirai, in Greek mythology.

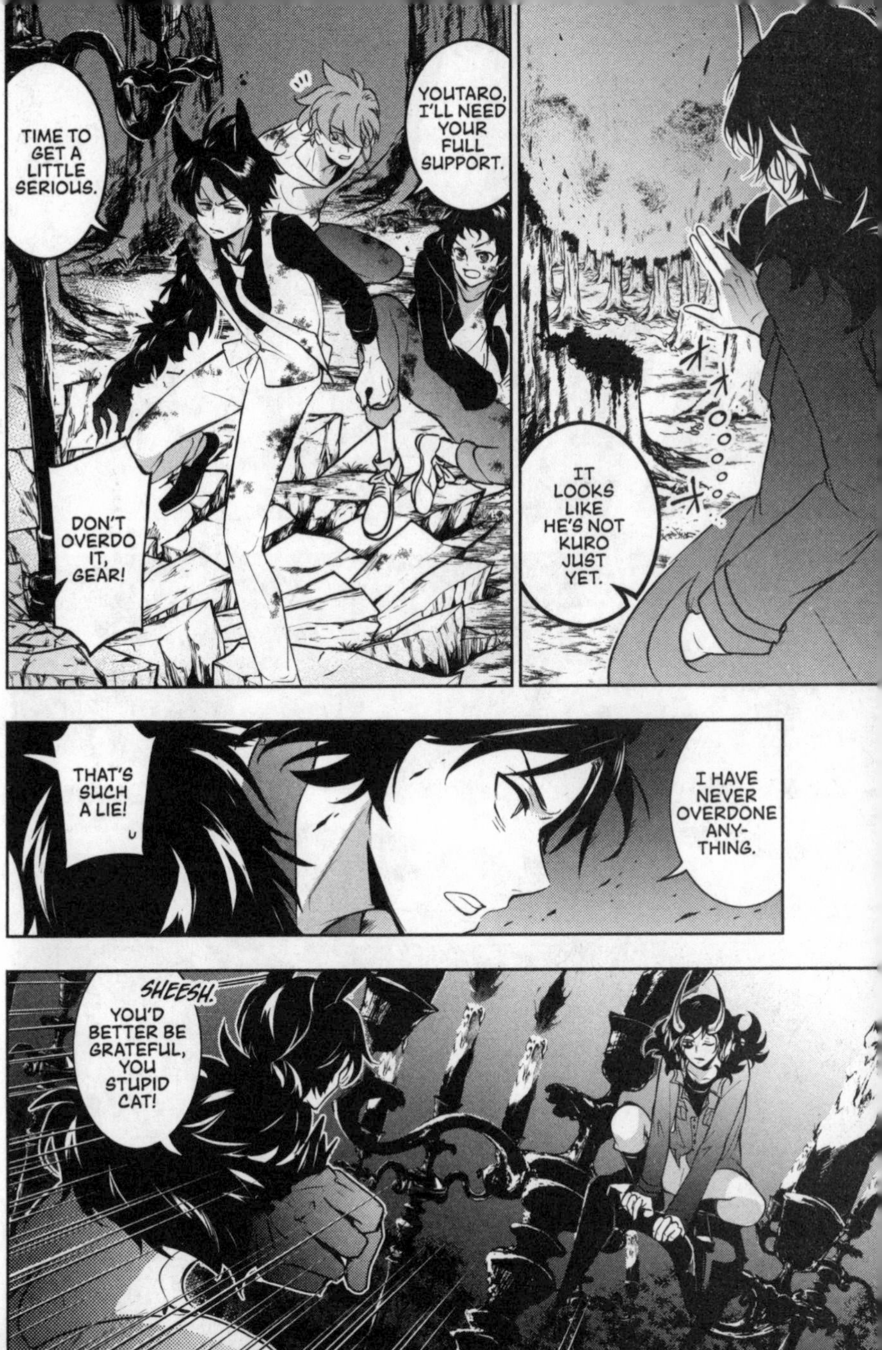
IT LOOKS LIKE HE'S NOT KURO JUST YET.
YOUTARO, I'LL NEED YOUR FULL SUPPORT.
TIME TO GET A LITTLE SERIOUS.
DON'T OVERDO IT, GEAR!
I HAVE NEVER OVERDONE ANYTHING.
THAT'S SUCH A LIE!
SHEESH.
YOU'D BETTER BE GRATEFUL, YOU STUPID CAT!

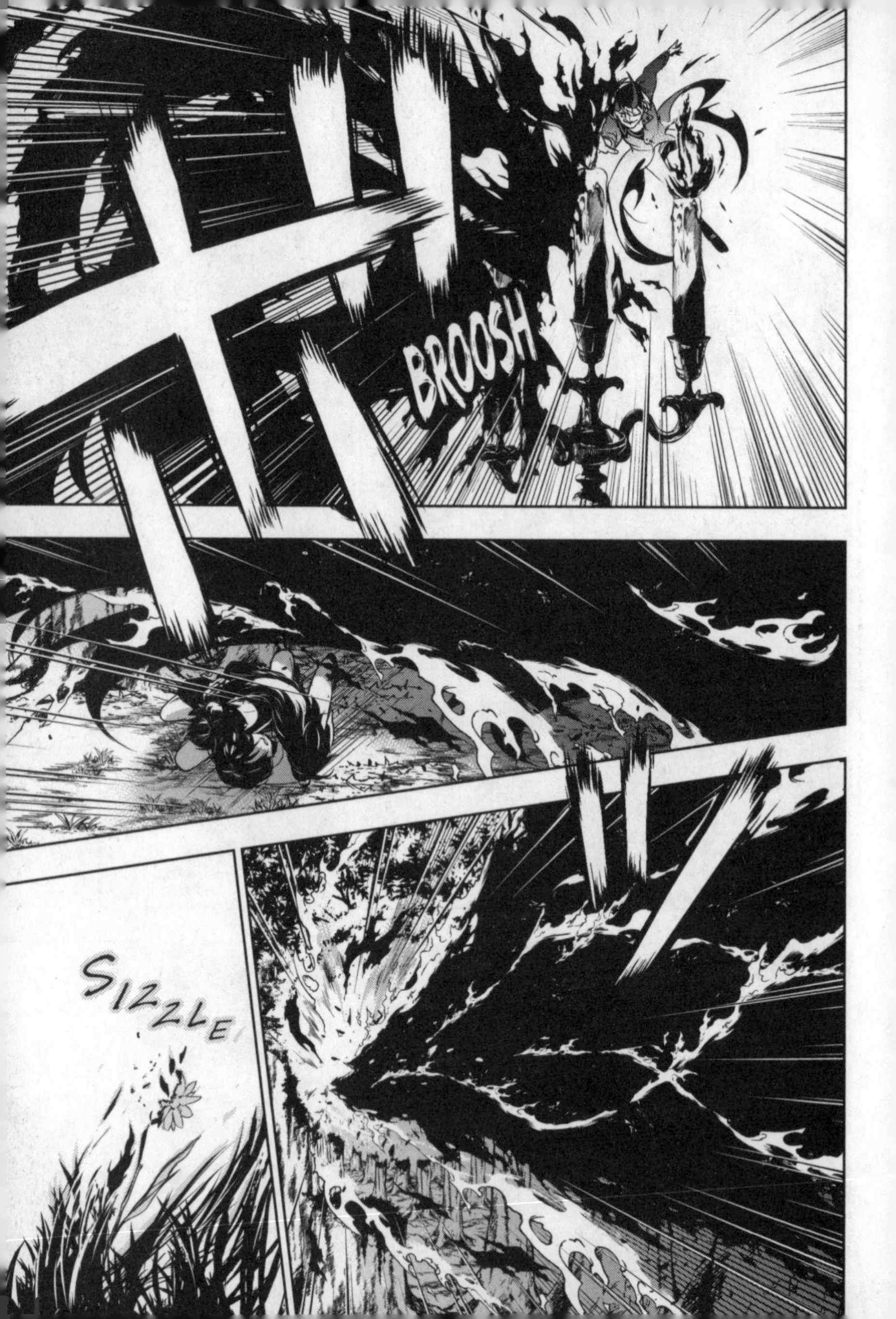
BROOSH
SIZZLE

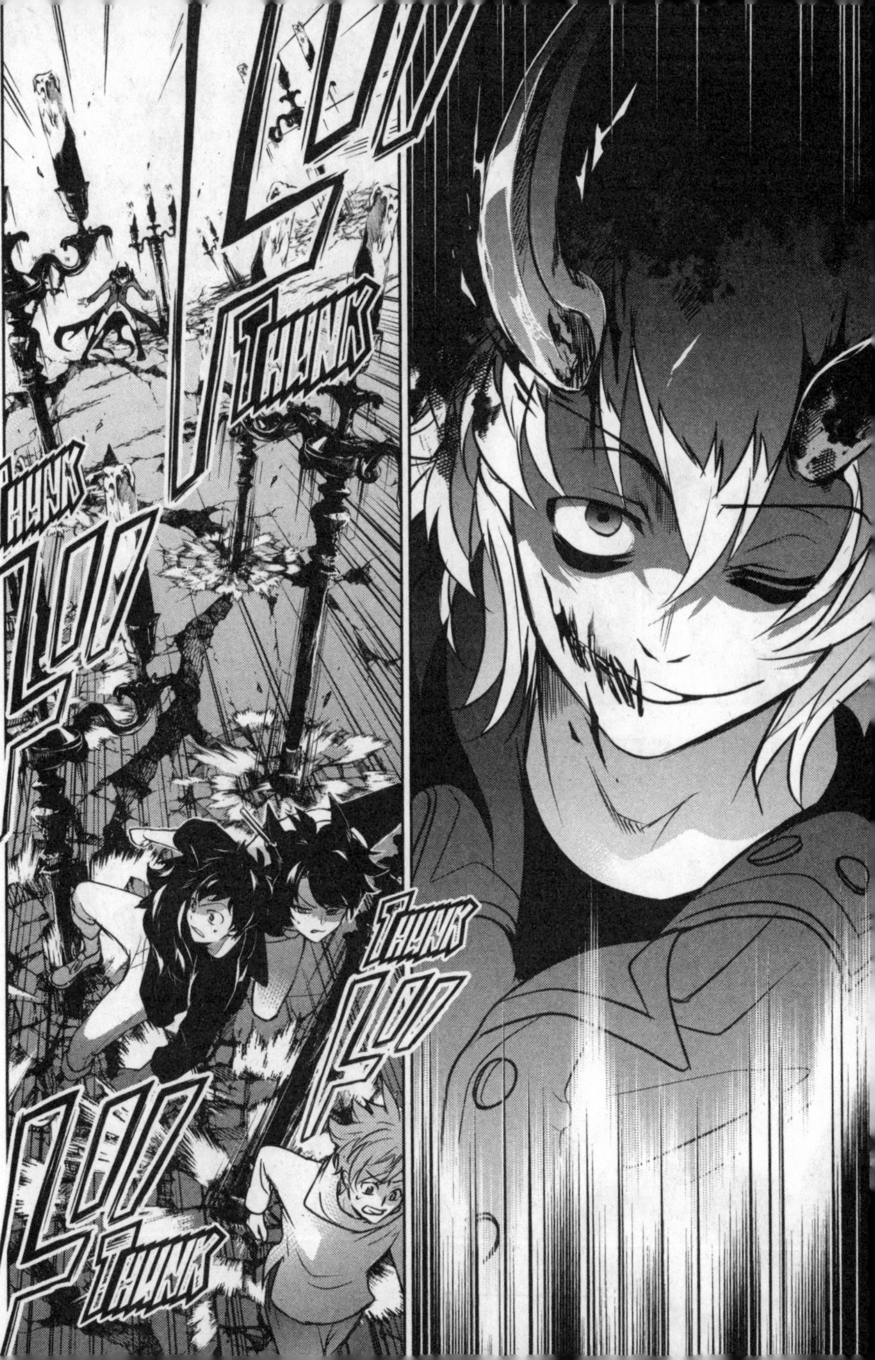
THUNK
THUNK
THUNK
THUNK

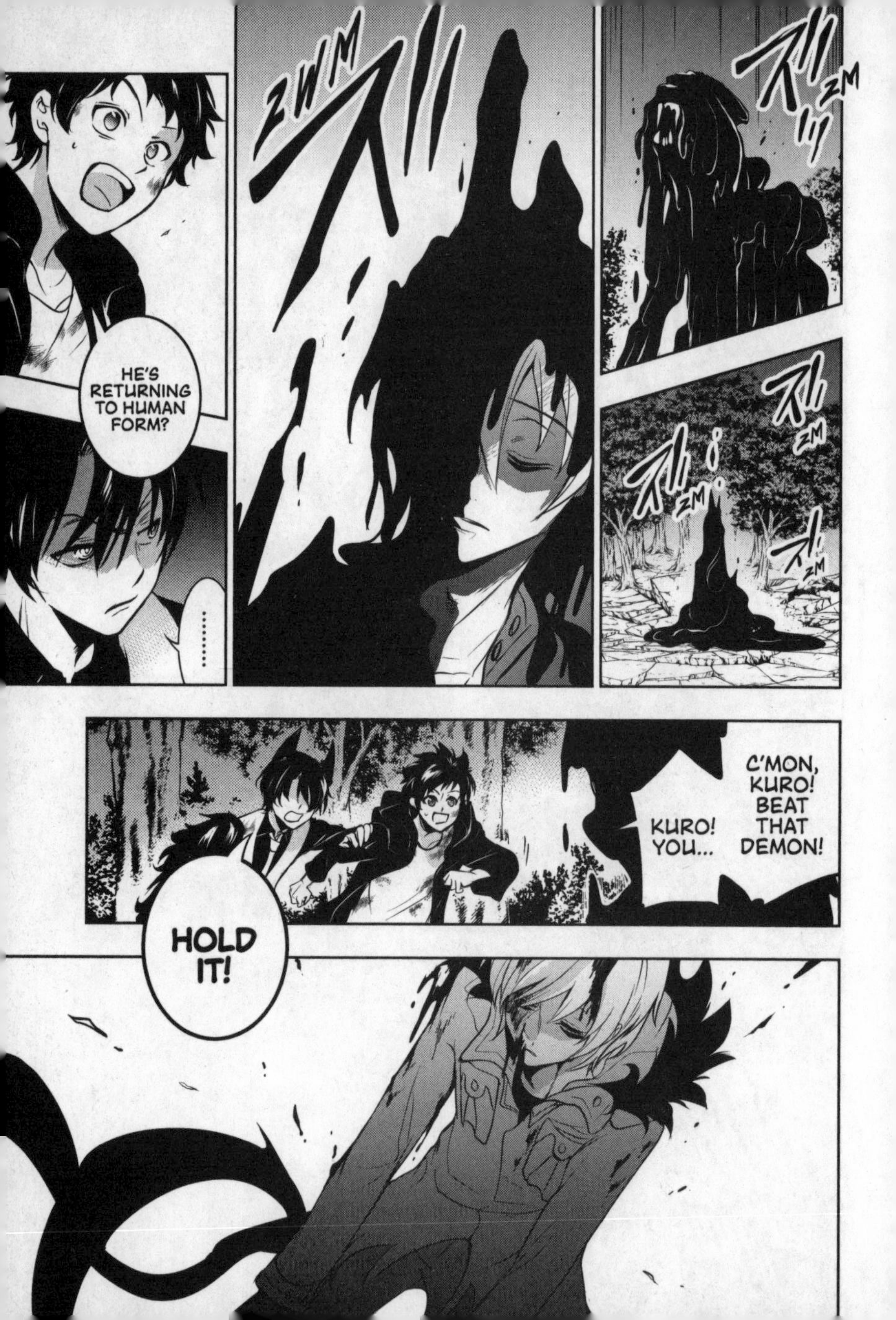
ZM
ZM
ZM
ZM
ZWM
HE'S RETURNING TO HUMAN FORM?
......
C'MON, KURO! BEAT THAT DEMON!
KURO! YOU...
HOLD IT!

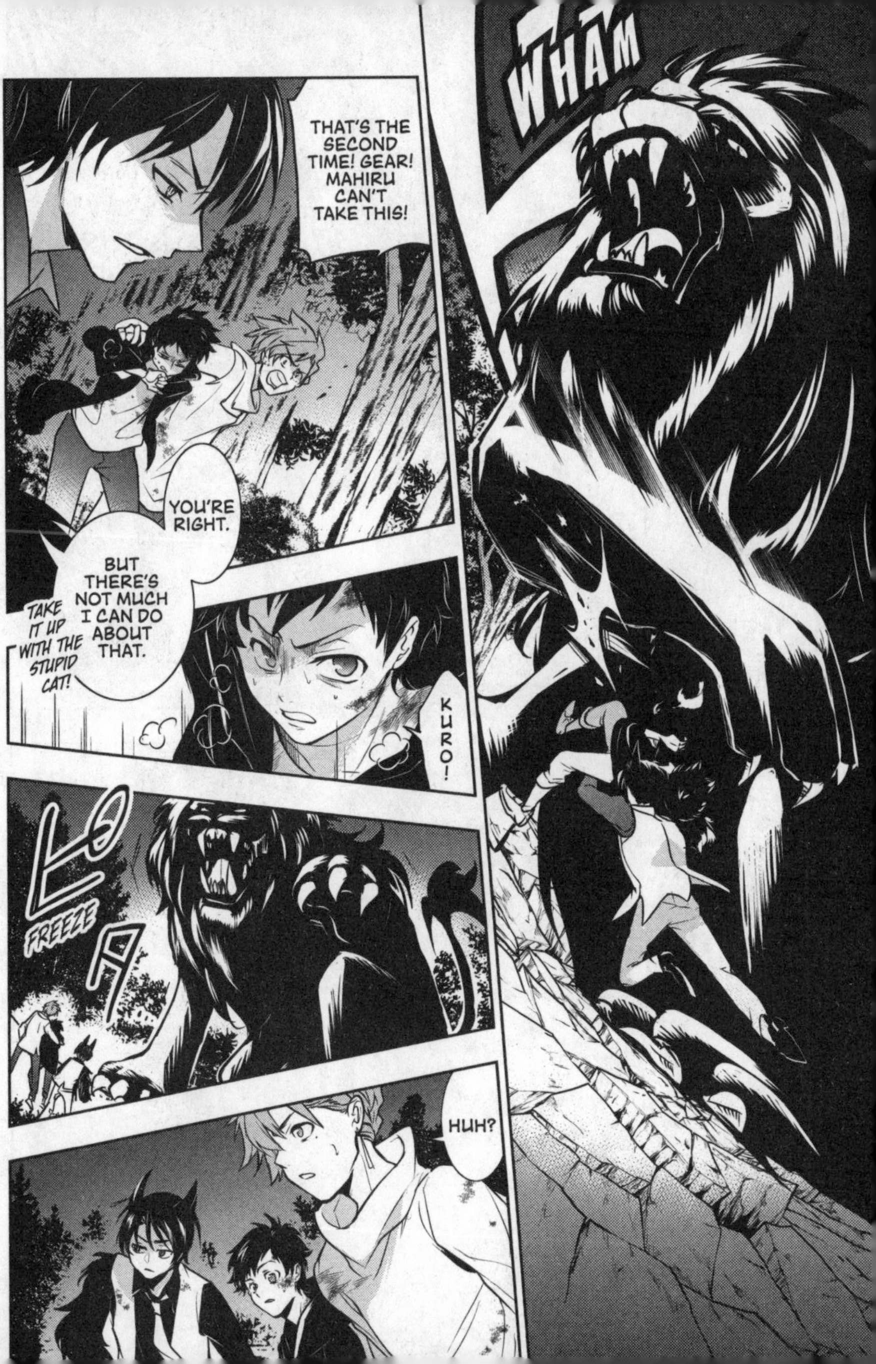
WHAM
THAT'S THE SECOND TIME! GEAR! MAHIRU CAN'T TAKE THIS!
YOU'RE RIGHT.
BUT THERE'S NOT MUCH I CAN DO ABOUT THAT.
TAKE IT UP WITH THE STUPID CAT!
KURO!
FREEZE
HUH?

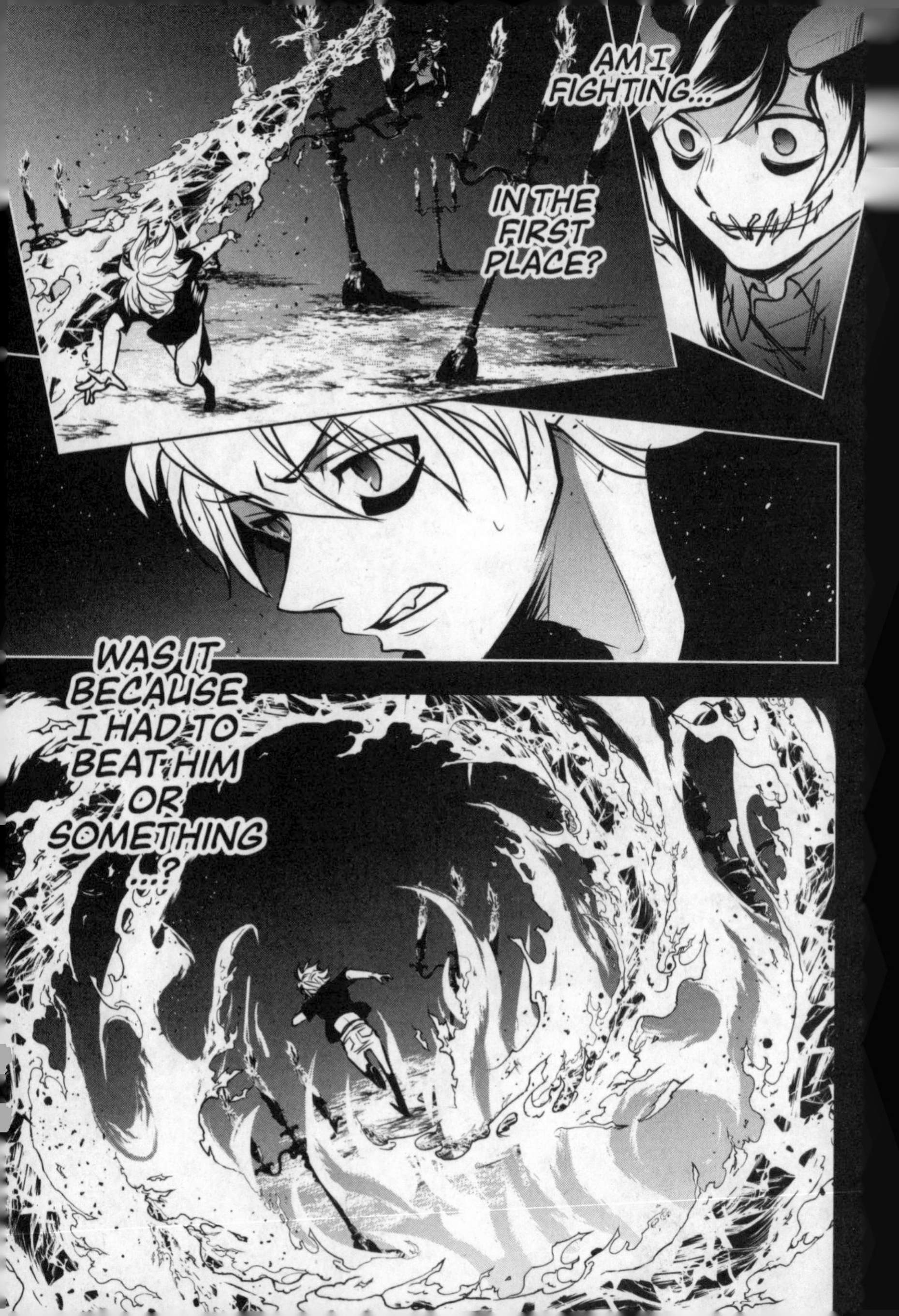
AM I FIGHTING...
IN THE FIRST PLACE?
WAS IT BECAUSE I HAD TO BEAT HIM OR SOMETHING ...?

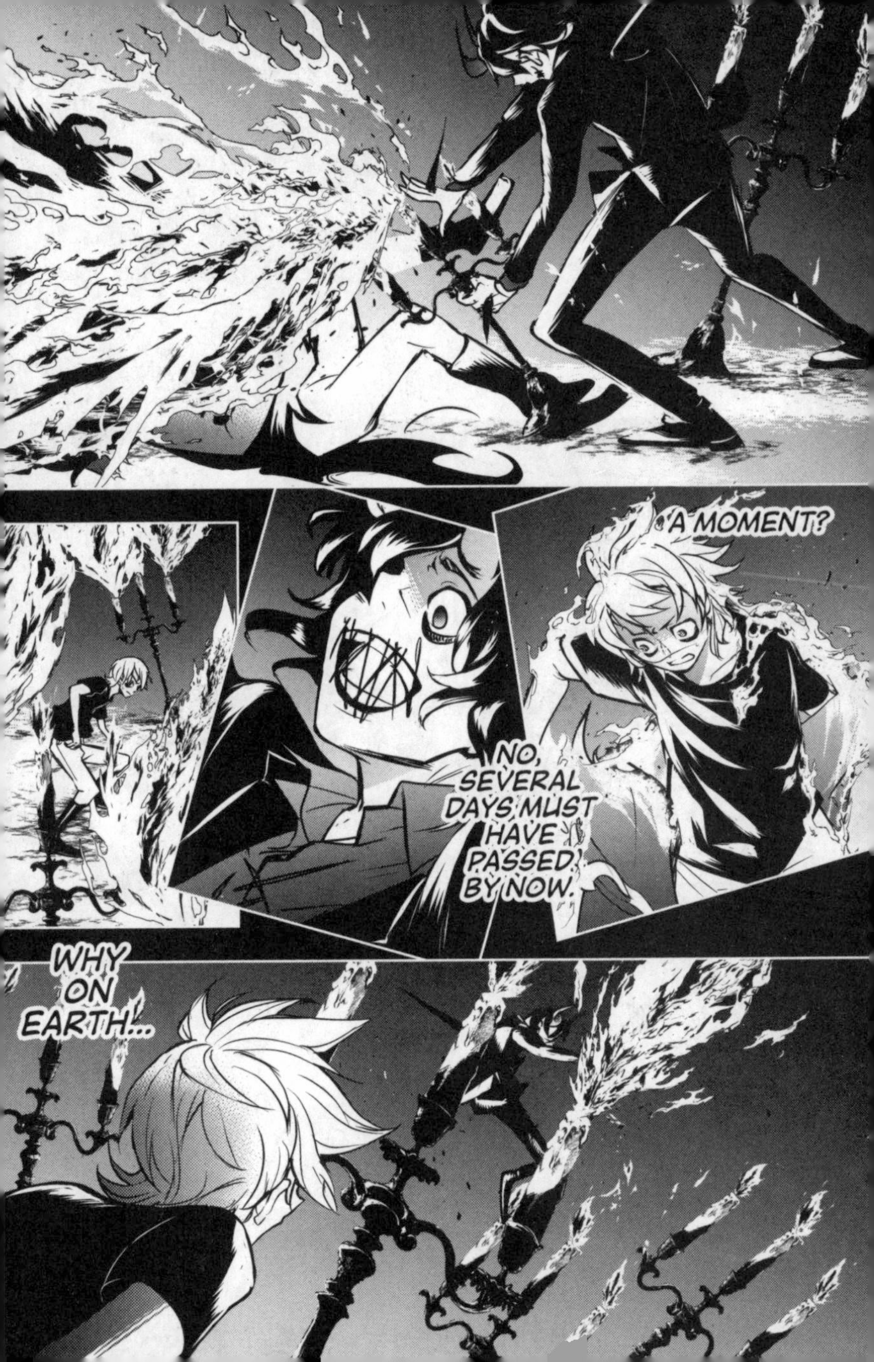
A MOMENT?
NO, SEVERAL DAYS MUST HAVE PASSED BY NOW.
WHY ON EARTH...

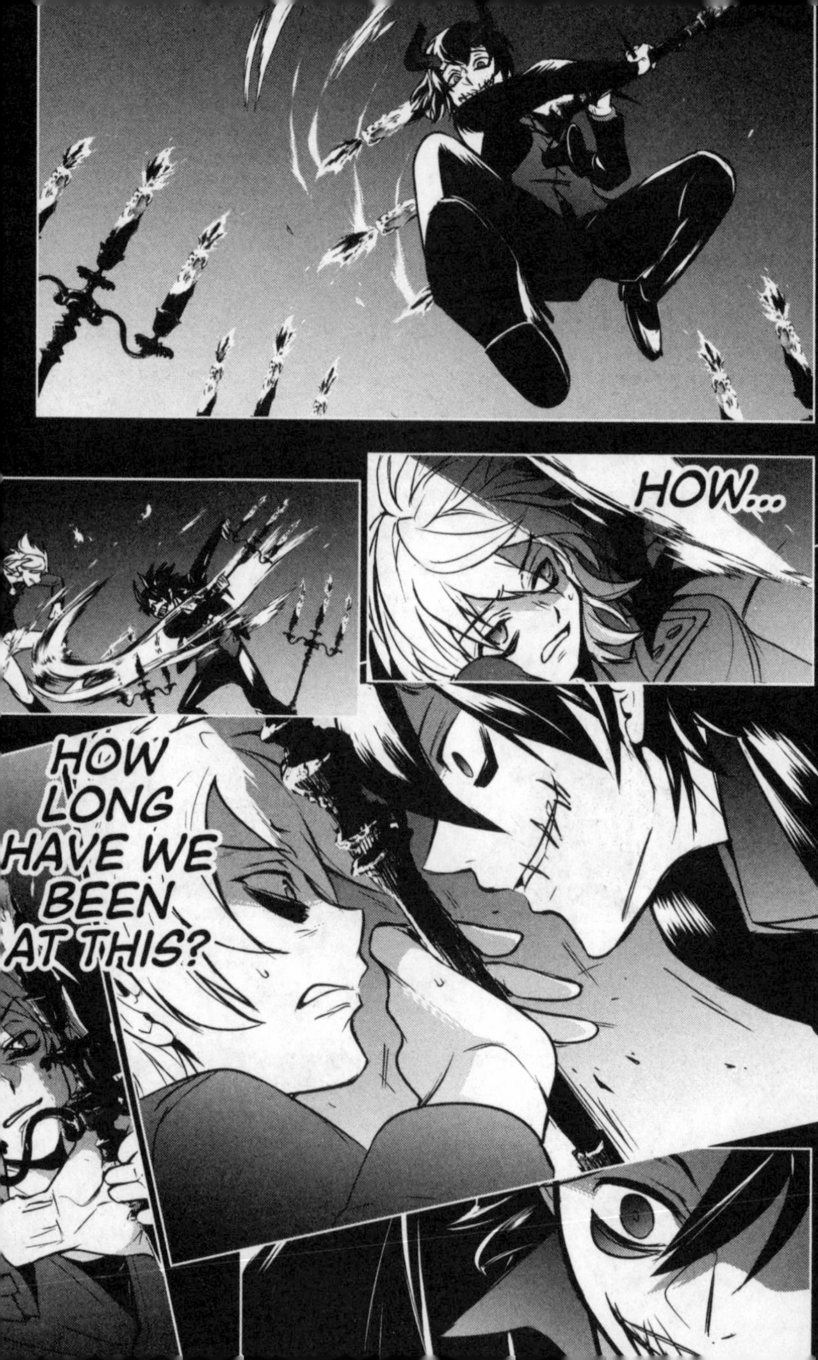
HOW...
HOW LONG HAVE WE BEEN AT THIS?

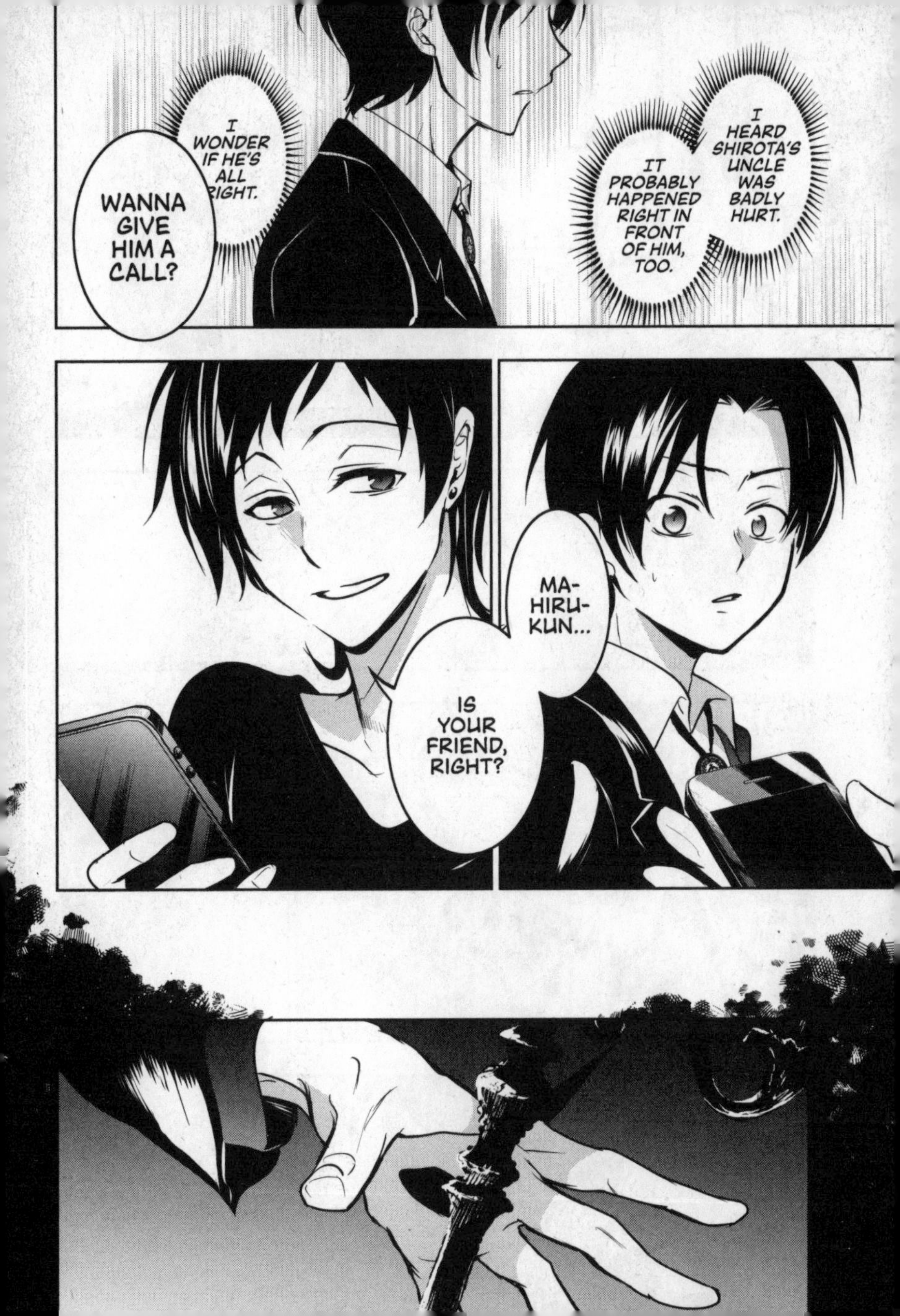
I HEARD SHIROTA'S UNCLE WAS BADLY HURT.
IT PROBABLY HAPPENED RIGHT IN FRONT OF HIM, TOO.
I WONDER IF HE'S ALL RIGHT.
WANNA GIVE HIM A CALL?
MA-HIRU-KUN...
IS YOUR FRIEND, RIGHT?

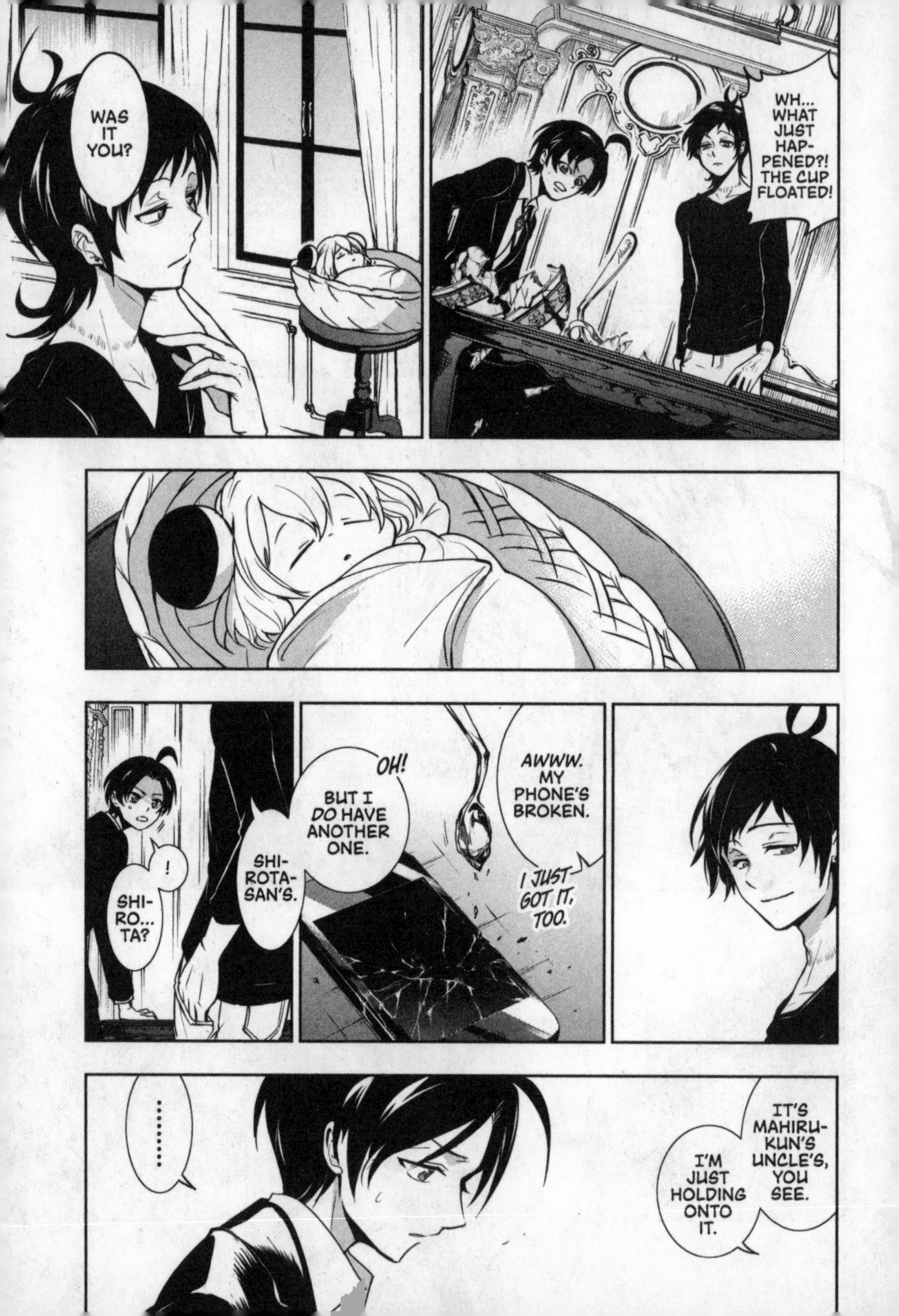
WH... WHAT JUST HAP-PENED?! THE CUP FLOATED!
WAS IT YOU?
AWWW. MY PHONE'S BROKEN.
I JUST GOT IT, TOO.
OH!
BUT I *DO* HAVE ANOTHER ONE.
SHI-ROTA-SAN'S.
!
SHI-RO... TA?
IT'S MAHIRU-KUN'S UNCLE'S, YOU SEE.
I'M JUST HOLDING ONTO IT.
....

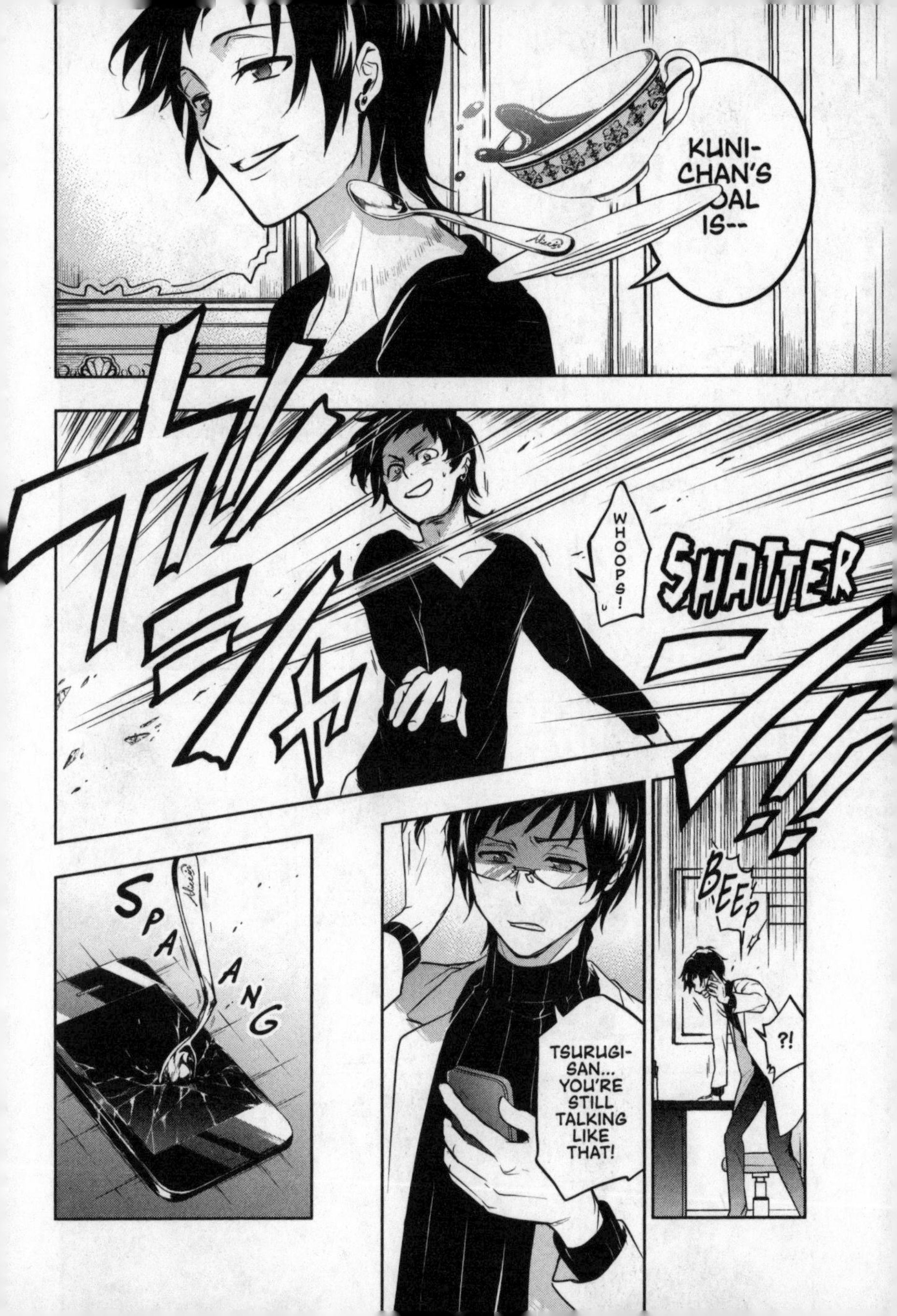
KUNI-CHAN'S OAL IS--
SHATTER
WHOOPS!
BEEP
?!
TSURUGI-SAN... YOU'RE STILL TALKING LIKE THAT!
SPAANG

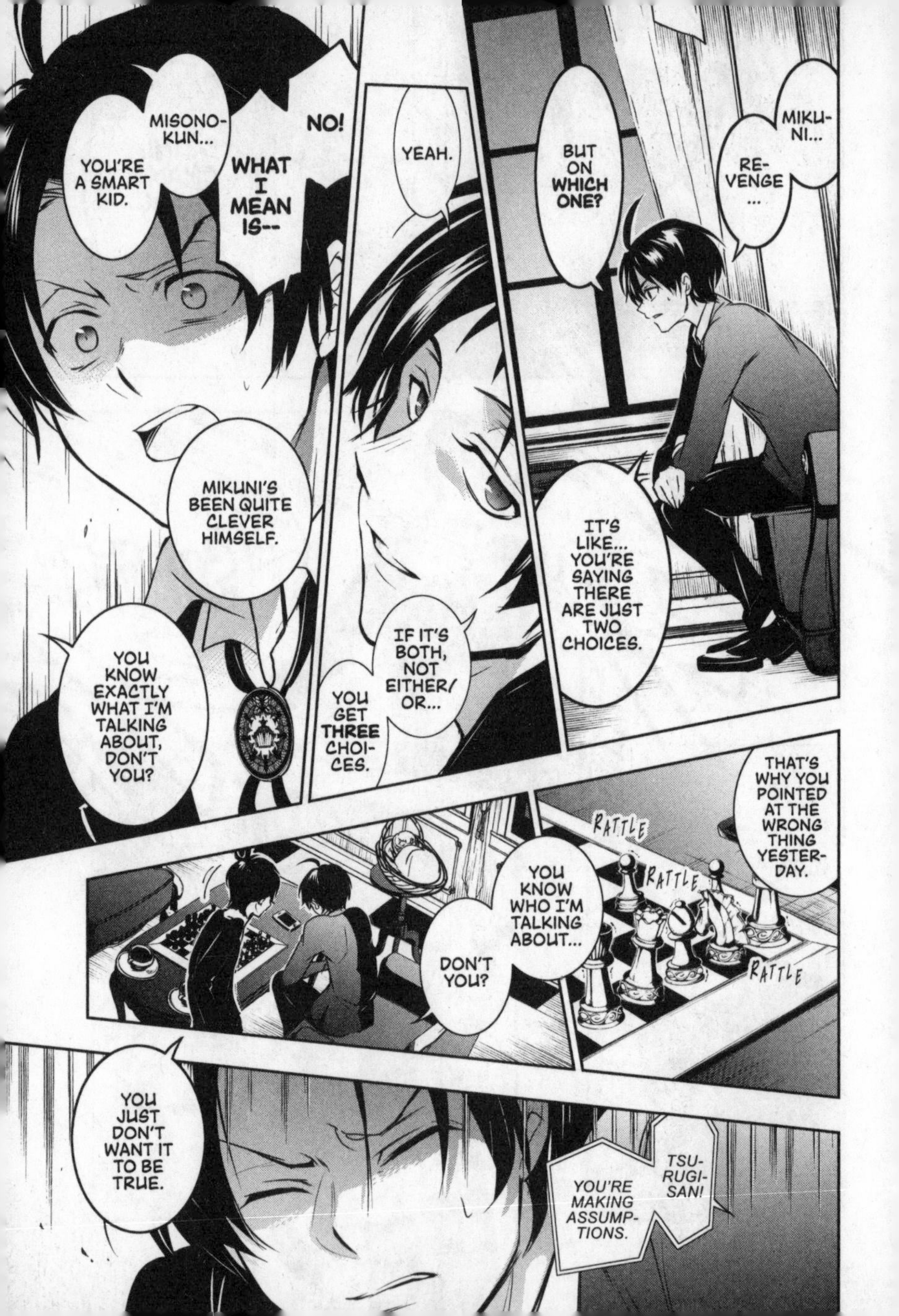
MIKUNI... REVENGE...
BUT ON WHICH ONE?
IT'S LIKE... YOU'RE SAYING THERE ARE JUST TWO CHOICES.
YEAH.
IF IT'S BOTH, NOT EITHER/OR...
YOU GET THREE CHOICES.
NO!
WHAT I MEAN IS--
MISONO-KUN...
YOU'RE A SMART KID.
MIKUNI'S BEEN QUITE CLEVER HIMSELF.
YOU KNOW EXACTLY WHAT I'M TALKING ABOUT, DON'T YOU?
THAT'S WHY YOU POINTED AT THE WRONG THING YESTERDAY.
RATTLE
RATTLE
RATTLE
YOU KNOW WHO I'M TALKING ABOUT...
DON'T YOU?
TSURUGI-SAN!
YOU'RE MAKING ASSUMPTIONS.
YOU JUST DON'T WANT IT TO BE TRUE.

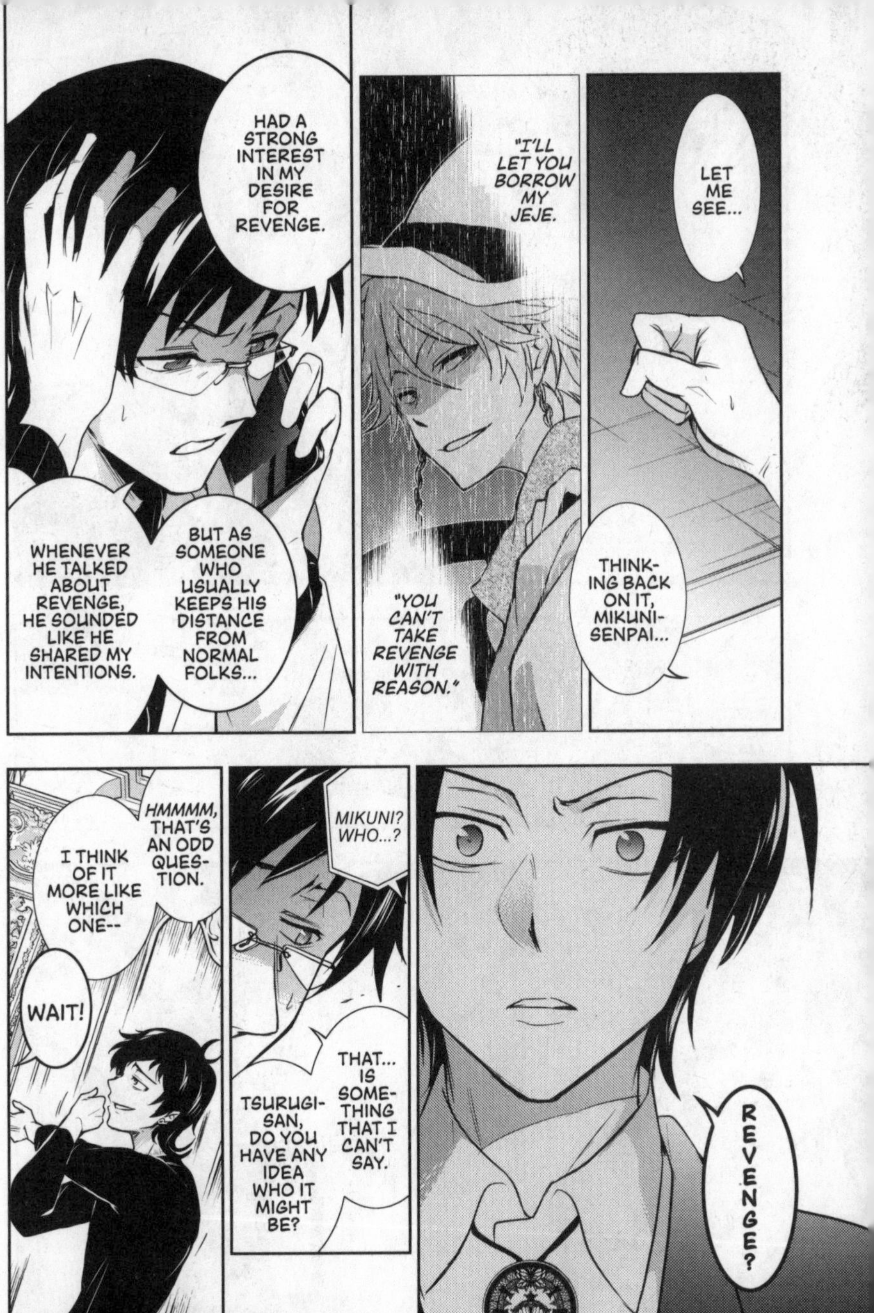
LET ME SEE...
THINKING BACK ON IT, MIKUNI-SENPAI...
"I'LL LET YOU BORROW MY JEJE.
"YOU CAN'T TAKE REVENGE WITH REASON."
HAD A STRONG INTEREST IN MY DESIRE FOR REVENGE.
BUT AS SOMEONE WHO USUALLY KEEPS HIS DISTANCE FROM NORMAL FOLKS...
WHENEVER HE TALKED ABOUT REVENGE, HE SOUNDED LIKE HE SHARED MY INTENTIONS.
REVENGE?
MIKUNI? WHO...?
THAT... IS SOMETHING THAT I CAN'T SAY.
TSURUGI-SAN, DO YOU HAVE ANY IDEA WHO IT MIGHT BE?
HMMMM, THAT'S AN ODD QUESTION.
I THINK OF IT MORE LIKE WHICH ONE--
WAIT!

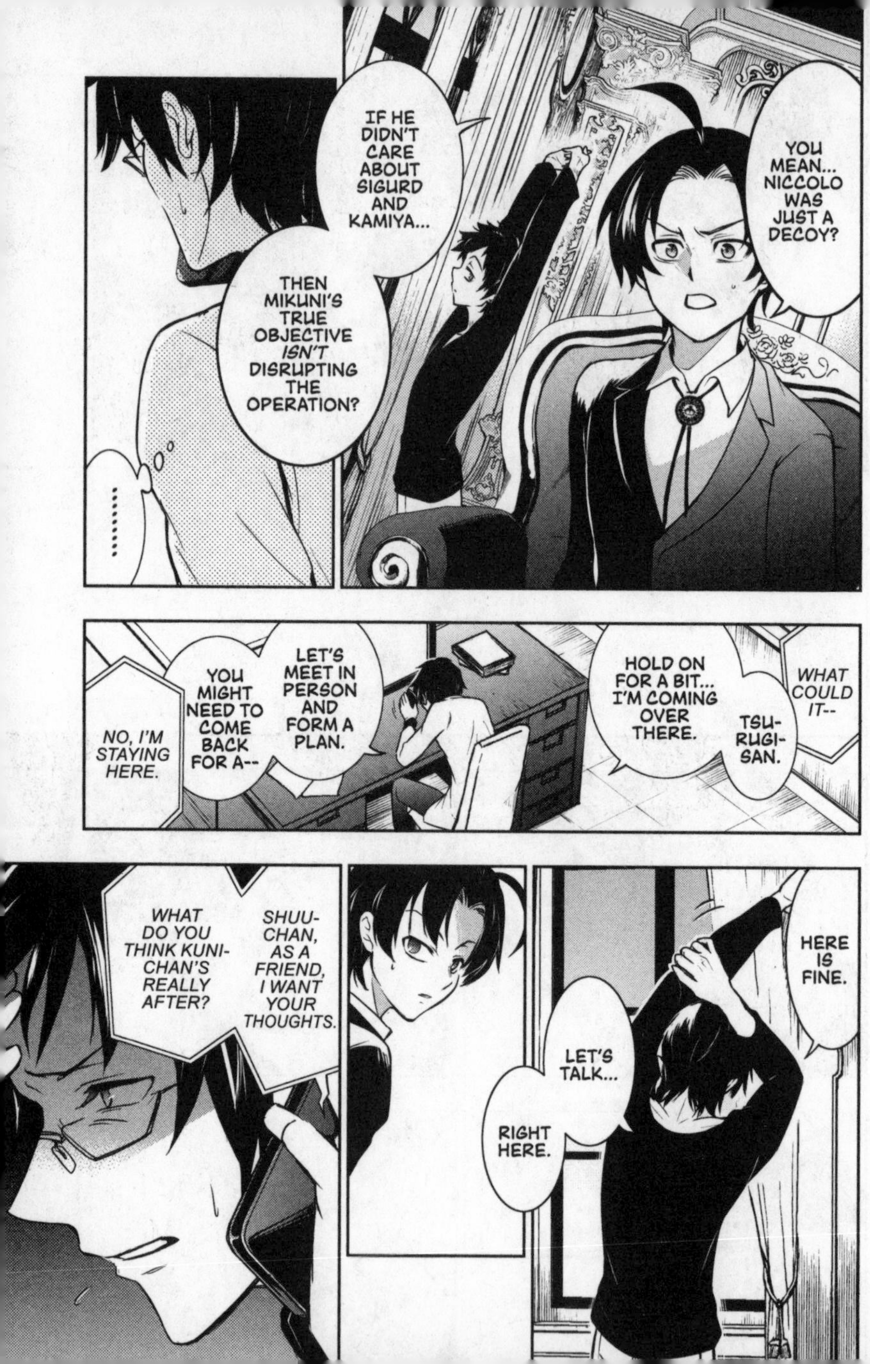
YOU MEAN... NICCOLO WAS JUST A DECOY?
IF HE DIDN'T CARE ABOUT SIGURD AND KAMIYA...
THEN MIKUNI'S TRUE OBJECTIVE *ISN'T* DISRUPTING THE OPERATION?
......
WHAT COULD IT--
TSU-RUGI-SAN.
HOLD ON FOR A BIT... I'M COMING OVER THERE.
LET'S MEET IN PERSON AND FORM A PLAN.
YOU MIGHT NEED TO COME BACK FOR A--
NO, I'M STAYING HERE.
HERE IS FINE.
LET'S TALK...
RIGHT HERE.
SHUU-CHAN, AS A FRIEND, I WANT YOUR THOUGHTS.
WHAT DO YOU THINK KUNI-CHAN'S REALLY AFTER?

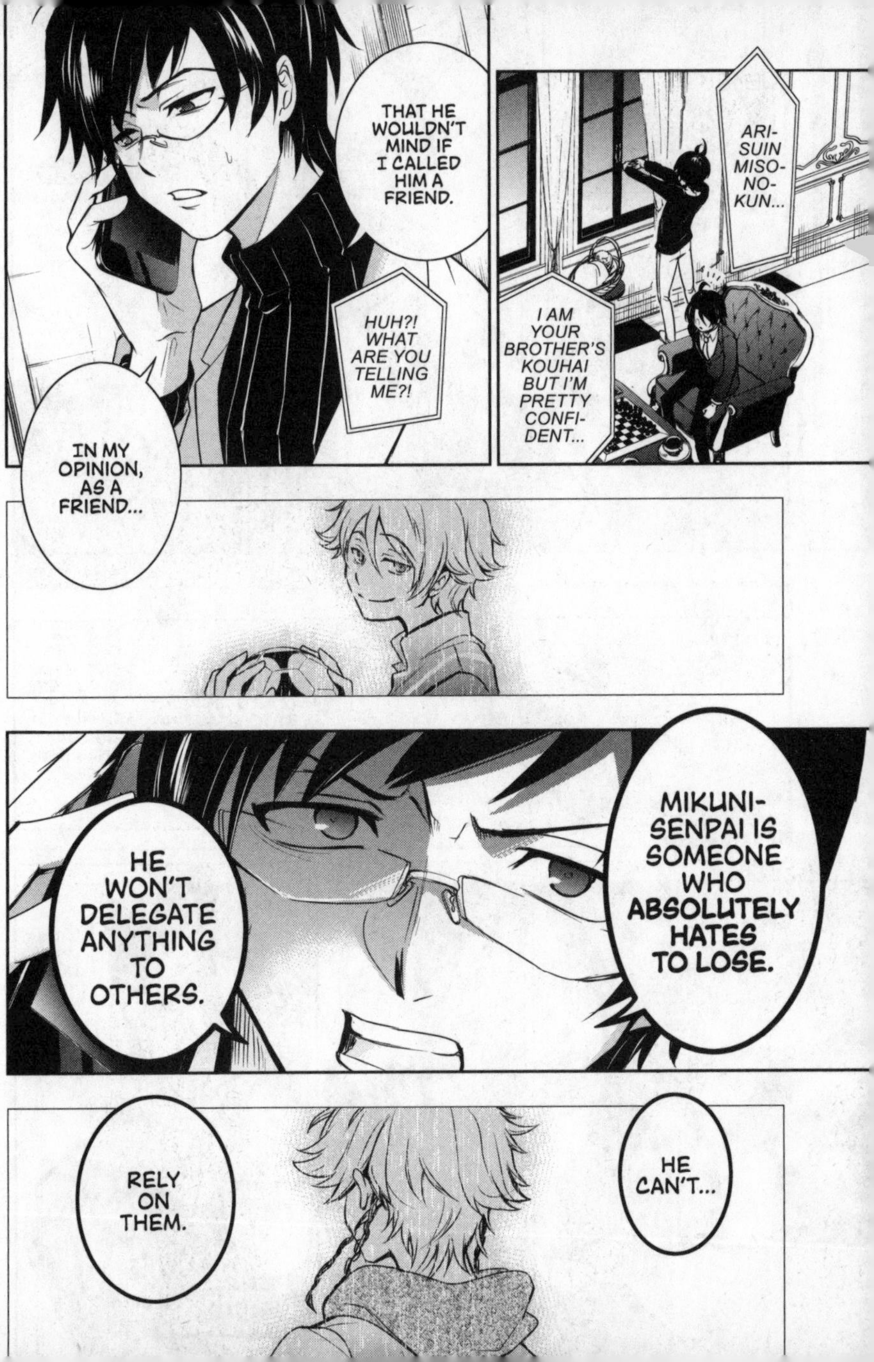
ARI-SUIN MISO-NO-KUN...
I AM YOUR BROTHER'S KOUHAI BUT I'M PRETTY CONFI-DENT...
THAT HE WOULDN'T MIND IF I CALLED HIM A FRIEND.
HUH?! WHAT ARE YOU TELLING ME?!
IN MY OPINION, AS A FRIEND...
MIKUNI-SENPAI IS SOMEONE WHO ABSOLUTELY HATES TO LOSE.
HE WON'T DELEGATE ANYTHING TO OTHERS.
HE CAN'T...
RELY ON THEM.

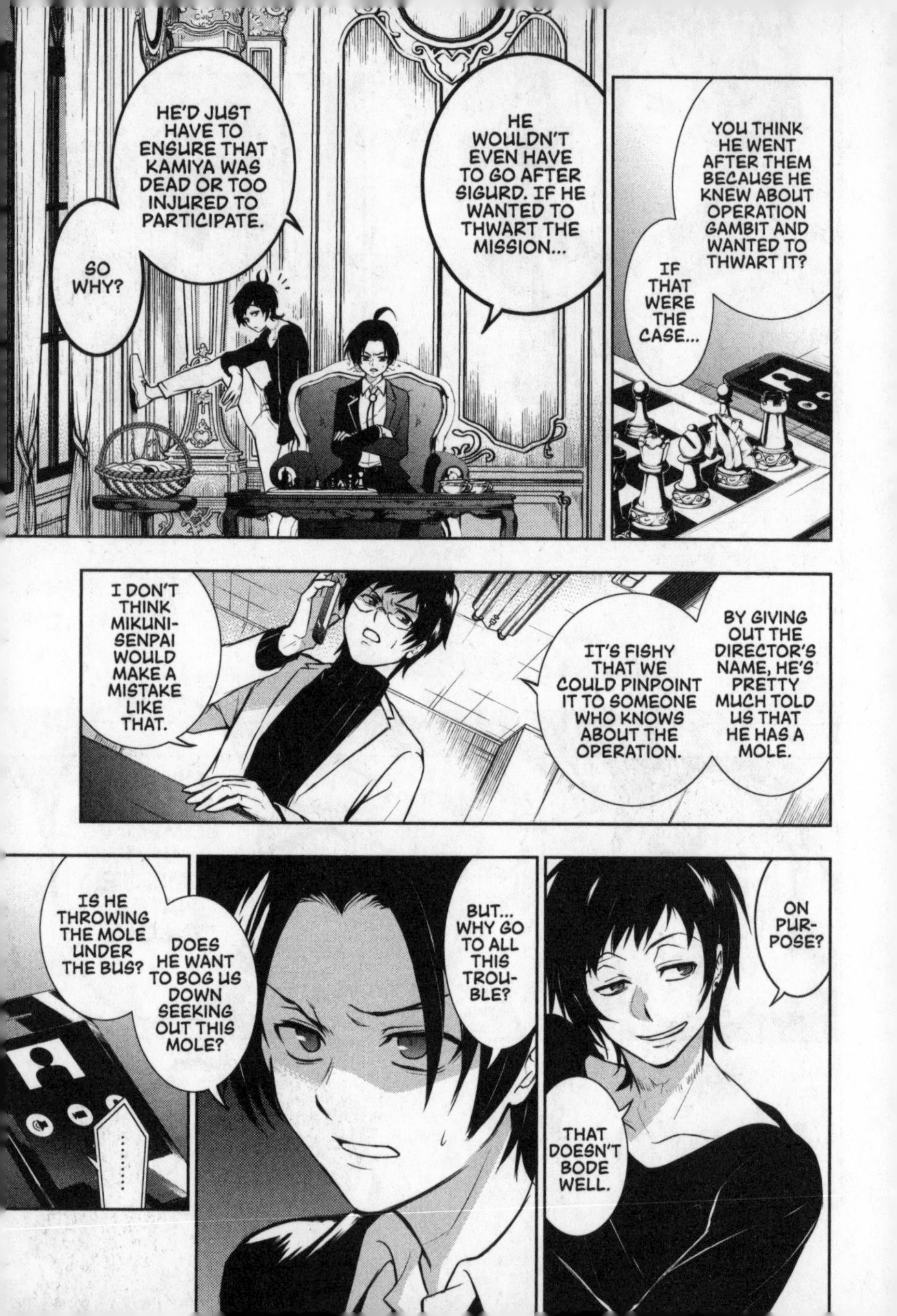
YOU THINK HE WENT AFTER THEM BECAUSE HE KNEW ABOUT OPERATION GAMBIT AND WANTED TO THWART IT?
IF THAT WERE THE CASE...
HE WOULDN'T EVEN HAVE TO GO AFTER SIGURD. IF HE WANTED TO THWART THE MISSION...
HE'D JUST HAVE TO ENSURE THAT KAMIYA WAS DEAD OR TOO INJURED TO PARTICIPATE.
SO WHY?
BY GIVING OUT THE DIRECTOR'S NAME, HE'S PRETTY MUCH TOLD US THAT HE HAS A MOLE.
IT'S FISHY THAT WE COULD PINPOINT IT TO SOMEONE WHO KNOWS ABOUT THE OPERATION.
I DON'T THINK MIKUNI-SENPAI WOULD MAKE A MISTAKE LIKE THAT.
ON PUR-POSE?
THAT DOESN'T BODE WELL.
BUT... WHY GO TO ALL THIS TROU-BLE?
IS HE THROWING THE MOLE UNDER THE BUS?
DOES HE WANT TO BOG US DOWN SEEKING OUT THIS MOLE?
......

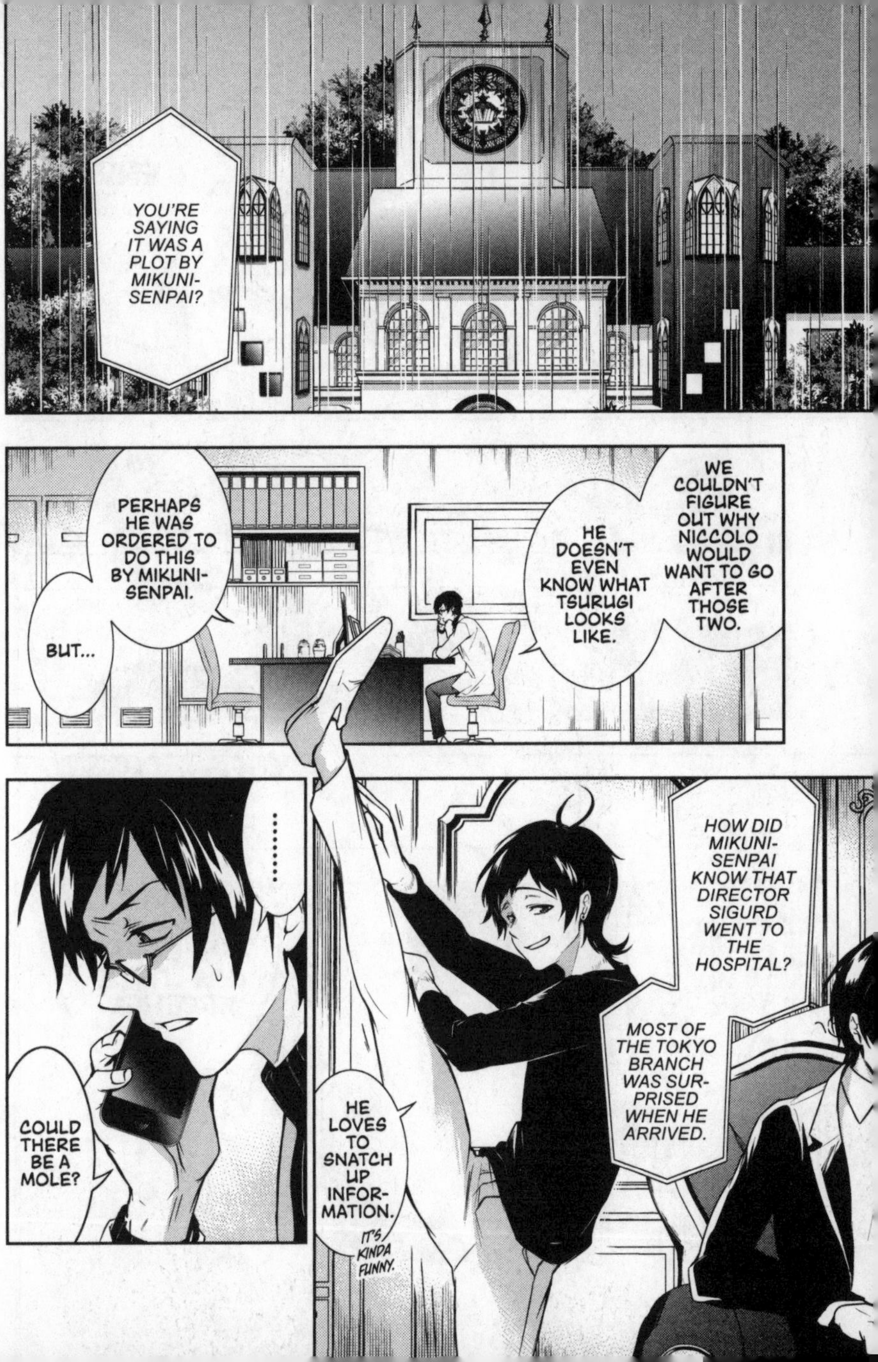
YOU'RE SAYING IT WAS A PLOT BY MIKUNI-SENPAI?
WE COULDN'T FIGURE OUT WHY NICCOLO WOULD WANT TO GO AFTER THOSE TWO.
HE DOESN'T EVEN KNOW WHAT TSURUGI LOOKS LIKE.
PERHAPS HE WAS ORDERED TO DO THIS BY MIKUNI-SENPAI.
BUT...
HOW DID MIKUNI-SENPAI KNOW THAT DIRECTOR SIGURD WENT TO THE HOSPITAL?
MOST OF THE TOKYO BRANCH WAS SURPRISED WHEN HE ARRIVED.
HE LOVES TO SNATCH UP INFORMATION.
IT'S KINDA FUNNY.
......
COULD THERE BE A MOLE?

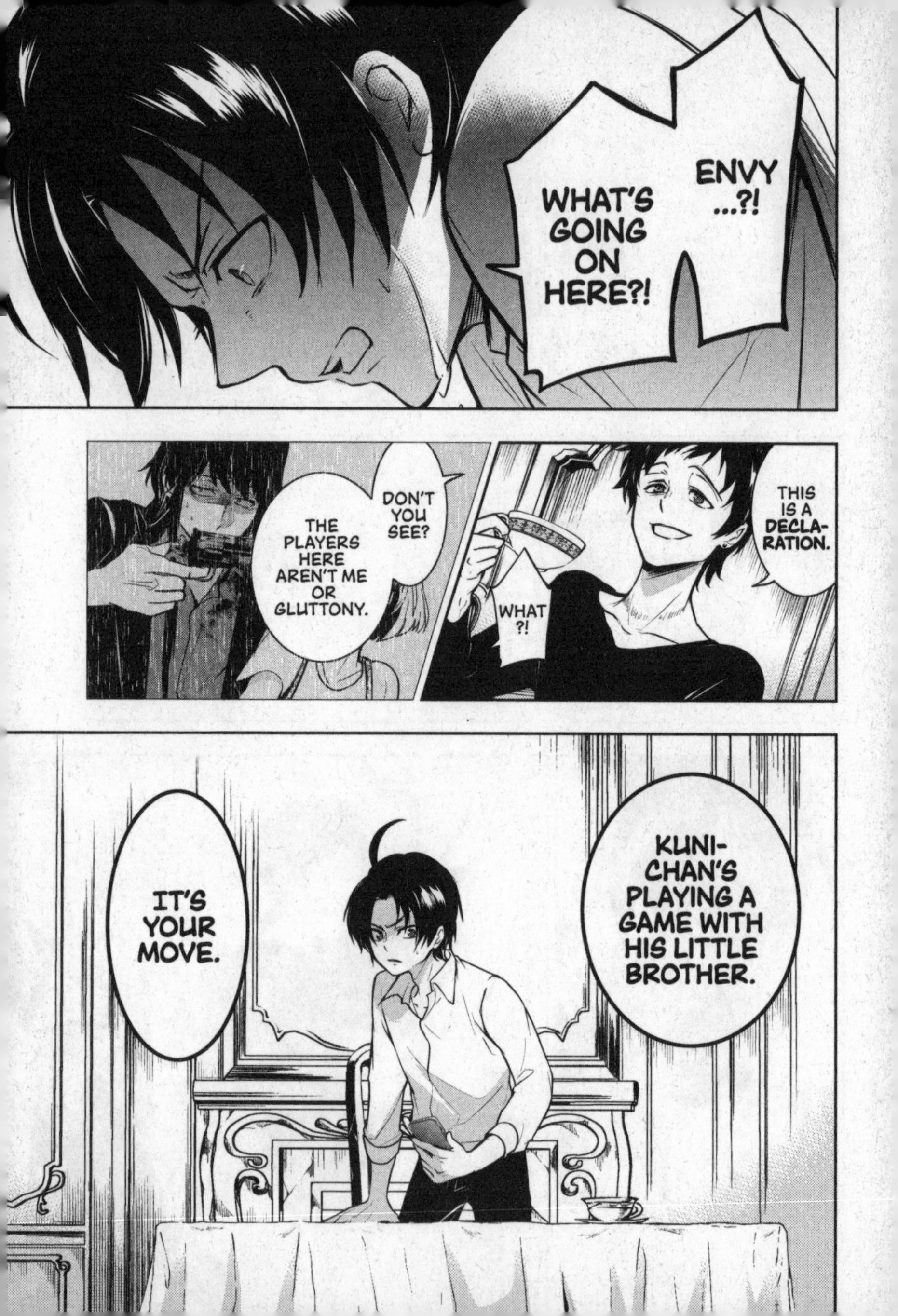
ENVY ...?!
WHAT'S GOING ON HERE?!
THIS IS A DECLARATION.
WHAT ?!
DON'T YOU SEE?
THE PLAYERS HERE AREN'T ME OR GLUTTONY.
KUNI-CHAN'S PLAYING A GAME WITH HIS LITTLE BROTHER.
IT'S YOUR MOVE.

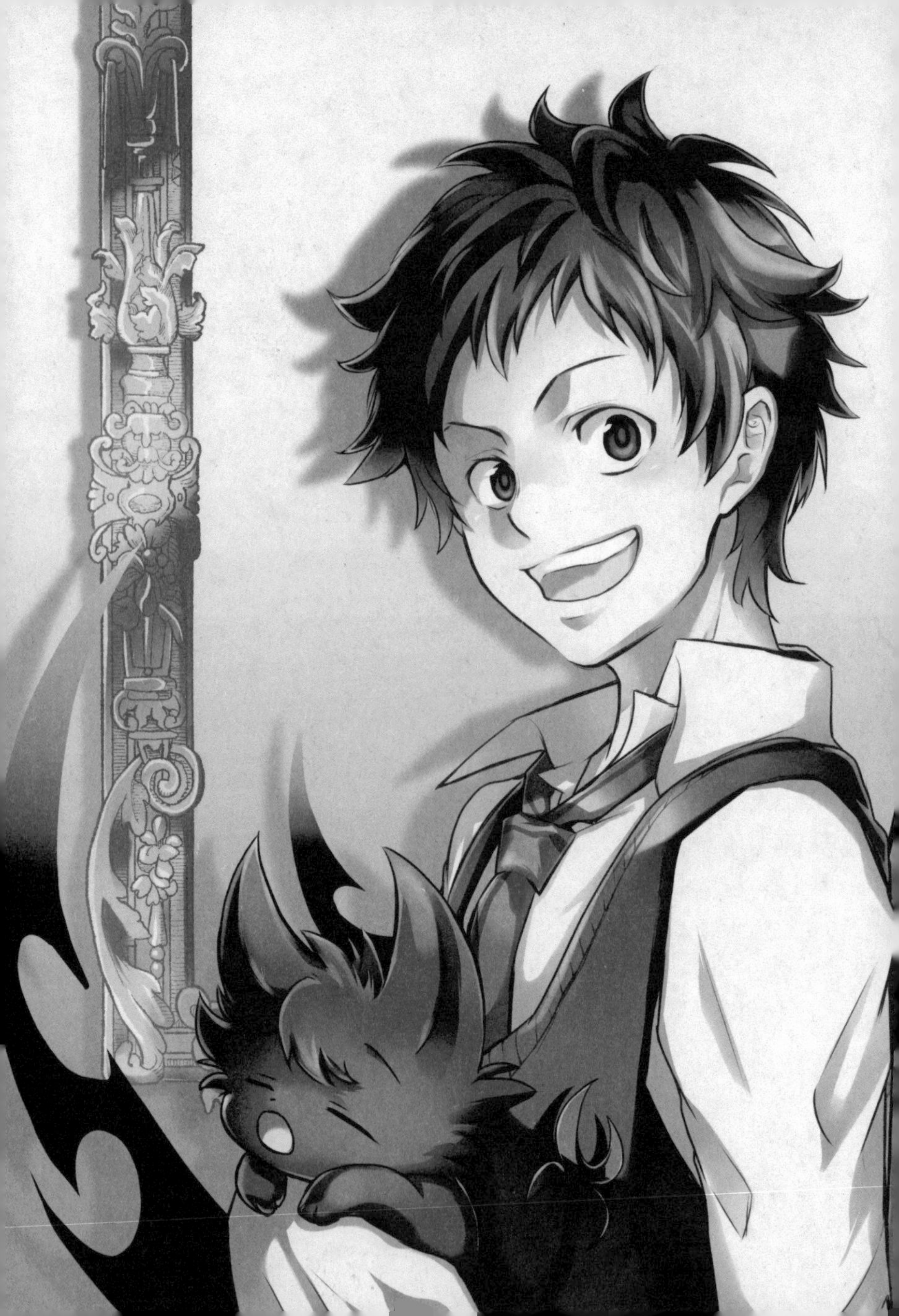

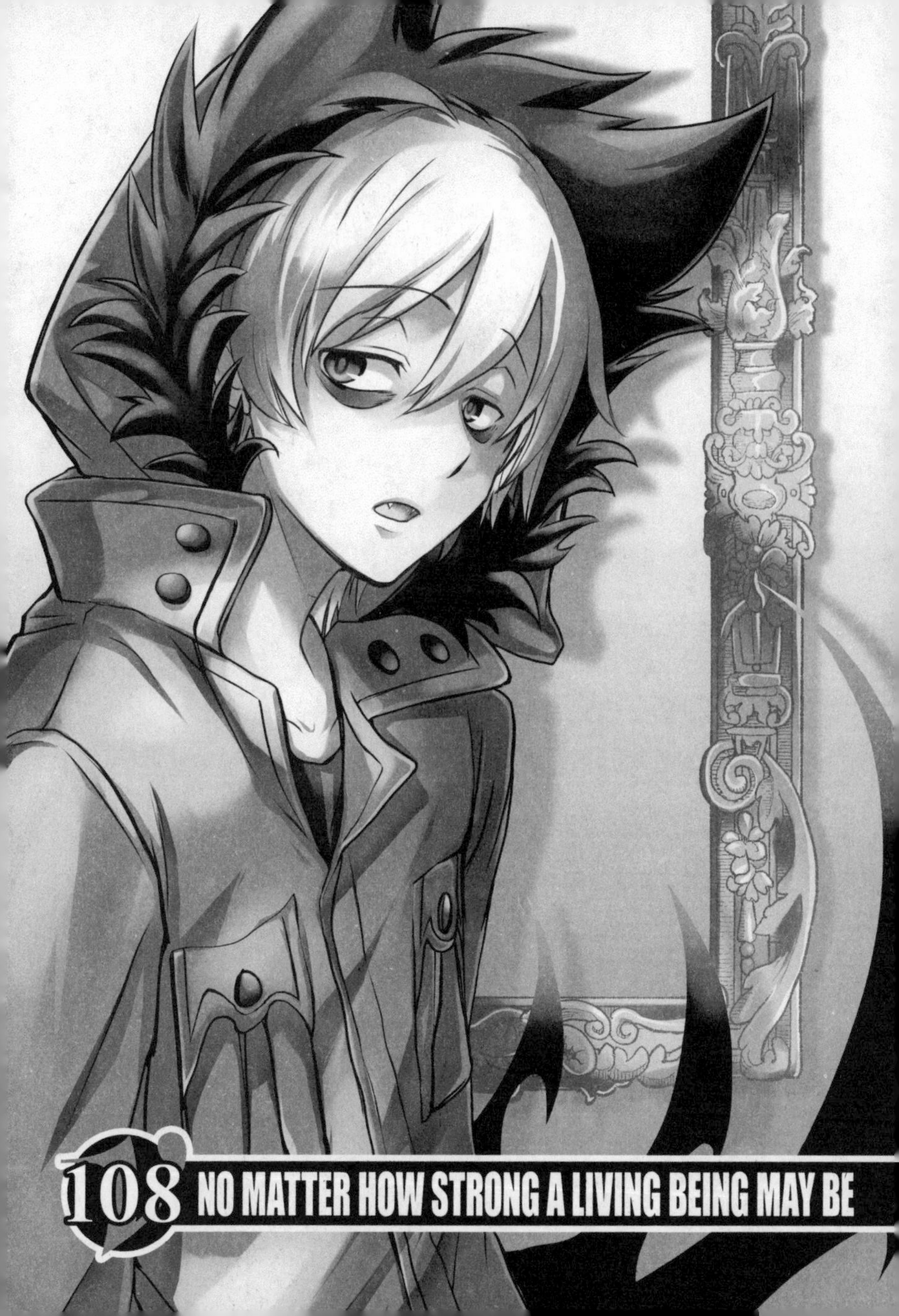

108 NO MATTER HOW STRONG A LIVING BEING MAY BE

SERVAMP

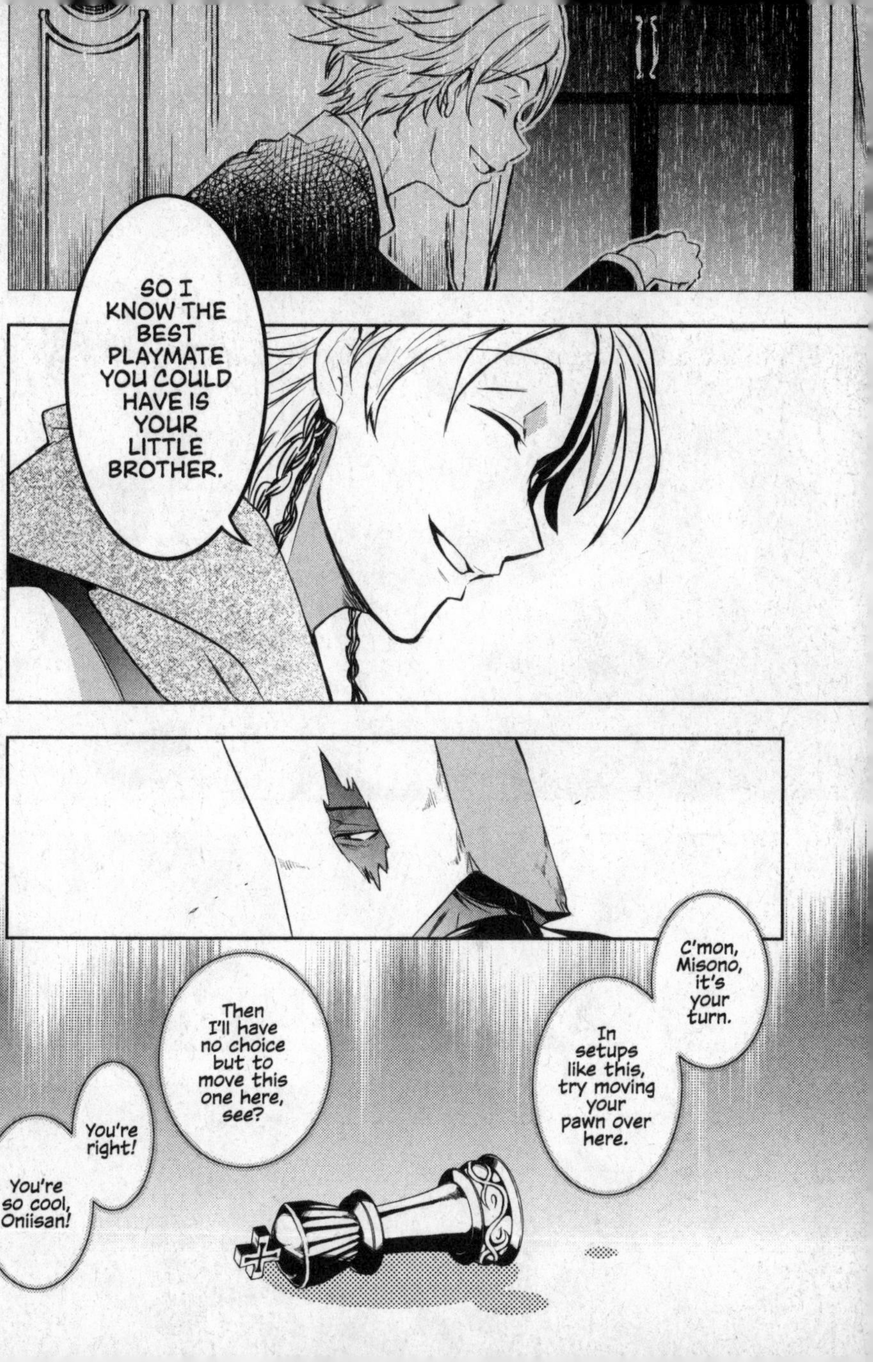
SO I KNOW THE BEST PLAYMATE YOU COULD HAVE IS YOUR LITTLE BROTHER.
C'mon, Misono, it's your turn.
In setups like this, try moving your pawn over here.
Then I'll have no choice but to move this one here, see?
You're right!
You're so cool, Oniisan!

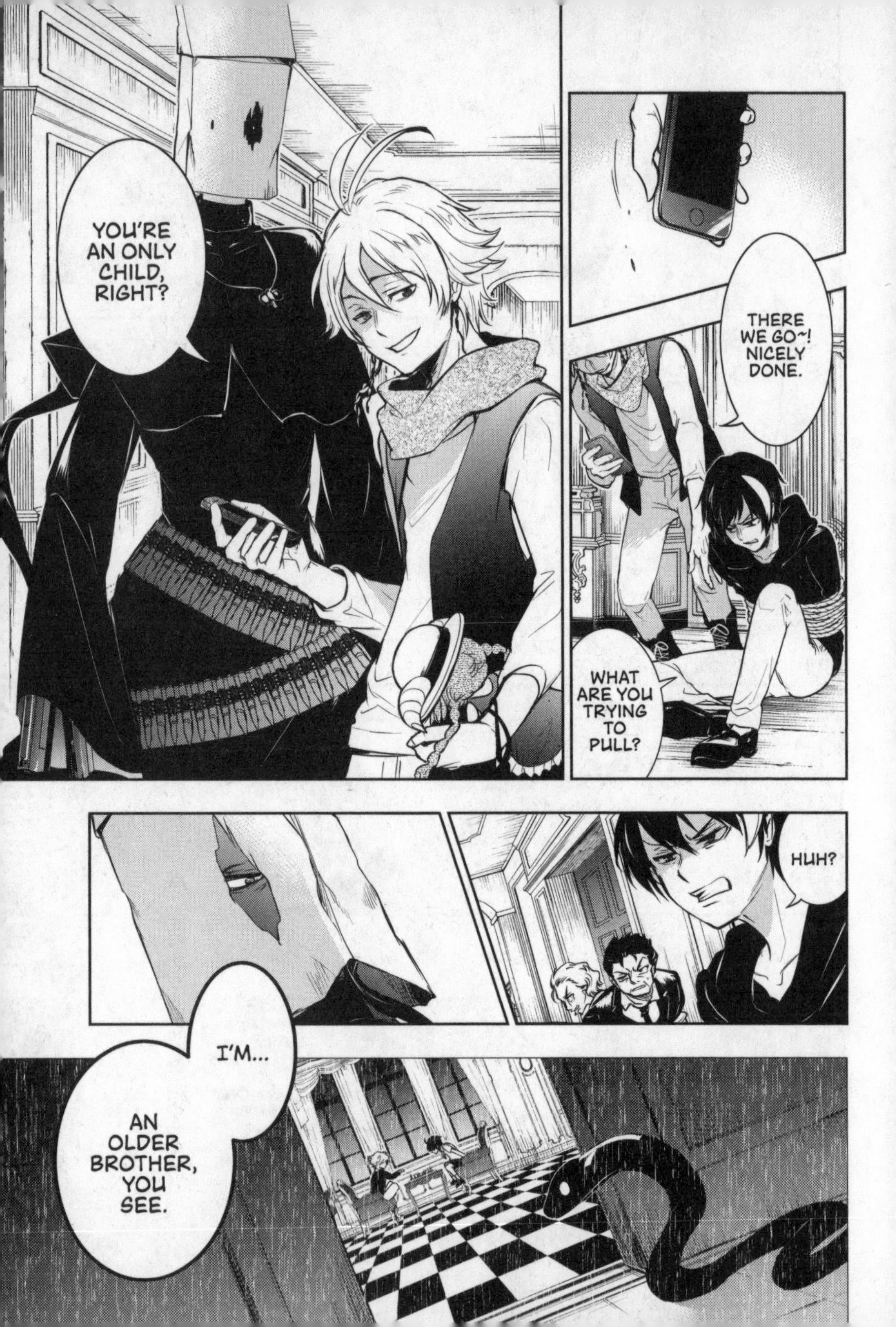
THERE WE GO~! NICELY DONE.
WHAT ARE YOU TRYING TO PULL?
YOU'RE AN ONLY CHILD, RIGHT?
HUH?
I'M...
AN OLDER BROTHER, YOU SEE.

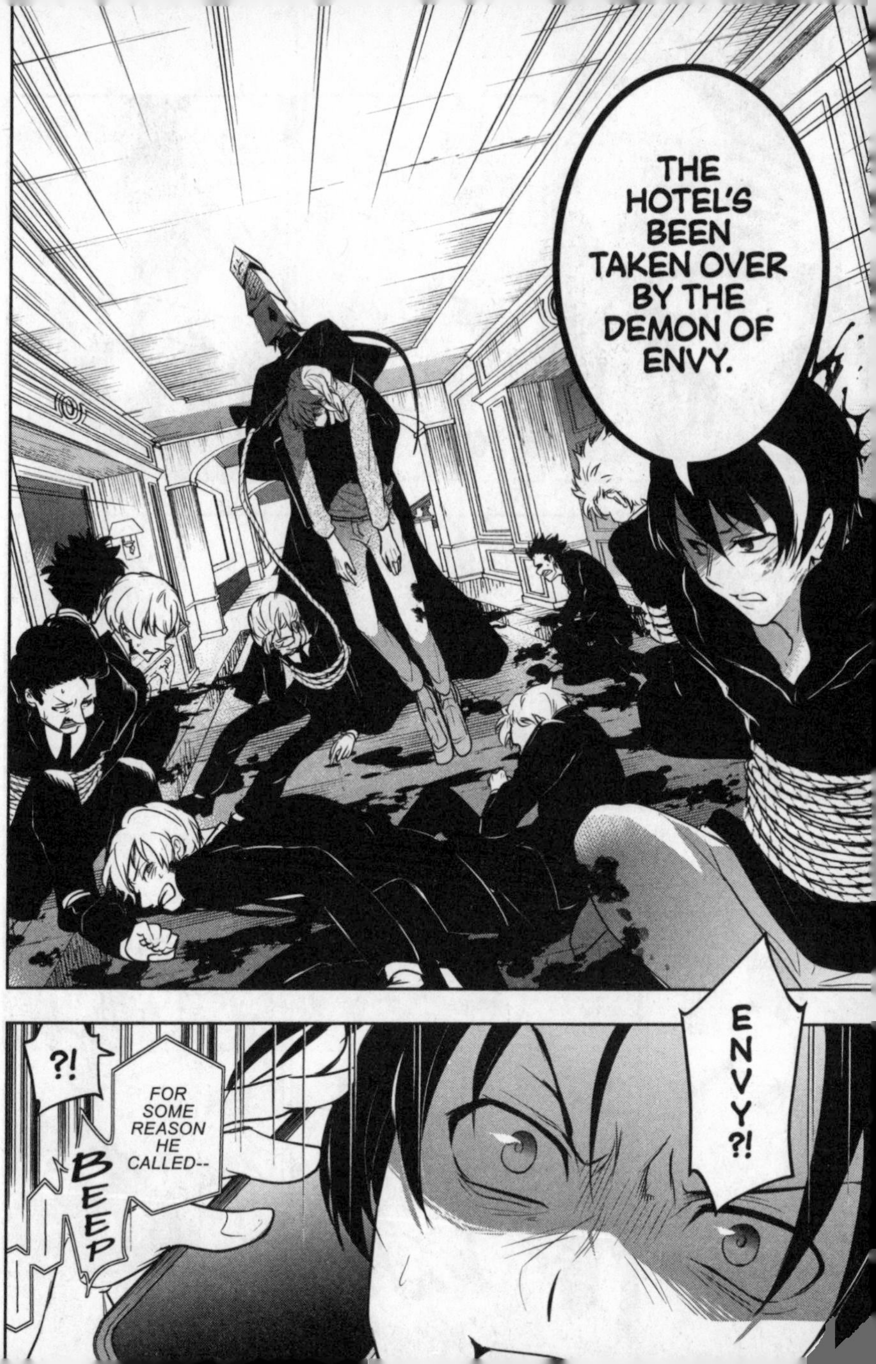
THE HOTEL'S BEEN TAKEN OVER BY THE DEMON OF ENVY.
ENVY?!
?!
FOR SOME REASON HE CALLED--
BEEP

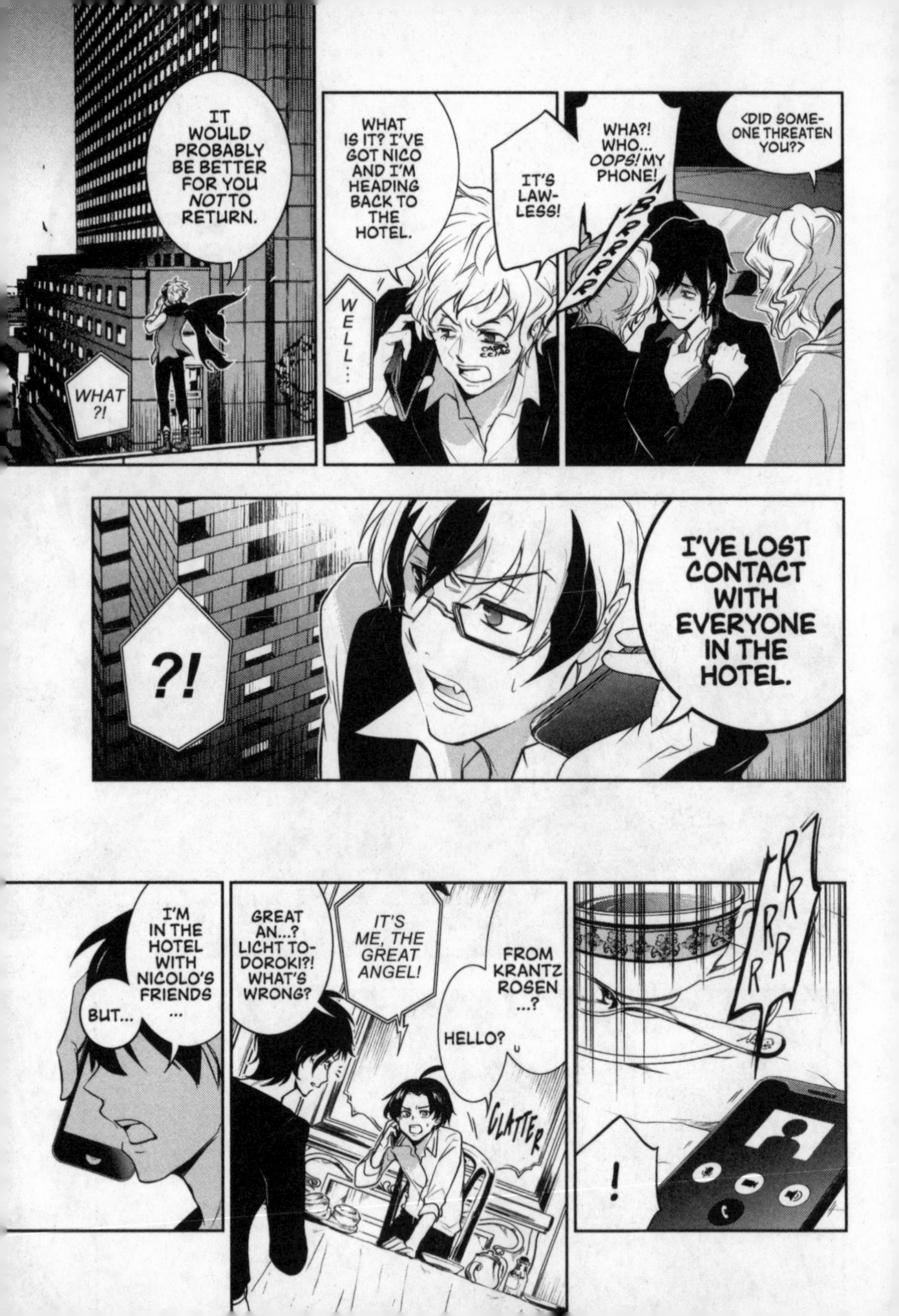
<DID SOME-ONE THREATEN YOU?>
WHA?! WHO... OOPS! MY PHONE!
IT'S LAW-LESS!
BRRRRR
WHAT IS IT? I'VE GOT NICO AND I'M HEADING BACK TO THE HOTEL.
WELL...
IT WOULD PROBABLY BE BETTER FOR YOU NOT TO RETURN.
WHAT?!
I'VE LOST CONTACT WITH EVERYONE IN THE HOTEL.
?!
RRRRR
!
FROM KRANTZ ROSEN...?
HELLO?
IT'S ME, THE GREAT ANGEL!
GREAT AN...? LICHT TO-DOROKI?! WHAT'S WRONG?
CLATTER
I'M IN THE HOTEL WITH NICOLO'S FRIENDS...
BUT...

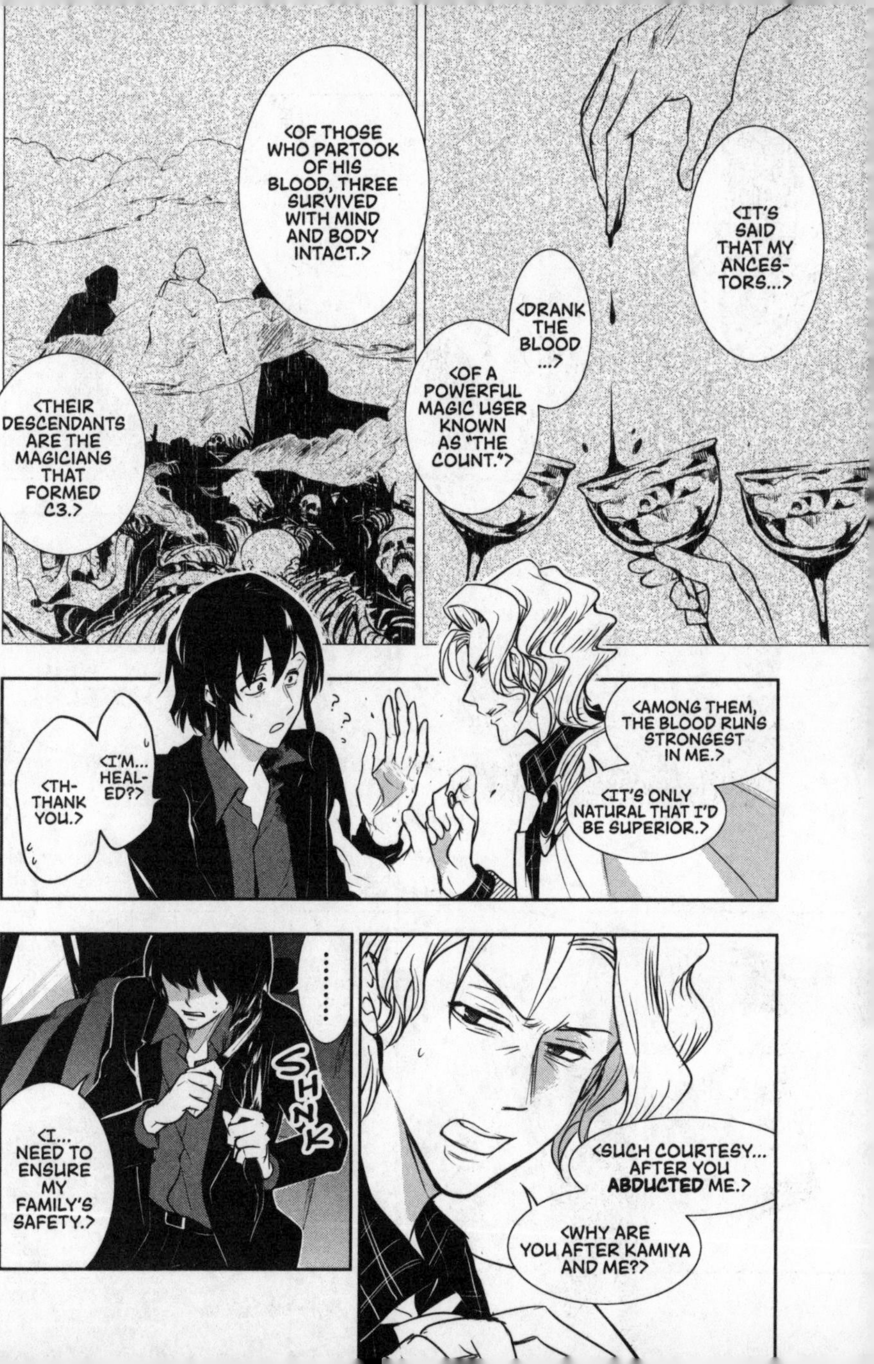
<IT'S SAID THAT MY ANCES-TORS...>
<DRANK THE BLOOD ...>
<OF A POWERFUL MAGIC USER KNOWN AS "THE COUNT.">
<OF THOSE WHO PARTOOK OF HIS BLOOD, THREE SURVIVED WITH MIND AND BODY INTACT.>
<THEIR DESCENDANTS ARE THE MAGICIANS THAT FORMED C3.>
<AMONG THEM, THE BLOOD RUNS STRONGEST IN ME.>
<IT'S ONLY NATURAL THAT I'D BE SUPERIOR.>
<I'M... HEAL-ED?>
<TH-THANK YOU.>
<SUCH COURTESY... AFTER YOU **ABDUCTED** ME.>
<WHY ARE YOU AFTER KAMIYA AND ME?>
......
SHNK
<I... NEED TO ENSURE MY FAMILY'S SAFETY.>

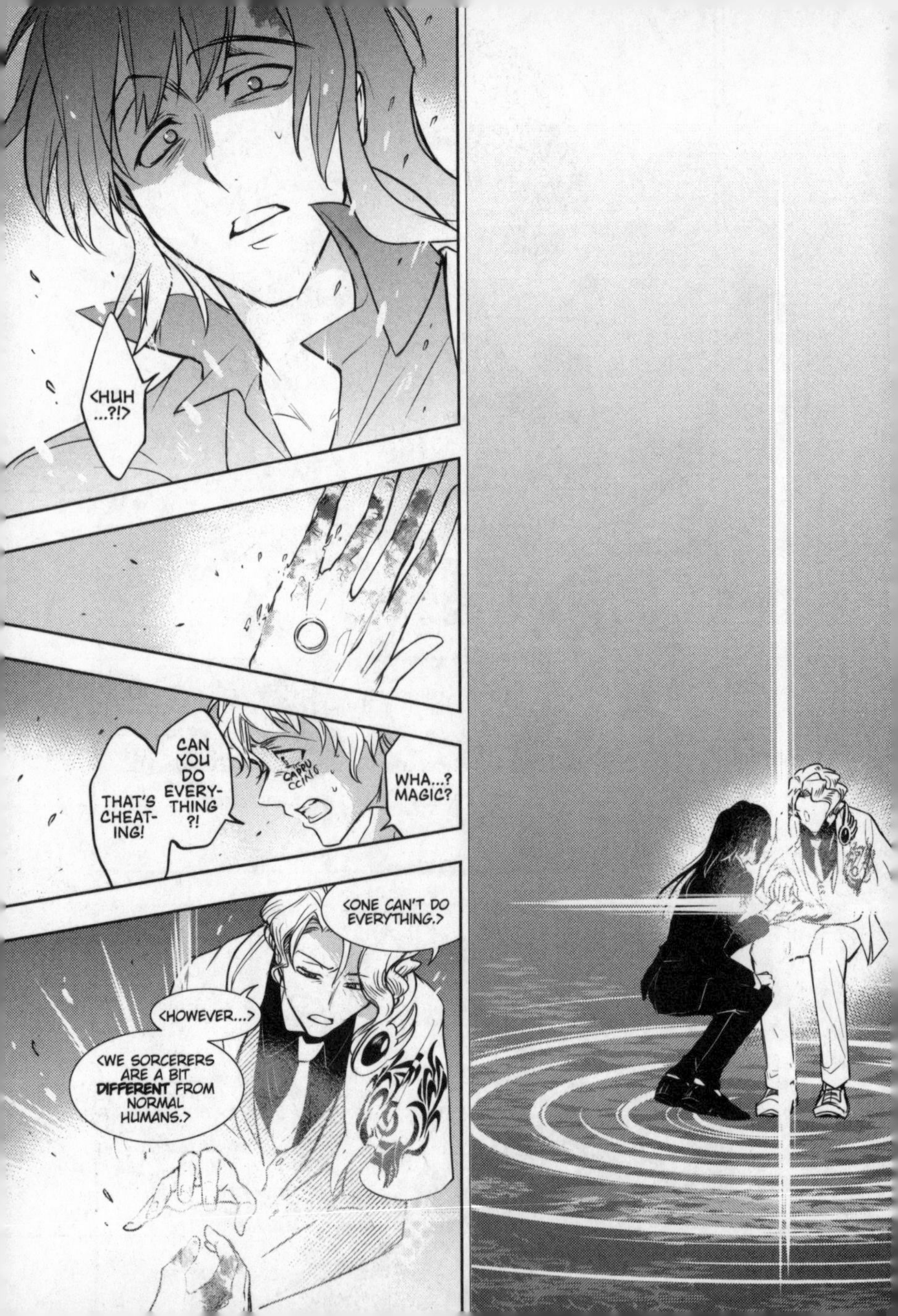
<HUH ...?!>
WHA...? MAGIC?
CAPPUCCINO
CAN YOU DO EVERYTHING ?!
THAT'S CHEATING!
<ONE CAN'T DO EVERYTHING.>
<HOWEVER...>
<WE SORCERERS ARE A BIT **DIFFERENT** FROM NORMAL HUMANS.>

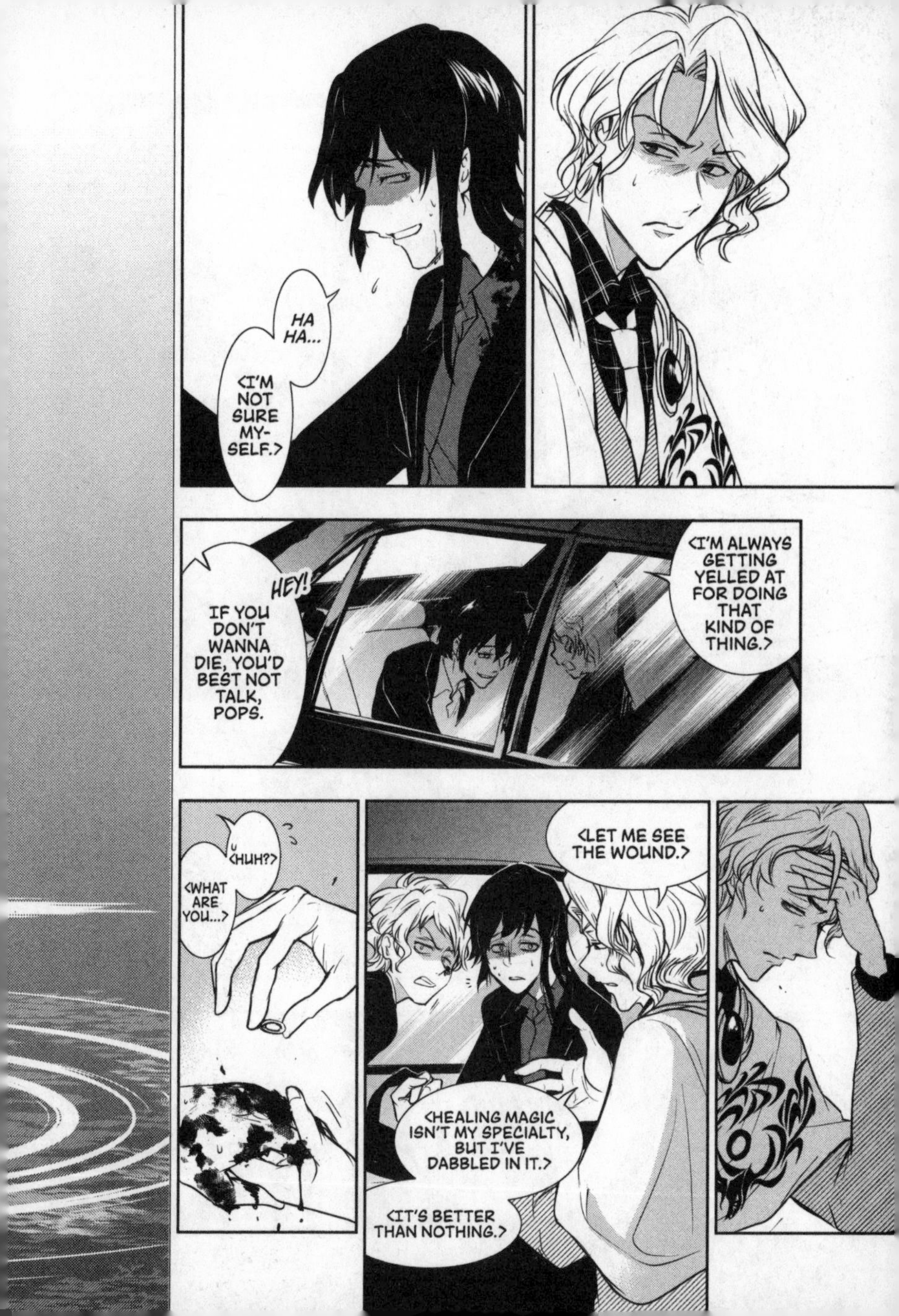
HA HA...
<I'M NOT SURE MYSELF.>
<I'M ALWAYS GETTING YELLED AT FOR DOING THAT KIND OF THING.>
HEY!
IF YOU DON'T WANNA DIE, YOU'D BEST NOT TALK, POPS.
<LET ME SEE THE WOUND.>
<HEALING MAGIC ISN'T MY SPECIALTY, BUT I'VE DABBLED IN IT.>
<IT'S BETTER THAN NOTHING.>
<HUH?>
<WHAT ARE YOU...>

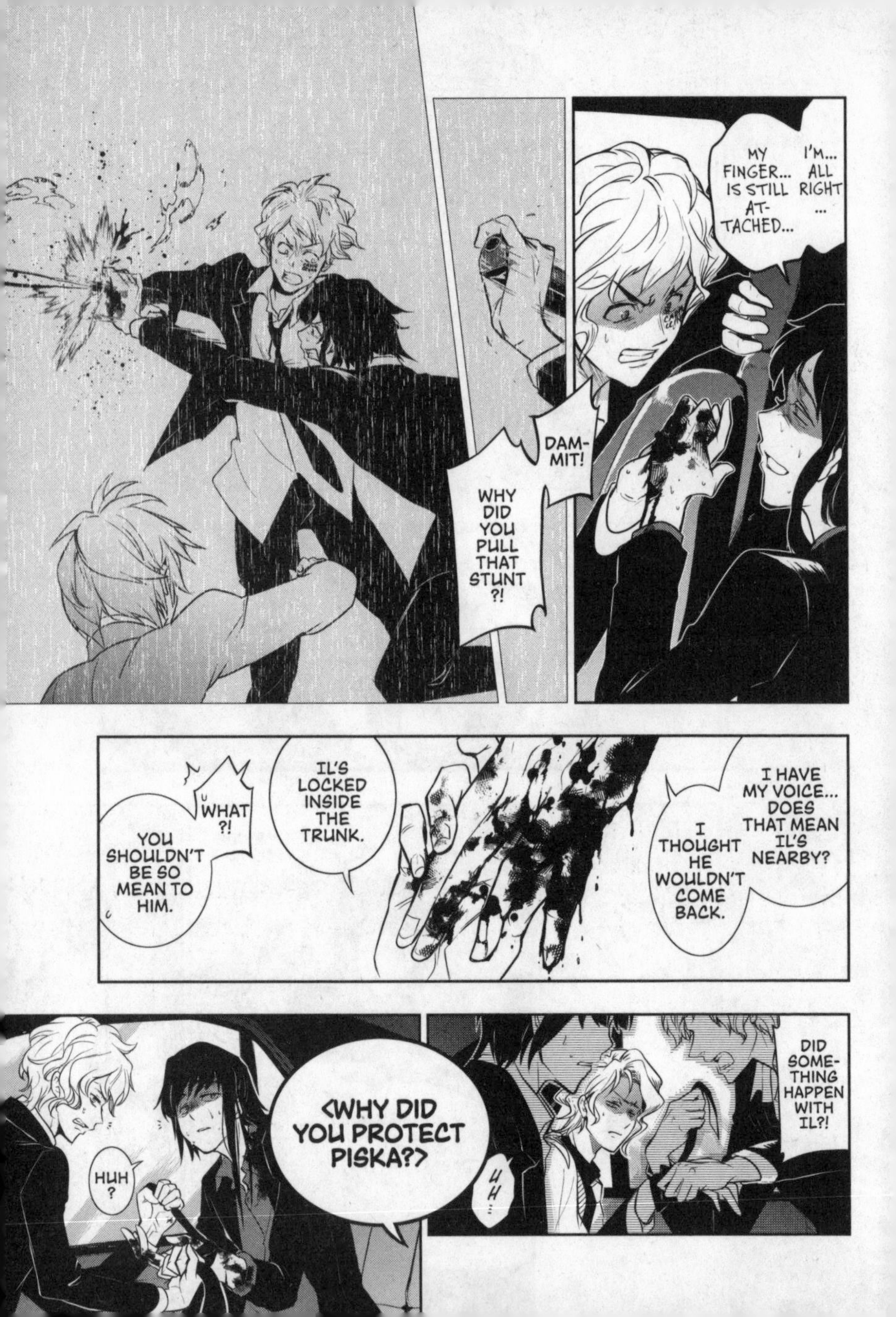
I'M... ALL RIGHT...
MY FINGER... IS STILL AT-TACHED...
DAM-MIT!
WHY DID YOU PULL THAT STUNT?!
I HAVE MY VOICE... DOES THAT MEAN IL'S NEARBY?
I THOUGHT HE WOULDN'T COME BACK.
IL'S LOCKED INSIDE THE TRUNK.
WHAT?!
YOU SHOULDN'T BE SO MEAN TO HIM.
DID SOMETHING HAPPEN WITH IL?!
UH...
<WHY DID YOU PROTECT PISKA?>
HUH?

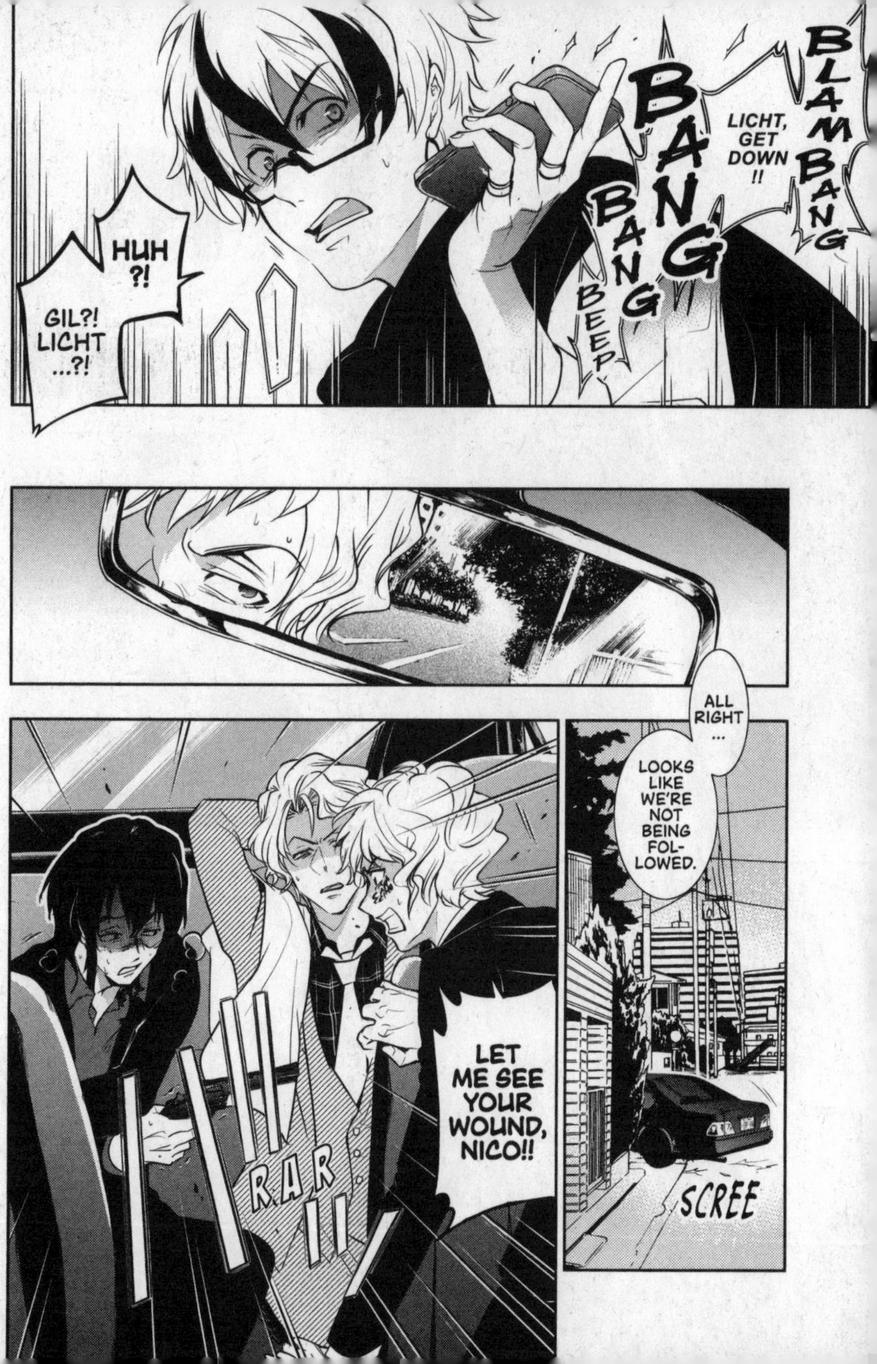
BLAM BANG
LICHT, GET DOWN !!
BANG
BANG
BEEP
HUH ?!
GIL?! LICHT ...?!
ALL RIGHT ...
LOOKS LIKE WE'RE NOT BEING FOL-LOWED.
SCREE
LET ME SEE YOUR WOUND, NICO!!
RAR !!

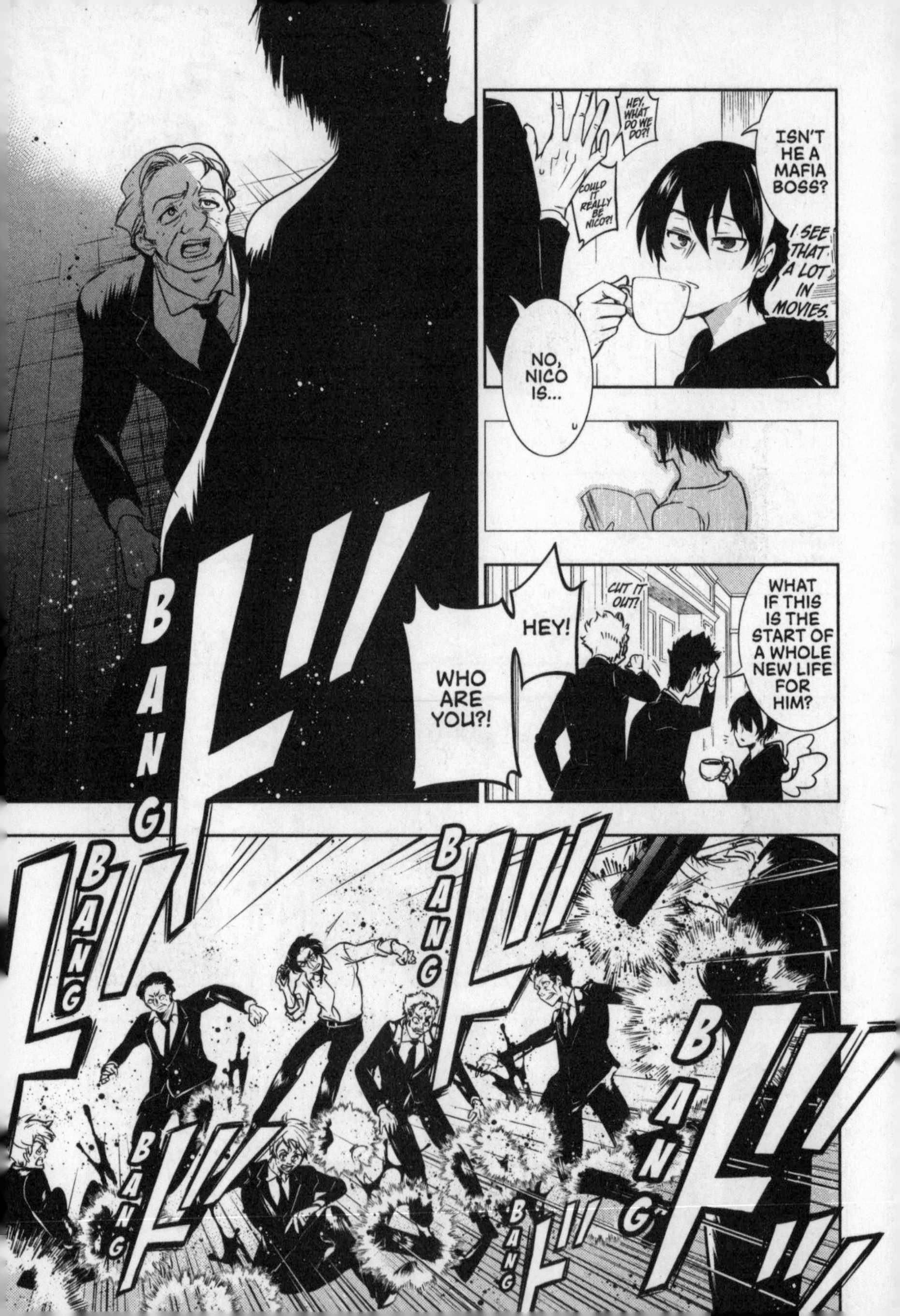

ISN'T HE A MAFIA BOSS?
I SEE THAT A LOT IN MOVIES.
HEY, WHAT DO WE DO?!
COULD IT REALLY BE NICO?!
NO, NICO IS...
WHAT IF THIS IS THE START OF A WHOLE NEW LIFE FOR HIM?
CUT IT OUT!
HEY!
WHO ARE YOU?!
BANG
BANG
BANG
BANG
BANG
BANG

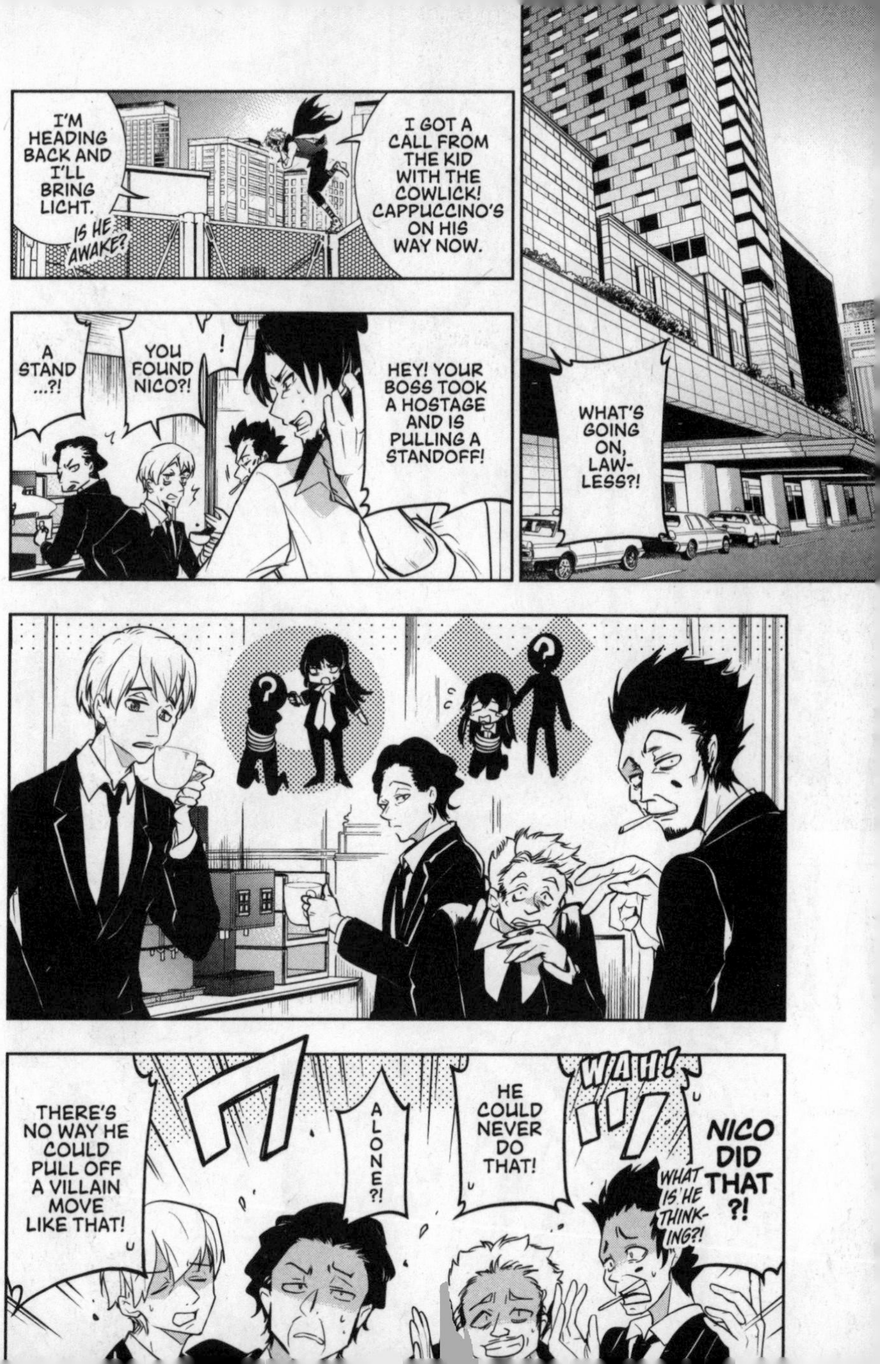
WHAT'S GOING ON, LAWLESS?!
I GOT A CALL FROM THE KID WITH THE COWLICK! CAPPUCCINO'S ON HIS WAY NOW.
I'M HEADING BACK AND I'LL BRING LICHT.
IS HE AWAKE?
HEY! YOUR BOSS TOOK A HOSTAGE AND IS PULLING A STANDOFF!
!
YOU FOUND NICO?!
A STAND...?!
NICO DID THAT?!
WHAT IS HE THINKING?!
WAH!
HE COULD NEVER DO THAT!
ALONE?!
THERE'S NO WAY HE COULD PULL OFF A VILLAIN MOVE LIKE THAT!

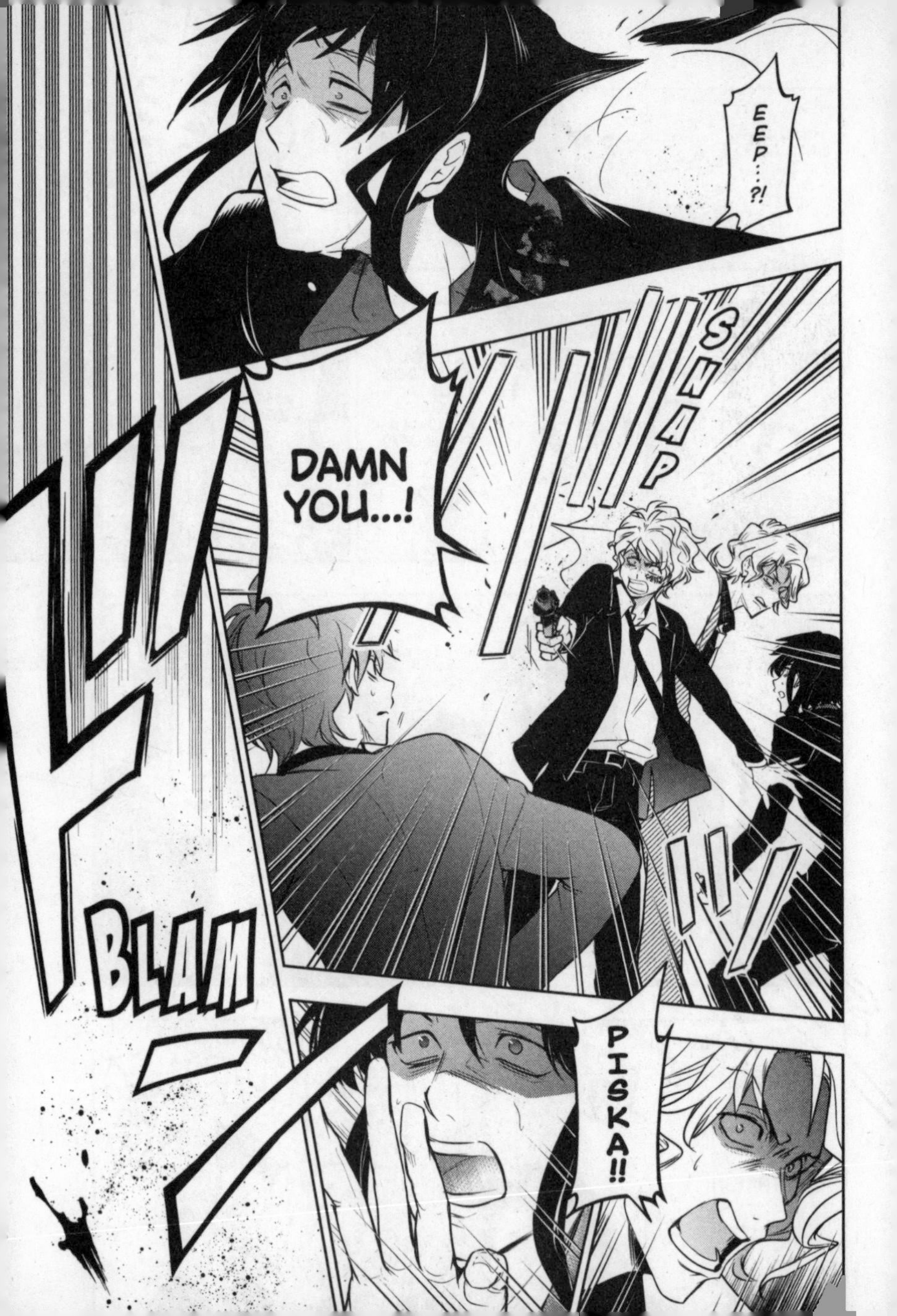
EEP...?!
SNAP
DAMN YOU...!
BLAM
PISKA!!

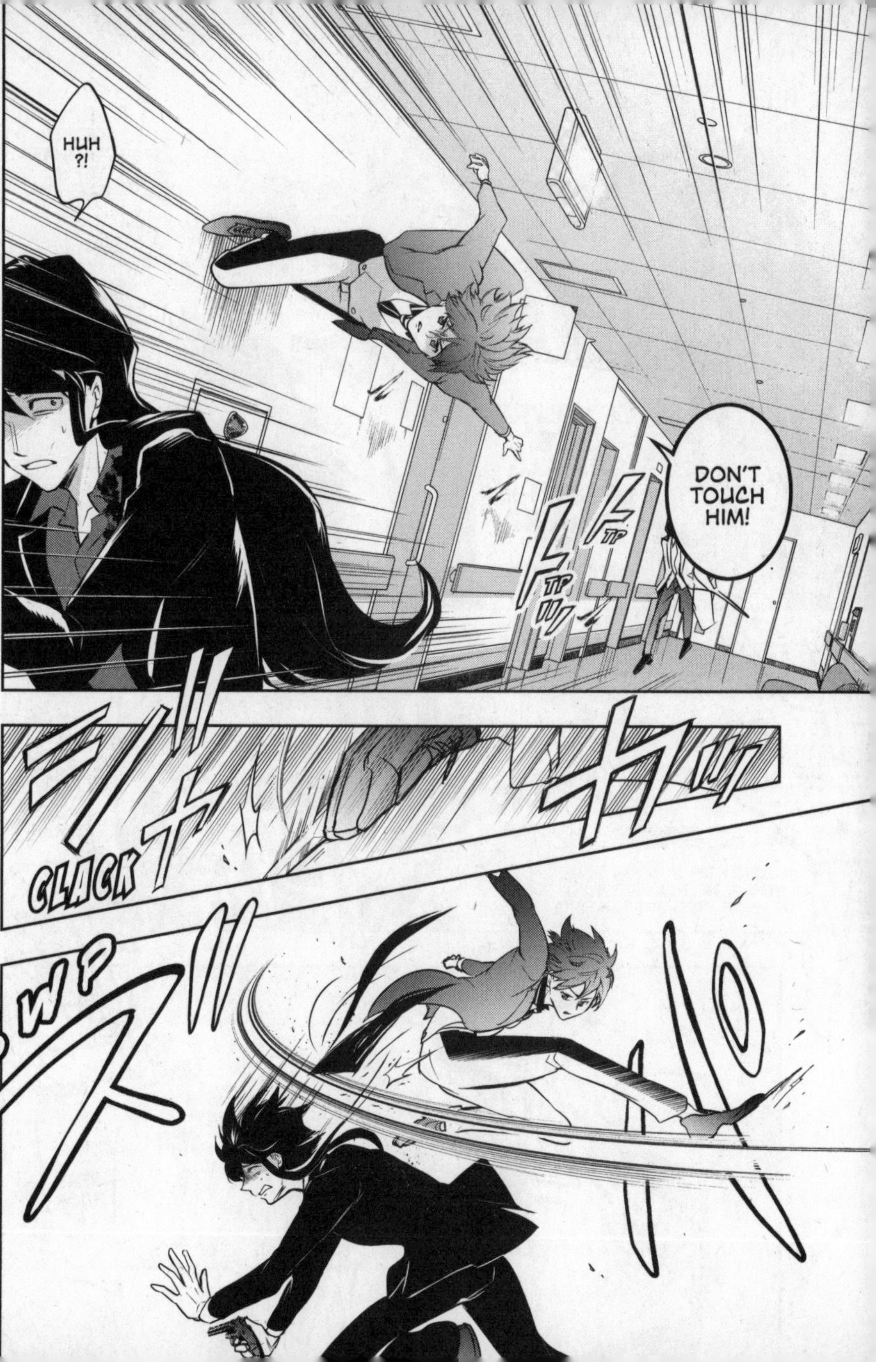
DON'T TOUCH HIM!
TP
TP
HUH ?!
CLACK
SWP

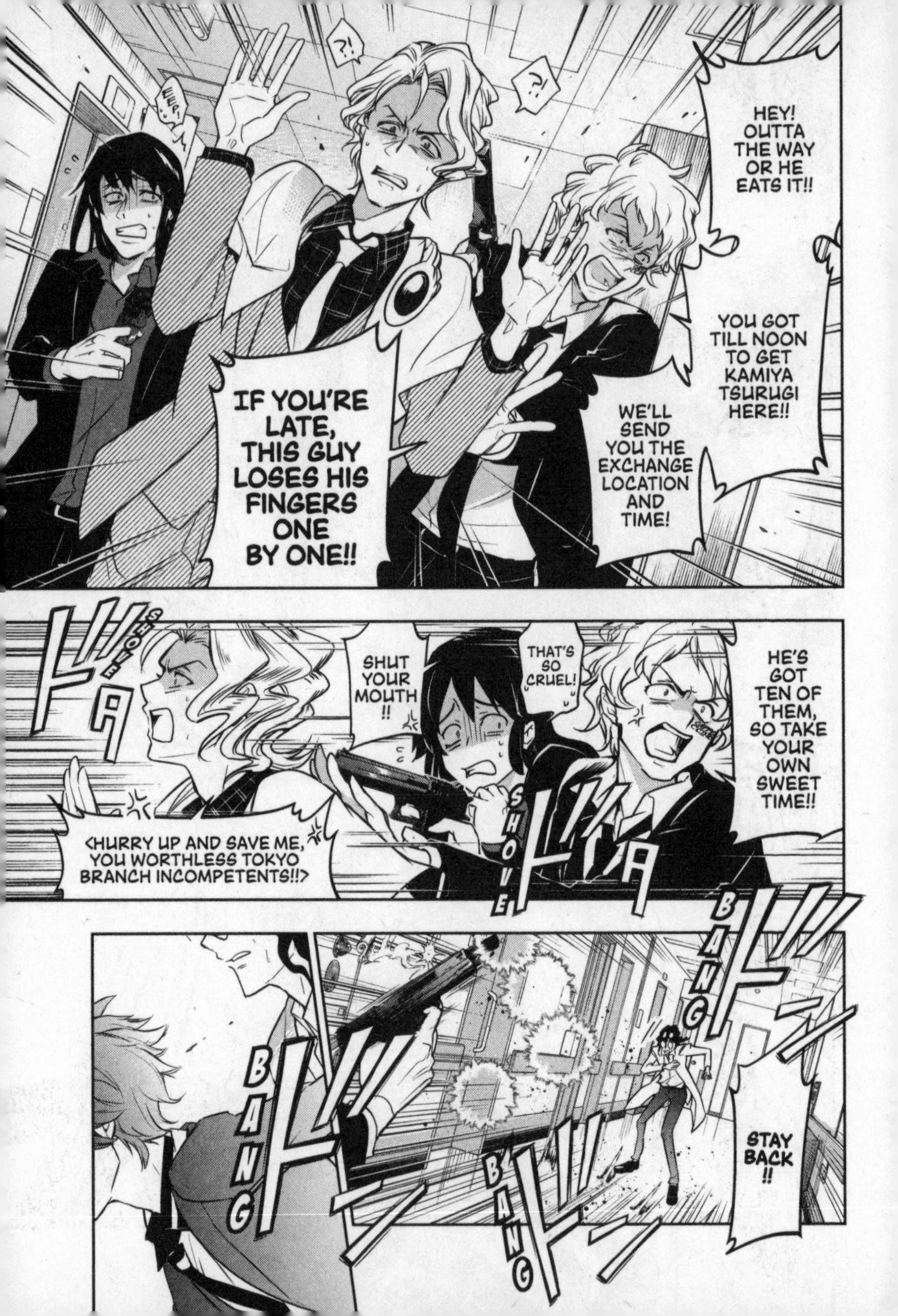
?!
?!
EEP!
HEY! OUTTA THE WAY OR HE EATS IT!!
YOU GOT TILL NOON TO GET KAMIYA TSURUGI HERE!!
WE'LL SEND YOU THE EXCHANGE LOCATION AND TIME!
IF YOU'RE LATE, THIS GUY LOSES HIS FINGERS ONE BY ONE!!
HE'S GOT TEN OF THEM, SO TAKE YOUR OWN SWEET TIME!!
THAT'S SO CRUEL!
SHOVE
SHUT YOUR MOUTH!!
SHOVE
<HURRY UP AND SAVE ME, YOU WORTHLESS TOKYO BRANCH INCOMPETENTS!!>
BANG
STAY BACK!!
BANG
BANG

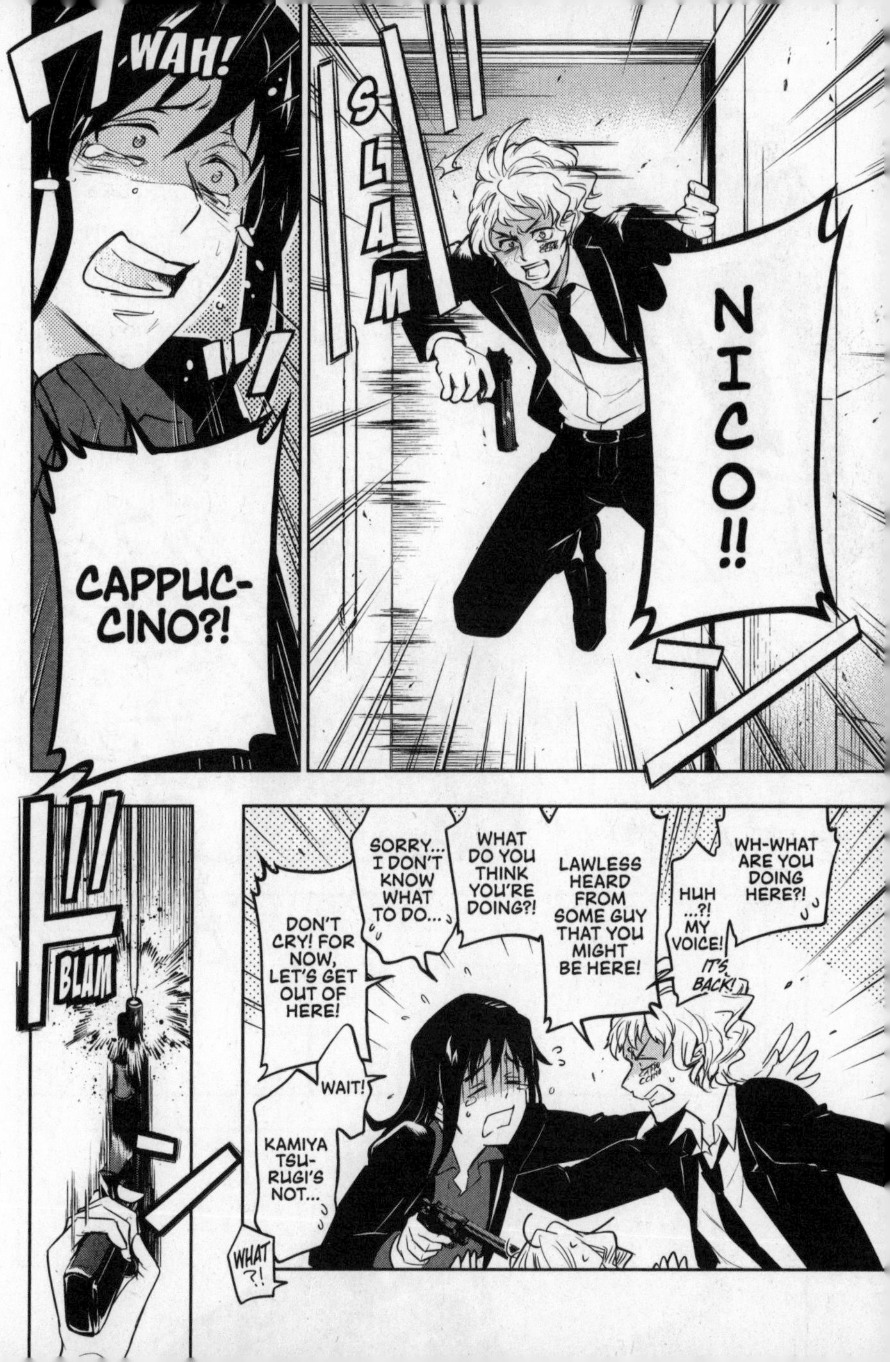
SLAM
NICO!!
WAH!
CAPPUCCINO?!
WH-WHAT ARE YOU DOING HERE?!
HUH ...?! MY VOICE!
IT'S BACK!
LAWLESS HEARD FROM SOME GUY THAT YOU MIGHT BE HERE!
WHAT DO YOU THINK YOU'RE DOING?!
SORRY... I DON'T KNOW WHAT TO DO...
DON'T CRY! FOR NOW, LET'S GET OUT OF HERE!
WAIT!
KAMIYA TSURUGI'S NOT...
WHAT ?!
BLAM

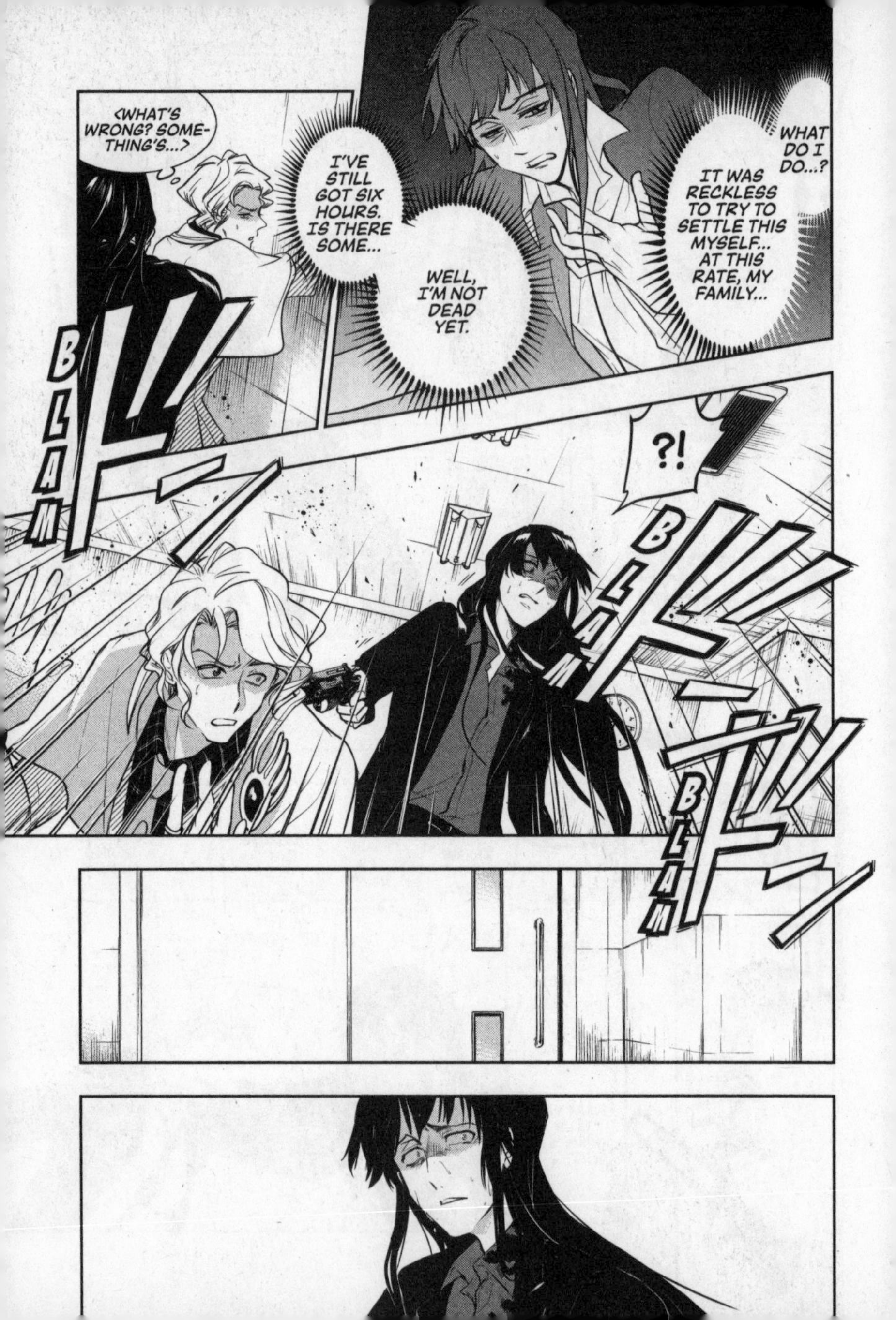
WHAT DO I DO...?
IT WAS RECKLESS TO TRY TO SETTLE THIS MYSELF... AT THIS RATE, MY FAMILY...
I'VE STILL GOT SIX HOURS. IS THERE SOME...
WELL, I'M NOT DEAD YET.
<WHAT'S WRONG? SOMETHING'S...>
BLLAM
?!
BLLAM
BLLAM

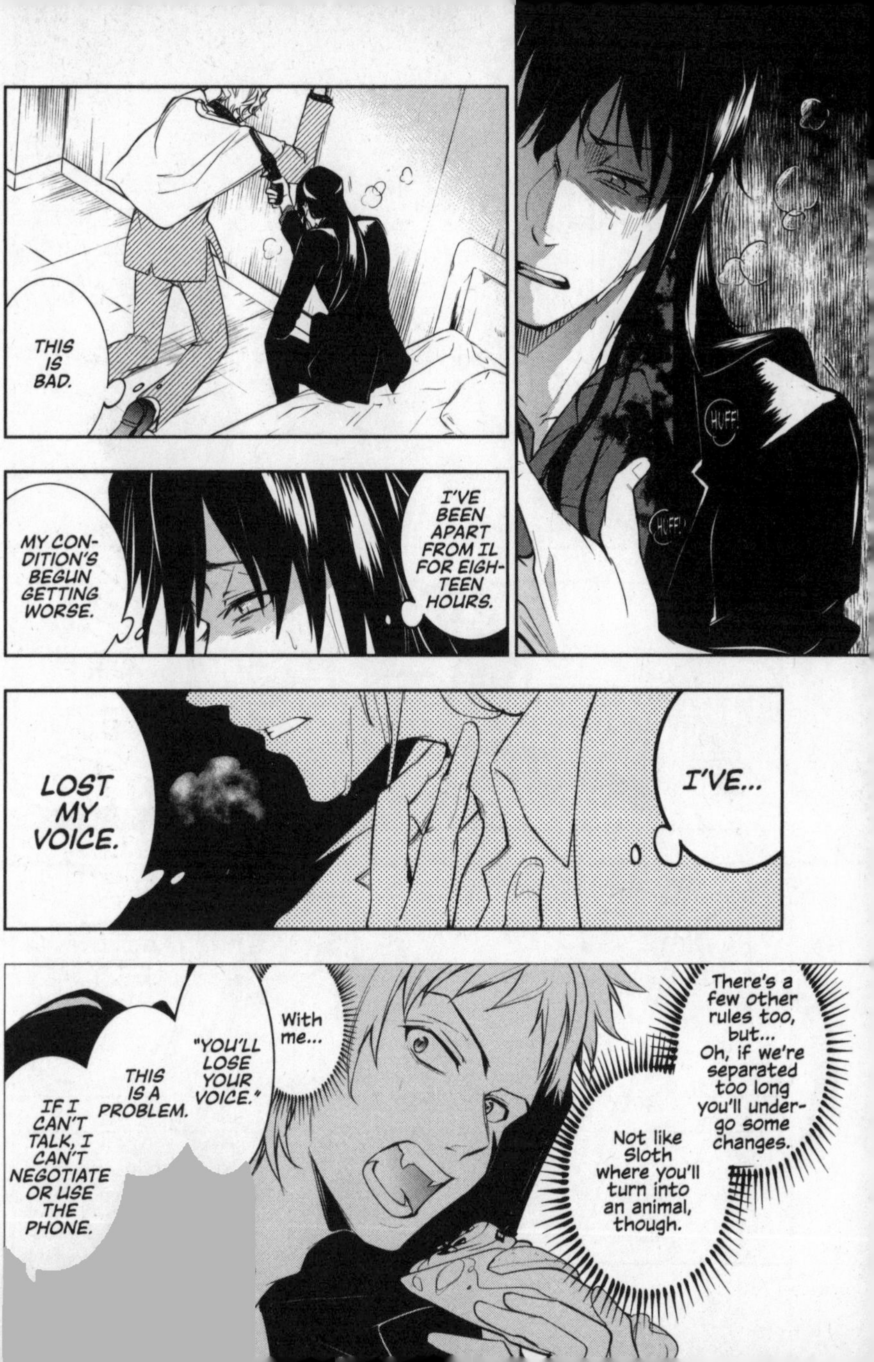
HUFF!
HUFF!
THIS IS BAD.
I'VE BEEN APART FROM IL FOR EIGHTEEN HOURS.
MY CONDITION'S BEGUN GETTING WORSE.
I'VE...
LOST MY VOICE.
There's a few other rules too, but... Oh, if we're separated too long you'll undergo some changes.
Not like Sloth where you'll turn into an animal, though.
With me...
"YOU'LL LOSE YOUR VOICE."
THIS IS A PROBLEM.
IF I CAN'T TALK, I CAN'T NEGOTIATE OR USE THE PHONE.

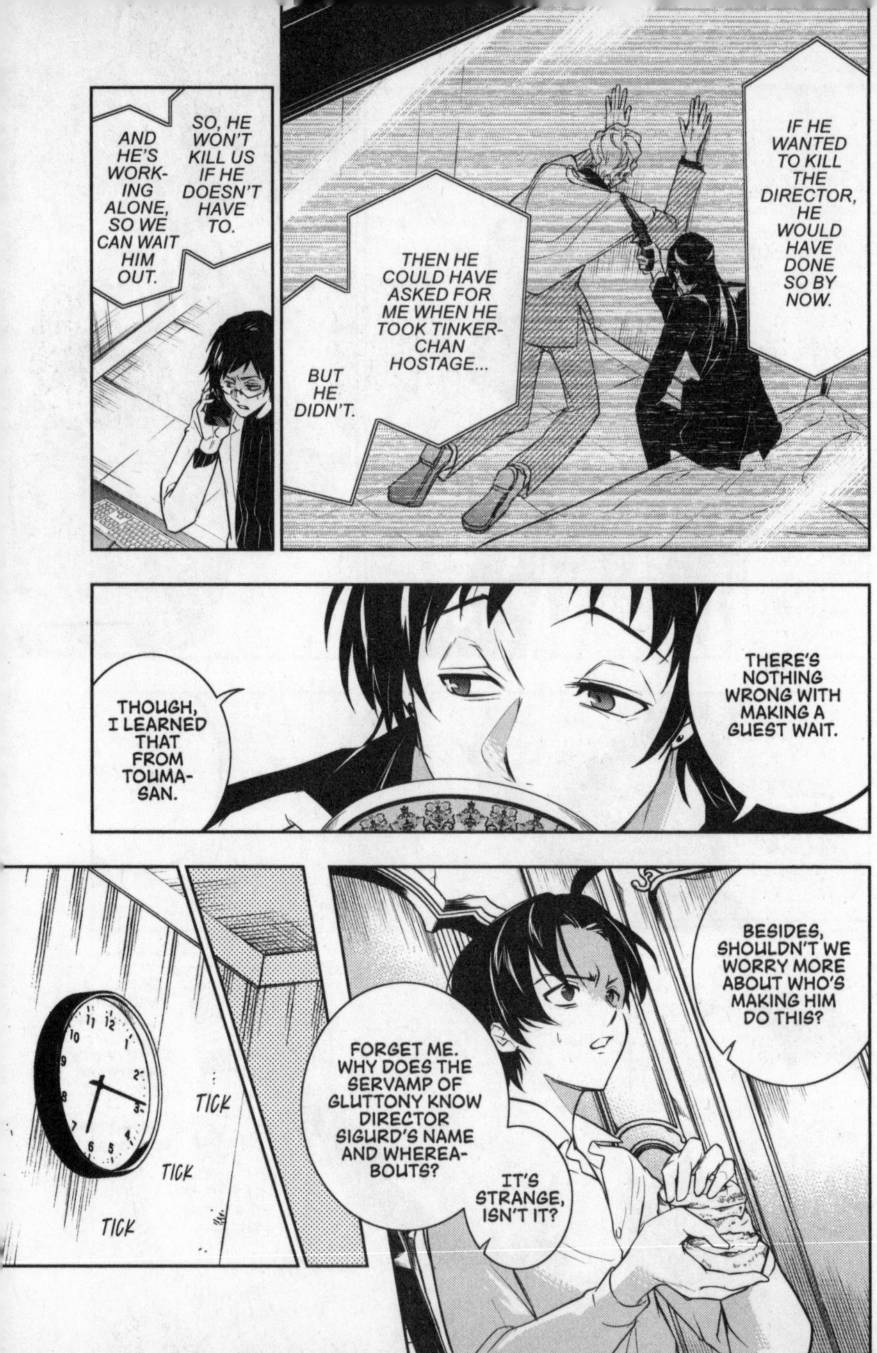
IF HE WANTED TO KILL THE DIRECTOR, HE WOULD HAVE DONE SO BY NOW.
THEN HE COULD HAVE ASKED FOR ME WHEN HE TOOK TINKER-CHAN HOSTAGE...
BUT HE DIDN'T.
SO, HE WON'T KILL US IF HE DOESN'T HAVE TO.
AND HE'S WORKING ALONE, SO WE CAN WAIT HIM OUT.
THERE'S NOTHING WRONG WITH MAKING A GUEST WAIT.
THOUGH, I LEARNED THAT FROM TOUMA-SAN.
BESIDES, SHOULDN'T WE WORRY MORE ABOUT WHO'S MAKING HIM DO THIS?
FORGET ME. WHY DOES THE SERVAMP OF GLUTTONY KNOW DIRECTOR SIGURD'S NAME AND WHEREABOUTS?
IT'S STRANGE, ISN'T IT?
TICK
TICK
TICK

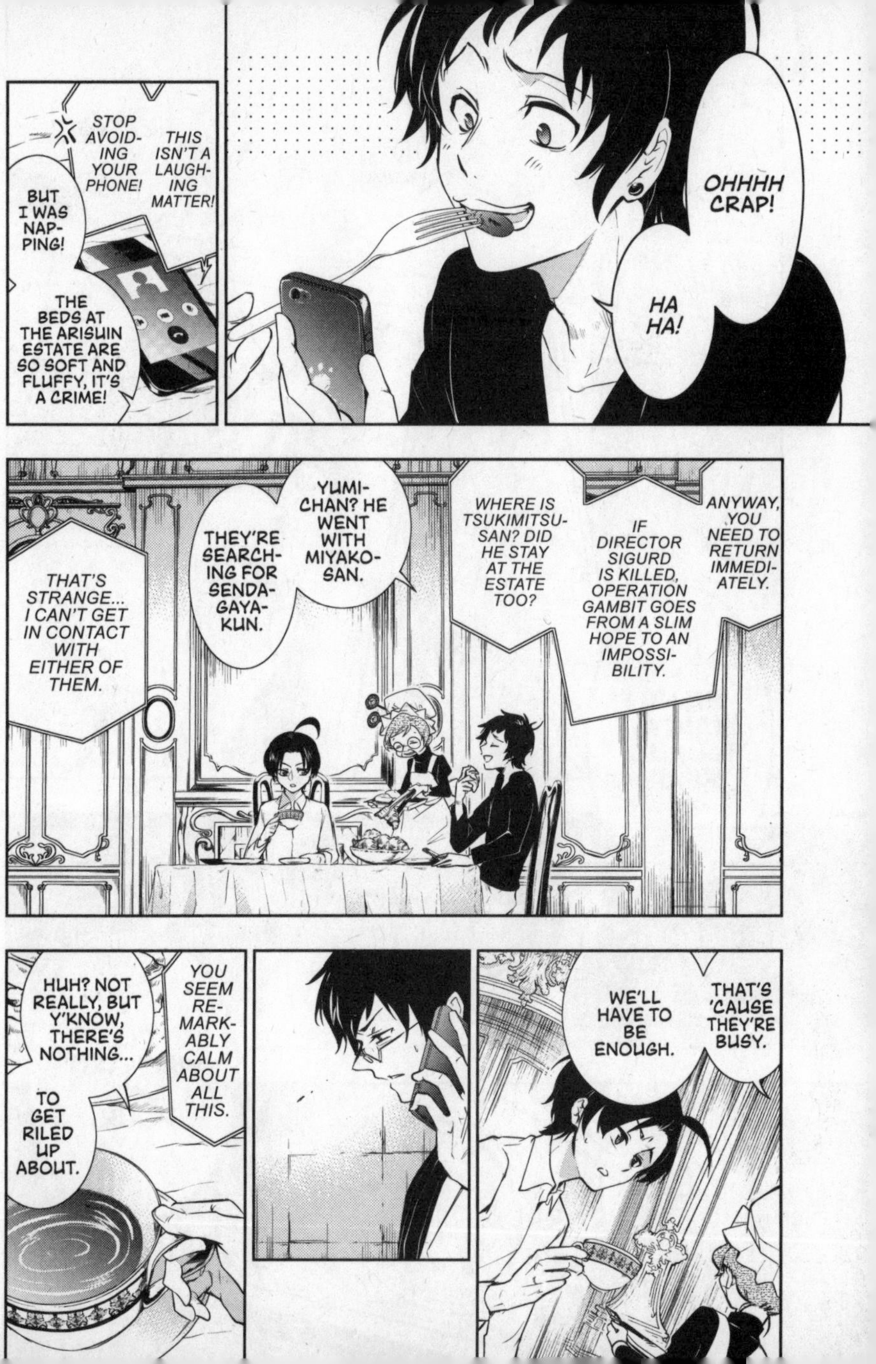
OHHHH CRAP!
HA HA!
THIS ISN'T A LAUGHING MATTER!
STOP AVOIDING YOUR PHONE!
BUT I WAS NAPPING!
THE BEDS AT THE ARISUIN ESTATE ARE SO SOFT AND FLUFFY, IT'S A CRIME!
ANYWAY, YOU NEED TO RETURN IMMEDIATELY.
IF DIRECTOR SIGURD IS KILLED, OPERATION GAMBIT GOES FROM A SLIM HOPE TO AN IMPOSSIBILITY.
WHERE IS TSUKIMITSU-SAN? DID HE STAY AT THE ESTATE TOO?
YUMI-CHAN? HE WENT WITH MIYAKO-SAN.
THEY'RE SEARCHING FOR SENDAGAYA-KUN.
THAT'S STRANGE... I CAN'T GET IN CONTACT WITH EITHER OF THEM.
THAT'S 'CAUSE THEY'RE BUSY.
WE'LL HAVE TO BE ENOUGH.
YOU SEEM REMARKABLY CALM ABOUT ALL THIS.
HUH? NOT REALLY, BUT Y'KNOW, THERE'S NOTHING...
TO GET RILED UP ABOUT.

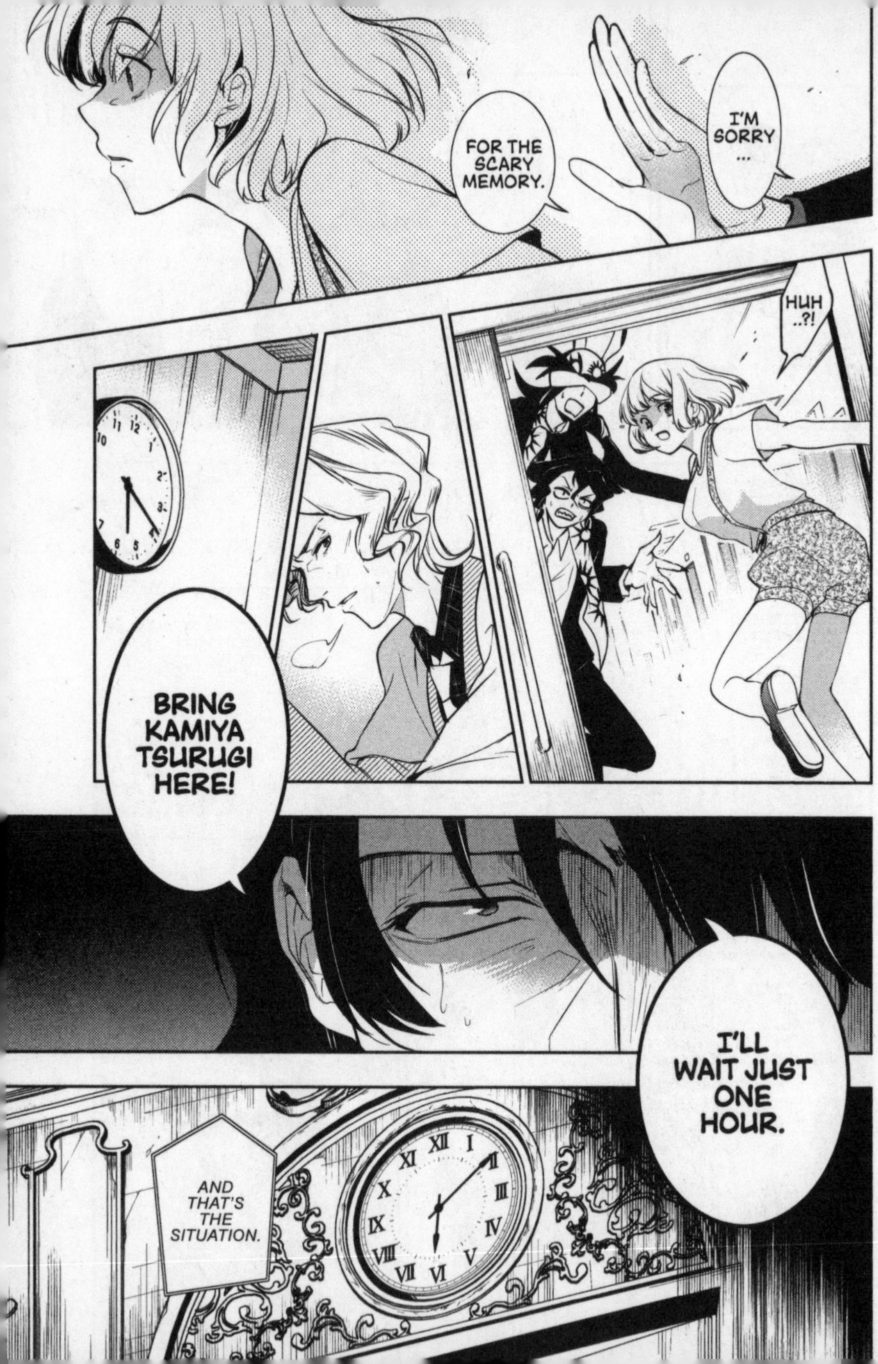

I'M SORRY ...
FOR THE SCARY MEMORY.
HUH ..?!
BRING KAMIYA TSURUGI HERE!
I'LL WAIT JUST ONE HOUR.
AND THAT'S THE SITUATION.

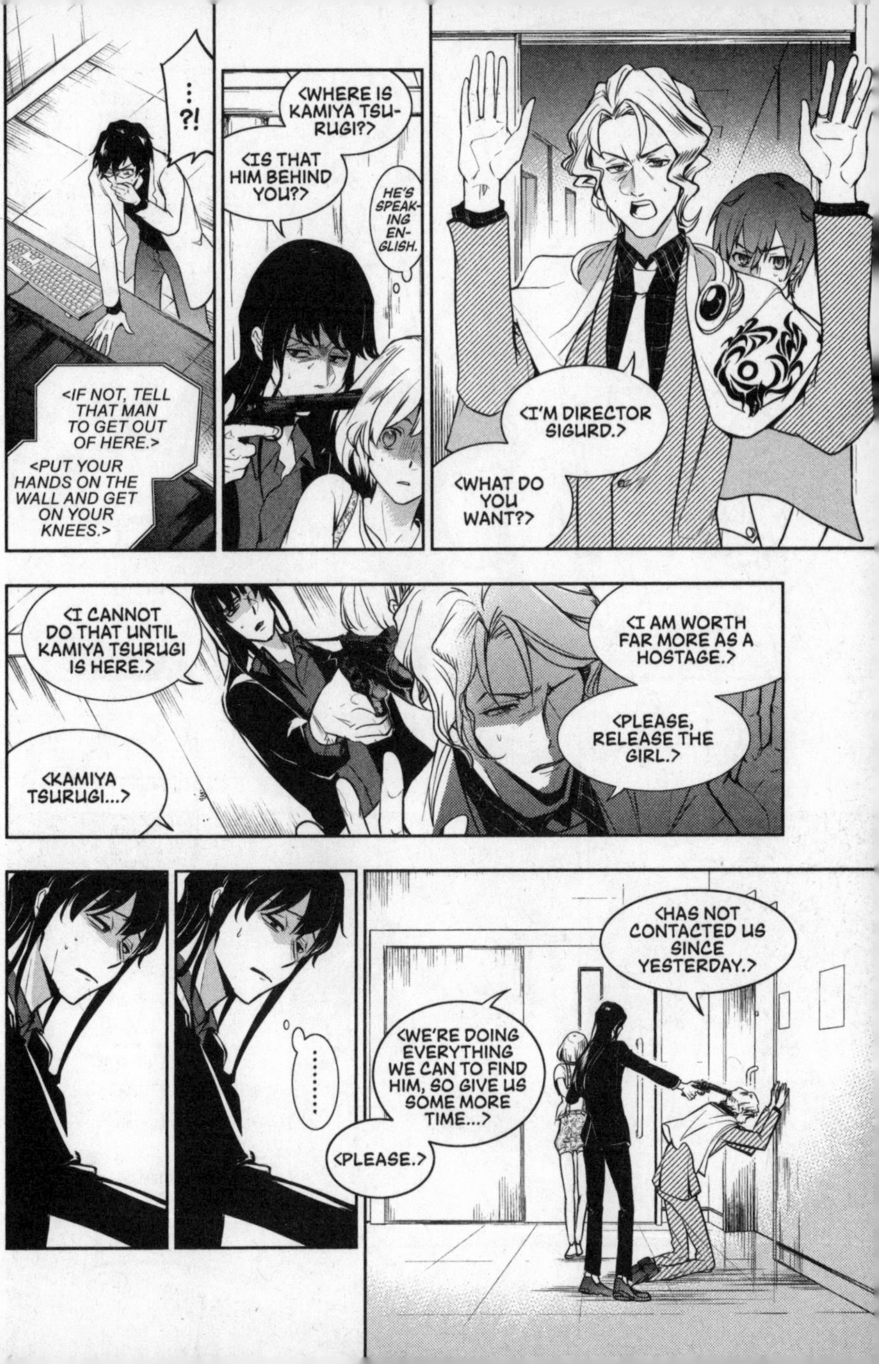
<I'M DIRECTOR SIGURD.>
<WHAT DO YOU WANT?>
<WHERE IS KAMIYA TSURUGI?>
<IS THAT HIM BEHIND YOU?>
HE'S SPEAKING ENGLISH.
...?!
<IF NOT, TELL THAT MAN TO GET OUT OF HERE.>
<PUT YOUR HANDS ON THE WALL AND GET ON YOUR KNEES.>
<I AM WORTH FAR MORE AS A HOSTAGE.>
<PLEASE, RELEASE THE GIRL.>
<I CANNOT DO THAT UNTIL KAMIYA TSURUGI IS HERE.>
<KAMIYA TSURUGI...>
<HAS NOT CONTACTED US SINCE YESTERDAY.>
<WE'RE DOING EVERYTHING WE CAN TO FIND HIM, SO GIVE US SOME MORE TIME...>
<PLEASE.>
....

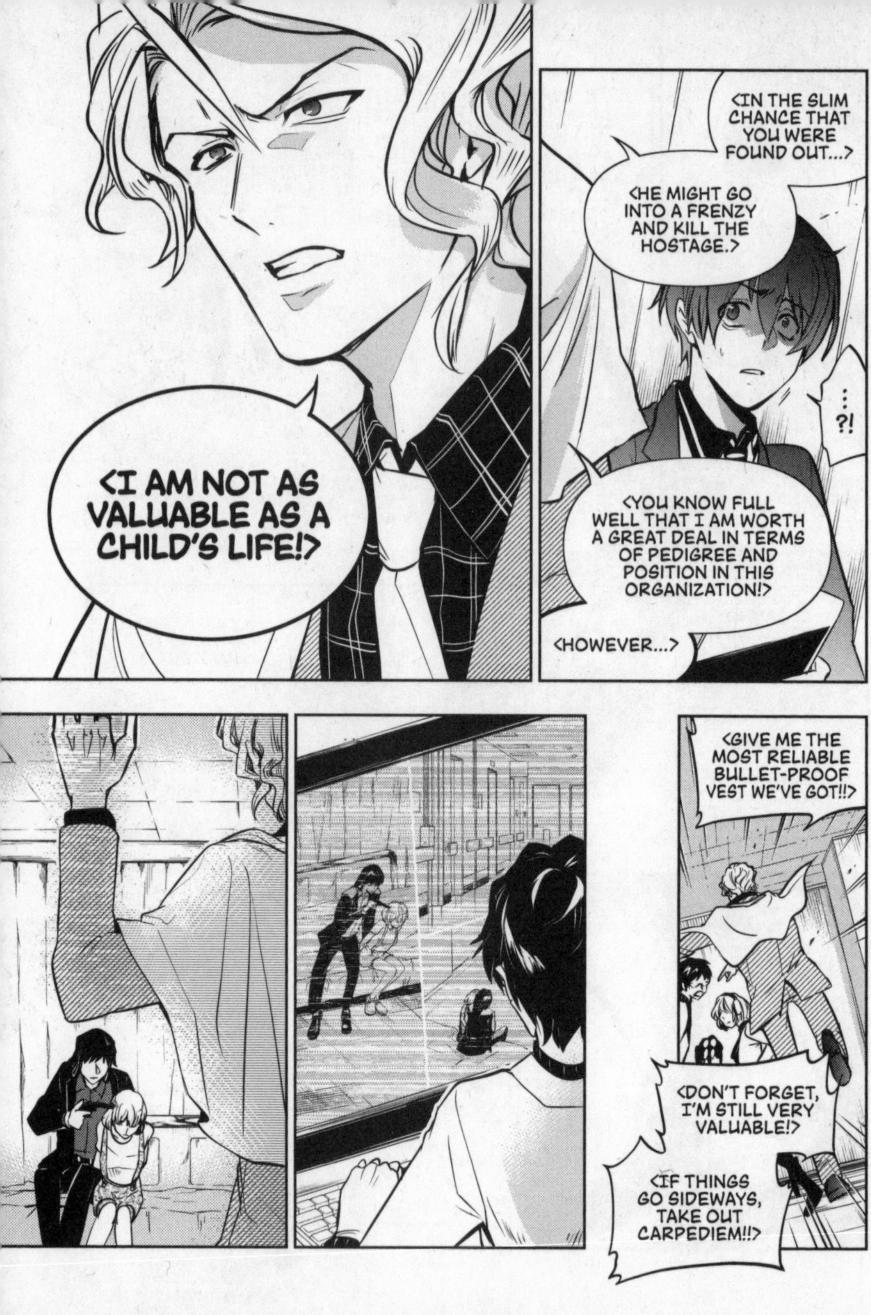
<IN THE SLIM CHANCE THAT YOU WERE FOUND OUT...>
<HE MIGHT GO INTO A FRENZY AND KILL THE HOSTAGE.>
...?!
<YOU KNOW FULL WELL THAT I AM WORTH A GREAT DEAL IN TERMS OF PEDIGREE AND POSITION IN THIS ORGANIZATION!>
<HOWEVER...>
<I AM NOT AS VALUABLE AS A CHILD'S LIFE!>
<GIVE ME THE MOST RELIABLE BULLET-PROOF VEST WE'VE GOT!!>
<DON'T FORGET, I'M STILL VERY VALUABLE!>
<IF THINGS GO SIDEWAYS, TAKE OUT CARPEDIEM!!>

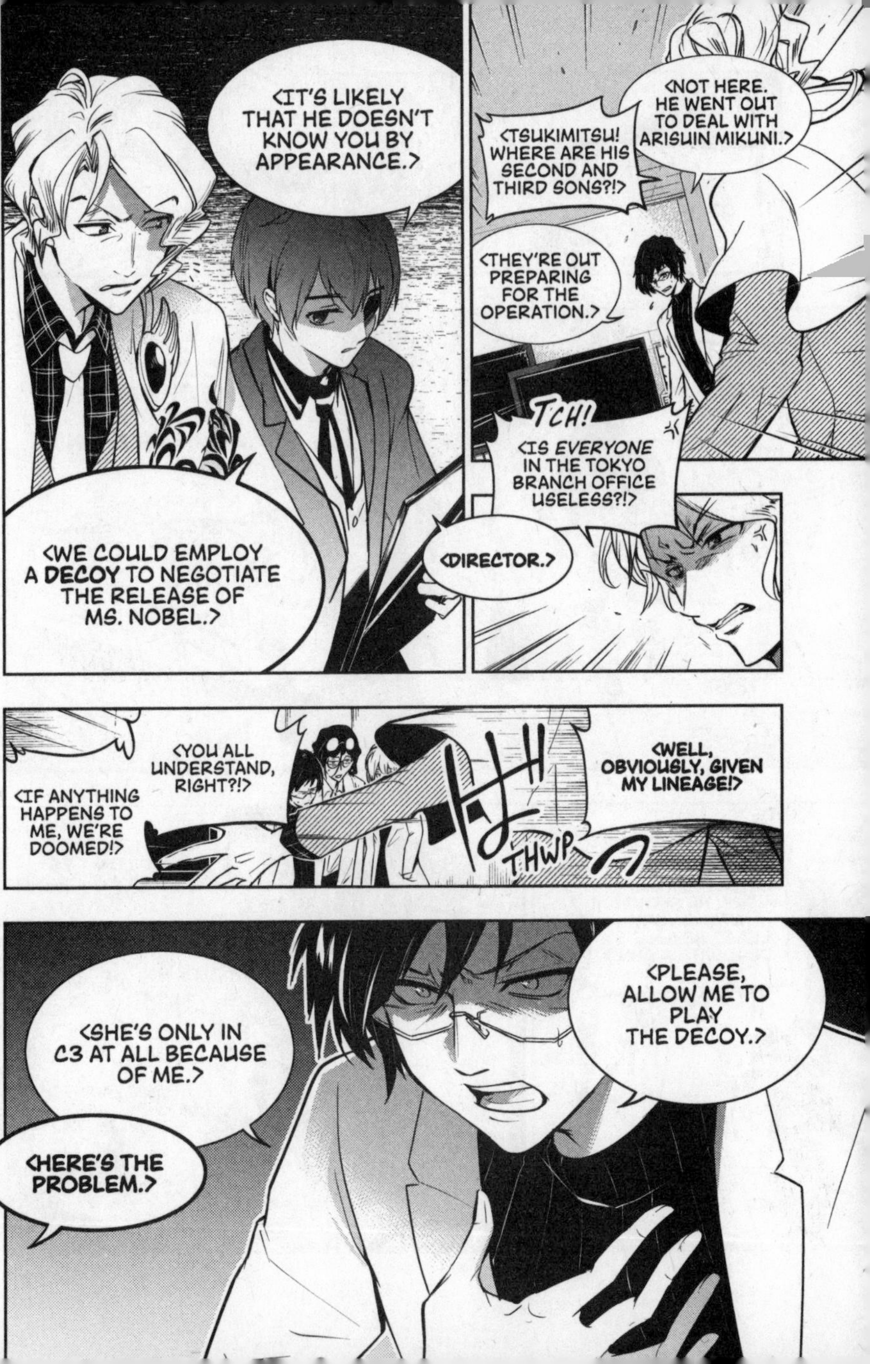
<TSUKIMITSU! WHERE ARE HIS SECOND AND THIRD SONS?!>
<NOT HERE. HE WENT OUT TO DEAL WITH ARISUIN MIKUNI.>
<THEY'RE OUT PREPARING FOR THE OPERATION.>
TCH!
<IS *EVERYONE* IN THE TOKYO BRANCH OFFICE USELESS?!>
<DIRECTOR.>
<IT'S LIKELY THAT HE DOESN'T KNOW YOU BY APPEARANCE.>
<WE COULD EMPLOY A **DECOY** TO NEGOTIATE THE RELEASE OF MS. NOBEL.>
<WELL, OBVIOUSLY, GIVEN MY LINEAGE!>
THWP
<YOU ALL UNDERSTAND, RIGHT?!>
<IF ANYTHING HAPPENS TO ME, WE'RE DOOMED!>
<PLEASE, ALLOW ME TO PLAY THE DECOY.>
<SHE'S ONLY IN C3 AT ALL BECAUSE OF ME.>
<HERE'S THE PROBLEM.>

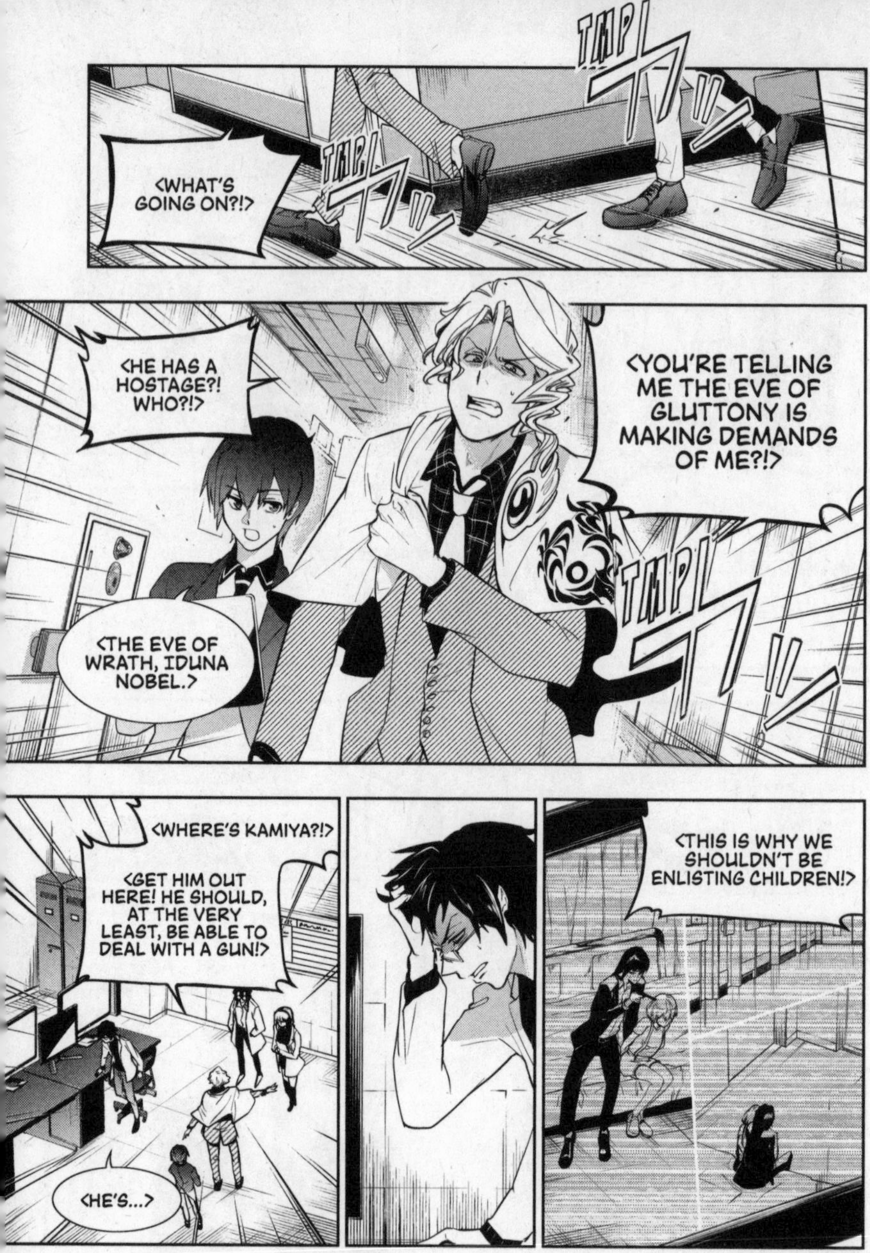
TMP!
TMP!
<WHAT'S GOING ON?!>
<YOU'RE TELLING ME THE EVE OF GLUTTONY IS MAKING DEMANDS OF ME?!>
<HE HAS A HOSTAGE?! WHO?!>
TMP!
<THE EVE OF WRATH, IDUNA NOBEL.>
<THIS IS WHY WE SHOULDN'T BE ENLISTING CHILDREN!>
<WHERE'S KAMIYA?!>
<GET HIM OUT HERE! HE SHOULD, AT THE VERY LEAST, BE ABLE TO DEAL WITH A GUN!>
<HE'S...>

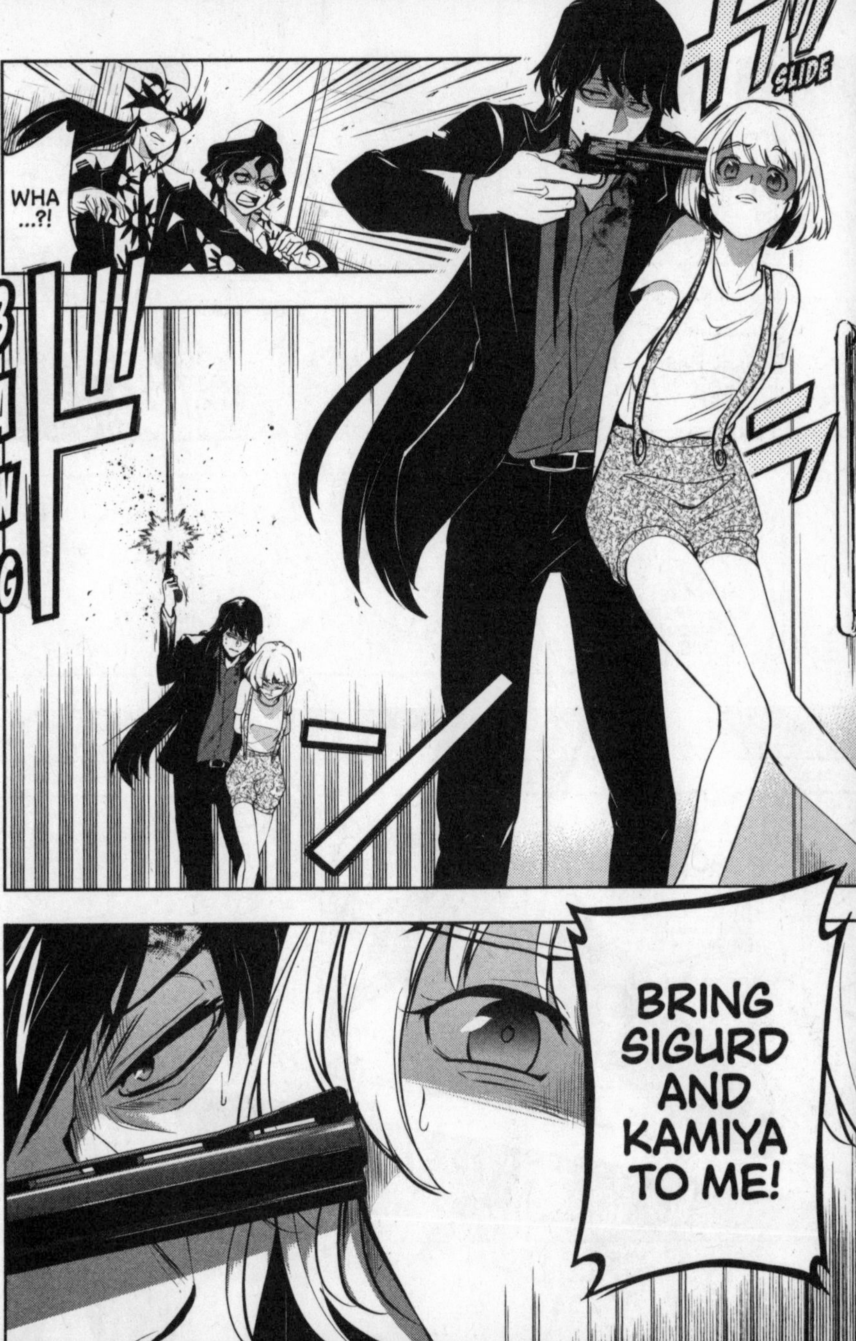
SLIDE
WHA ...?!
BANG
BRING SIGURD AND KAMIYA TO ME!

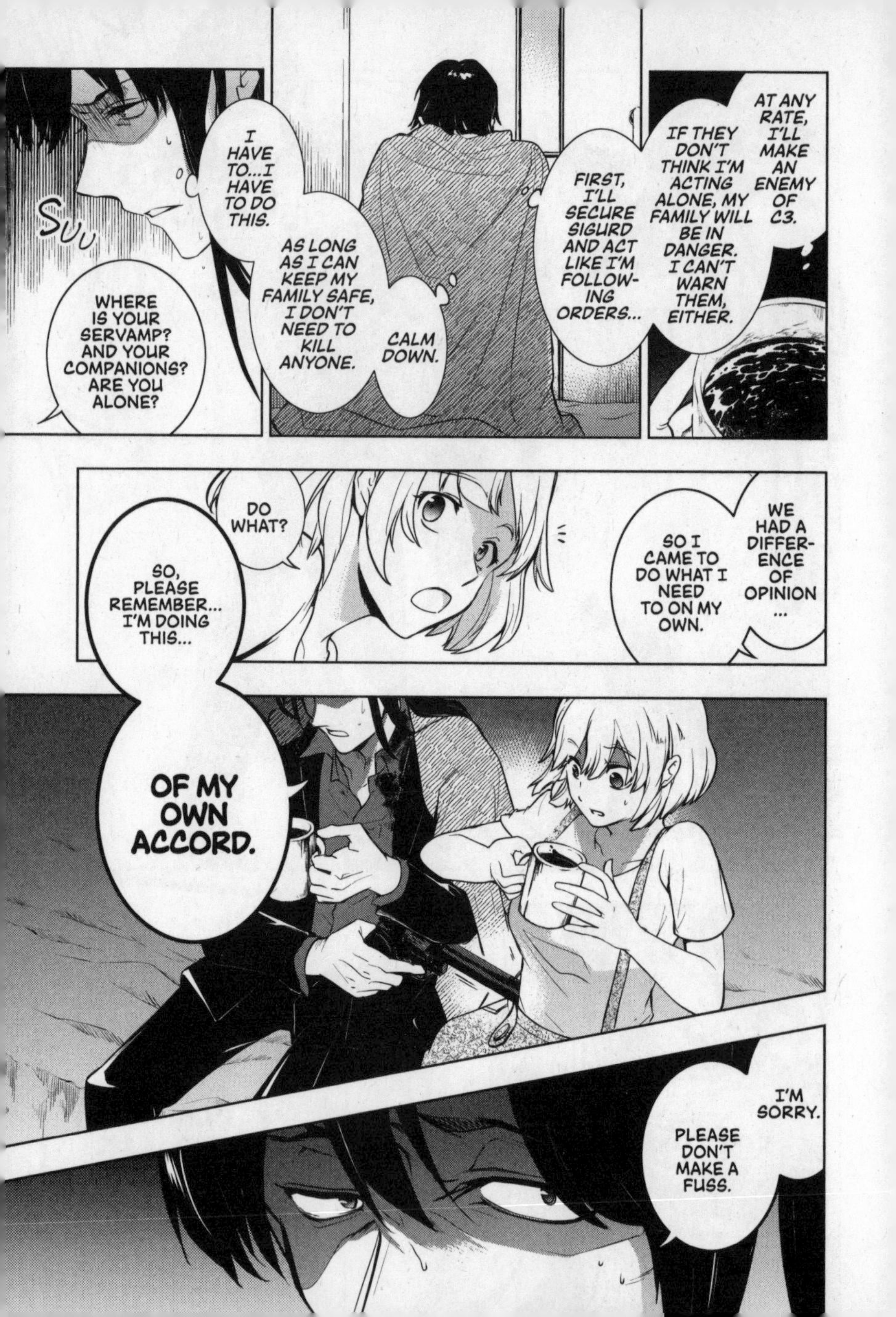
AT ANY RATE, I'LL MAKE AN ENEMY OF C3.
IF THEY DON'T THINK I'M ACTING ALONE, MY FAMILY WILL BE IN DANGER. I CAN'T WARN THEM, EITHER.
FIRST, I'LL SECURE SIGURD AND ACT LIKE I'M FOLLOWING ORDERS...
I HAVE TO...I HAVE TO DO THIS.
AS LONG AS I CAN KEEP MY FAMILY SAFE, I DON'T NEED TO KILL ANYONE.
CALM DOWN.
SUU
WHERE IS YOUR SERVAMP? AND YOUR COMPANIONS? ARE YOU ALONE?
WE HAD A DIFFERENCE OF OPINION...
SO I CAME TO DO WHAT I NEED TO ON MY OWN.
DO WHAT?
SO, PLEASE REMEMBER... I'M DOING THIS...
OF MY OWN ACCORD.
I'M SORRY.
PLEASE DON'T MAKE A FUSS.

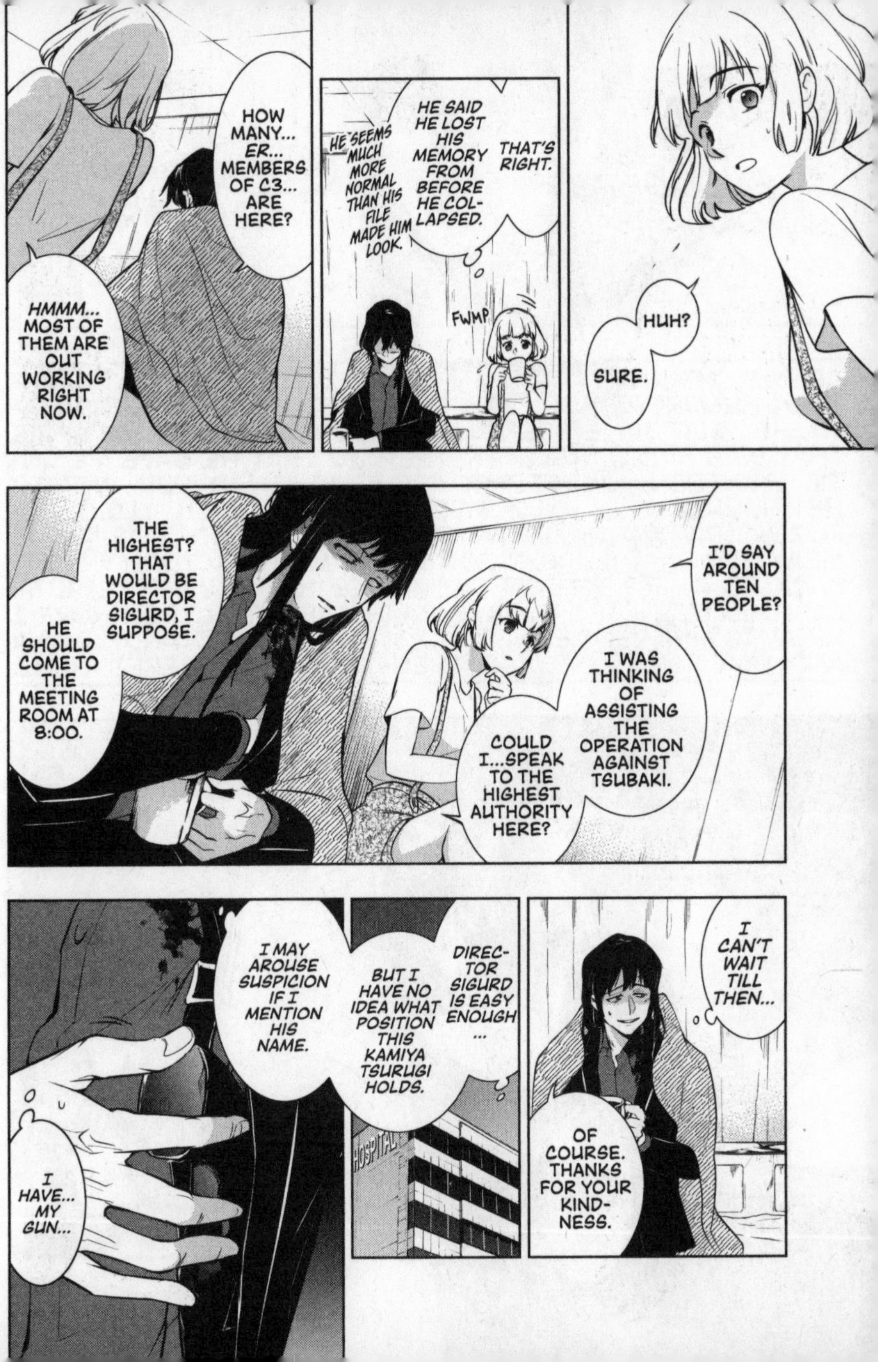
HUH?
SURE.
THAT'S RIGHT.
HE SAID HE LOST HIS MEMORY FROM BEFORE HE COL-LAPSED.
HE SEEMS MUCH MORE NORMAL THAN HIS FILE MADE HIM LOOK.
FWMP
HOW MANY... ER... MEMBERS OF C3... ARE HERE?
HMMM... MOST OF THEM ARE OUT WORKING RIGHT NOW.
I'D SAY AROUND TEN PEOPLE?
I WAS THINKING OF ASSISTING THE OPERATION AGAINST TSUBAKI.
COULD I...SPEAK TO THE HIGHEST AUTHORITY HERE?
THE HIGHEST? THAT WOULD BE DIRECTOR SIGURD, I SUPPOSE.
HE SHOULD COME TO THE MEETING ROOM AT 8:00.
I CAN'T WAIT TILL THEN...
OF COURSE. THANKS FOR YOUR KIND-NESS.
DIREC-TOR SIGURD IS EASY ENOUGH...
BUT I HAVE NO IDEA WHAT POSITION THIS KAMIYA TSURUGI HOLDS.
I MAY AROUSE SUSPICION IF I MENTION HIS NAME.
HOSPITAL
I HAVE... MY GUN...

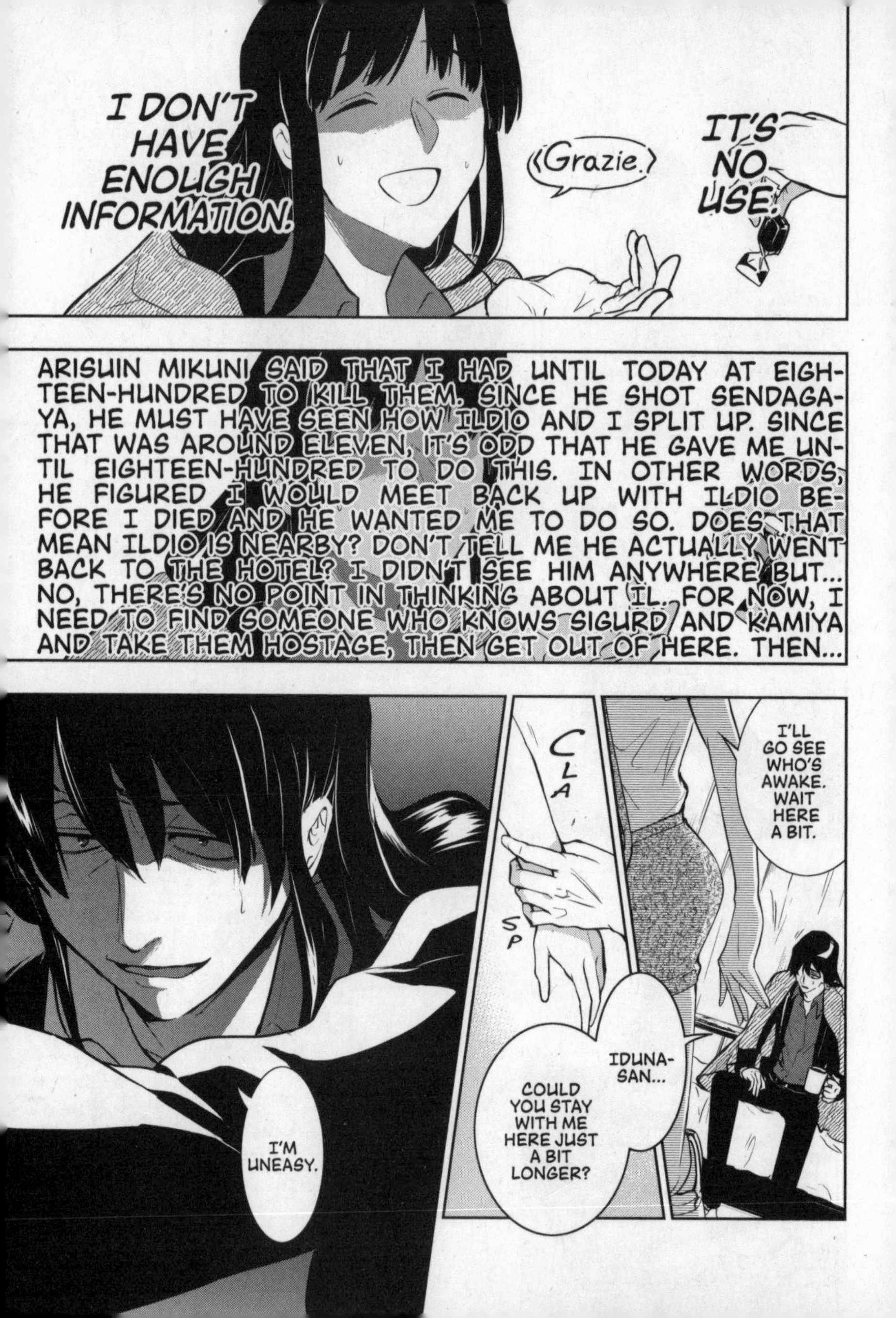
IT'S NO USE!
Grazie.
I DON'T HAVE ENOUGH INFORMATION.
ARISUIN MIKUNI SAID THAT I HAD UNTIL TODAY AT EIGHTEEN-HUNDRED TO KILL THEM. SINCE HE SHOT SENDAGAYA, HE MUST HAVE SEEN HOW ILDIO AND I SPLIT UP. SINCE THAT WAS AROUND ELEVEN, IT'S ODD THAT HE GAVE ME UNTIL EIGHTEEN-HUNDRED TO DO THIS. IN OTHER WORDS, HE FIGURED I WOULD MEET BACK UP WITH ILDIO BEFORE I DIED AND HE WANTED ME TO DO SO. DOES THAT MEAN ILDIO IS NEARBY? DON'T TELL ME HE ACTUALLY WENT BACK TO THE HOTEL? I DIDN'T SEE HIM ANYWHERE BUT... NO, THERE'S NO POINT IN THINKING ABOUT IL. FOR NOW, I NEED TO FIND SOMEONE WHO KNOWS SIGURD AND KAMIYA AND TAKE THEM HOSTAGE, THEN GET OUT OF HERE. THEN...
I'LL GO SEE WHO'S AWAKE. WAIT HERE A BIT.
CLA
SP
IDUNA-SAN...
COULD YOU STAY WITH ME HERE JUST A BIT LONGER?
I'M UNEASY.

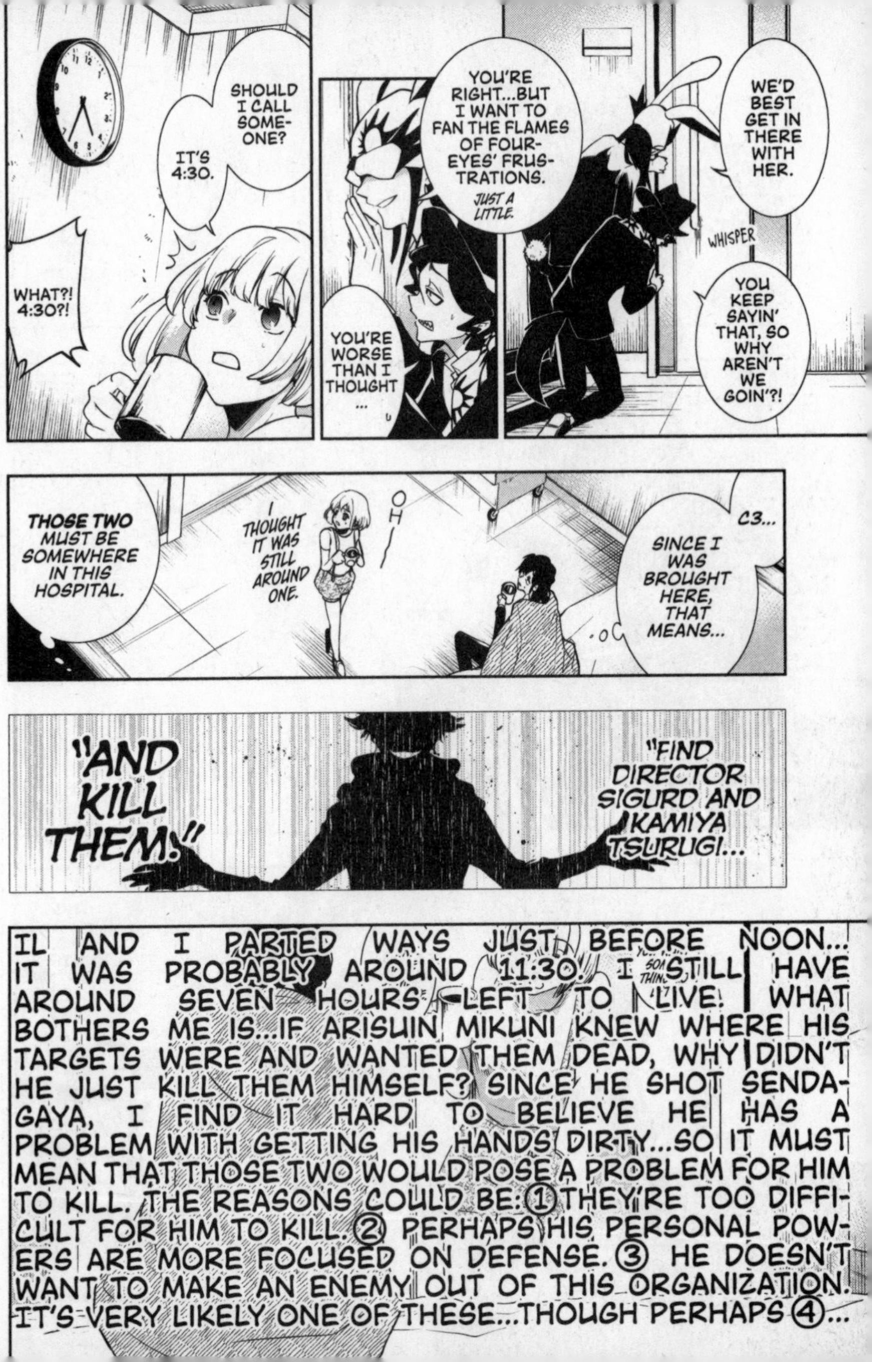
WE'D BEST GET IN THERE WITH HER.
WHISPER
YOU KEEP SAYIN' THAT, SO WHY AREN'T WE GOIN'?!
YOU'RE RIGHT...BUT I WANT TO FAN THE FLAMES OF FOUR-EYES' FRUSTRATIONS.
JUST A LITTLE.
YOU'RE WORSE THAN I THOUGHT...
SHOULD I CALL SOMEONE?
IT'S 4:30.
WHAT?! 4:30?!
C3...
SINCE I WAS BROUGHT HERE, THAT MEANS...
OH!
I THOUGHT IT WAS STILL AROUND ONE.
THOSE TWO MUST BE SOMEWHERE IN THIS HOSPITAL.
"FIND DIRECTOR SIGURD AND KAMIYA TSURUGI...
"AND KILL THEM!"
IL AND I PARTED WAYS JUST BEFORE NOON... IT WAS PROBABLY AROUND 11:30. I STILL HAVE AROUND SEVEN HOURS LEFT TO LIVE. WHAT BOTHERS ME IS...IF ARISUIN MIKUNI KNEW WHERE HIS TARGETS WERE AND WANTED THEM DEAD, WHY DIDN'T HE JUST KILL THEM HIMSELF? SINCE HE SHOT SENDA-GAYA, I FIND IT HARD TO BELIEVE HE HAS A PROBLEM WITH GETTING HIS HANDS DIRTY...SO IT MUST MEAN THAT THOSE TWO WOULD POSE A PROBLEM FOR HIM TO KILL. THE REASONS COULD BE: ① THEY'RE TOO DIFFI-CULT FOR HIM TO KILL. ② PERHAPS HIS PERSONAL POW-ERS ARE MORE FOCUSED ON DEFENSE. ③ HE DOESN'T WANT TO MAKE AN ENEMY OUT OF THIS ORGANIZATION. IT'S VERY LIKELY ONE OF THESE...THOUGH PERHAPS ④...

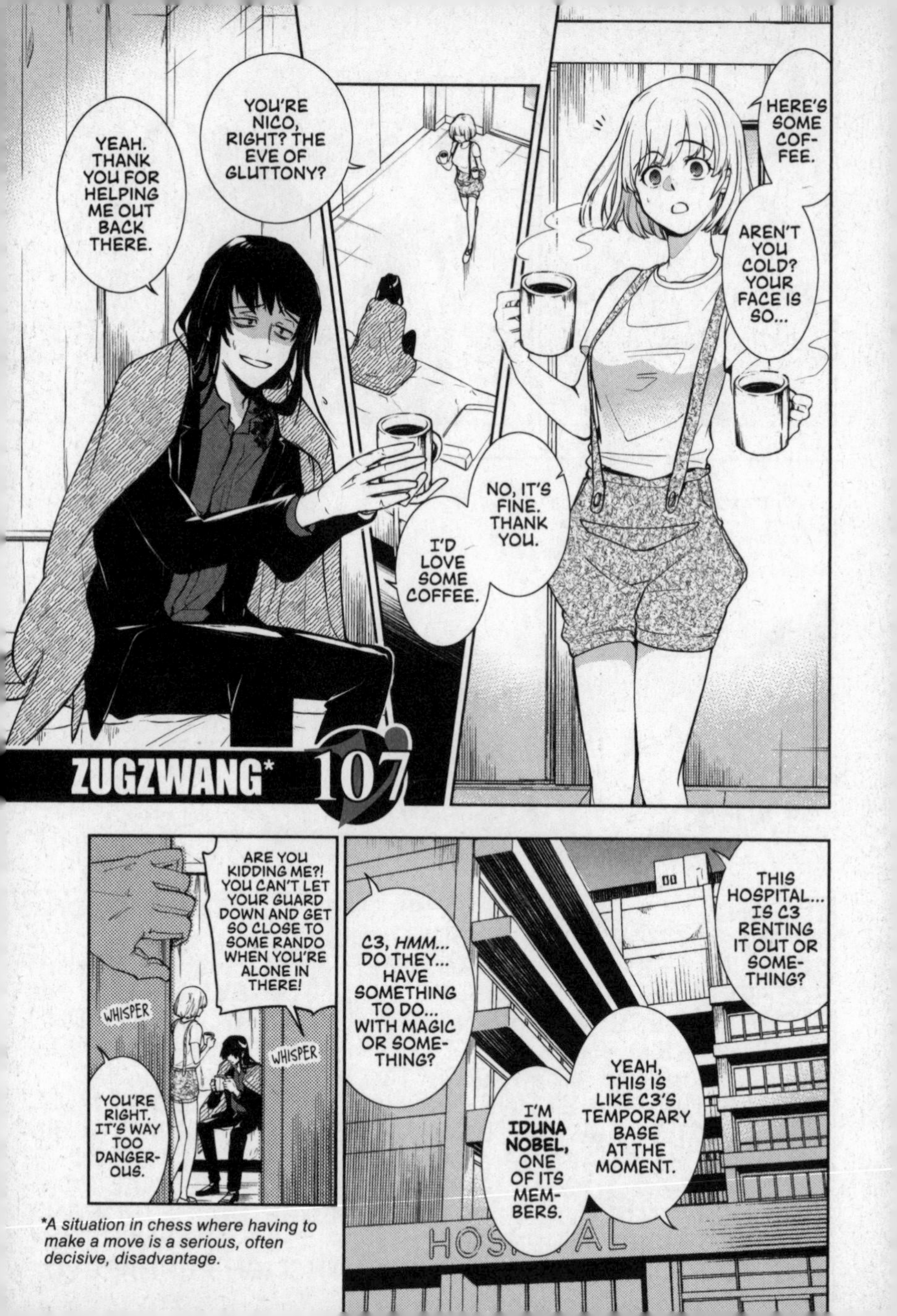
HERE'S SOME COFFEE.
AREN'T YOU COLD? YOUR FACE IS SO...
NO, IT'S FINE. THANK YOU.
I'D LOVE SOME COFFEE.
YOU'RE NICO, RIGHT? THE EVE OF GLUTTONY?
YEAH. THANK YOU FOR HELPING ME OUT BACK THERE.
ZUGZWANG* 107
THIS HOSPITAL... IS C3 RENTING IT OUT OR SOMETHING?
YEAH, THIS IS LIKE C3'S TEMPORARY BASE AT THE MOMENT.
I'M **IDUNA NOBEL,** ONE OF ITS MEMBERS.
C3, *HMM*... DO THEY... HAVE SOMETHING TO DO... WITH MAGIC OR SOMETHING?
ARE YOU KIDDING ME?! YOU CAN'T LET YOUR GUARD DOWN AND GET SO CLOSE TO SOME RANDO WHEN YOU'RE ALONE IN THERE!
WHISPER
WHISPER
YOU'RE RIGHT. IT'S WAY TOO DANGEROUS.

**A situation in chess where having to make a move is a serious, often decisive, disadvantage.*

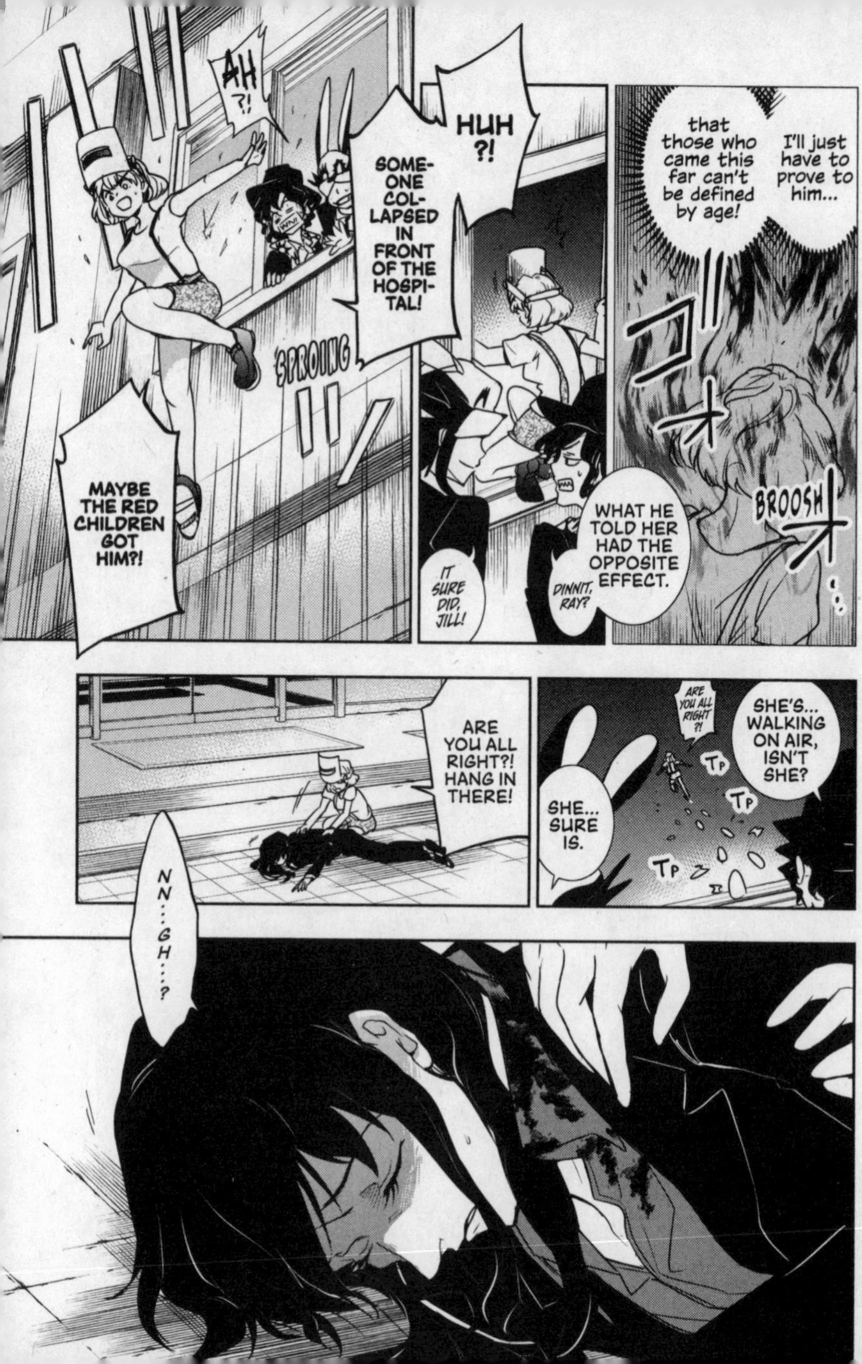
I'll just have to prove to him...
that those who came this far can't be defined by age!
BROOSH
WHAT HE TOLD HER HAD THE OPPOSITE EFFECT.
DINNIT, RAY?
IT SURE DID, JILL!
HUH ?!
SOME-ONE COL-LAPSED IN FRONT OF THE HOSPI-TAL!
AH ?!
SPROING
MAYBE THE RED CHILDREN GOT HIM?!
SHE'S... WALKING ON AIR, ISN'T SHE?
ARE YOU ALL RIGHT ?!
SHE... SURE IS.
TP
TP
TP
ARE YOU ALL RIGHT?! HANG IN THERE!
NN...GH...?

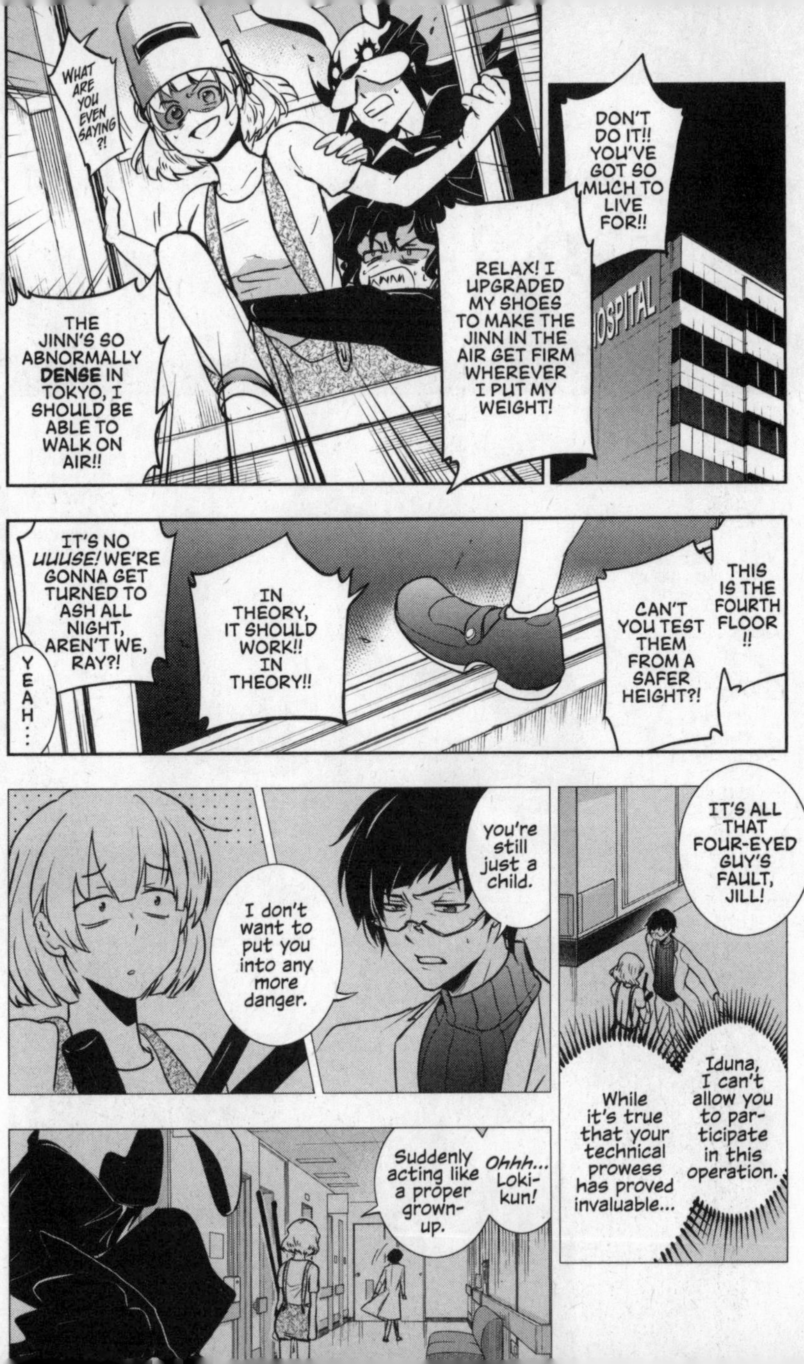
DON'T DO IT!! YOU'VE GOT SO MUCH TO LIVE FOR!!
RELAX! I UPGRADED MY SHOES TO MAKE THE JINN IN THE AIR GET FIRM WHEREVER I PUT MY WEIGHT!
HOSPITAL
WHAT ARE YOU EVEN SAYING?!
THE JINN'S SO ABNORMALLY **DENSE** IN TOKYO, I SHOULD BE ABLE TO WALK ON AIR!!
THIS IS THE FOURTH FLOOR!!
CAN'T YOU TEST THEM FROM A SAFER HEIGHT?!
IN THEORY, IT SHOULD WORK!! IN THEORY!!
IT'S NO *UUUSE!* WE'RE GONNA GET TURNED TO ASH ALL NIGHT, AREN'T WE, RAY?!
YEAH...
IT'S ALL THAT FOUR-EYED GUY'S FAULT, JILL!
Iduna, I can't allow you to participate in this operation.
While it's true that your technical prowess has proved invaluable...
you're still just a child.
I don't want to put you into any more danger.
Ohhh... Loki-kun!
Suddenly acting like a proper grown-up.

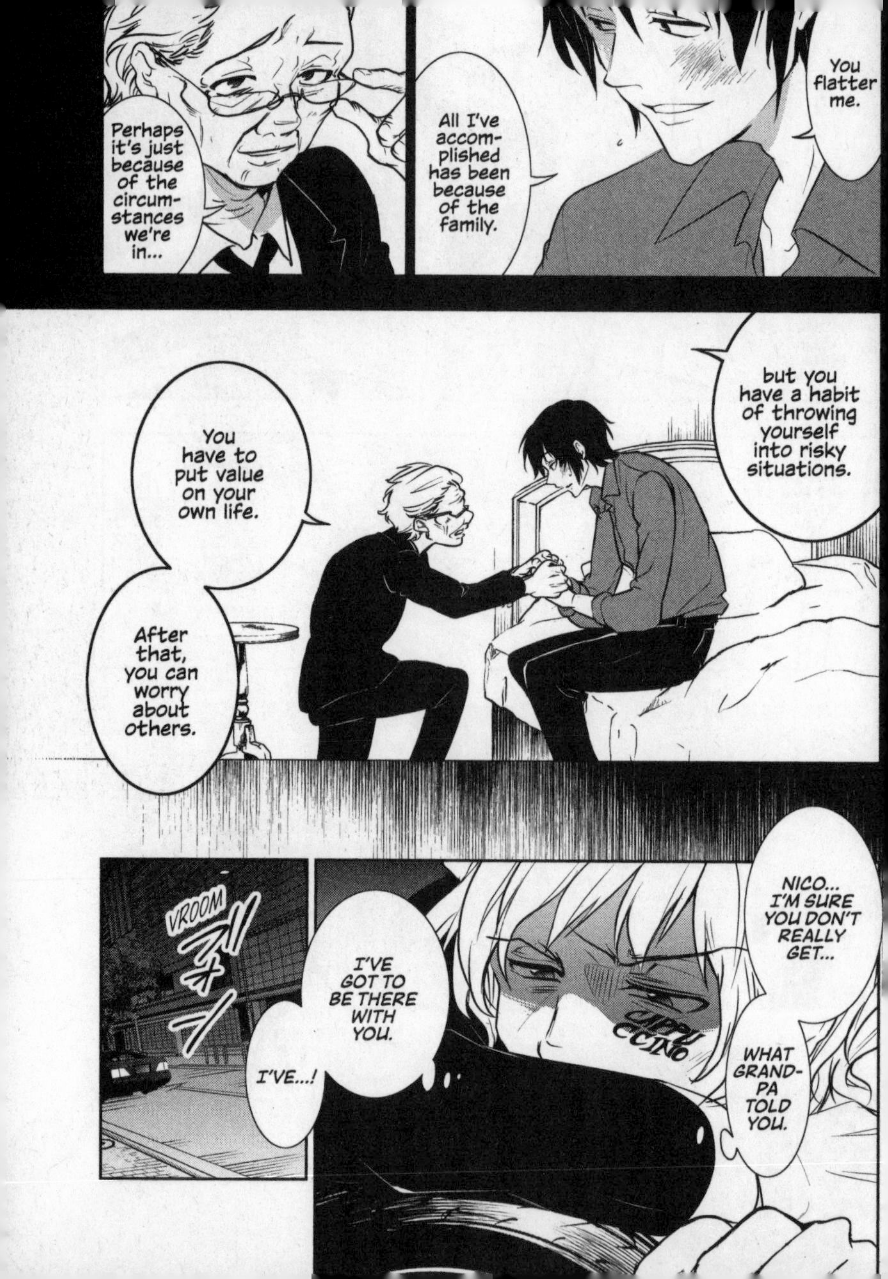
You flatter me.
All I've accomplished has been because of the family.
Perhaps it's just because of the circumstances we're in...
but you have a habit of throwing yourself into risky situations.
You have to put value on your own life.
After that, you can worry about others.
NICO... I'M SURE YOU DON'T REALLY GET...
WHAT GRAND-PA TOLD YOU.
CAPPU CCINO
I'VE GOT TO BE THERE WITH YOU.
I'VE...!
VROOM

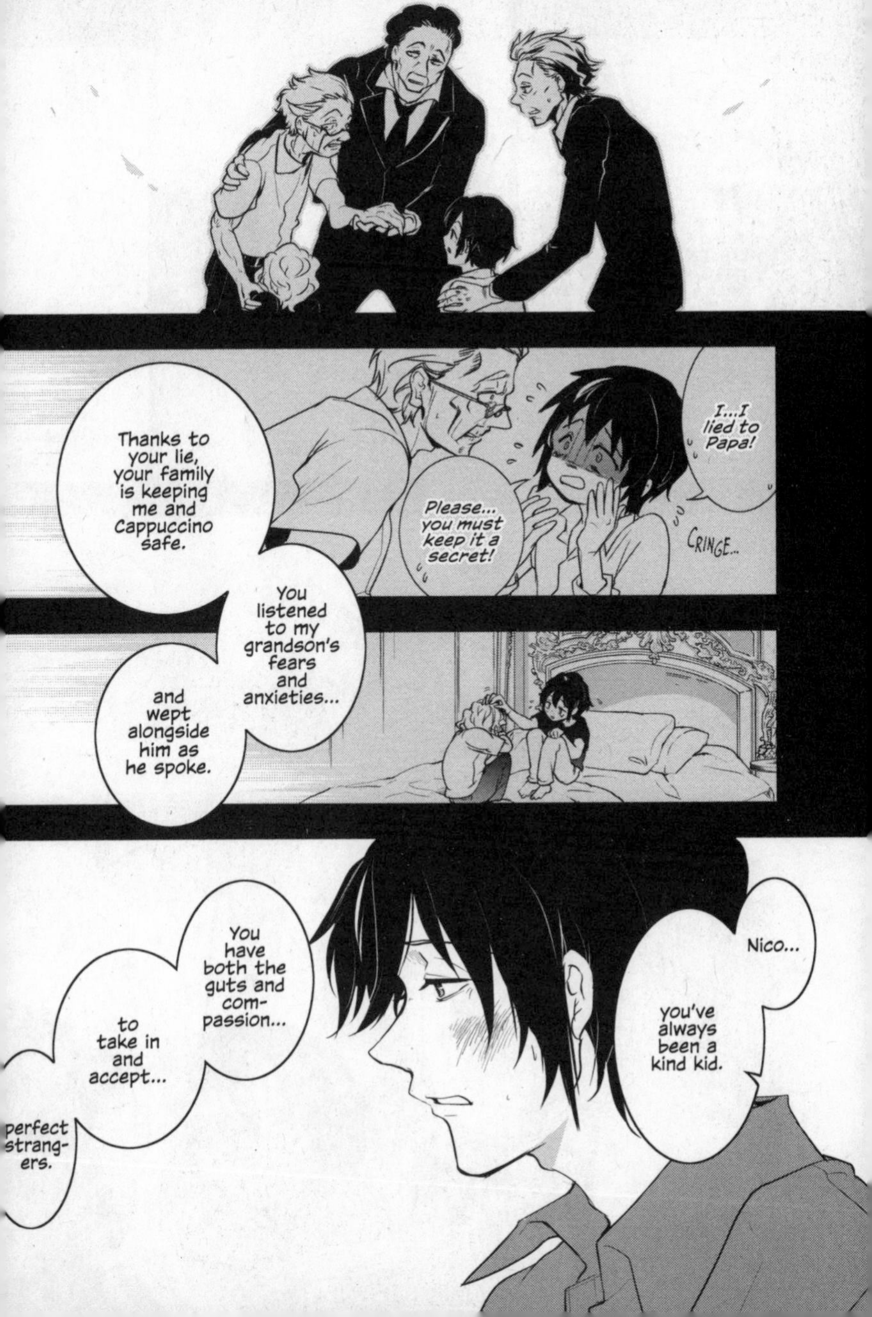
I...I lied to Papa!
CRINGE...
Please... you must keep it a secret!
Thanks to your lie, your family is keeping me and Cappuccino safe.
You listened to my grandson's fears and anxieties...
and wept alongside him as he spoke.
Nico...
you've always been a kind kid.
You have both the guts and com-passion...
to take in and accept...
perfect strang-ers.

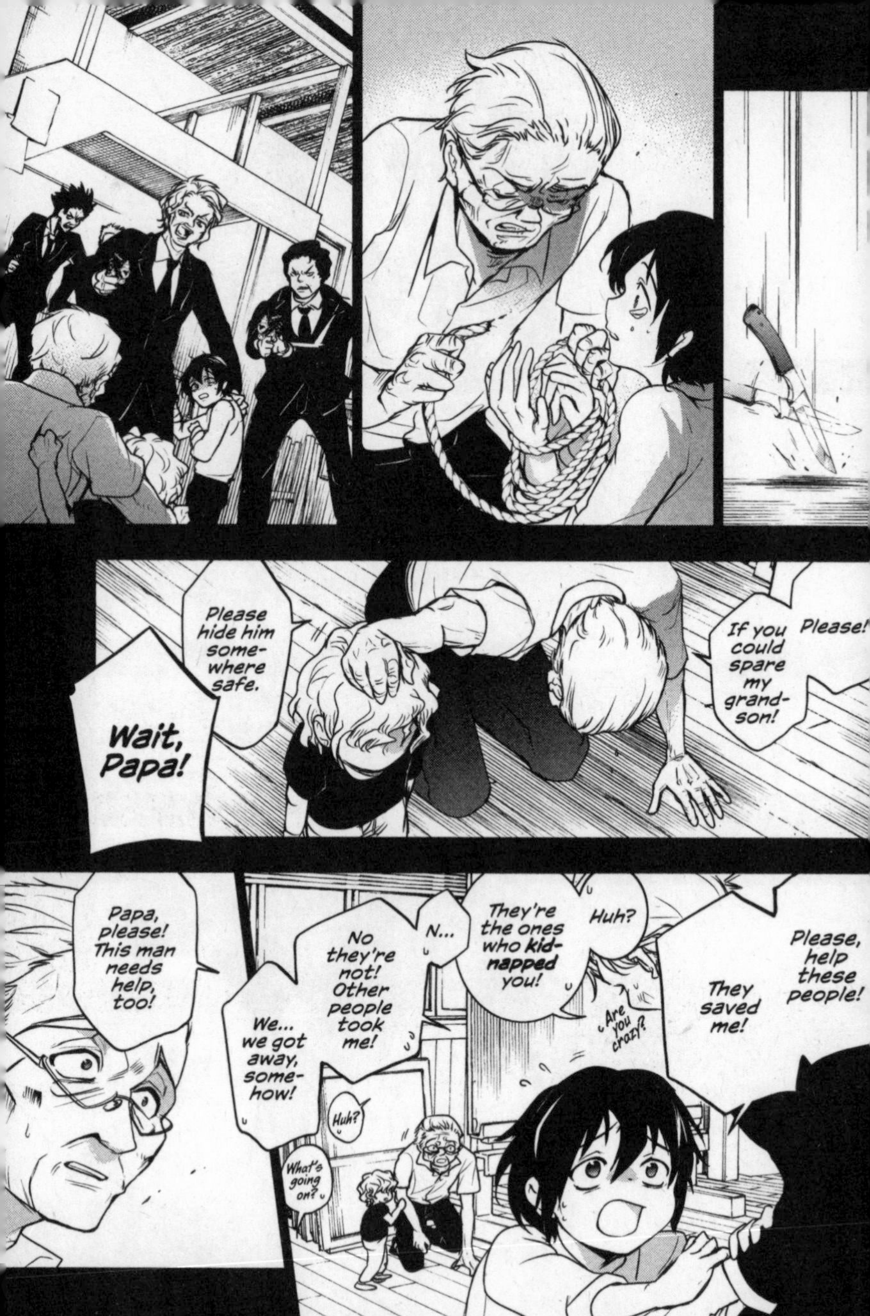

Please!
If you could spare my grand-son!
Please hide him some-where safe.
Wait, Papa!
Please, help these people!
They saved me!
Huh?
Are you crazy?
They're the ones who kid-napped you!
N...
No they're not! Other people took me!
We... we got away, some-how!
Huh?
What's going on?
Papa, please! This man needs help, too!

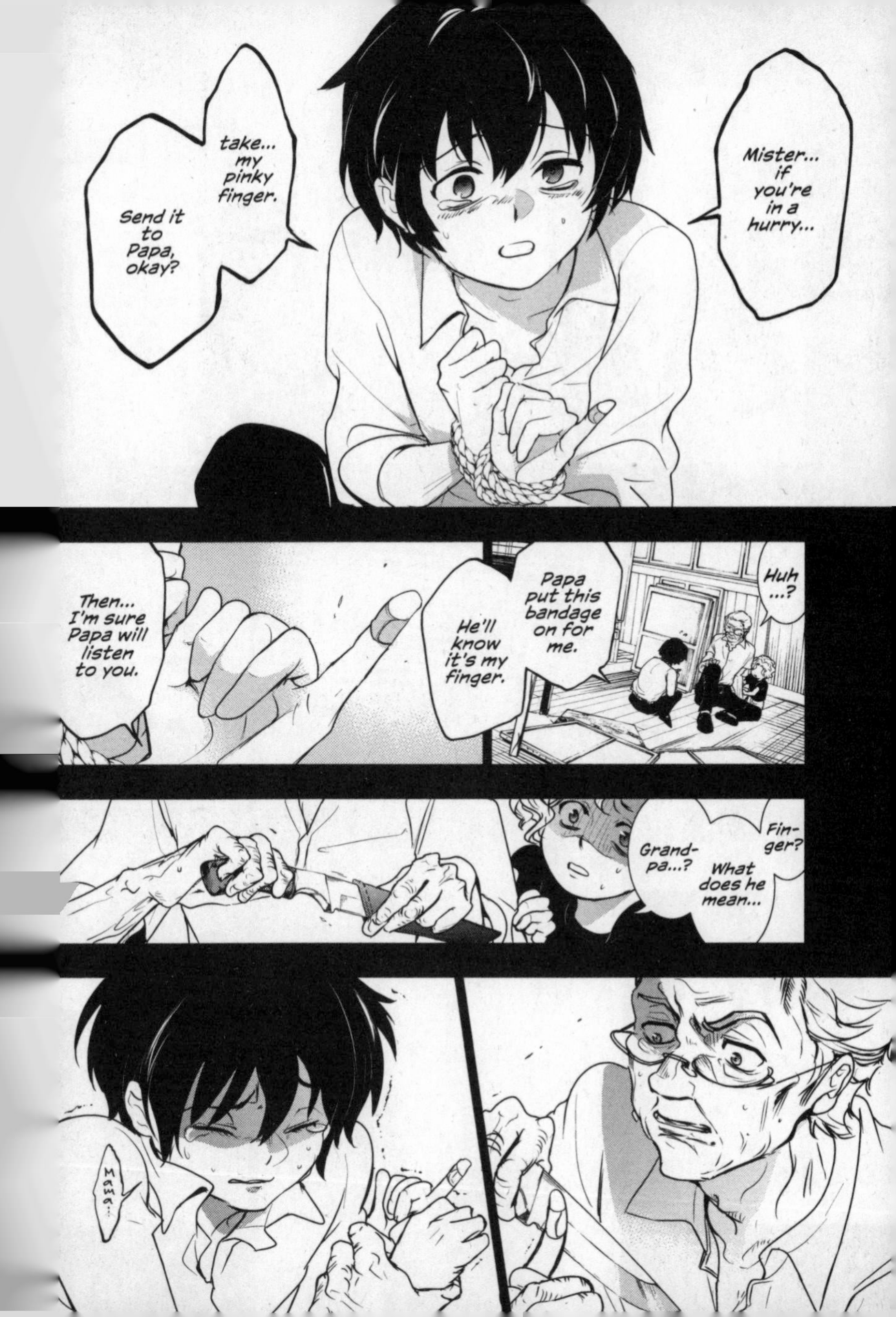

Mister... if you're in a hurry...
take... my pinky finger.
Send it to Papa, okay?
Huh...?
Papa put this bandage on for me.
He'll know it's my finger.
Then... I'm sure Papa will listen to you.
Fin-ger? What does he mean...
Grand-pa...?
Mama...

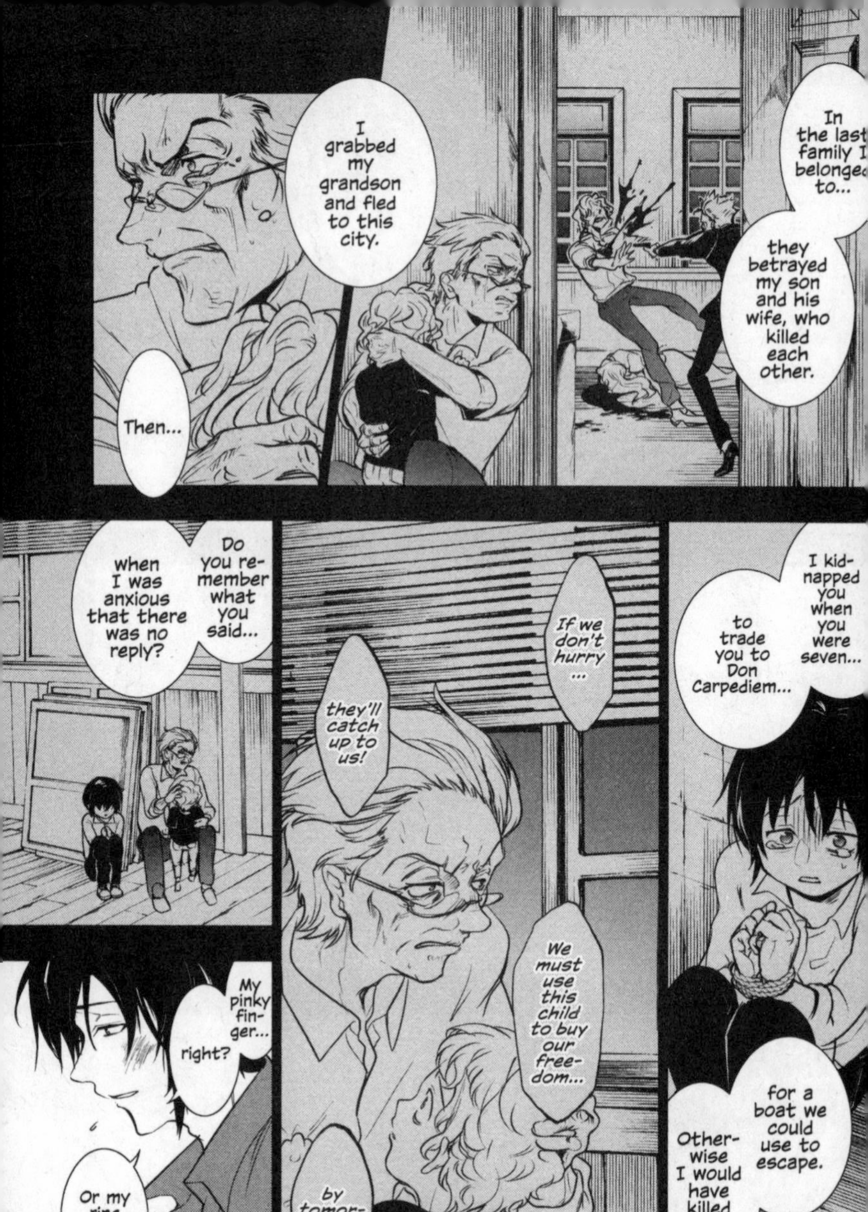
In the last family I belonged to...
they betrayed my son and his wife, who killed each other.
I grabbed my grandson and fled to this city.
Then...
I kidnapped you when you were seven...
to trade you to Don Carpediem...
for a boat we could use to escape.
Otherwise I would have killed you.
If we don't hurry...
they'll catch up to us!
We must use this child to buy our freedom...
by tomorrow.
Do you remember what you said...
when I was anxious that there was no reply?
My pinky finger...
right?
Or my ring finger?

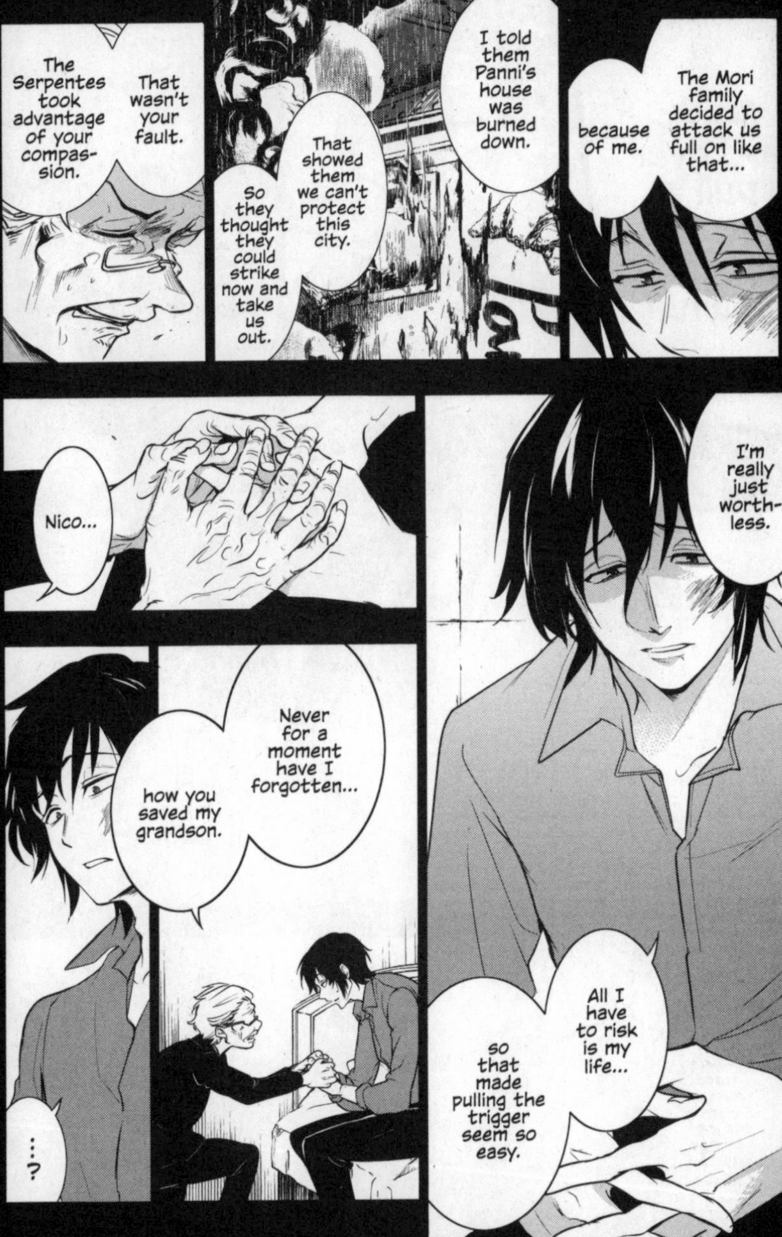
The Mori family decided to attack us full on like that...
because of me.
I told them Panni's house was burned down.
That showed them we can't protect this city.
So they thought they could strike now and take us out.
That wasn't your fault.
The Serpentes took advantage of your compassion.
I'm really just worthless.
All I have to risk is my life...
so that made pulling the trigger seem so easy.
Nico...
Never for a moment have I forgotten...
how you saved my grandson.
...?

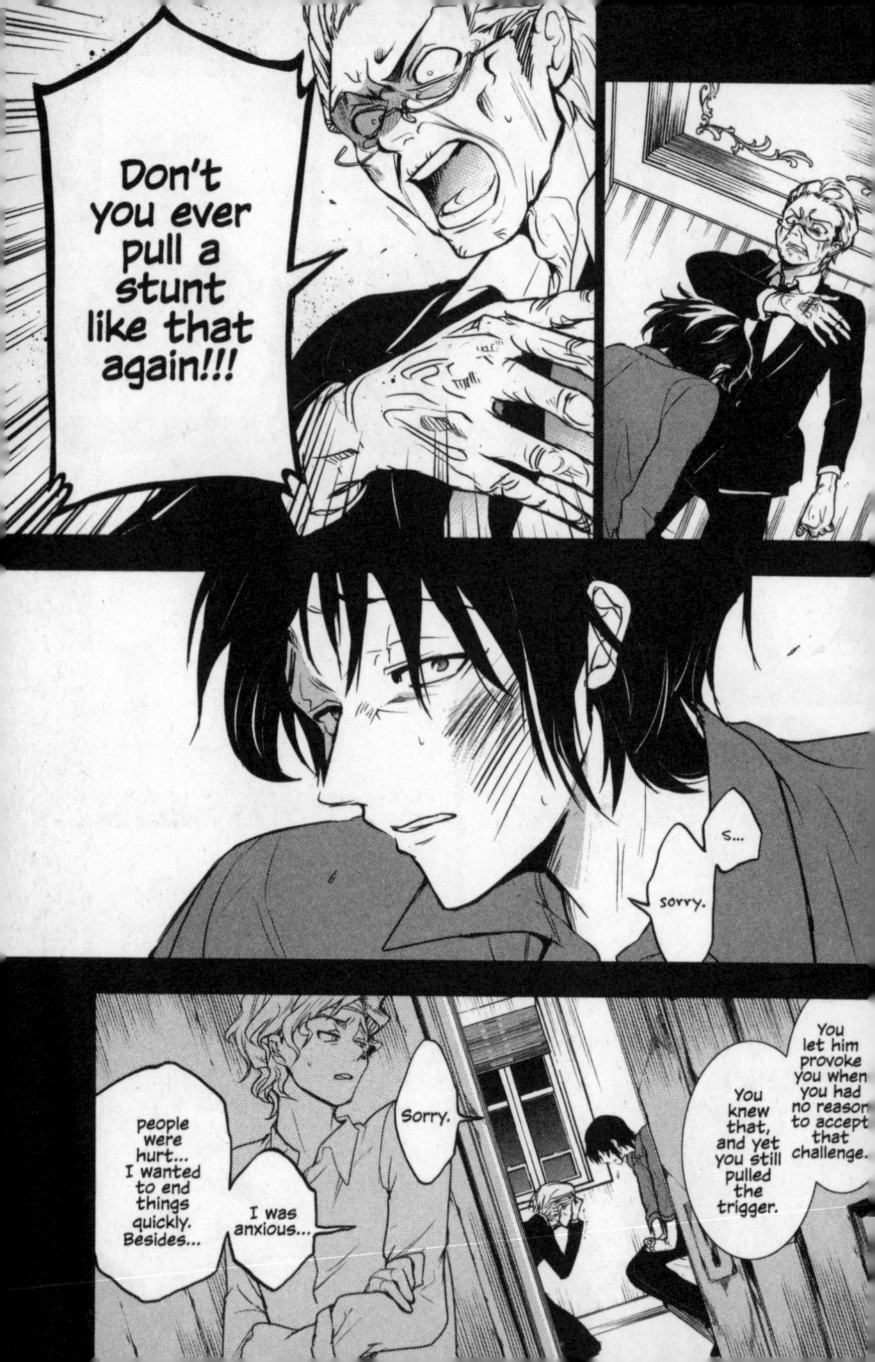
Don't you ever pull a stunt like that again!!!
S...
sorry.
You let him provoke you when you had no reason to accept that challenge.
You knew that, and yet you still pulled the trigger.
Sorry.
I was anxious...
people were hurt... I wanted to end things quickly. Besides...

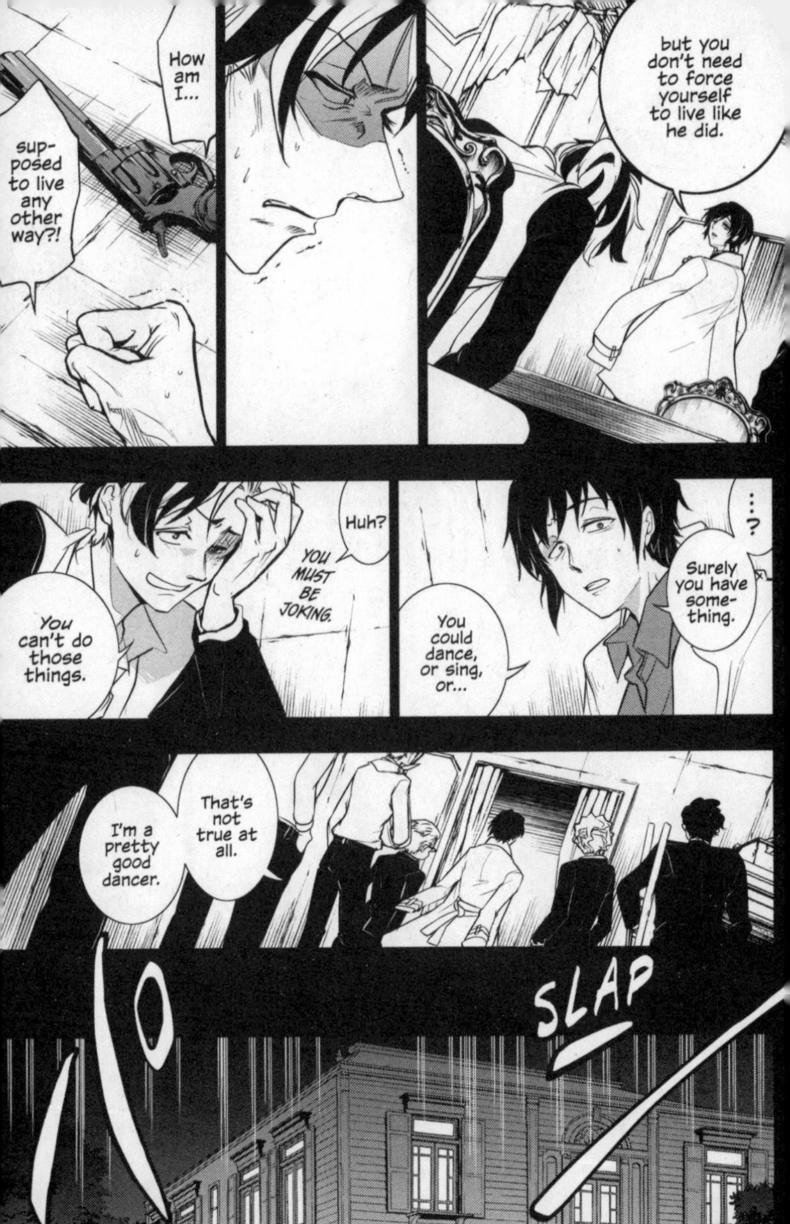

but you don't need to force yourself to live like he did.
How am I...
sup-posed to live any other way?!
...?
Surely you have some-thing.
You could dance, or sing, or...
Huh?
YOU MUST BE JOKING.
You can't do those things.
That's not true at all.
I'm a pretty good dancer.
SLAP

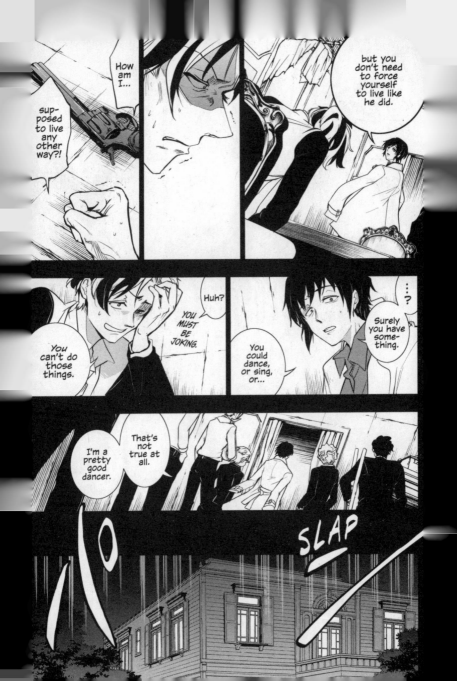

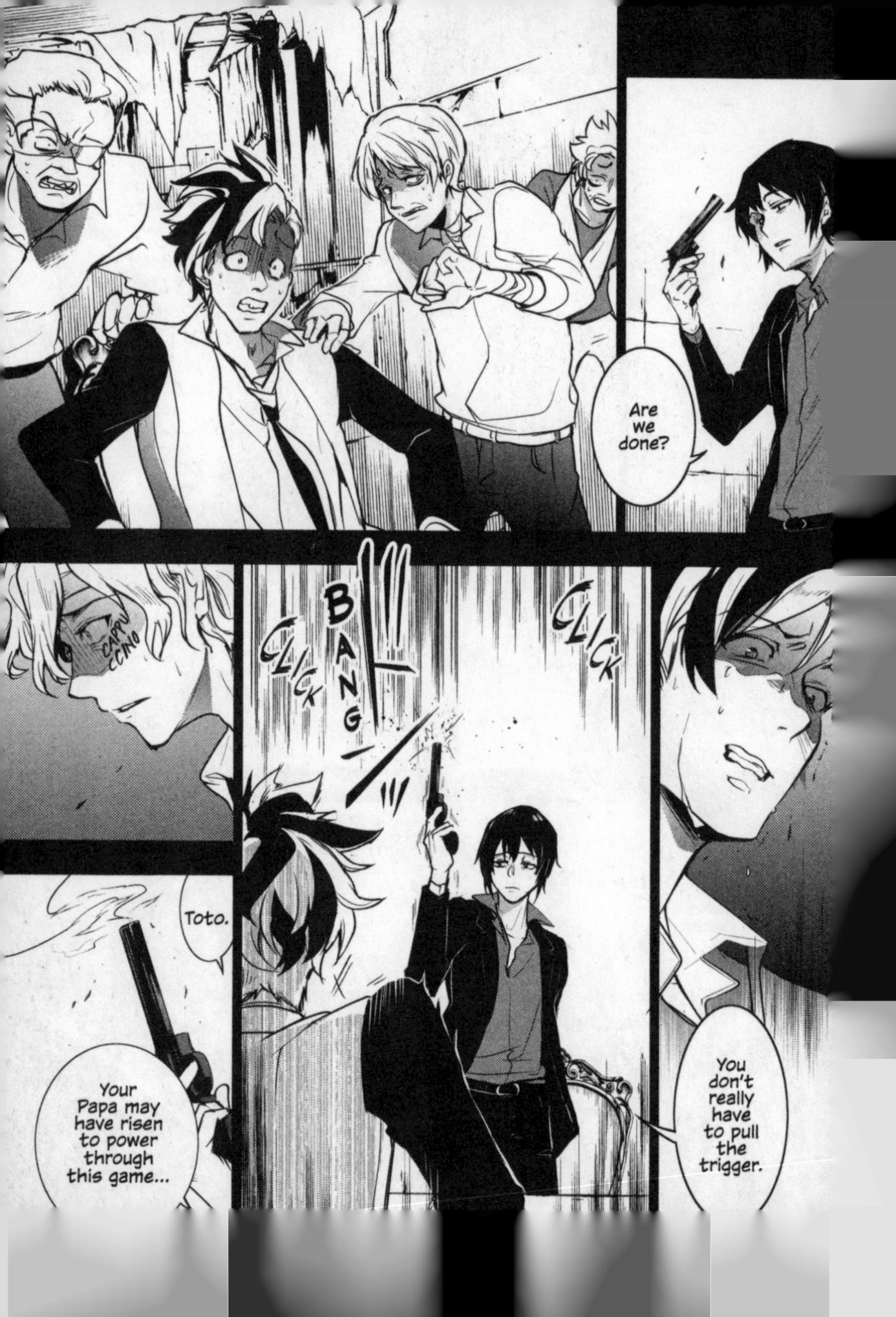
Are we done?
You don't really have to pull the trigger.
CLICK
BANG!!
CLICK
CAPPUCCINO
Toto.
Your Papa may have risen to power through this game...

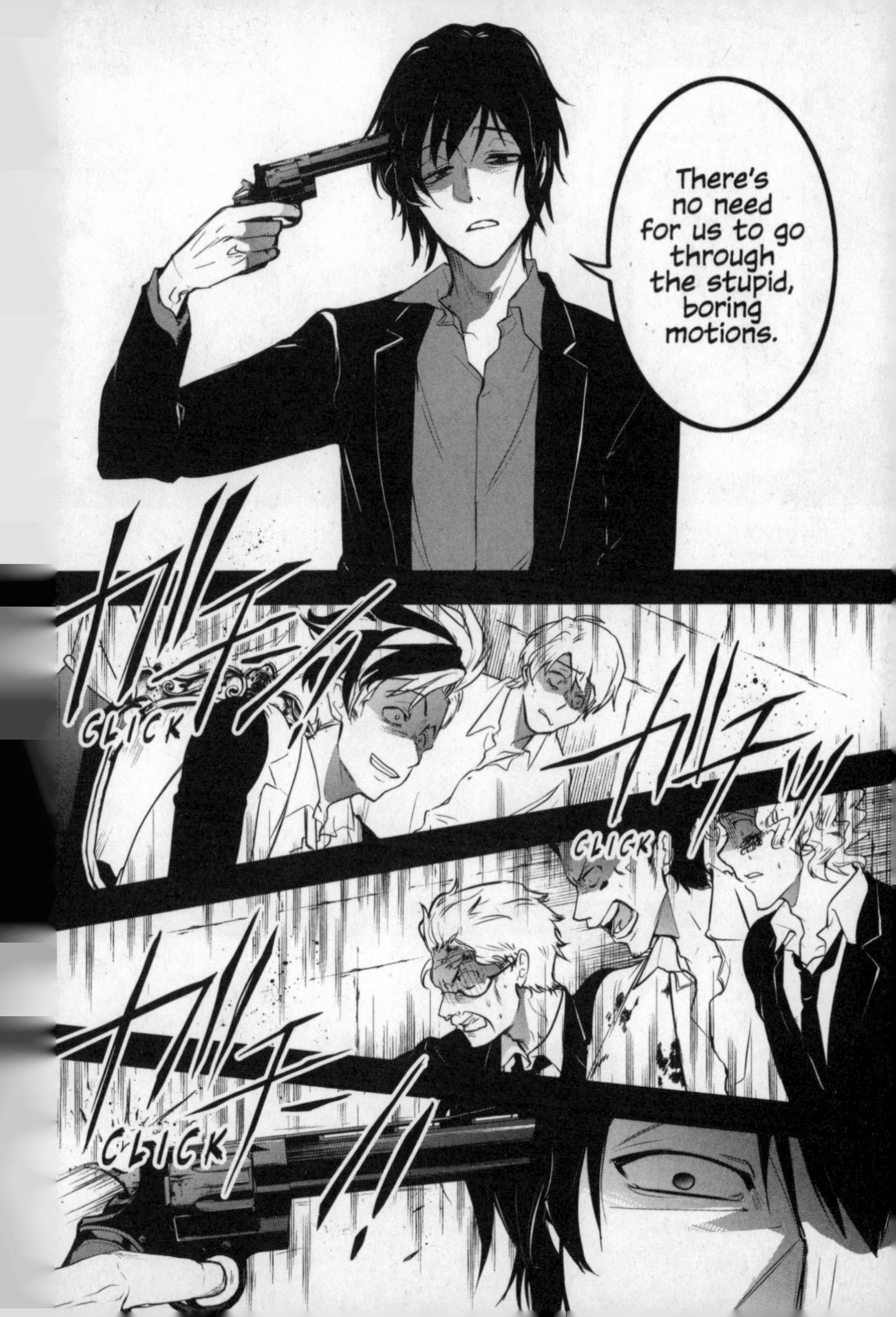
There's no need for us to go through the stupid, boring motions.
CLICK
CLICK
CLICK

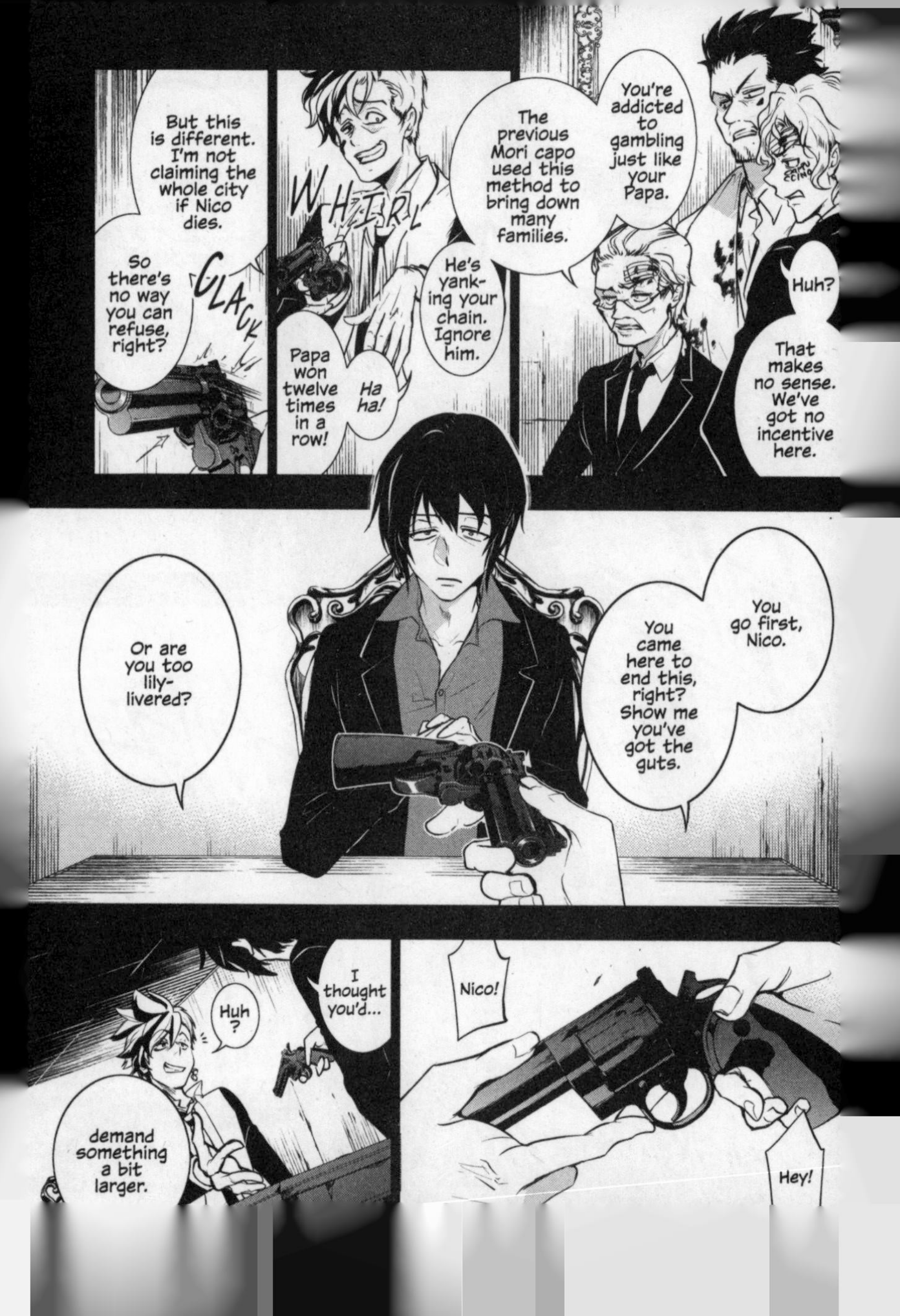
Huh?
That makes no sense. We've got no incentive here.
You're addicted to gambling just like your Papa.
The previous Mori capo used this method to bring down many families.
He's yanking your chain. Ignore him.
Ha ha!
Papa won twelve times in a row!
WHIRL
But this is different. I'm not claiming the whole city if Nico dies.
CLACK
So there's no way you can refuse, right?
You go first, Nico.
You came here to end this, right? Show me you've got the guts.
Or are you too lily-livered?
Nico!
Hey!
I thought you'd...
Huh?
demand something a bit larger.

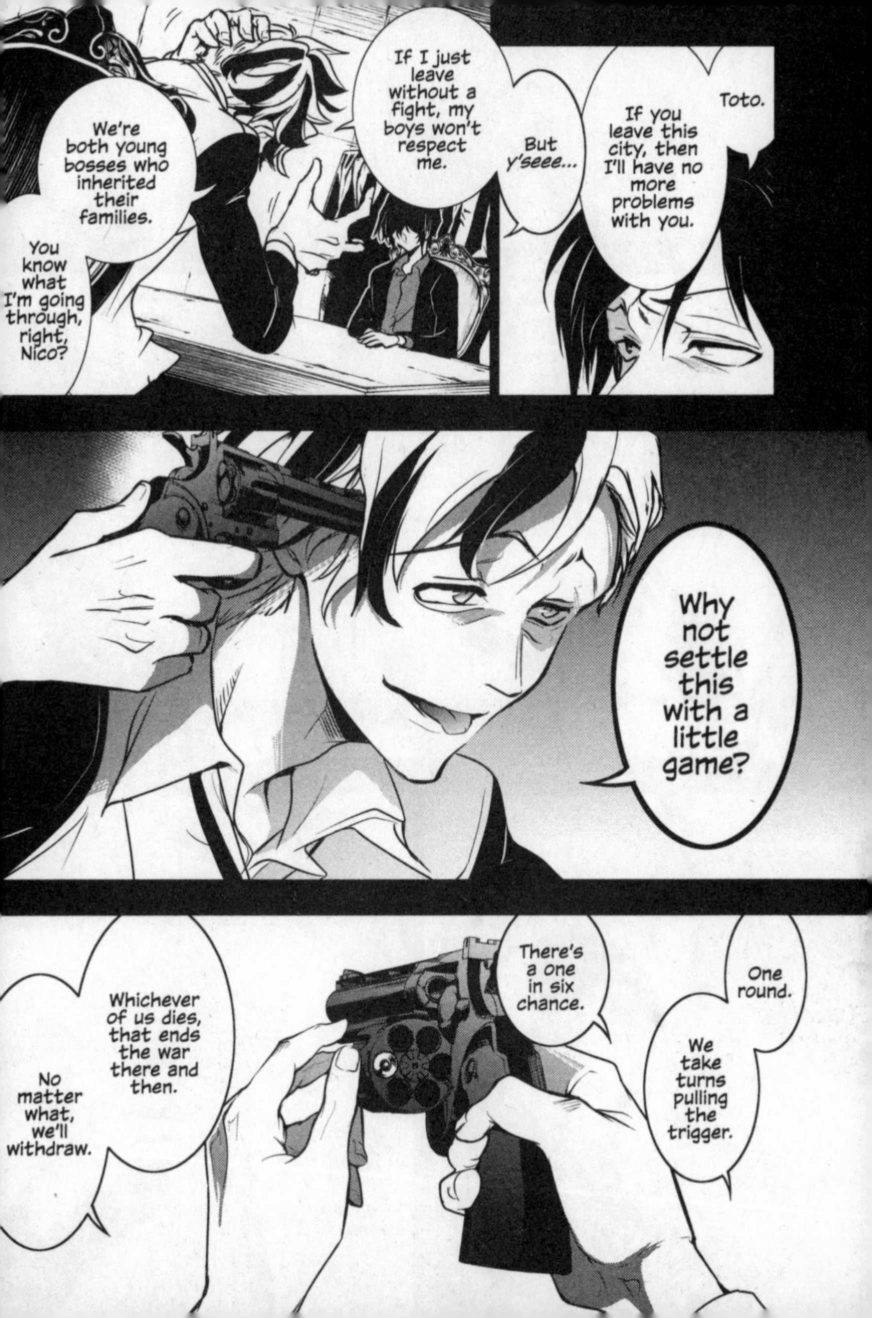
Toto.
If you leave this city, then I'll have no more problems with you.
But y'seee...
If I just leave without a fight, my boys won't respect me.
We're both young bosses who inherited their families.
You know what I'm going through, right, Nico?
Why not settle this with a little game?
One round.
We take turns pulling the trigger.
There's a one in six chance.
Whichever of us dies, that ends the war there and then.
No matter what, we'll withdraw.

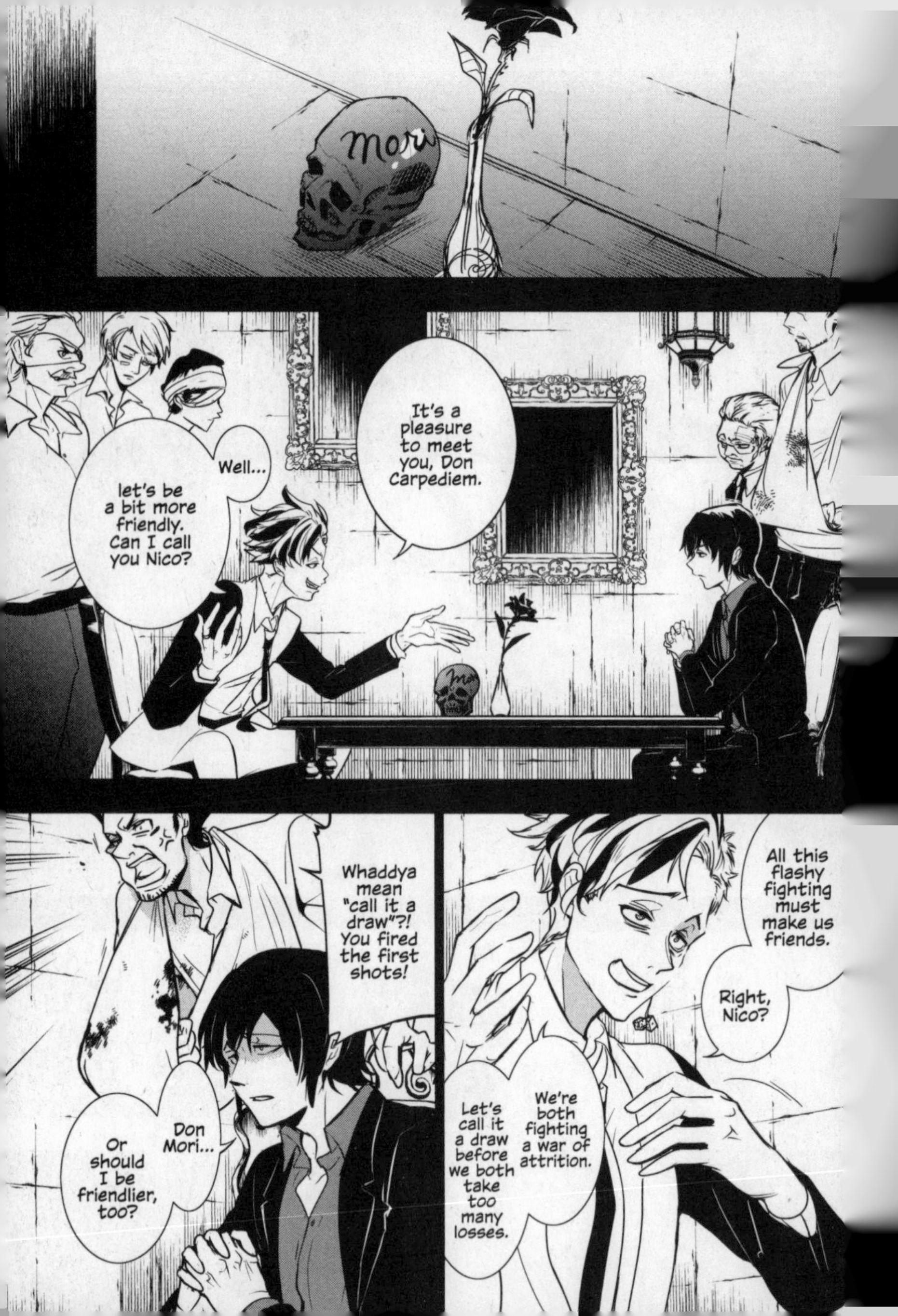
mori
It's a pleasure to meet you, Don Carpediem.
Well...
let's be a bit more friendly. Can I call you Nico?
All this flashy fighting must make us friends.
Right, Nico?
We're both fighting a war of attrition.
Let's call it a draw before we both take too many losses.
Whaddya mean "call it a draw"?! You fired the first shots!
Don Mori...
Or should I be friendlier, too?

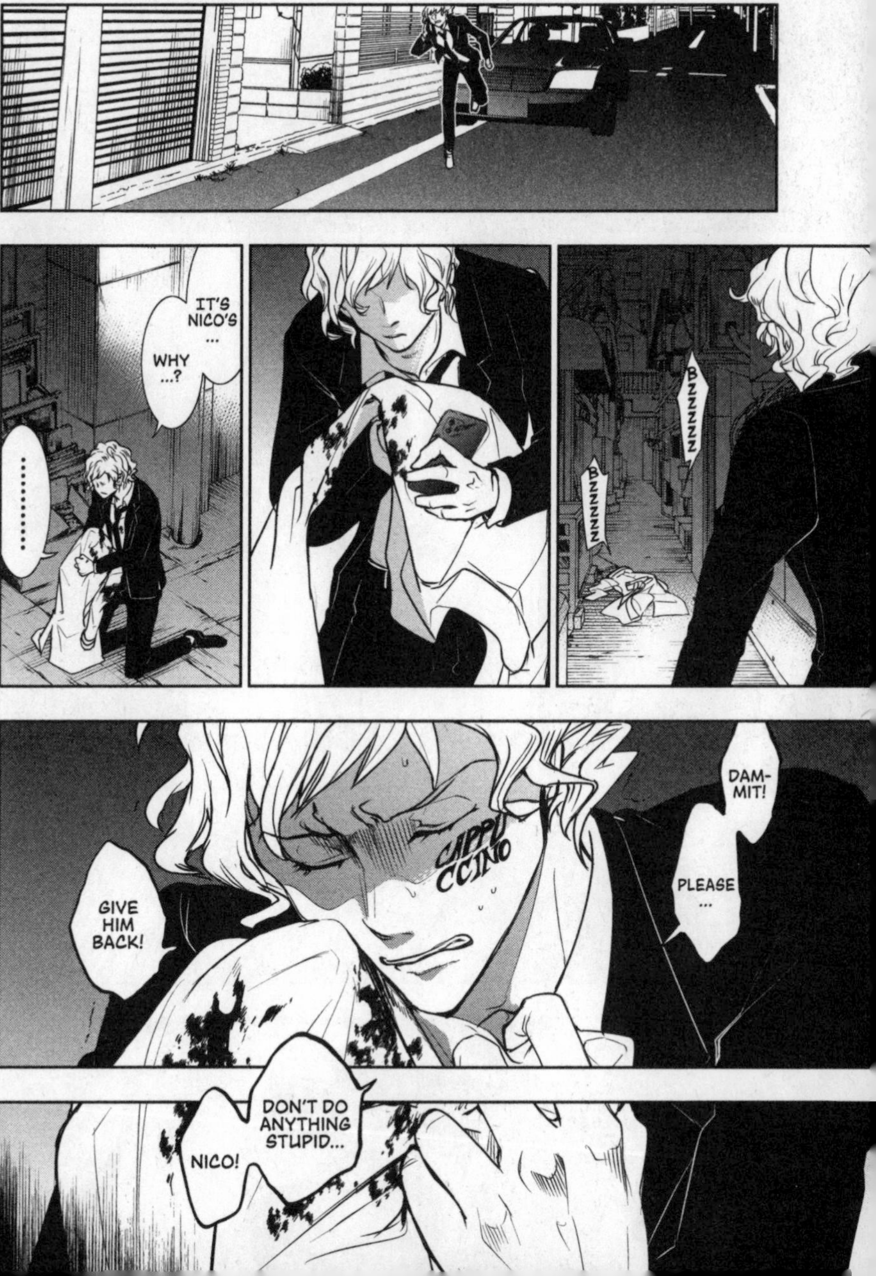
BZZZZZ
BZZZZZ
IT'S NICO'S...
WHY...?
....
DAM-MIT!
PLEASE...
CAPPUCCINO
GIVE HIM BACK!
DON'T DO ANYTHING STUPID...
NICO!

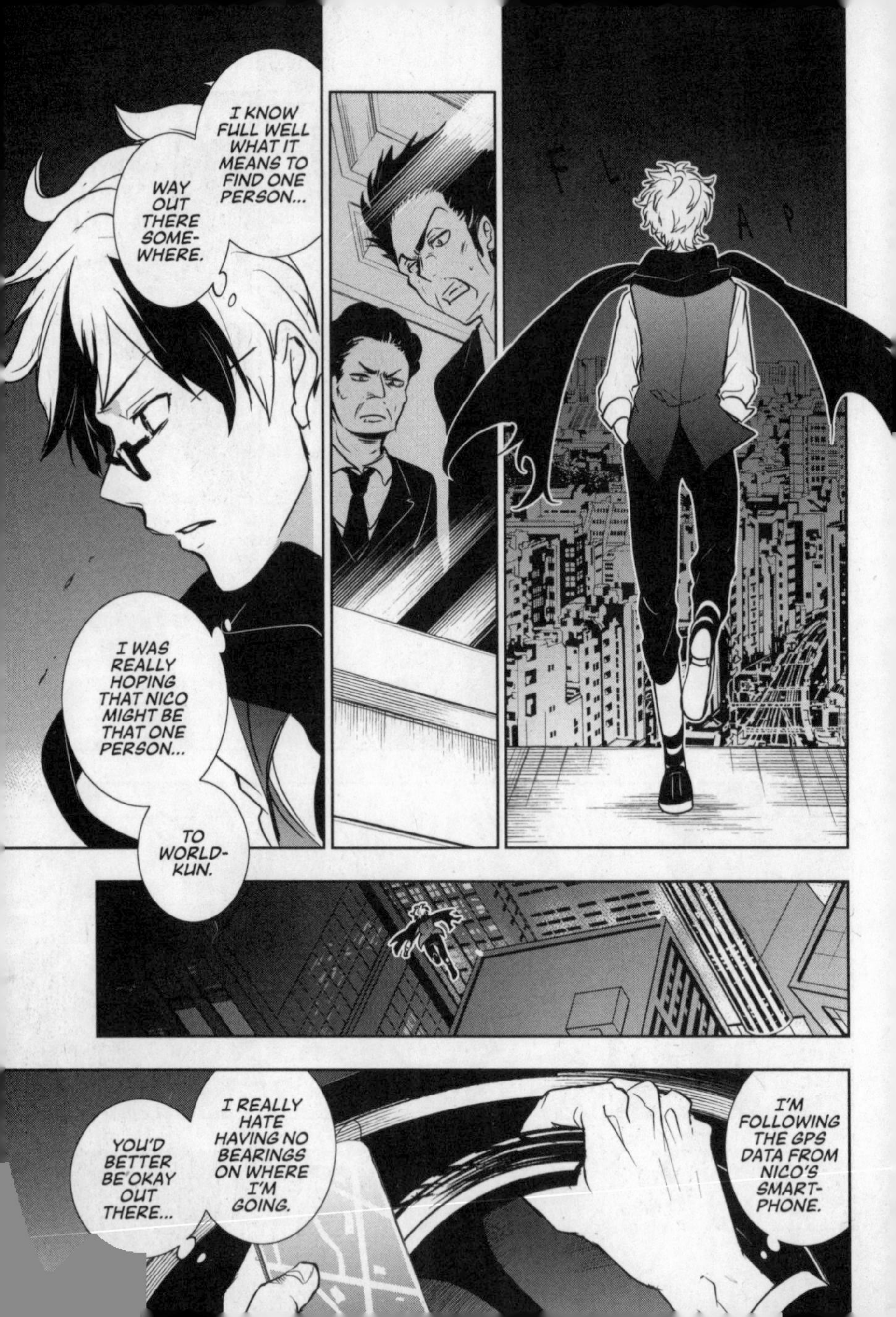
FLAP
I KNOW FULL WELL WHAT IT MEANS TO FIND ONE PERSON...
WAY OUT THERE SOME-WHERE.
I WAS REALLY HOPING THAT NICO MIGHT BE THAT ONE PERSON...
TO WORLD-KUN.
I'M FOLLOWING THE GPS DATA FROM NICO'S SMART-PHONE.
I REALLY HATE HAVING NO BEARINGS ON WHERE I'M GOING.
YOU'D BETTER BE OKAY OUT THERE...

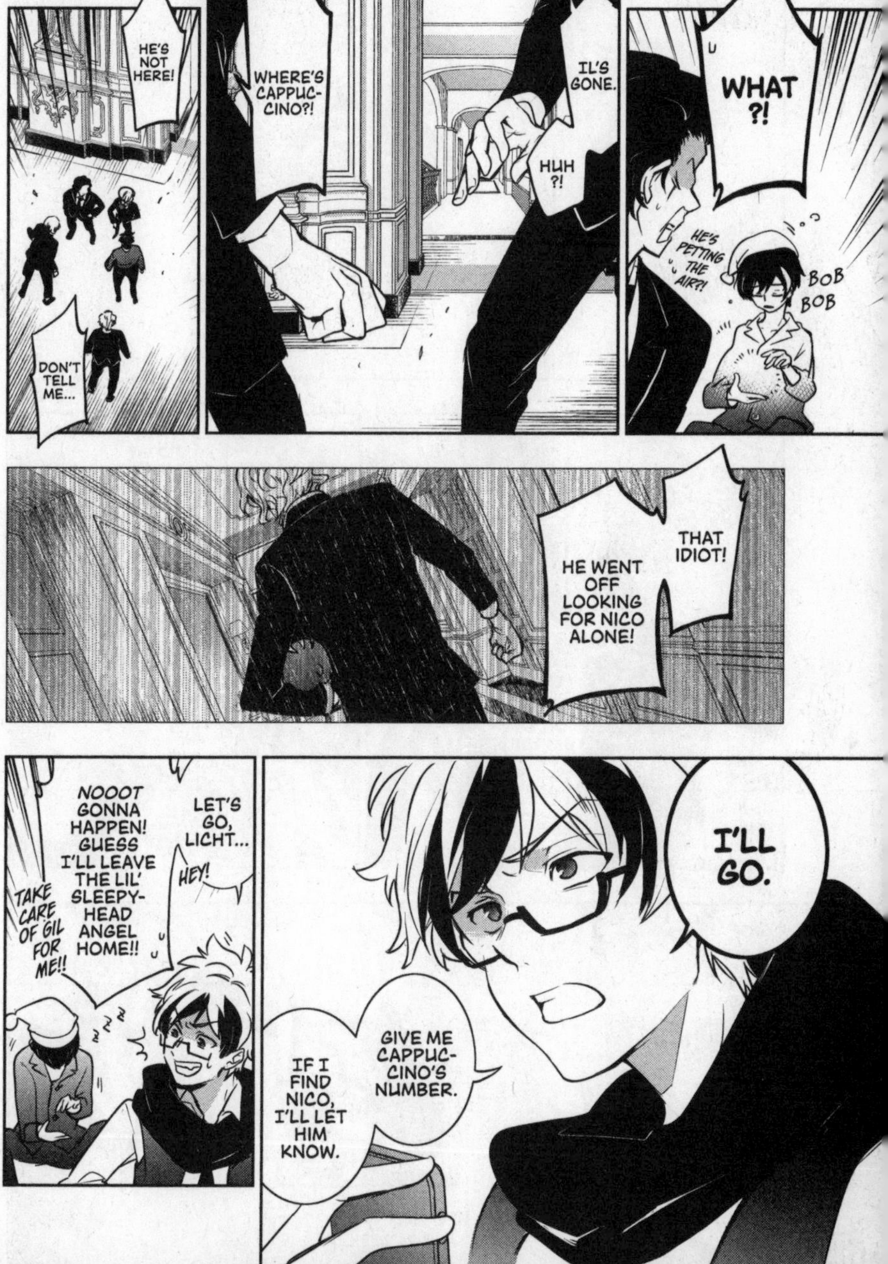
WHAT?!
HE'S PETTING THE AIR?!
BOB BOB
IL'S GONE.
WHERE'S CAPPUCCINO?!
HUH?!
HE'S NOT HERE!
DON'T TELL ME...
THAT IDIOT!
HE WENT OFF LOOKING FOR NICO ALONE!
I'LL GO.
GIVE ME CAPPUCCINO'S NUMBER.
IF I FIND NICO, I'LL LET HIM KNOW.
LET'S GO, LICHT...
HEY!
NOOOT GONNA HAPPEN! GUESS I'LL LEAVE THE LIL' SLEEPYHEAD ANGEL HOME!!
TAKE CARE OF GIL FOR ME!!

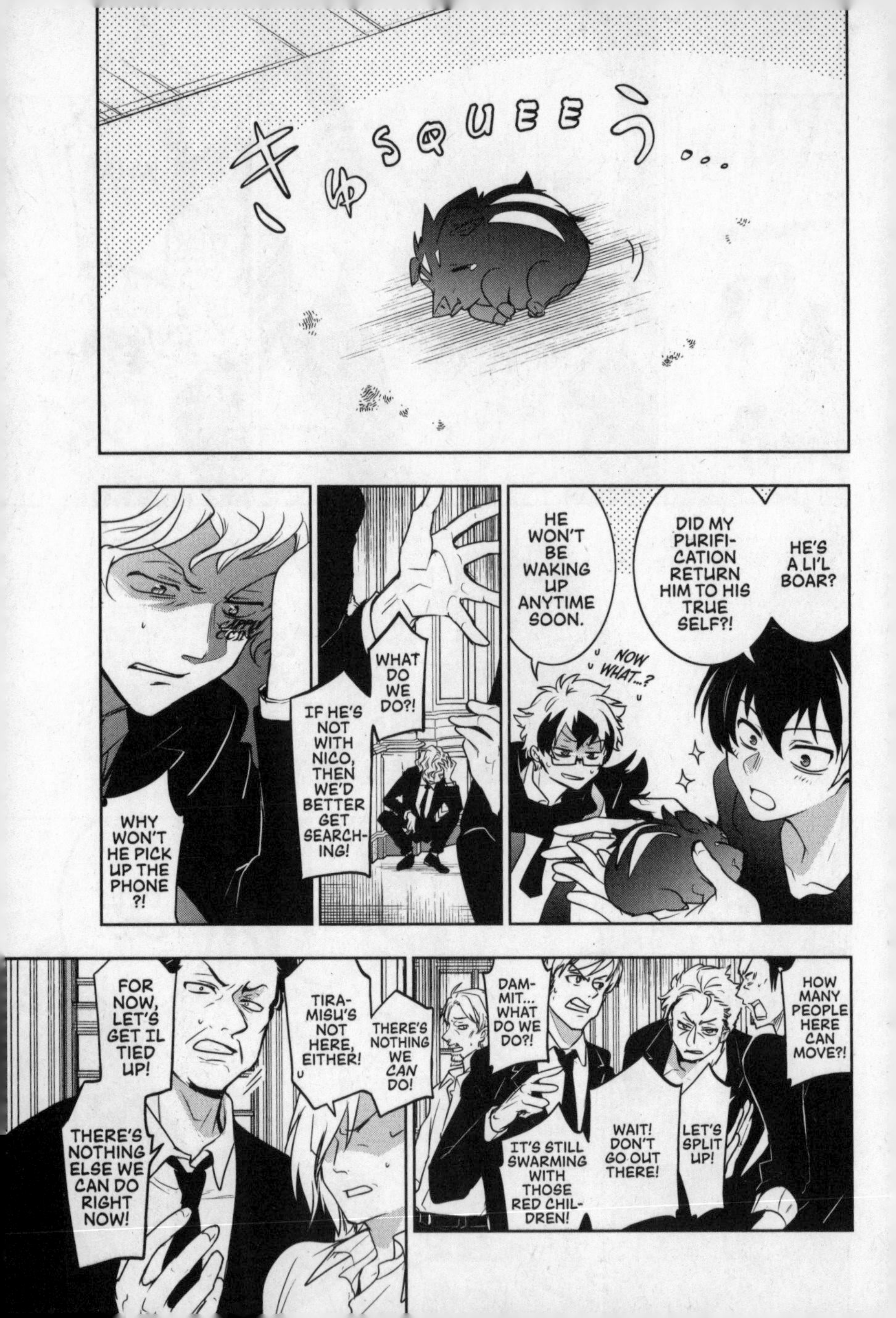
キゅSQUEEう...
HE'S A LI'L BOAR?
DID MY PURIFICATION RETURN HIM TO HIS TRUE SELF?!
HE WON'T BE WAKING UP ANYTIME SOON.
NOW WHAT...?
WHAT DO WE DO?!
IF HE'S NOT WITH NICO, THEN WE'D BETTER GET SEARCHING!
WHY WON'T HE PICK UP THE PHONE?!
HOW MANY PEOPLE HERE CAN MOVE?!
DAMMIT... WHAT DO WE DO?!
LET'S SPLIT UP!
WAIT! DON'T GO OUT THERE!
IT'S STILL SWARMING WITH THOSE RED CHILDREN!
THERE'S NOTHING WE CAN DO!
TIRAMISU'S NOT HERE, EITHER!
FOR NOW, LET'S GET IL TIED UP!
THERE'S NOTHING ELSE WE CAN DO RIGHT NOW!

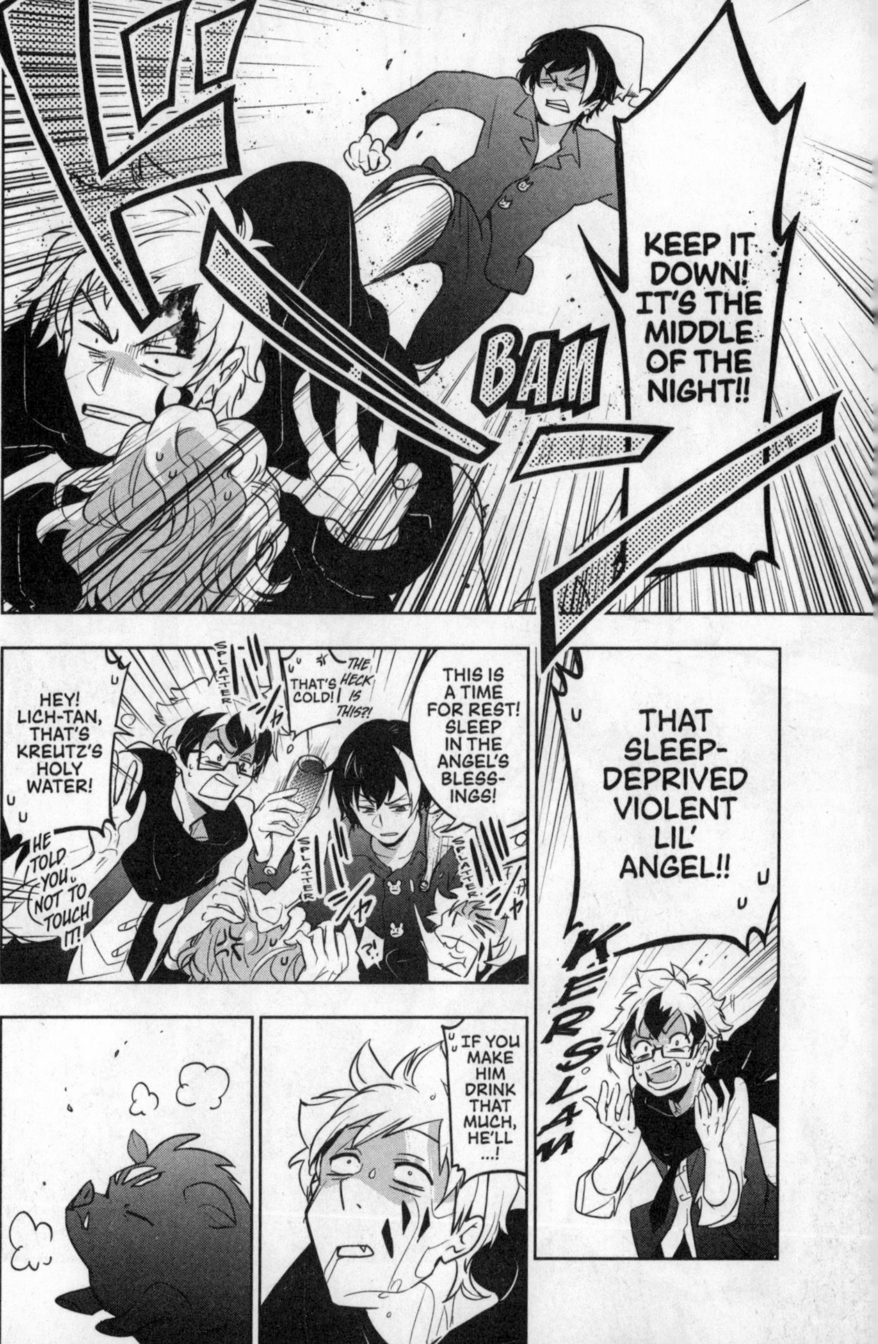
KEEP IT DOWN! IT'S THE MIDDLE OF THE NIGHT!!
BAM
THAT SLEEP-DEPRIVED VIOLENT LIL' ANGEL!!
KERSLAM
THIS IS A TIME FOR REST! SLEEP IN THE ANGEL'S BLESSINGS!
THE HECK IS THIS?!
THAT'S COLD!
SPLATTER
SPLATTER
SPLATTER
HEY! LICH-TAN, THAT'S KREUTZ'S HOLY WATER!
HE TOLD YOU NOT TO TOUCH IT!
IF YOU MAKE HIM DRINK THAT MUCH, HE'LL ...!

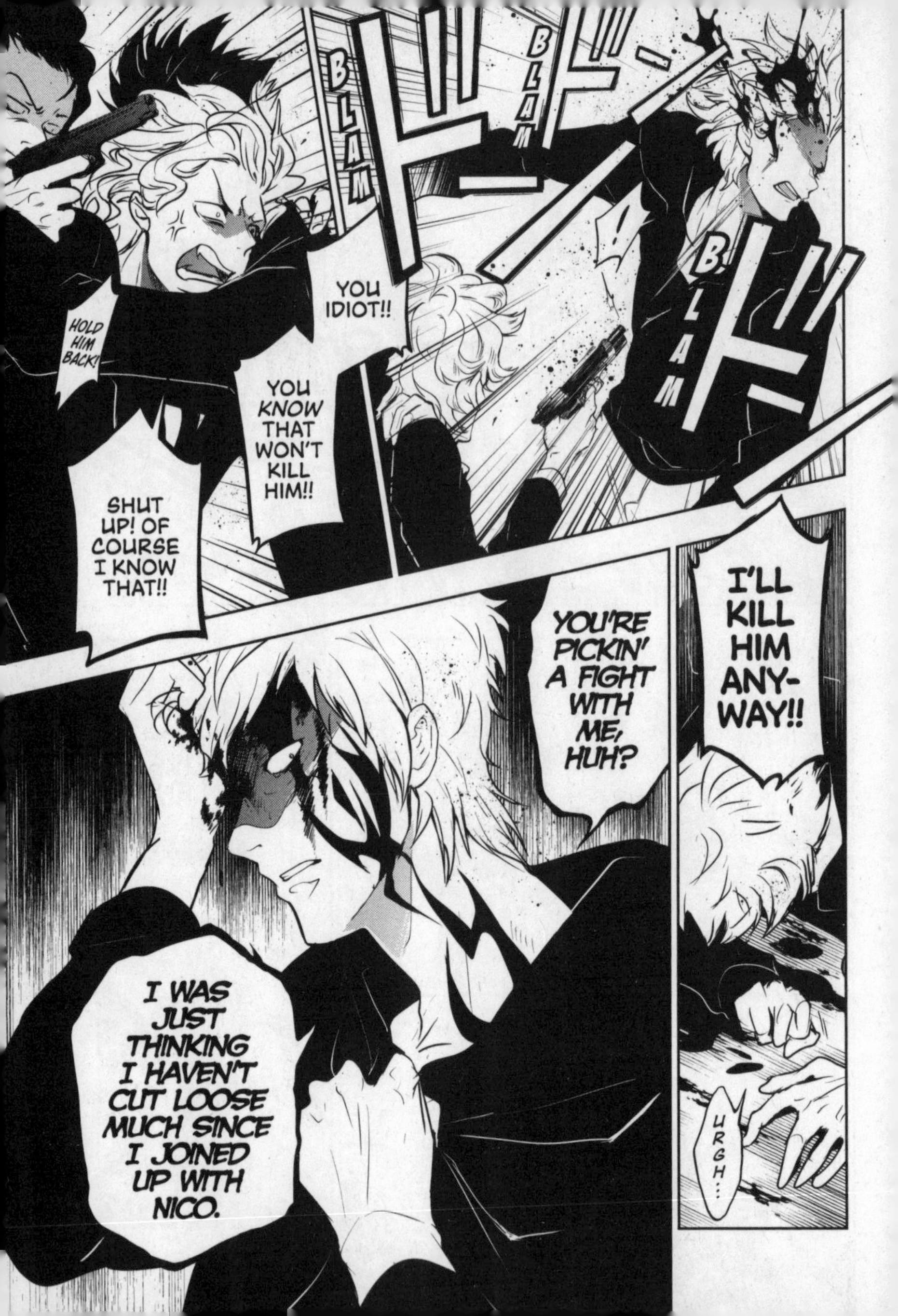
BLAM
B,
BLAM
BLAM
YOU IDIOT!!
HOLD HIM BACK!
YOU KNOW THAT WON'T KILL HIM!!
SHUT UP! OF COURSE I KNOW THAT!!
I'LL KILL HIM ANY-WAY!!
URGH...
YOU'RE PICKIN' A FIGHT WITH ME, HUH?
I WAS JUST THINKING I HAVEN'T CUT LOOSE MUCH SINCE I JOINED UP WITH NICO.

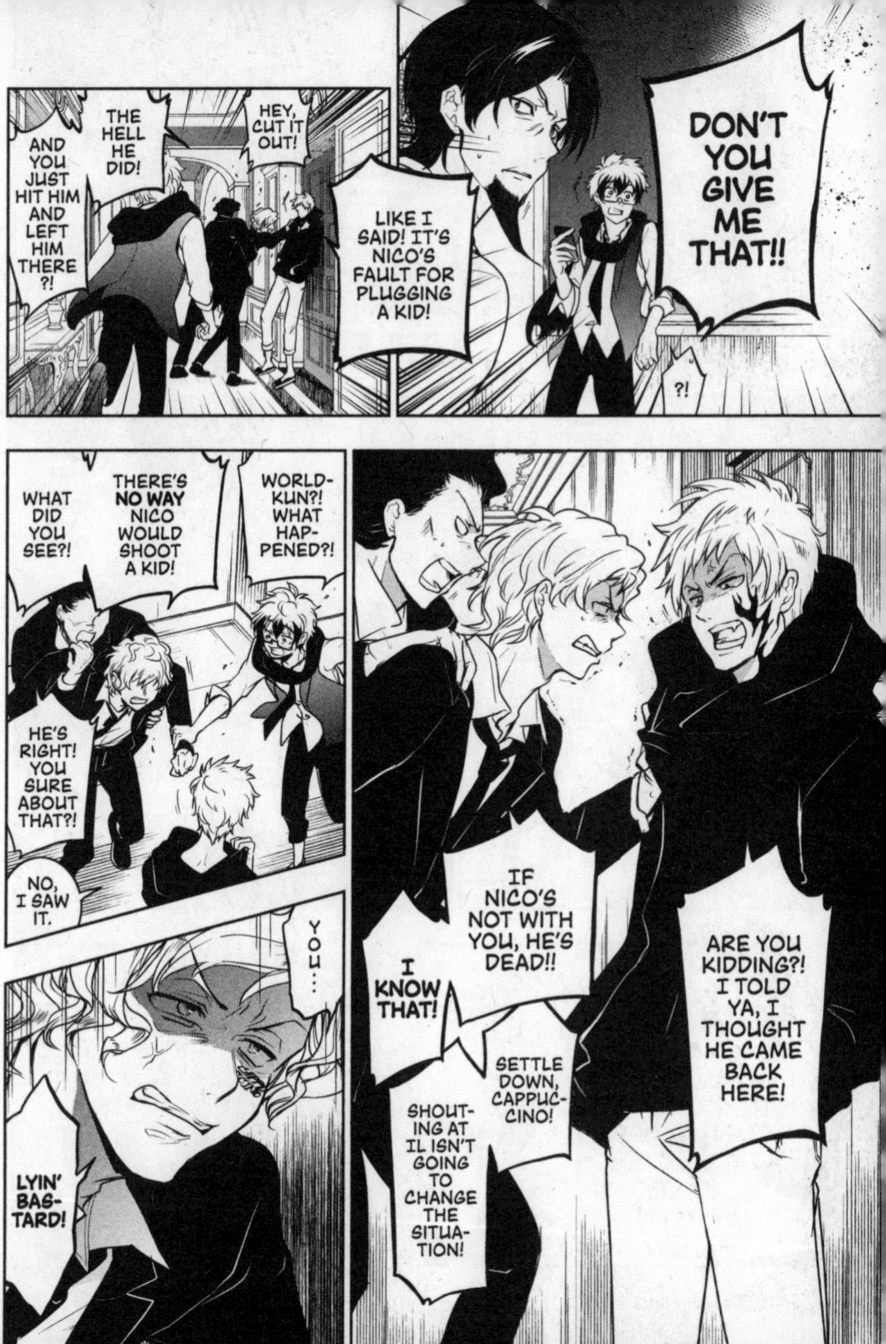

DON'T YOU GIVE ME THAT!!
?!
LIKE I SAID! IT'S NICO'S FAULT FOR PLUGGING A KID!
HEY, CUT IT OUT!
THE HELL HE DID!
AND YOU JUST HIT HIM AND LEFT HIM THERE?!
ARE YOU KIDDING?! I TOLD YA, I THOUGHT HE CAME BACK HERE!
IF NICO'S NOT WITH YOU, HE'S DEAD!!
I KNOW THAT!
SETTLE DOWN, CAPPUCCINO!
SHOUTING AT IL ISN'T GOING TO CHANGE THE SITUATION!
WORLD-KUN?! WHAT HAPPENED?!
THERE'S NO WAY NICO WOULD SHOOT A KID!
WHAT DID YOU SEE?!
HE'S RIGHT! YOU SURE ABOUT THAT?!
NO, I SAW IT.
YOU...
LYIN' BASTARD!

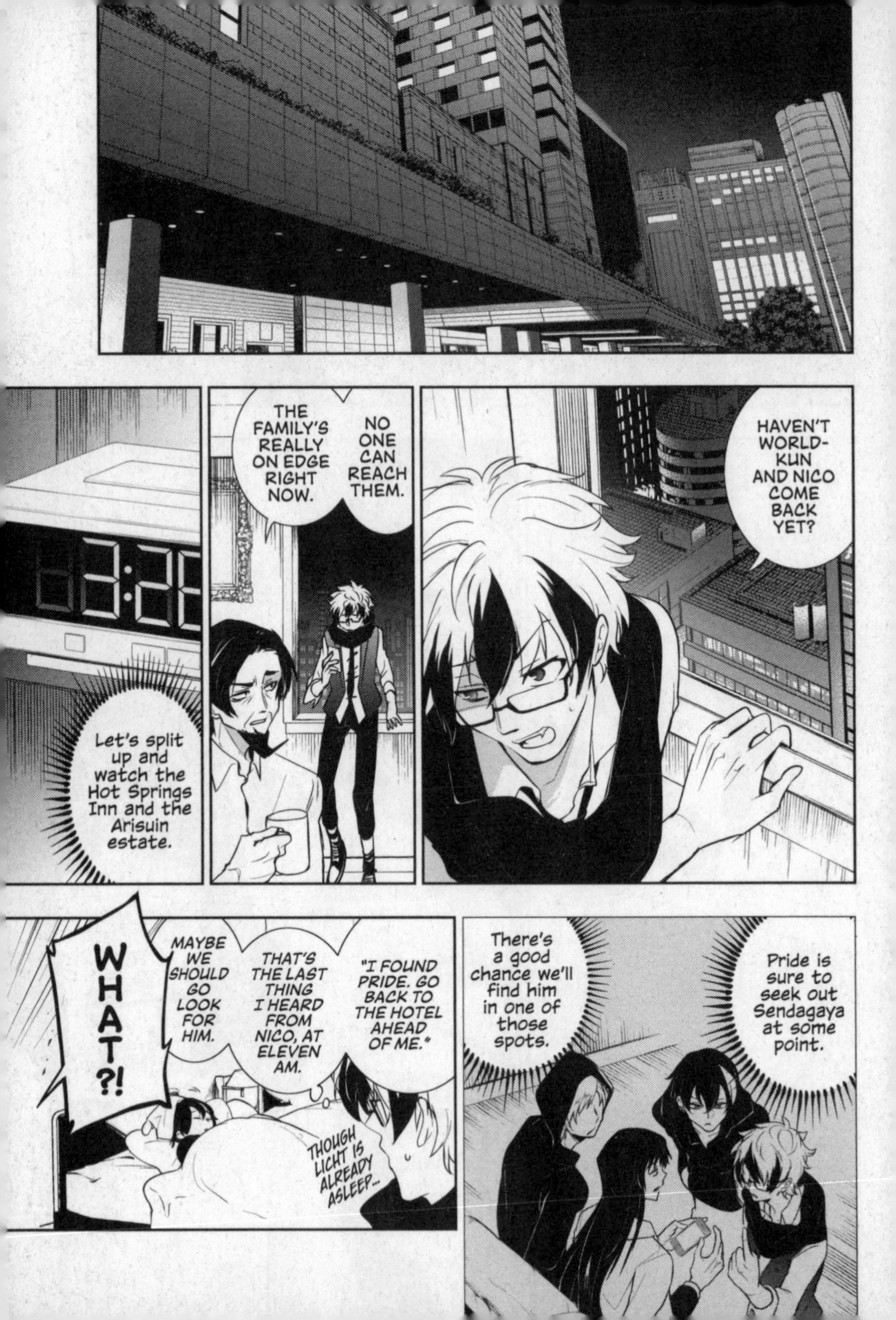
HAVEN'T WORLD-KUN AND NICO COME BACK YET?
NO ONE CAN REACH THEM.
THE FAMILY'S REALLY ON EDGE RIGHT NOW.
Let's split up and watch the Hot Springs Inn and the Arisuin estate.
Pride is sure to seek out Sendagaya at some point.
There's a good chance we'll find him in one of those spots.
"I FOUND PRIDE. GO BACK TO THE HOTEL AHEAD OF ME."
THAT'S THE LAST THING I HEARD FROM NICO, AT ELEVEN AM.
MAYBE WE SHOULD GO LOOK FOR HIM.
THOUGH LICHT IS ALREADY ASLEEP...
WHAT?!

SERVAMP

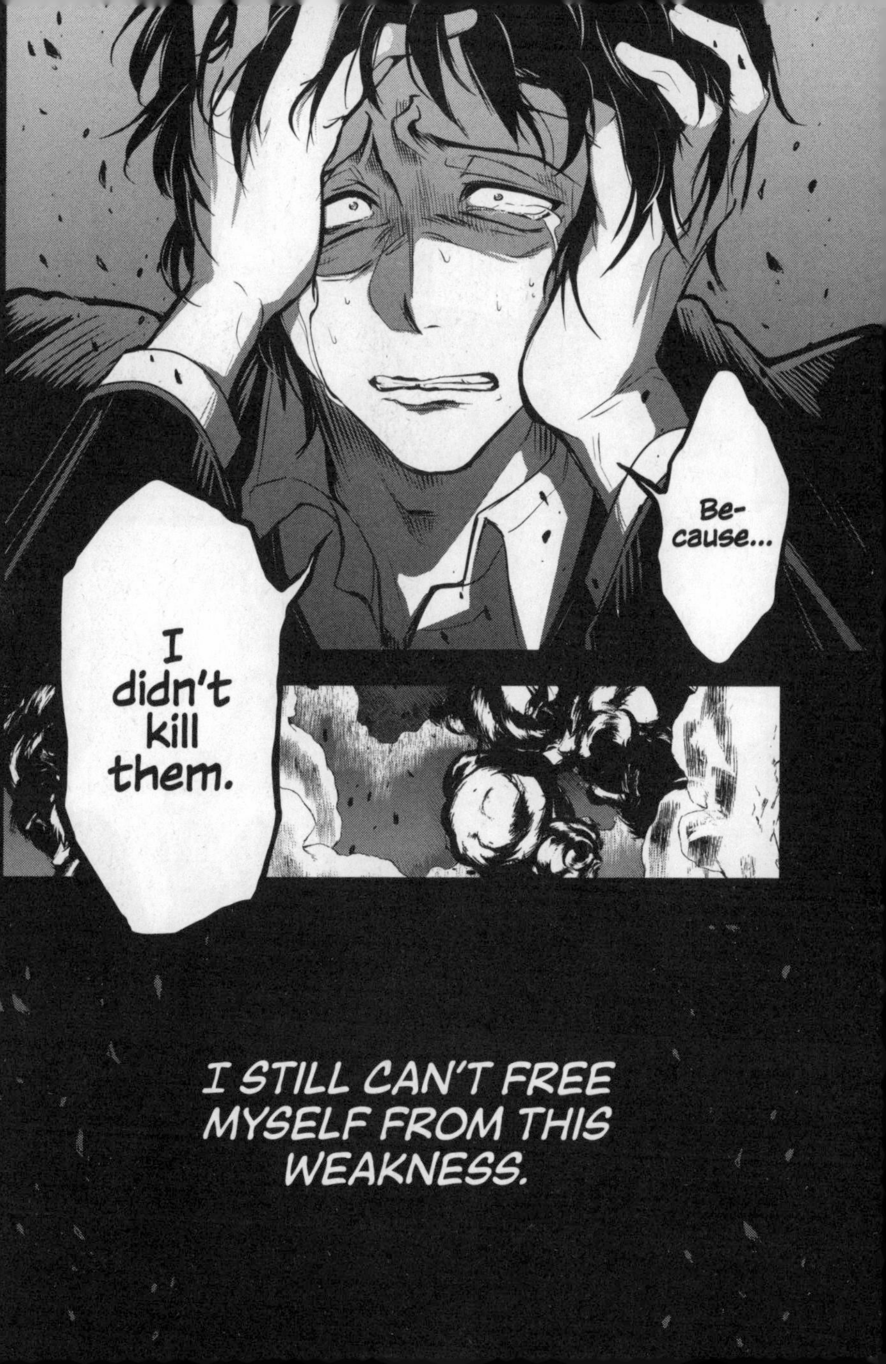
Be-cause...
I didn't kill them.
I STILL CAN'T FREE MYSELF FROM THIS WEAKNESS.

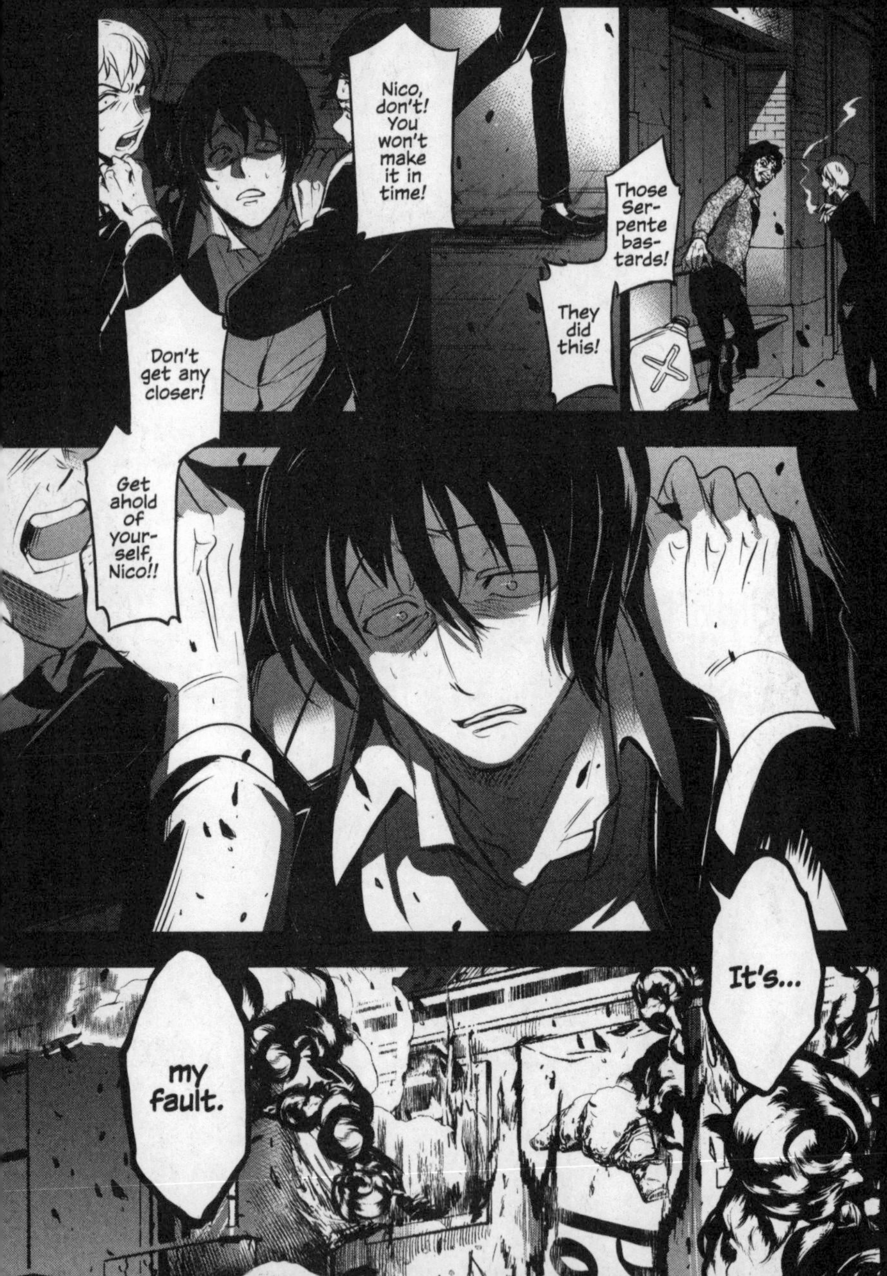
Those Serpente bastards!
They did this!
Nico, don't! You won't make it in time!
Don't get any closer!
Get ahold of yourself, Nico!!
It's...
my fault.

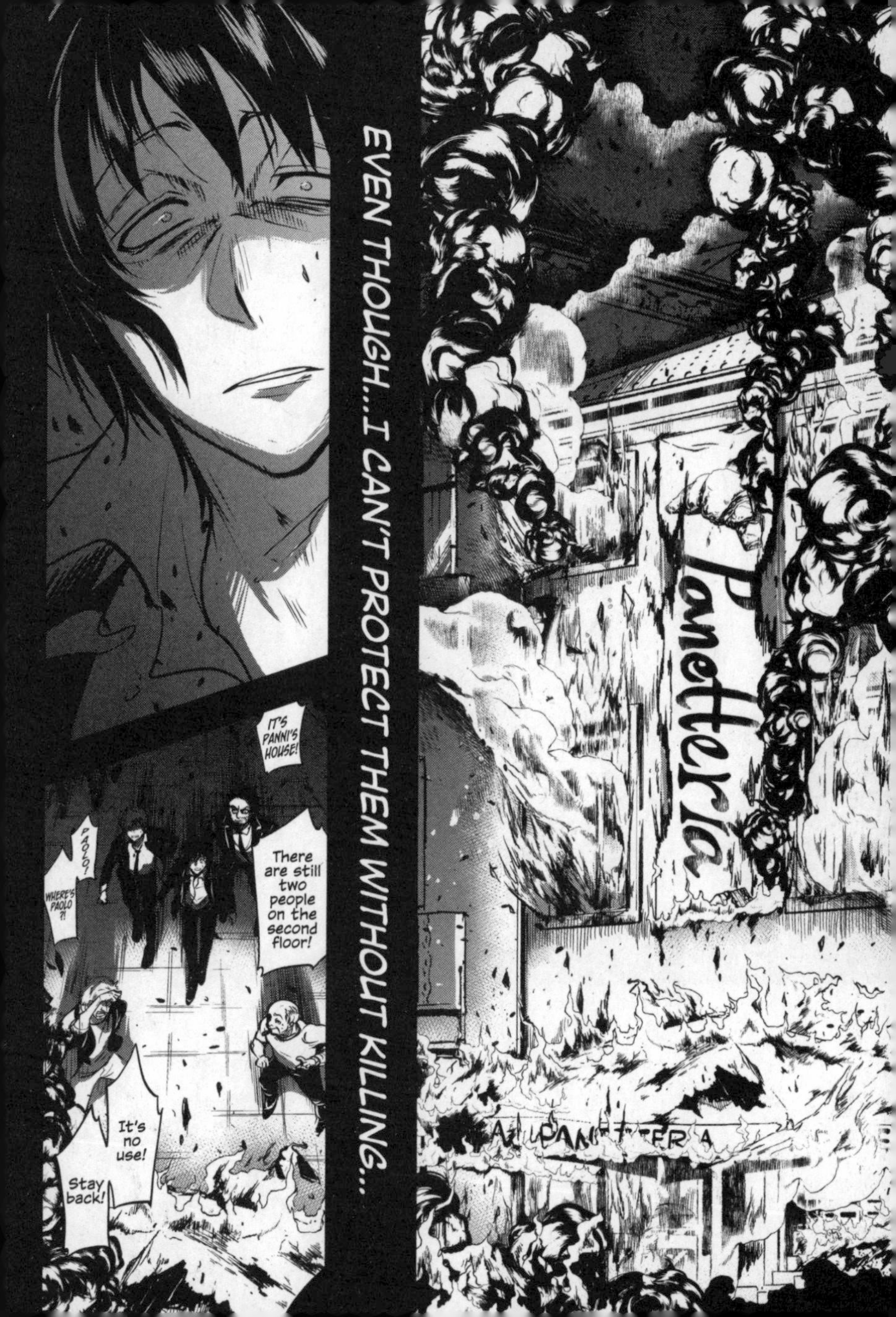
Panetteria
EVEN THOUGH...I CAN'T PROTECT THEM WITHOUT KILLING...
IT'S PANNI'S HOUSE!
There are still two people on the second floor!
PAOLO!
WHERE'S PAOLO?!
It's no use!
Stay back!

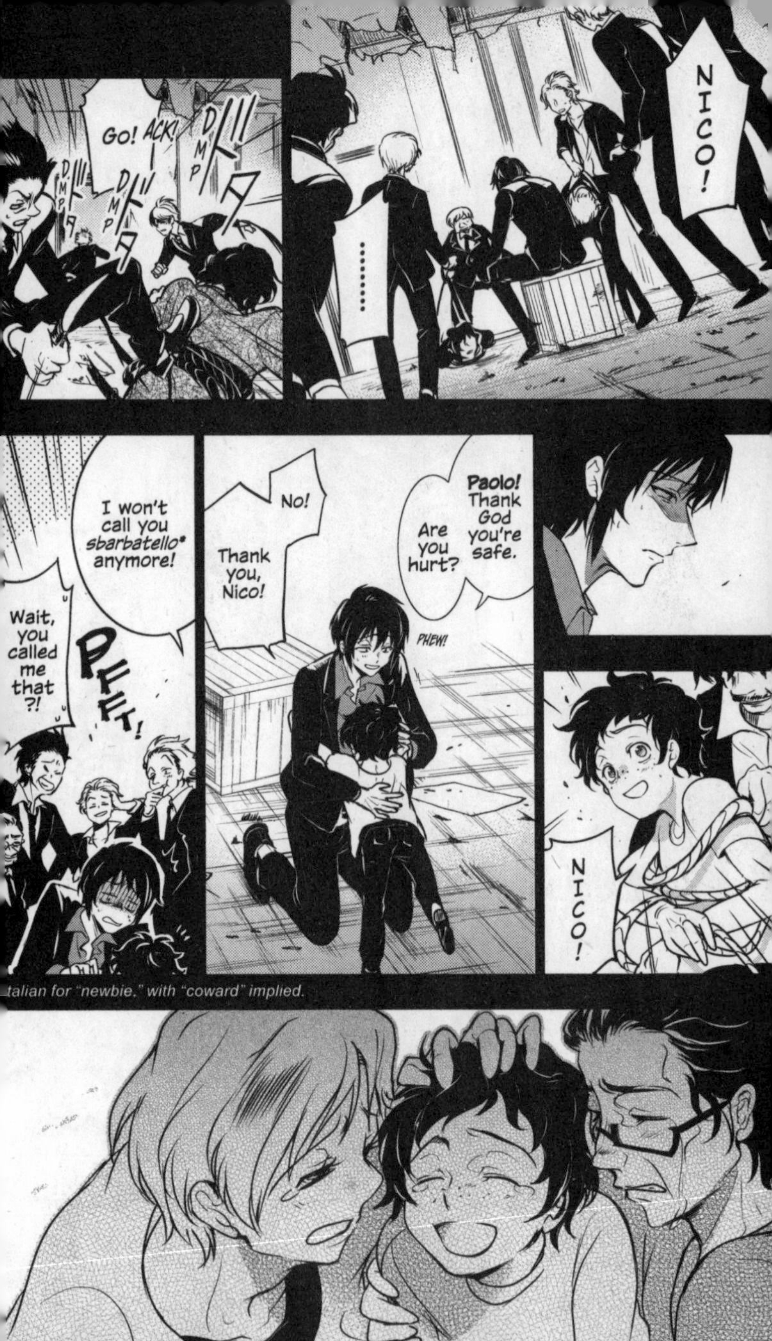
NICO!
......
Go!
ACK!
DMP
DMP
DMP
DMP
NICO!
Paolo! Thank God you're safe.
Are you hurt?
No!
Thank you, Nico!
PHEW!
I won't call you sbarbatello* anymore!
Wait, you called me that?!
PFFT!

*Italian for "newbie," with "coward" implied.

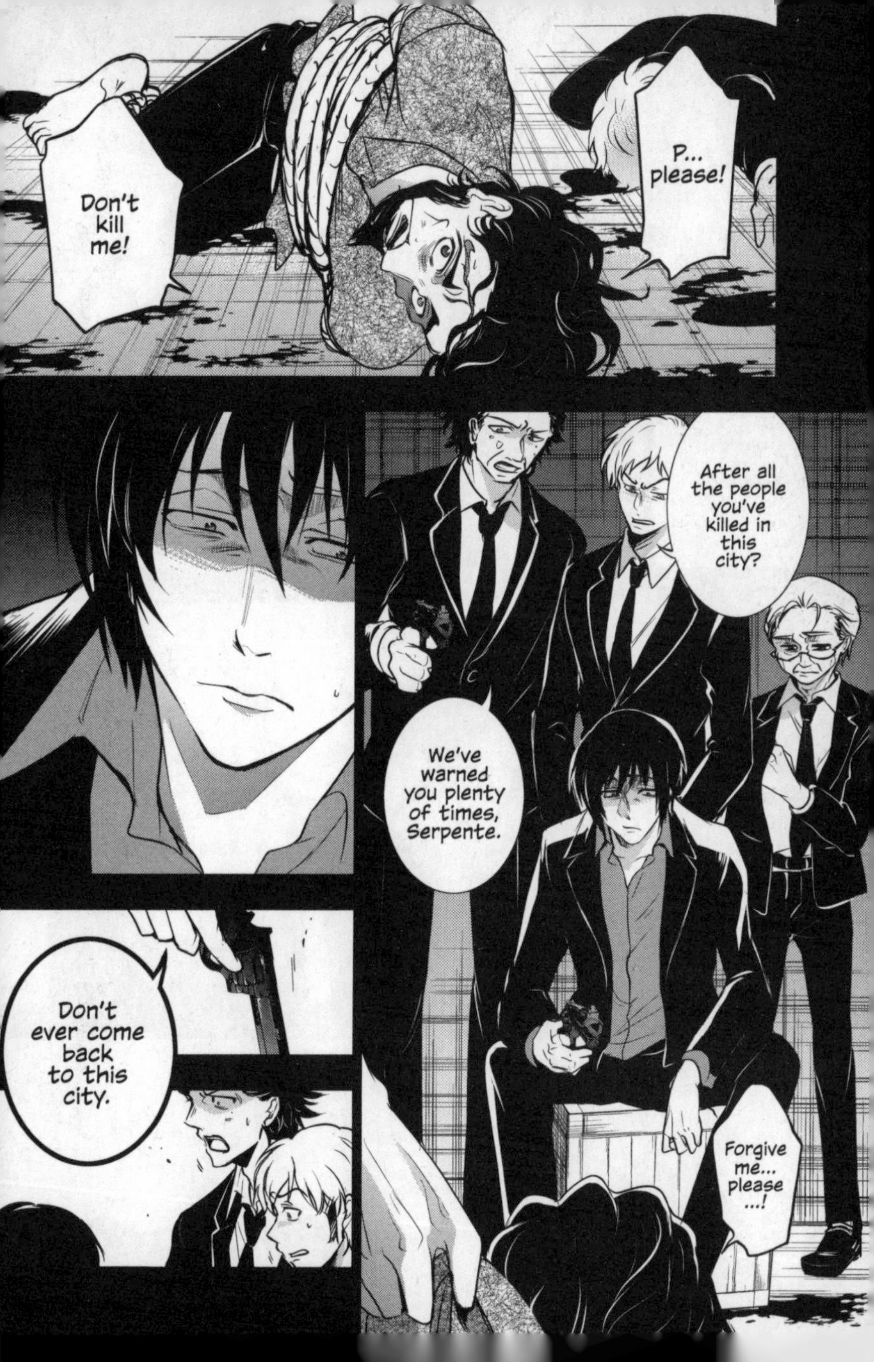
P... please!
Don't kill me!
After all the people you've killed in this city?
We've warned you plenty of times, Serpente.
Forgive me... please ...!
Don't ever come back to this city.

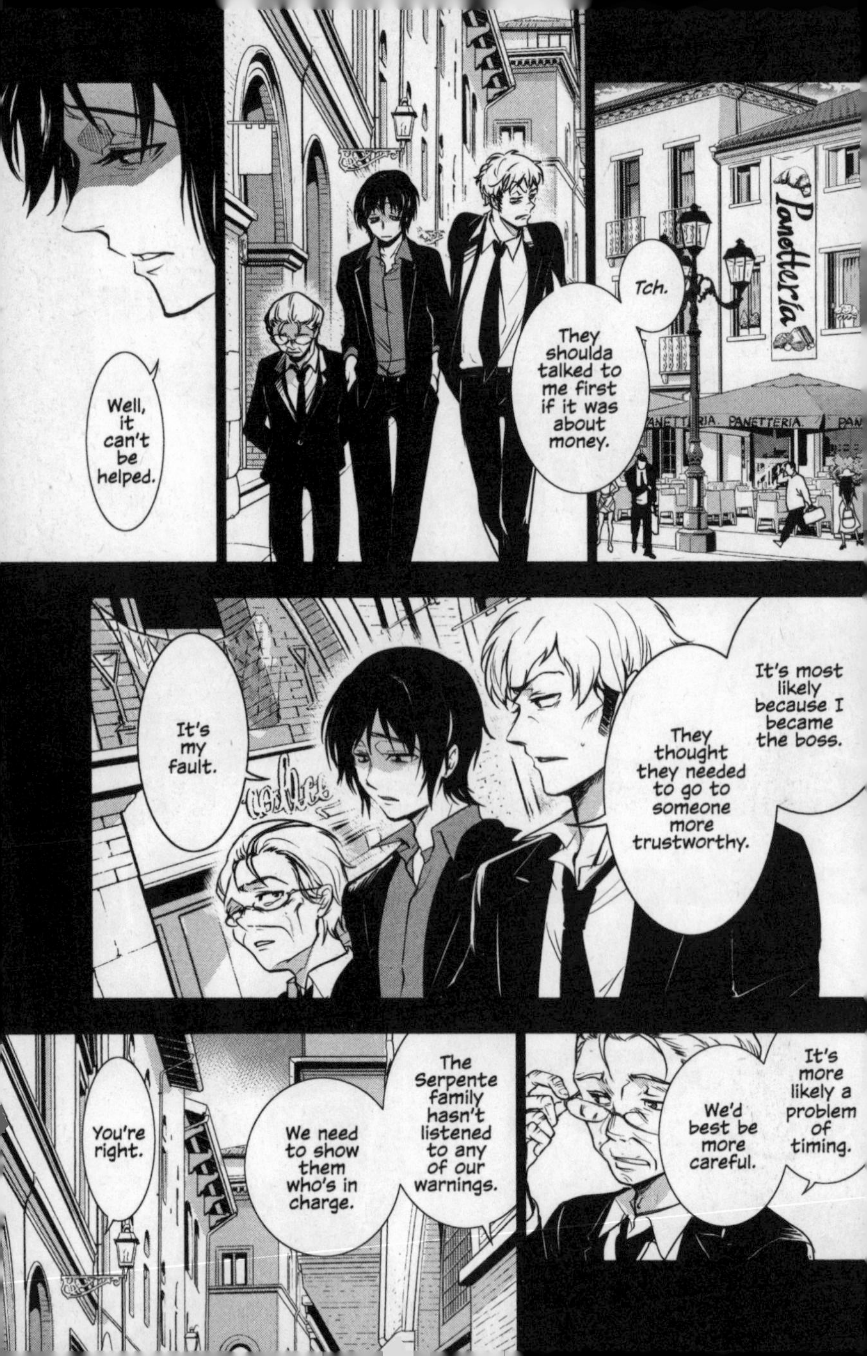
Panetteria
PANETTERIA PANETTERIA PA
Tch.
They shoulda talked to me first if it was about money.
Well, it can't be helped.
It's most likely because I became the boss.
They thought they needed to go to someone more trustworthy.
It's my fault.
It's more likely a problem of timing.
We'd best be more careful.
The Serpente family hasn't listened to any of our warnings.
We need to show them who's in charge.
You're right.

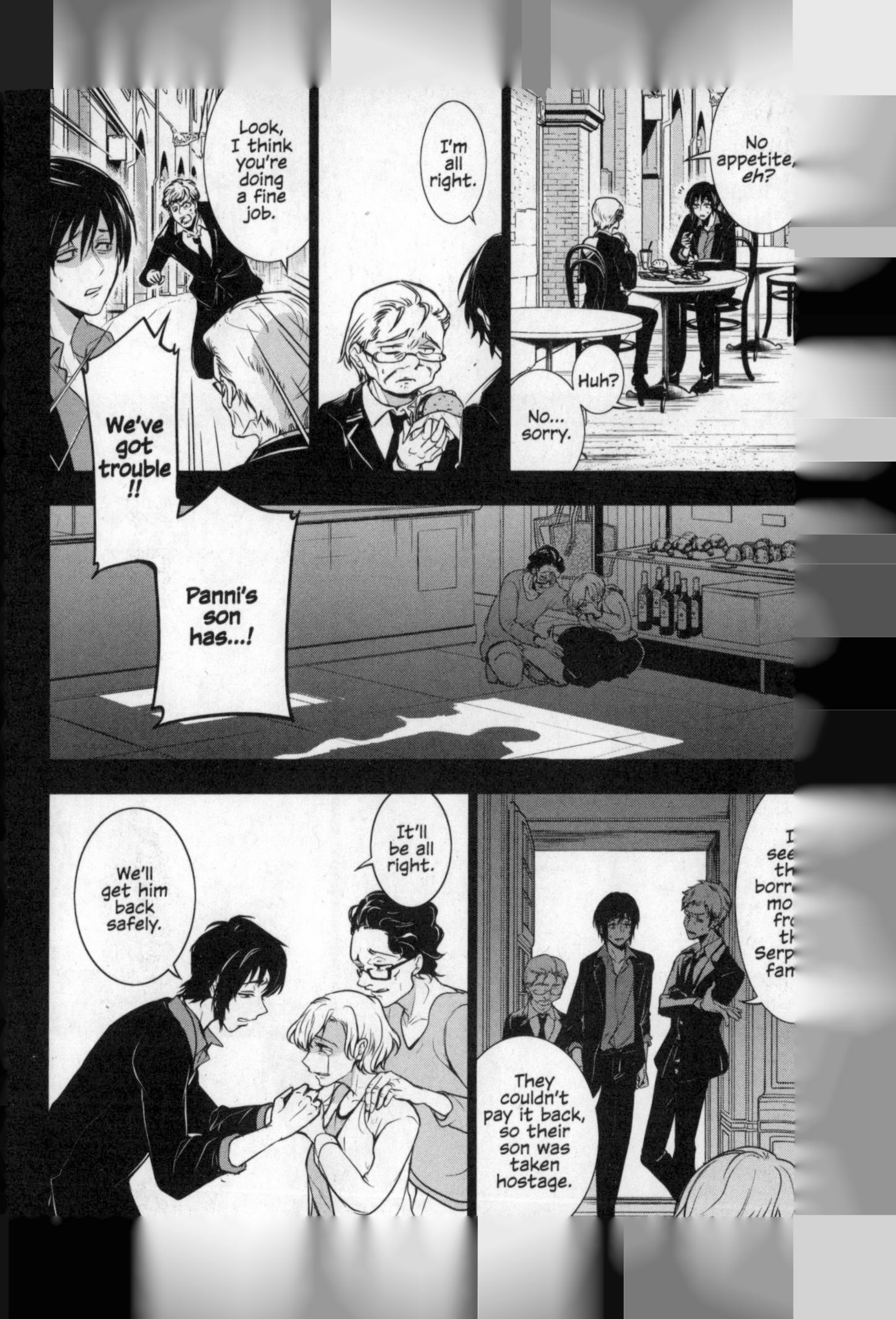
No appetite, eh?
Huh?
No... sorry.
I'm all right.
Look, I think you're doing a fine job.
We've got trouble !!
Panni's son has...!
They couldn't pay it back, so their son was taken hostage.
It'll be all right.
We'll get him back safely.

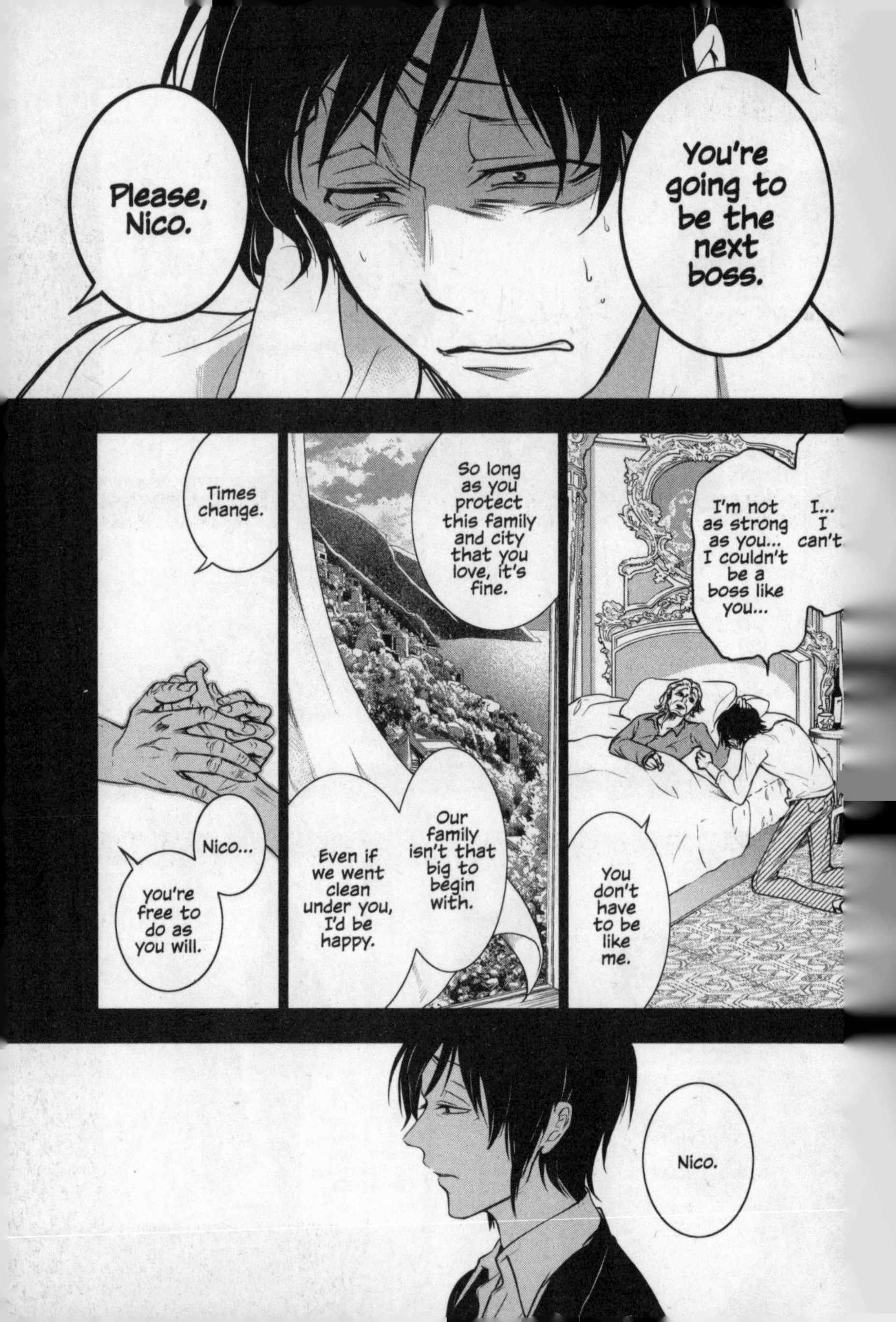

You're going to be the next boss.
Please, Nico.
I... I can't.
I'm not as strong as you... I couldn't be a boss like you...
You don't have to be like me.
So long as you protect this family and city that you love, it's fine.
Our family isn't that big to begin with.
Even if we went clean under you, I'd be happy.
Times change.
Nico...
you're free to do as you will.
Nico.

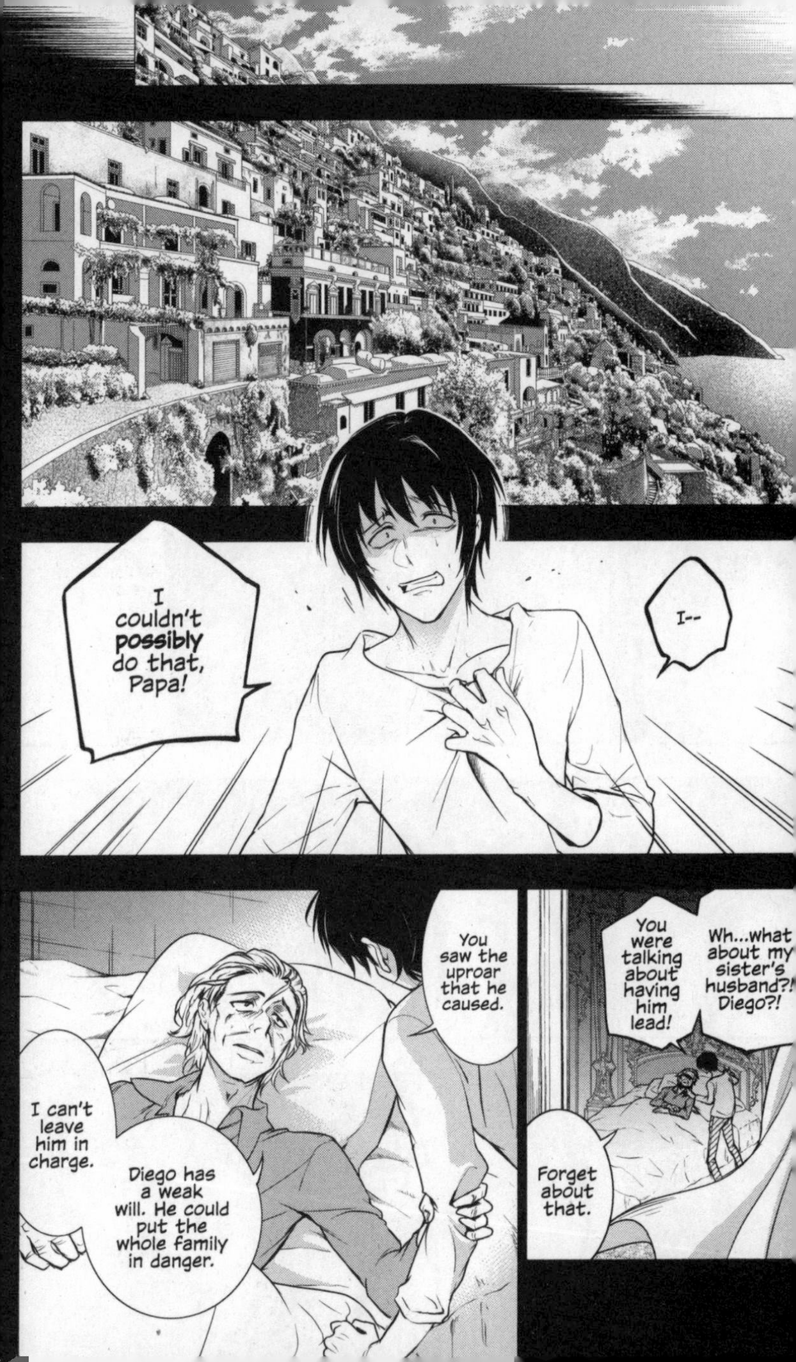
I--
I couldn't possibly do that, Papa!
Wh...what about my sister's husband?! Diego?!
You were talking about having him lead!
Forget about that.
You saw the uproar that he caused.
I can't leave him in charge.
Diego has a weak will. He could put the whole family in danger.

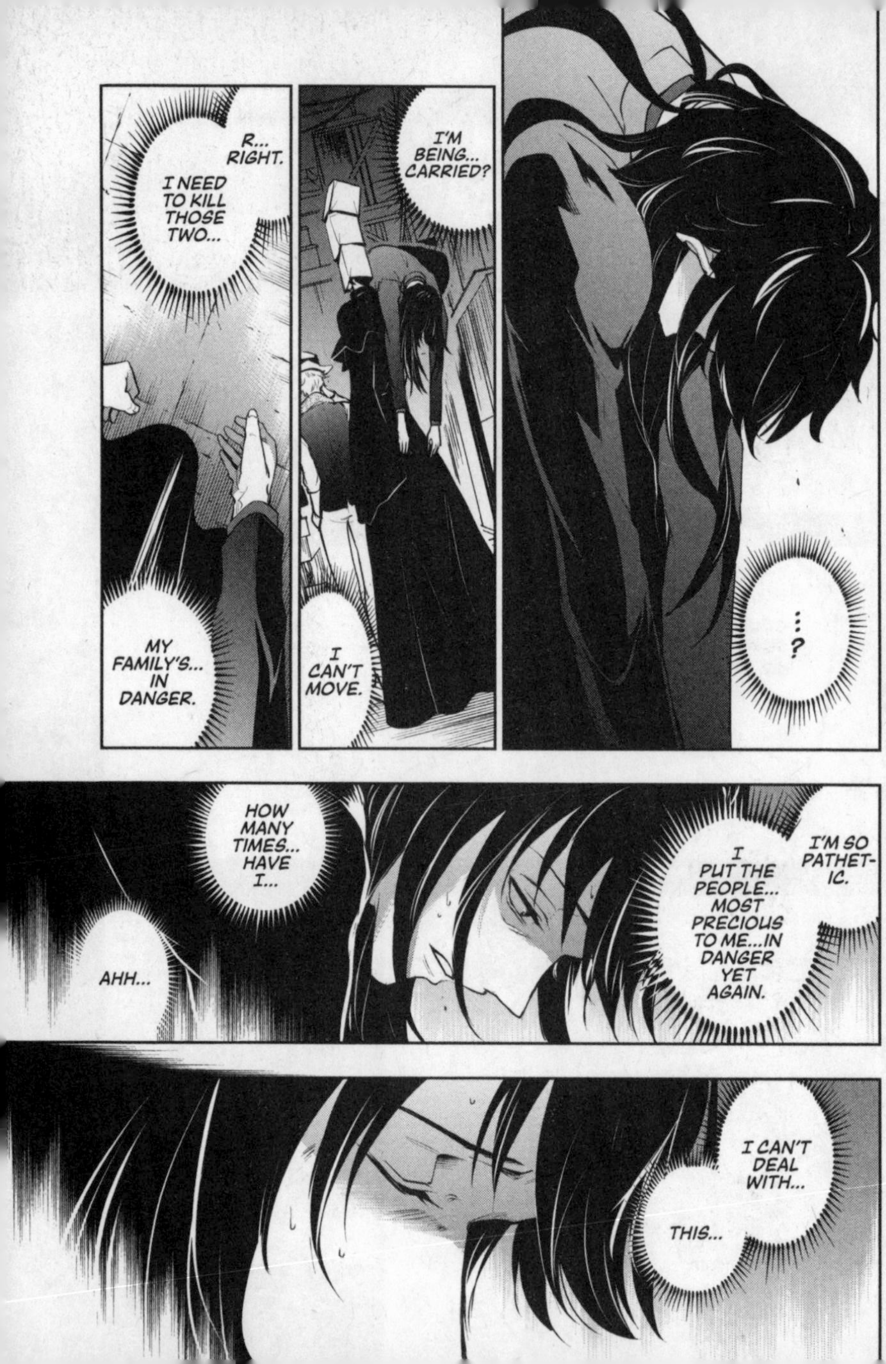
...?
I'M BEING... CARRIED?
I CAN'T MOVE.
R... RIGHT.
I NEED TO KILL THOSE TWO...
MY FAMILY'S... IN DANGER.
I'M SO PATHET-IC.
I PUT THE PEOPLE... MOST PRECIOUS TO ME...IN DANGER YET AGAIN.
HOW MANY TIMES... HAVE I...
AHH...
I CAN'T DEAL WITH...
THIS...

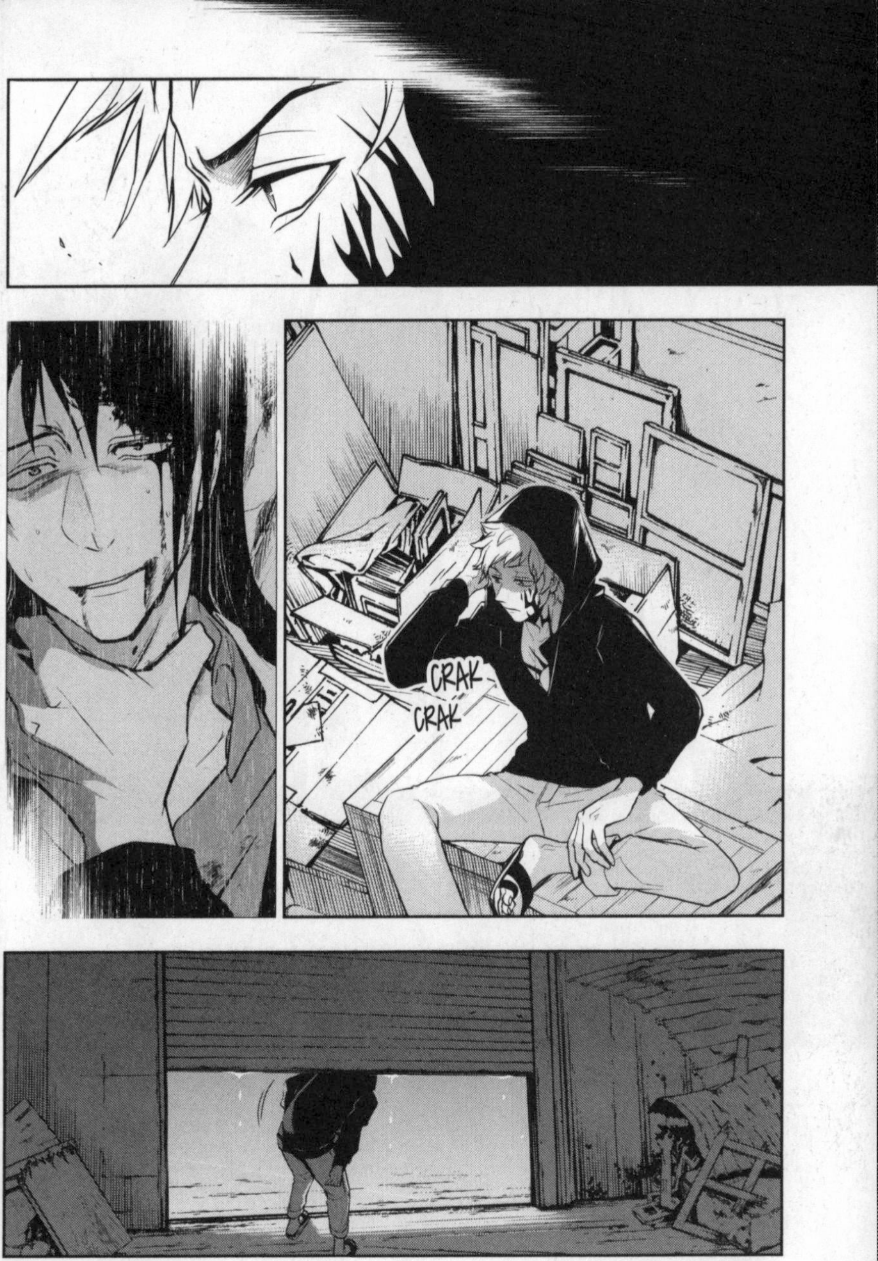
CRAK
CRAK

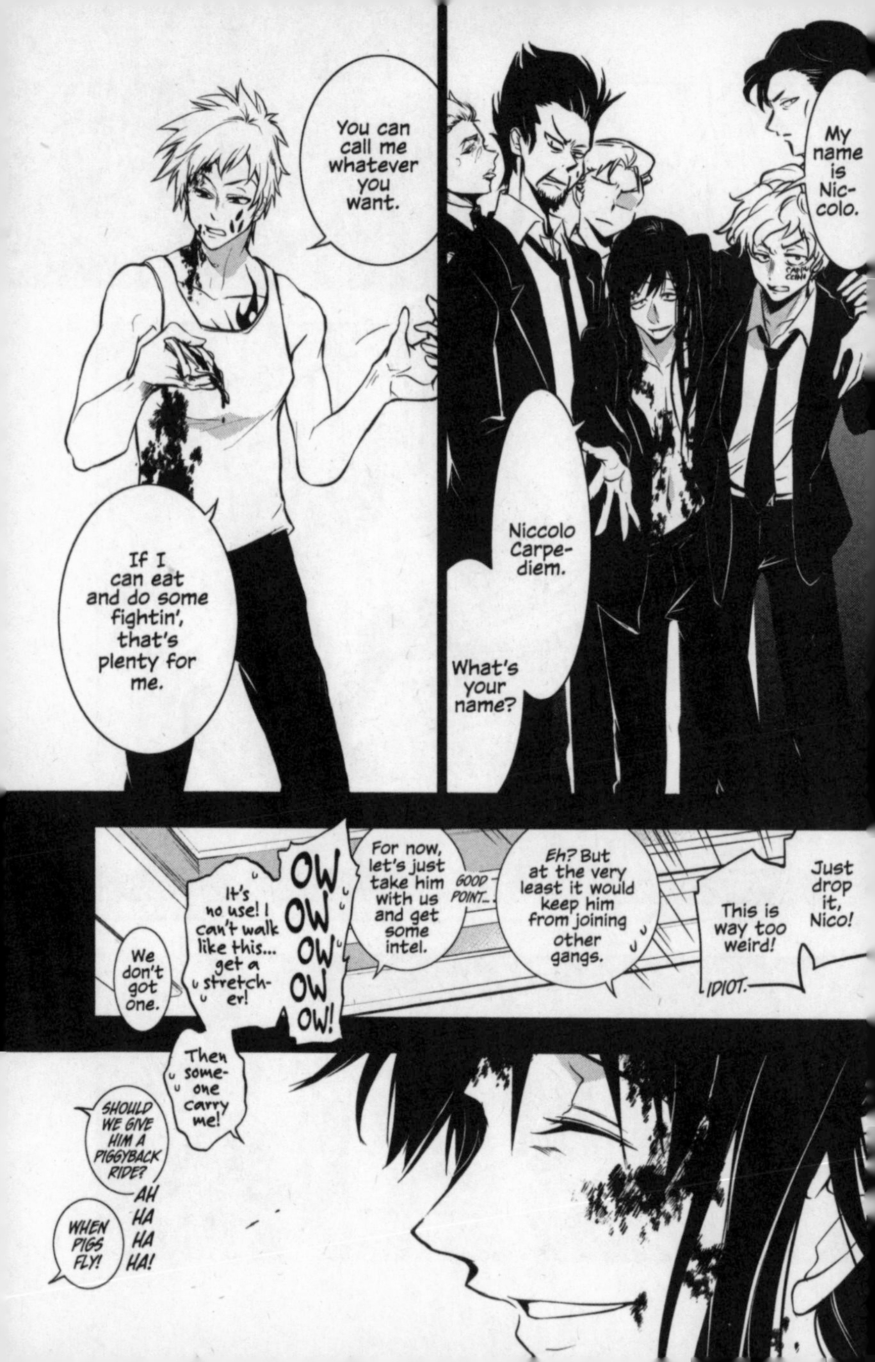
My name is Nic-colo.
Niccolo Carpe-diem.
What's your name?
You can call me whatever you want.
If I can eat and do some fightin', that's plenty for me.
Just drop it, Nico!
This is way too weird!
IDIOT.
Eh? But at the very least it would keep him from joining other gangs.
GOOD POINT...
For now, let's just take him with us and get some intel.
OW OW OW OW OW!
It's no use! I can't walk like this... get a stretch-er!
We don't got one.
Then some-one carry me!
SHOULD WE GIVE HIM A PIGGYBACK RIDE?
AH HA HA HA!
WHEN PIGS FLY!

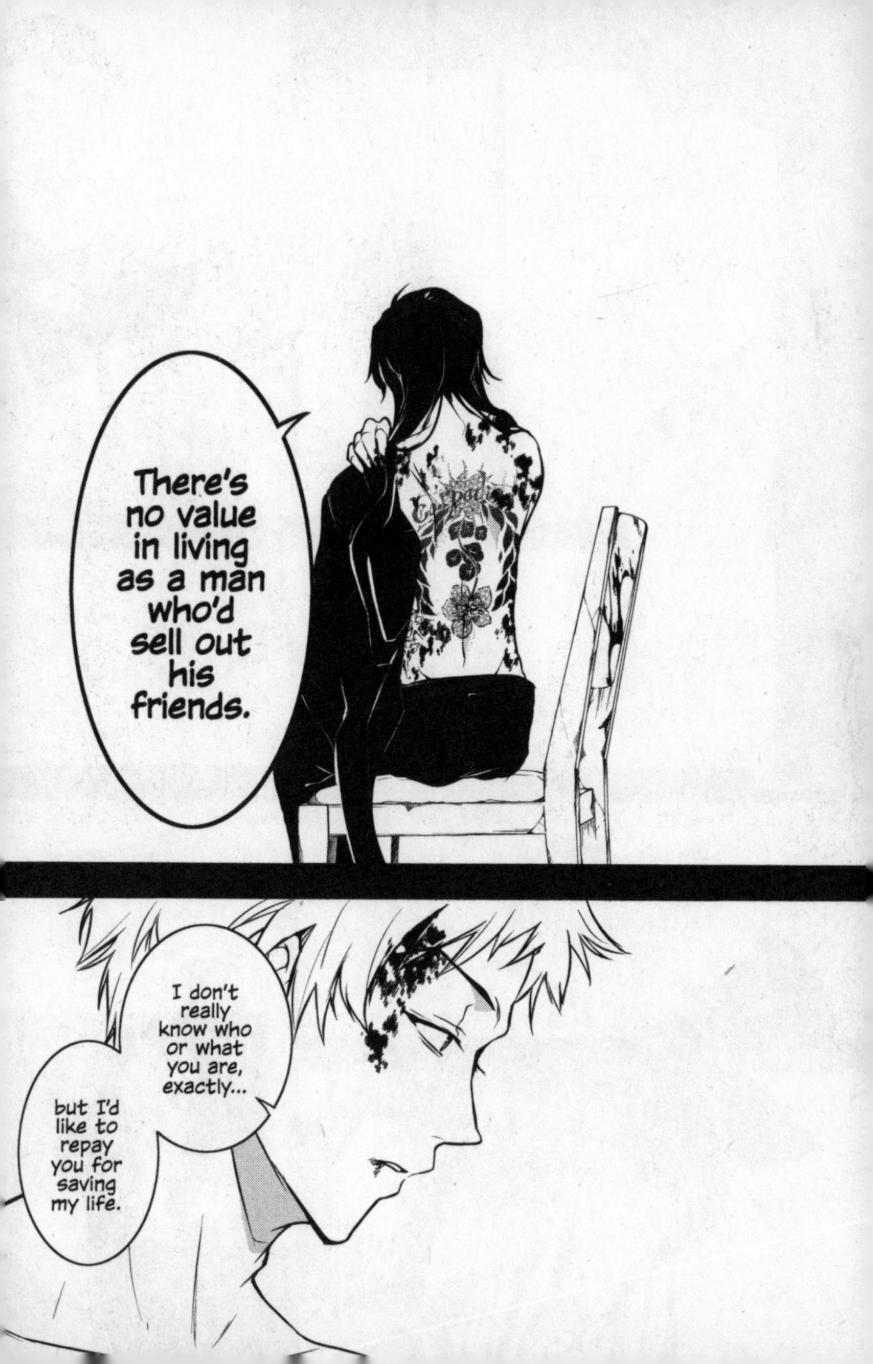
There's no value in living as a man who'd sell out his friends.
I don't really know who or what you are, exactly...
but I'd like to repay you for saving my life.

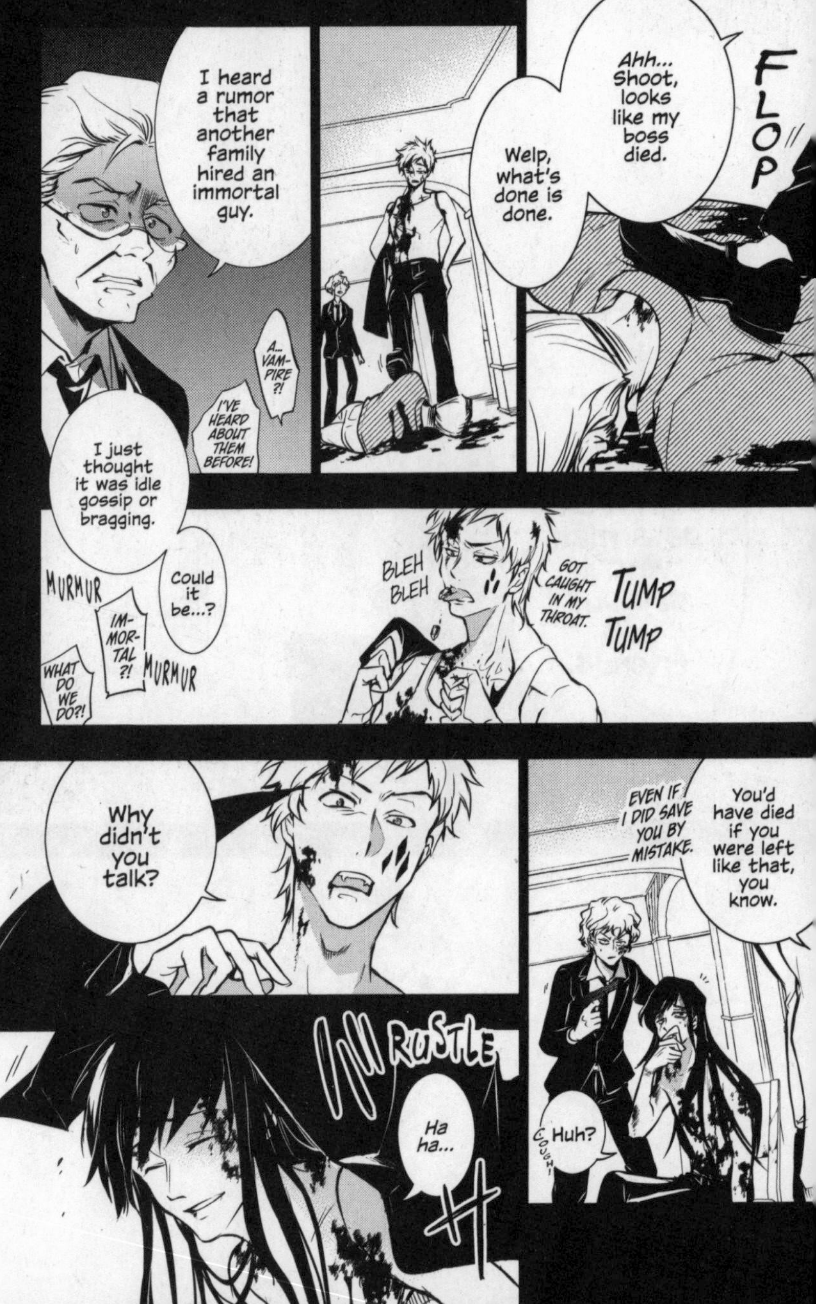
FLOP
Ahh... Shoot, looks like my boss died.
Welp, what's done is done.
I heard a rumor that another family hired an immortal guy.
A... VAMPIRE?!
I'VE HEARD ABOUT THEM BEFORE!
I just thought it was idle gossip or bragging.
TUMP TUMP
GOT CAUGHT IN MY THROAT.
BLEH BLEH
Could it be...?
MURMUR
IMMORTAL?!
MURMUR
WHAT DO WE DO?!
You'd have died if you were left like that, you know.
EVEN IF I DID SAVE YOU BY MISTAKE.
Huh?
COUGH
Why didn't you talk?
RUSTLE
Ha ha...

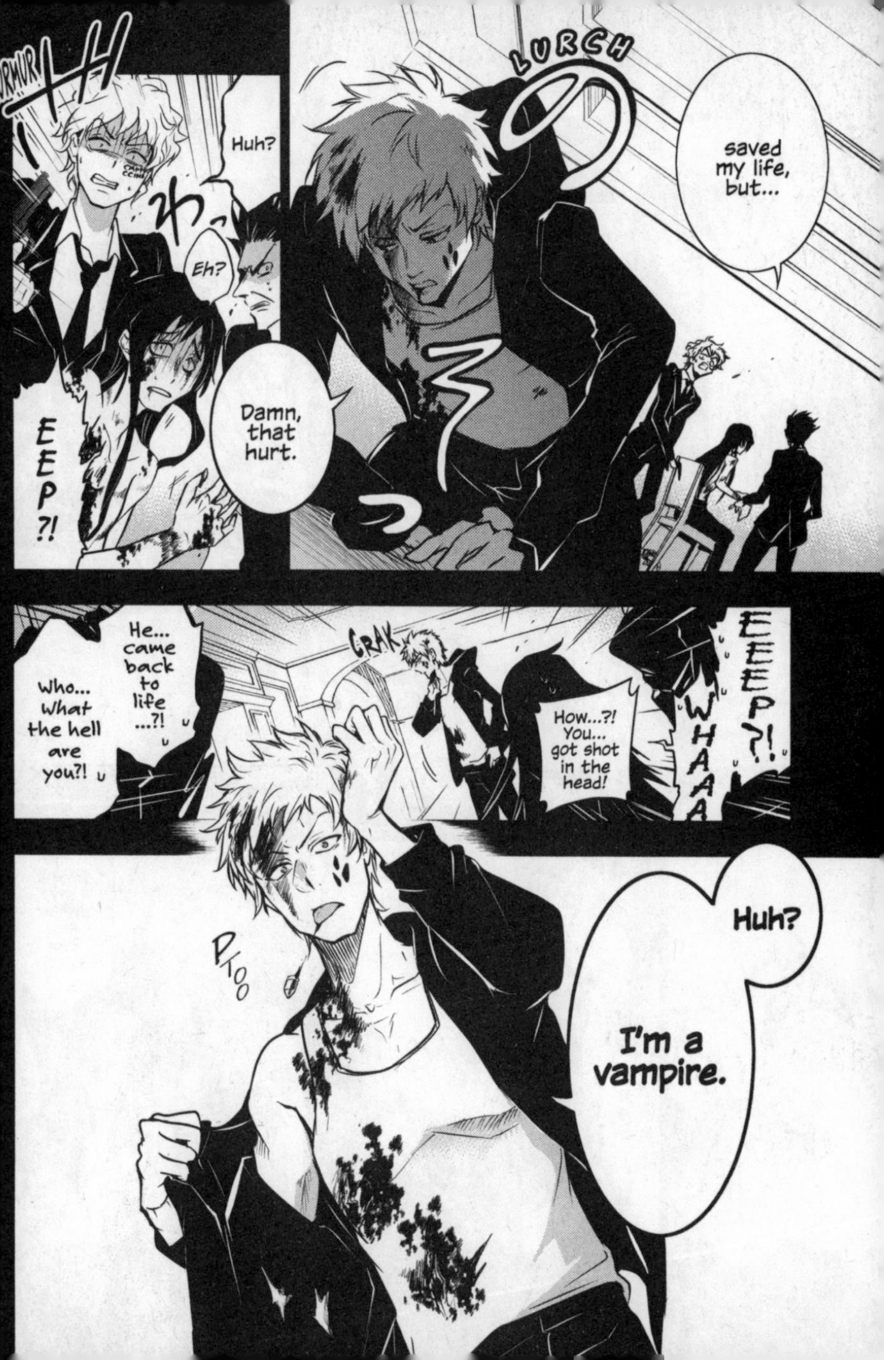
LURCH
saved my life, but...
Damn, that hurt.
Huh?
Eh?
EEP?!
EEEP?!
WHAAA
How...?! You... got shot in the head!
CRAK
He... came back to life...?!
Who... what the hell are you?!
Huh?
I'm a vampire.
PTOO

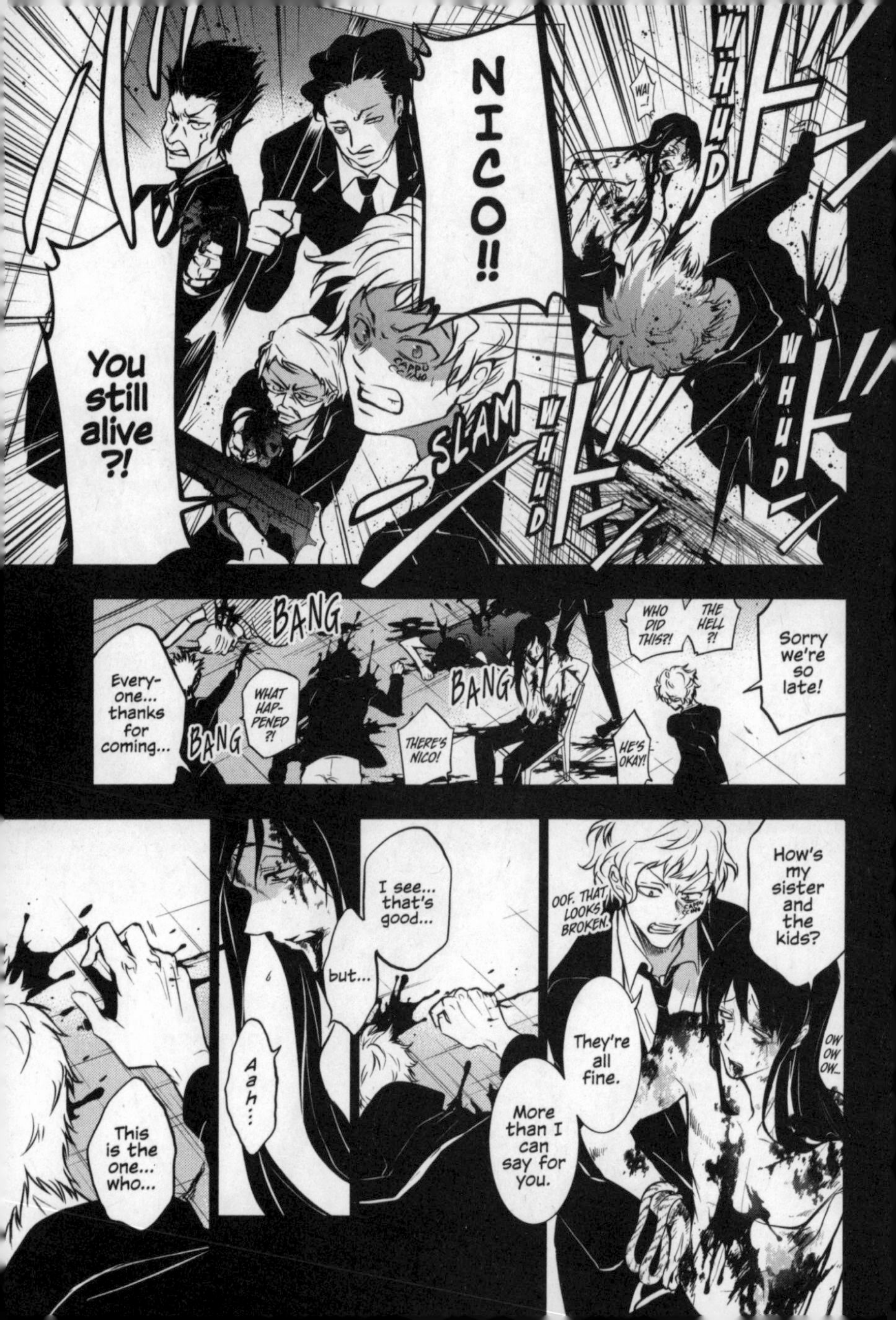
WAI—!
WHUD
WHUD
NICO!!
SLAM
WHUD
You still alive?!
Sorry we're so late!
THE HELL?!
WHO DID THIS?!
HE'S OKAY!
BANG
THERE'S NICO!
WHAT HAPPENED?!
BANG
BANG
Every-one... thanks for coming...
How's my sister and the kids?
OOF. THAT LOOKS BROKEN.
OW OW OW...
They're all fine.
More than I can say for you.
I see... that's good...
but...
Aah...
This is the one... who...

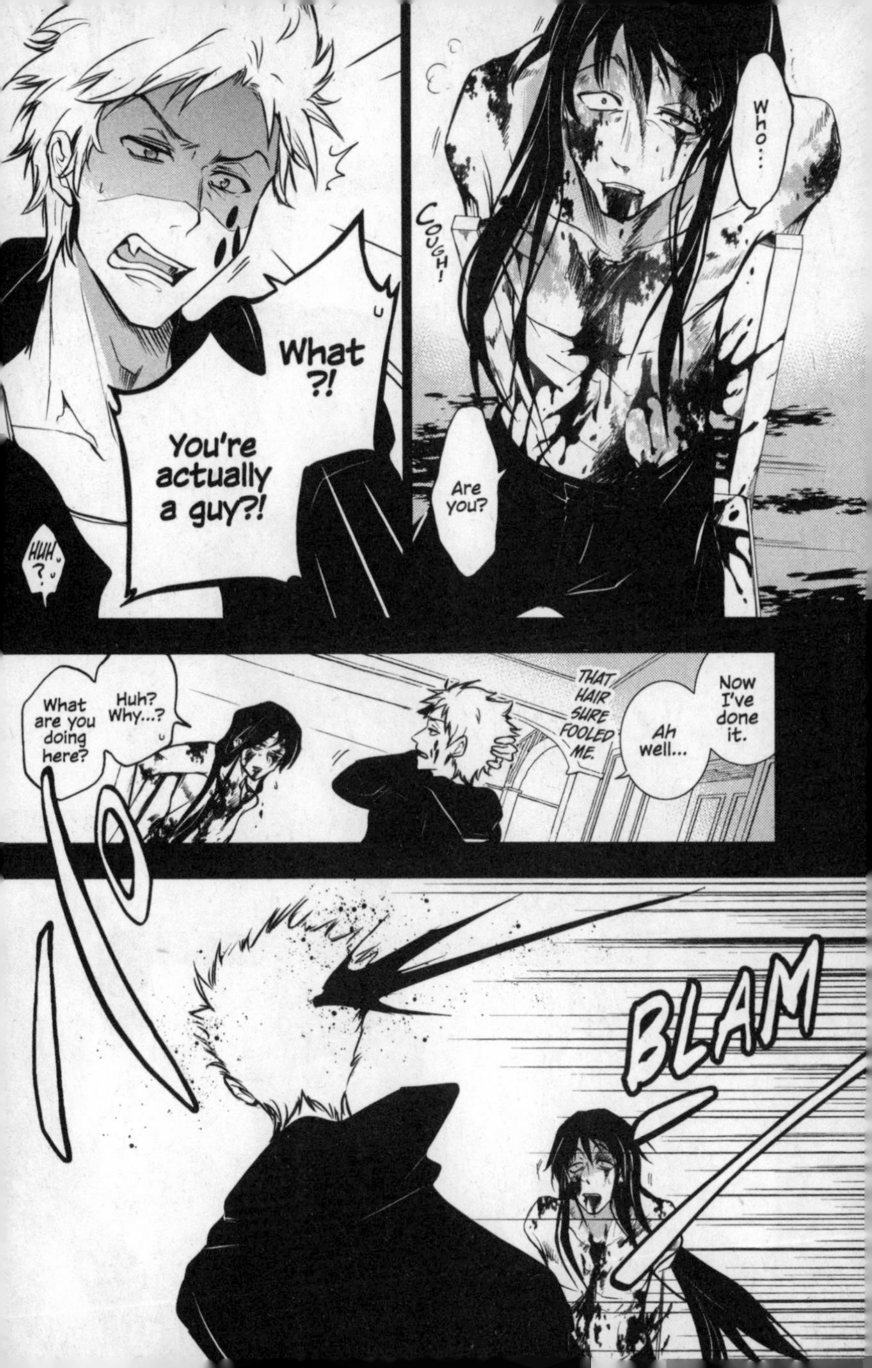
Who...
COUGH!
Are you?
What ?!
You're actually a guy?!
HUH ?
Now I've done it.
Ah well...
THAT HAIR SURE FOOLED ME.
Huh? Why...?
What are you doing here?
BLAM

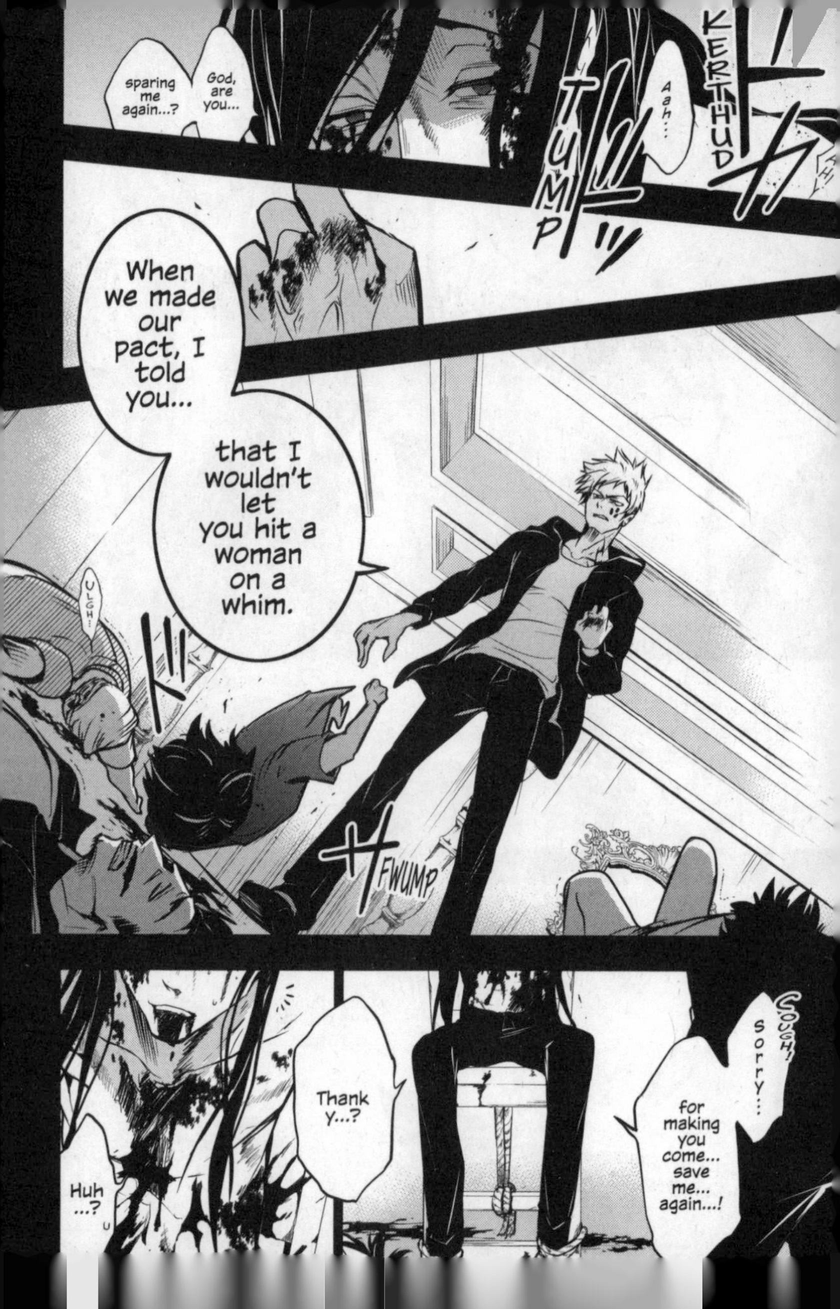
KERTHUD
Aah...
TUMP
God, are you...
sparing me again...?
When we made our pact, I told you...
that I wouldn't let you hit a woman on a whim.
ULGH!
FWUMP
COUGH!
Sorry...
for making you come... save me... again...!
Thank y...?
Huh ...?

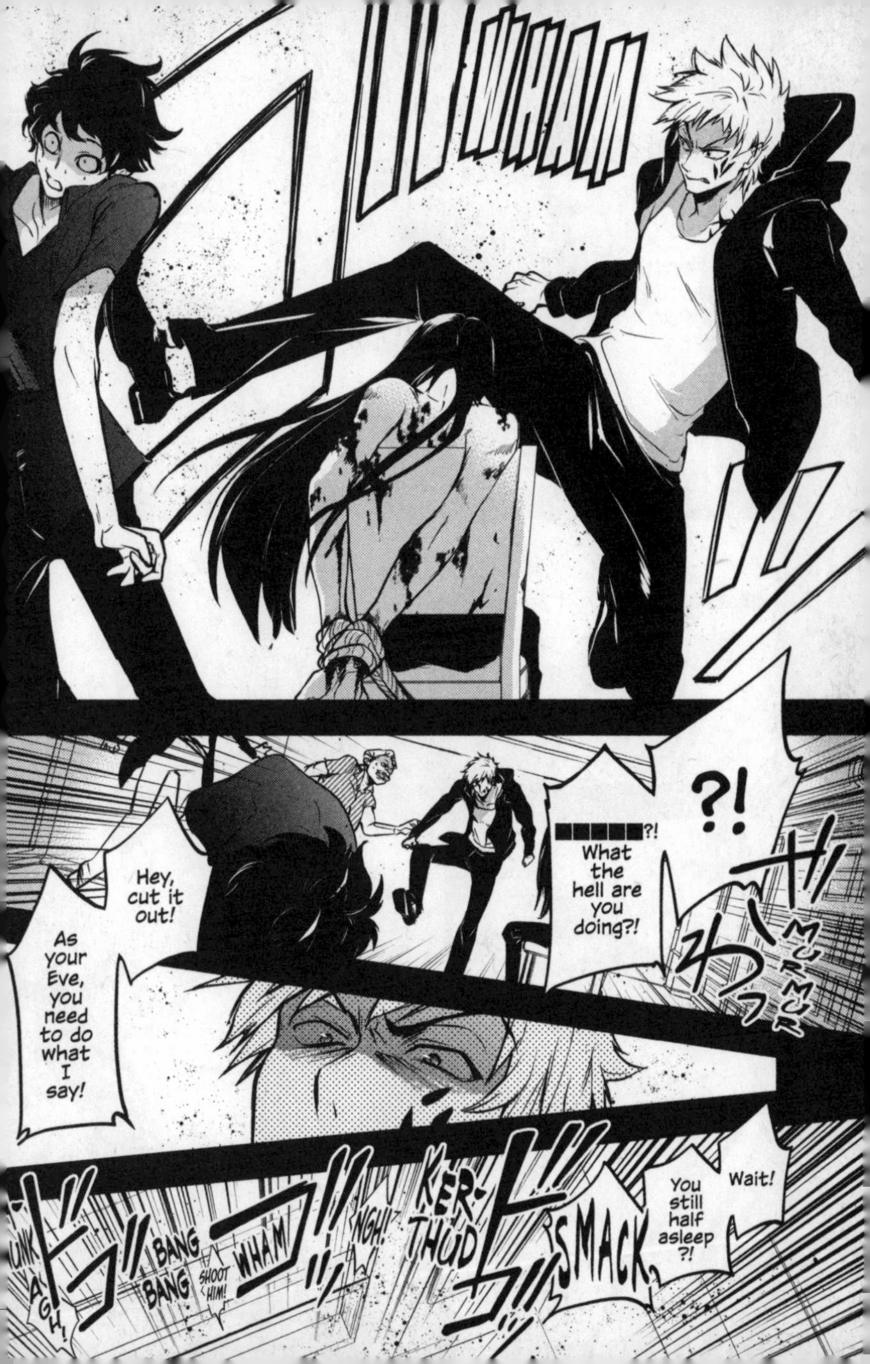
?!
[redacted]?! What the hell are you doing?!
Hey, cut it out!
As your Eve, you need to do what I say!
MURMUR
Wait!
You still half asleep?!
SMACK
KER-THUD
NGH!
WHAM
SHOOT HIM!
BANG BANG
AGH!

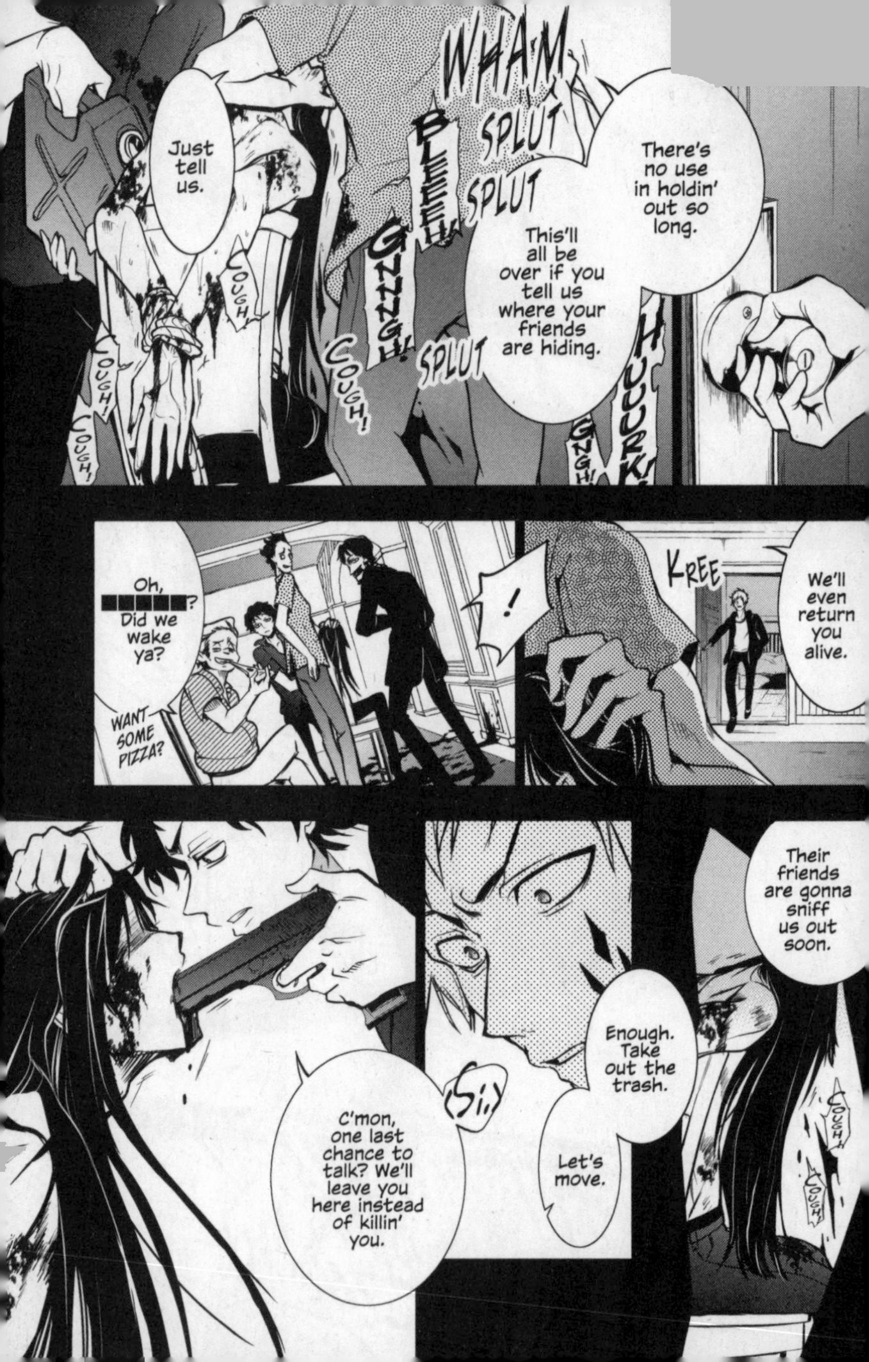

There's no use in holdin' out so long.
HUUURK!
WHAM
SPLUT
SPLUT
This'll all be over if you tell us where your friends are hiding.
GNGH!
SPLUT
BLEEEH!
GNNNGH!
COUGH!
Just tell us.
COUGH!
COUGH!
COUGH!
We'll even return you alive.
KREE
!
Oh, [redacted]? Did we wake ya?
WANT SOME PIZZA?
Their friends are gonna sniff us out soon.
COUGH
COUGH!
Enough. Take out the trash.
Let's move.
Si.
C'mon, one last chance to talk? We'll leave you here instead of killin' you.

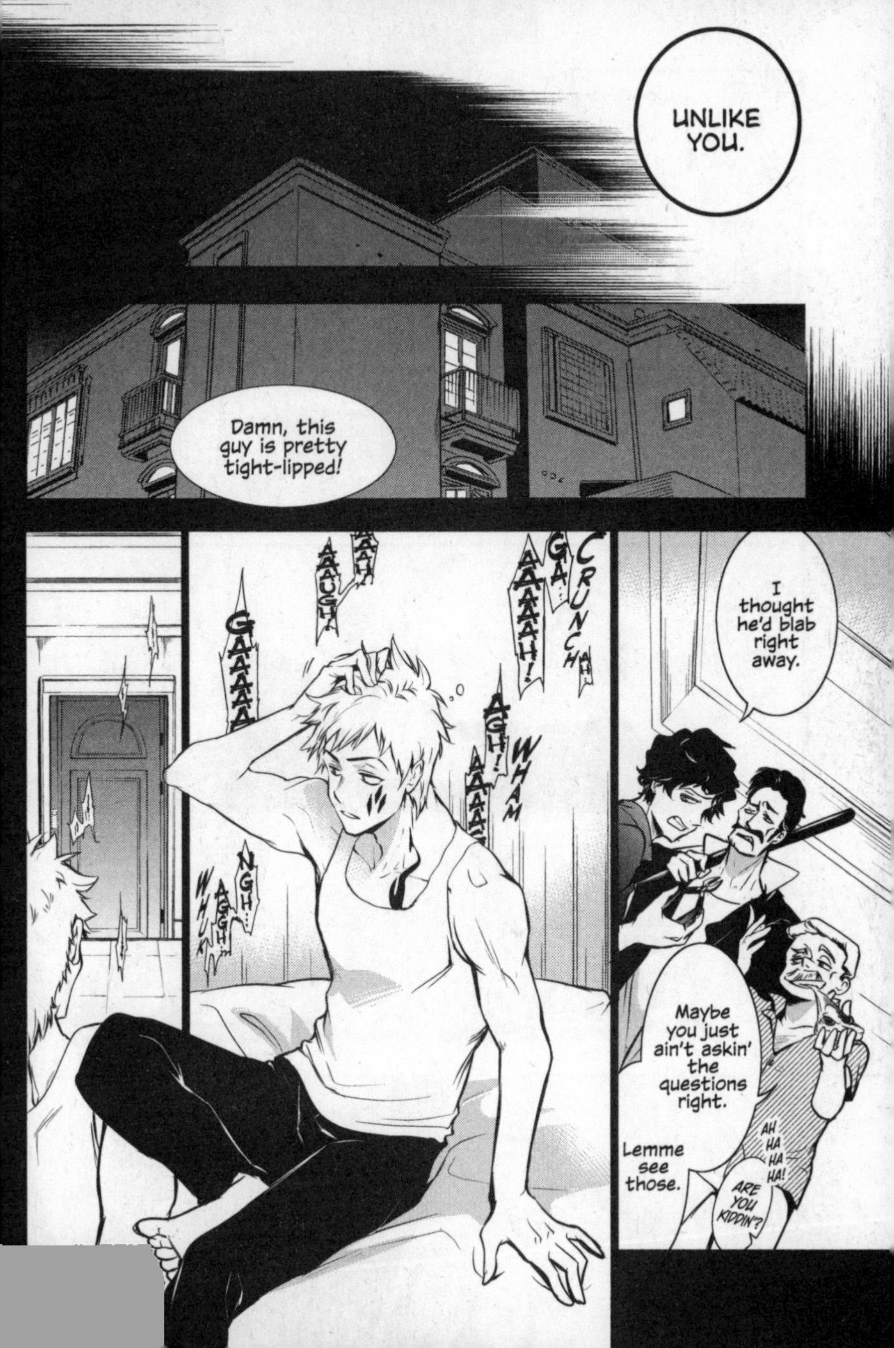
UNLIKE YOU.
Damn, this guy is pretty tight-lipped!
I thought he'd blab right away.
Maybe you just ain't askin' the questions right.
AH HA HA HA!
ARE YOU KIDDIN'?
Lemme see those.
CRUNCH
GA...
AAAAAAH!
AAAH!
AAUGH!
GAAAAAA
AGH!
WHAM
NGH...
AAGGH...
WHUK

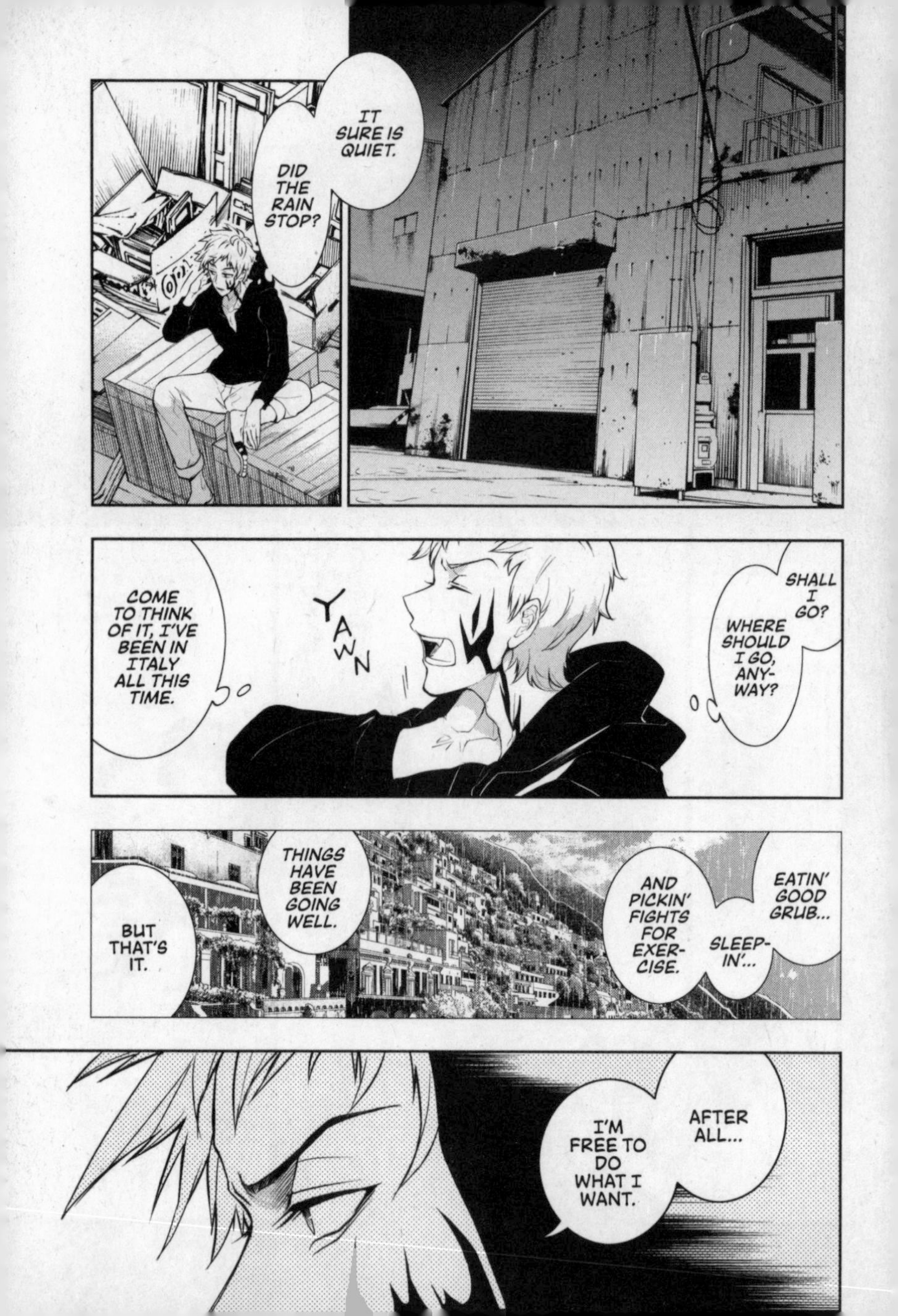
IT SURE IS QUIET.
DID THE RAIN STOP?
SHALL I GO?
WHERE SHOULD I GO, ANYWAY?
YAWN
COME TO THINK OF IT, I'VE BEEN IN ITALY ALL THIS TIME.
EATIN' GOOD GRUB...
SLEEPIN'...
AND PICKIN' FIGHTS FOR EXERCISE.
THINGS HAVE BEEN GOING WELL.
BUT THAT'S IT.
AFTER ALL...
I'M FREE TO DO WHAT I WANT.

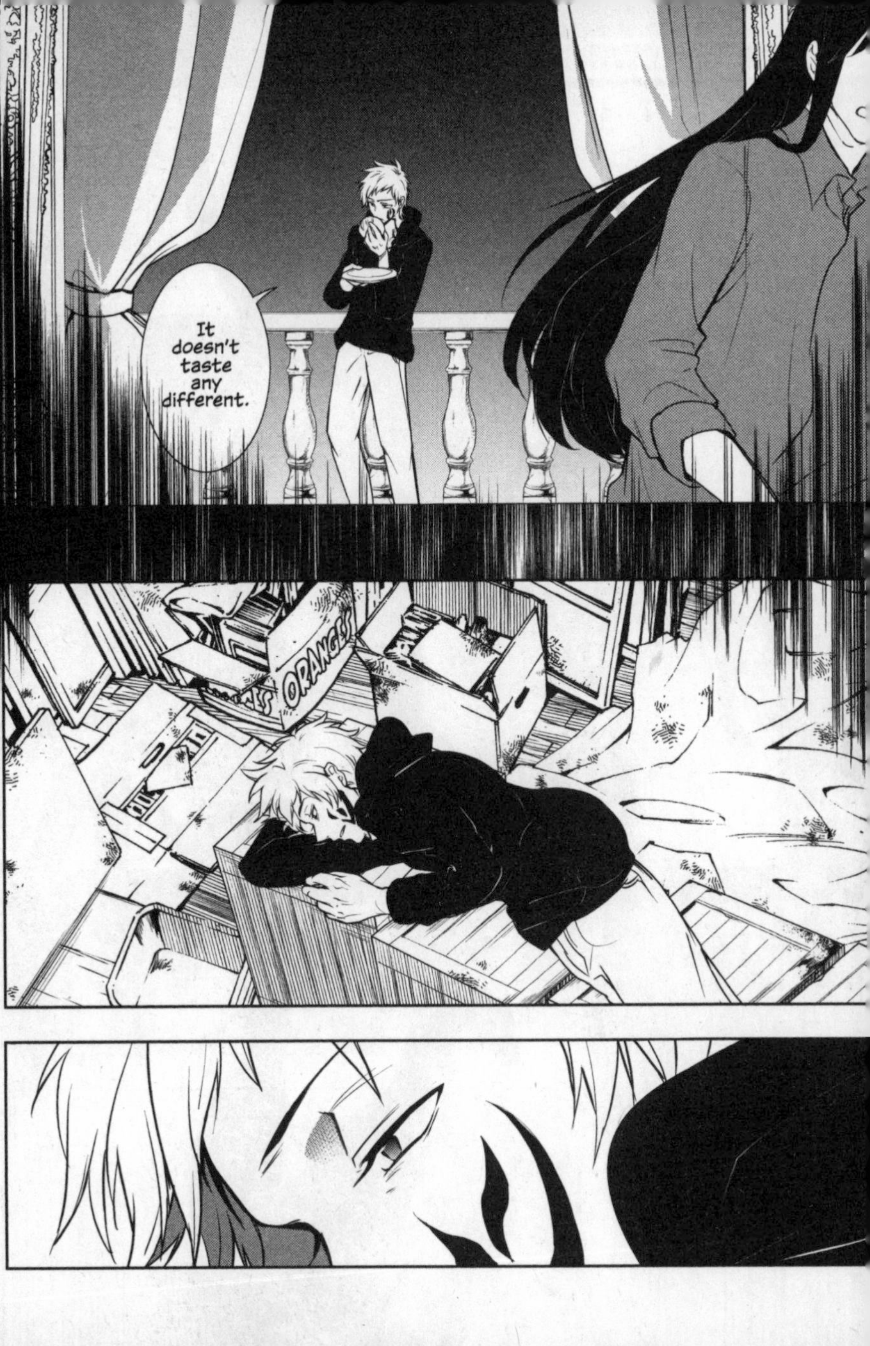
It doesn't taste any different.
ORANGES

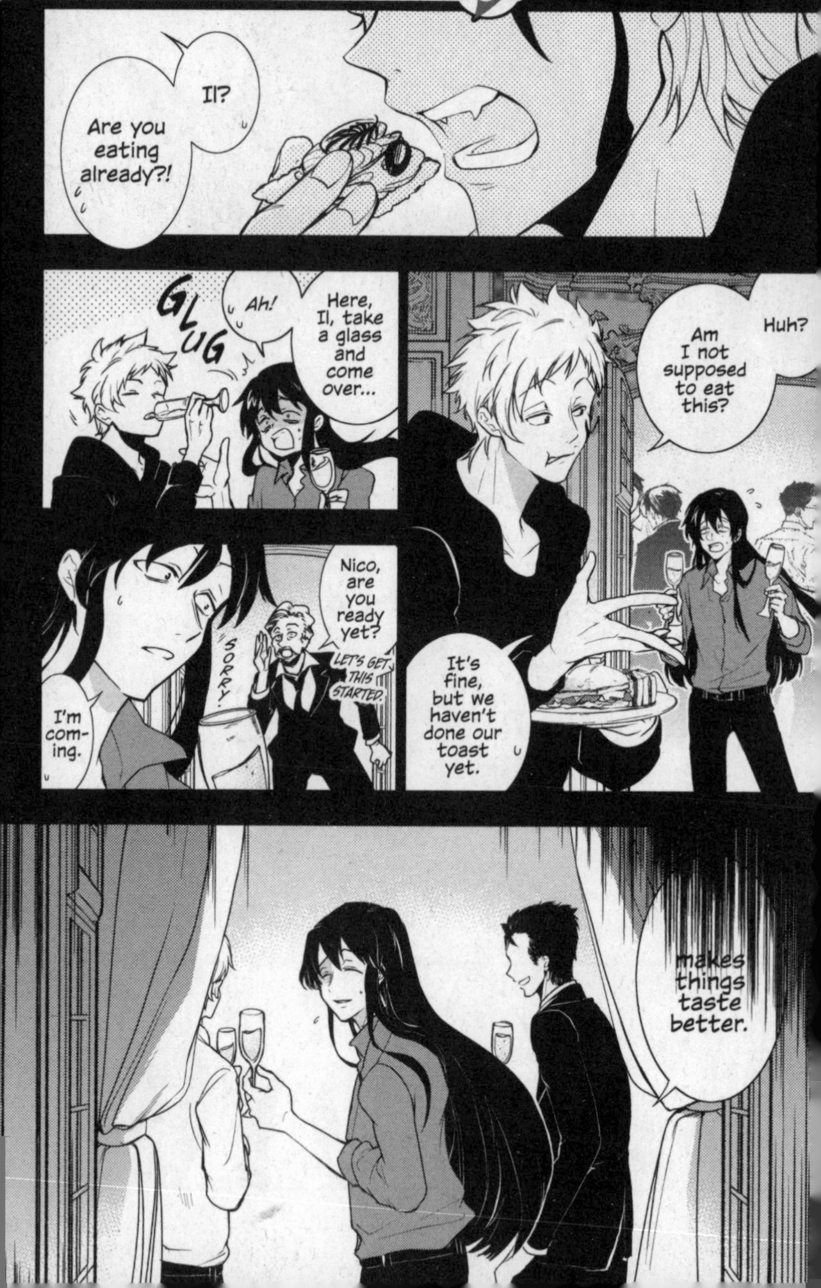
Il?
Are you eating already?!
Huh?
Am I not supposed to eat this?
It's fine, but we haven't done our toast yet.
Here, Il, take a glass and come over...
Ah!
GLUG
Nico, are you ready yet?
LET'S GET THIS STARTED.
SORRY.
I'm com- ing.
makes things taste better.

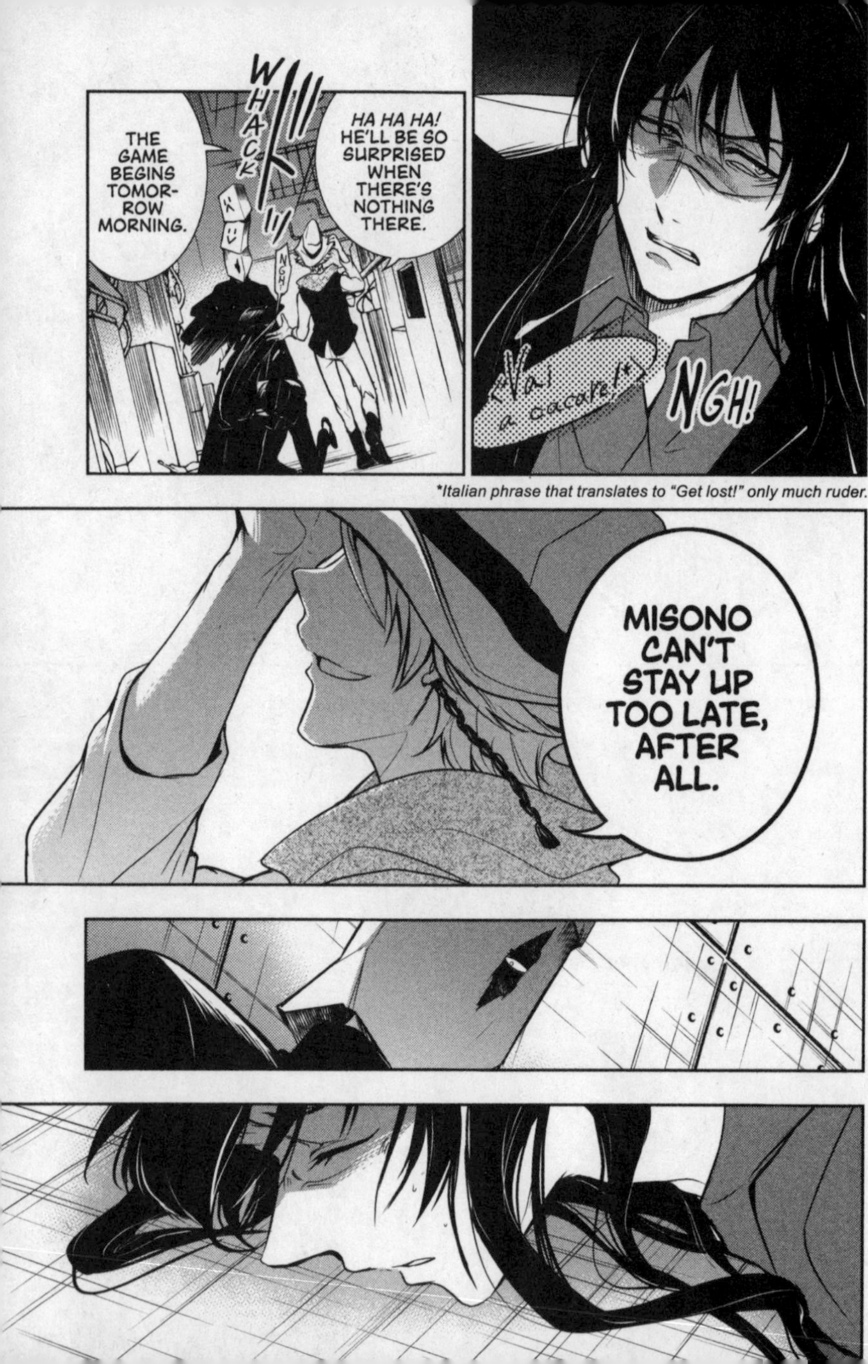
Vai a cacare!*
NGH!
HA HA HA! HE'LL BE SO SURPRISED WHEN THERE'S NOTHING THERE.
WHACK
THE GAME BEGINS TOMORROW MORNING.
NGH!
MISONO CAN'T STAY UP TOO LATE, AFTER ALL.

*Italian phrase that translates to "Get lost!" only much ruder.

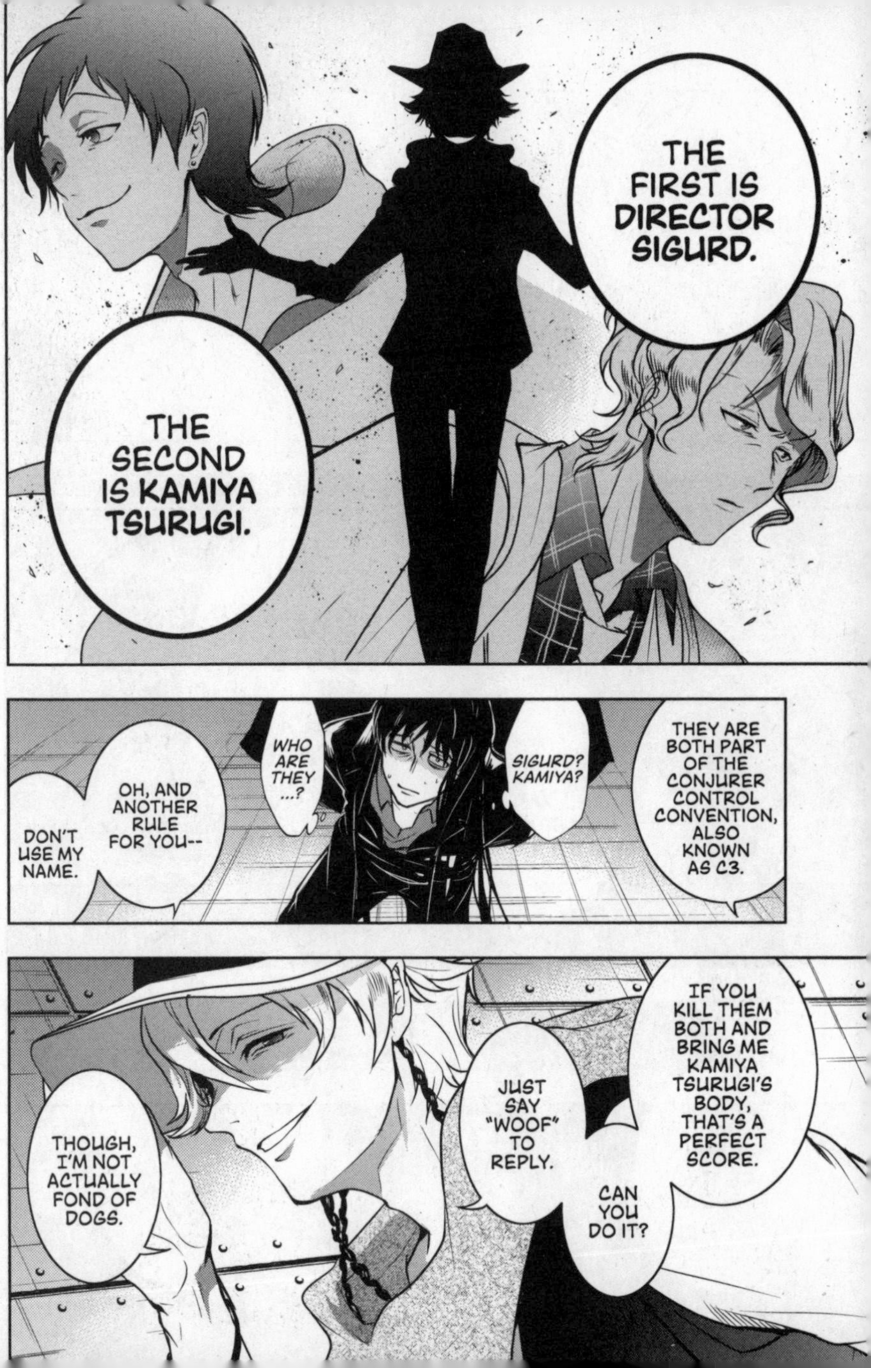
THE FIRST IS DIRECTOR SIGURD.
THE SECOND IS KAMIYA TSURUGI.
THEY ARE BOTH PART OF THE CONJURER CONTROL CONVENTION, ALSO KNOWN AS C3.
SIGURD? KAMIYA?
WHO ARE THEY ...?
OH, AND ANOTHER RULE FOR YOU--
DON'T USE MY NAME.
IF YOU KILL THEM BOTH AND BRING ME KAMIYA TSURUGI'S BODY, THAT'S A PERFECT SCORE.
CAN YOU DO IT?
JUST SAY "WOOF" TO REPLY.
THOUGH, I'M NOT ACTUALLY FOND OF DOGS.

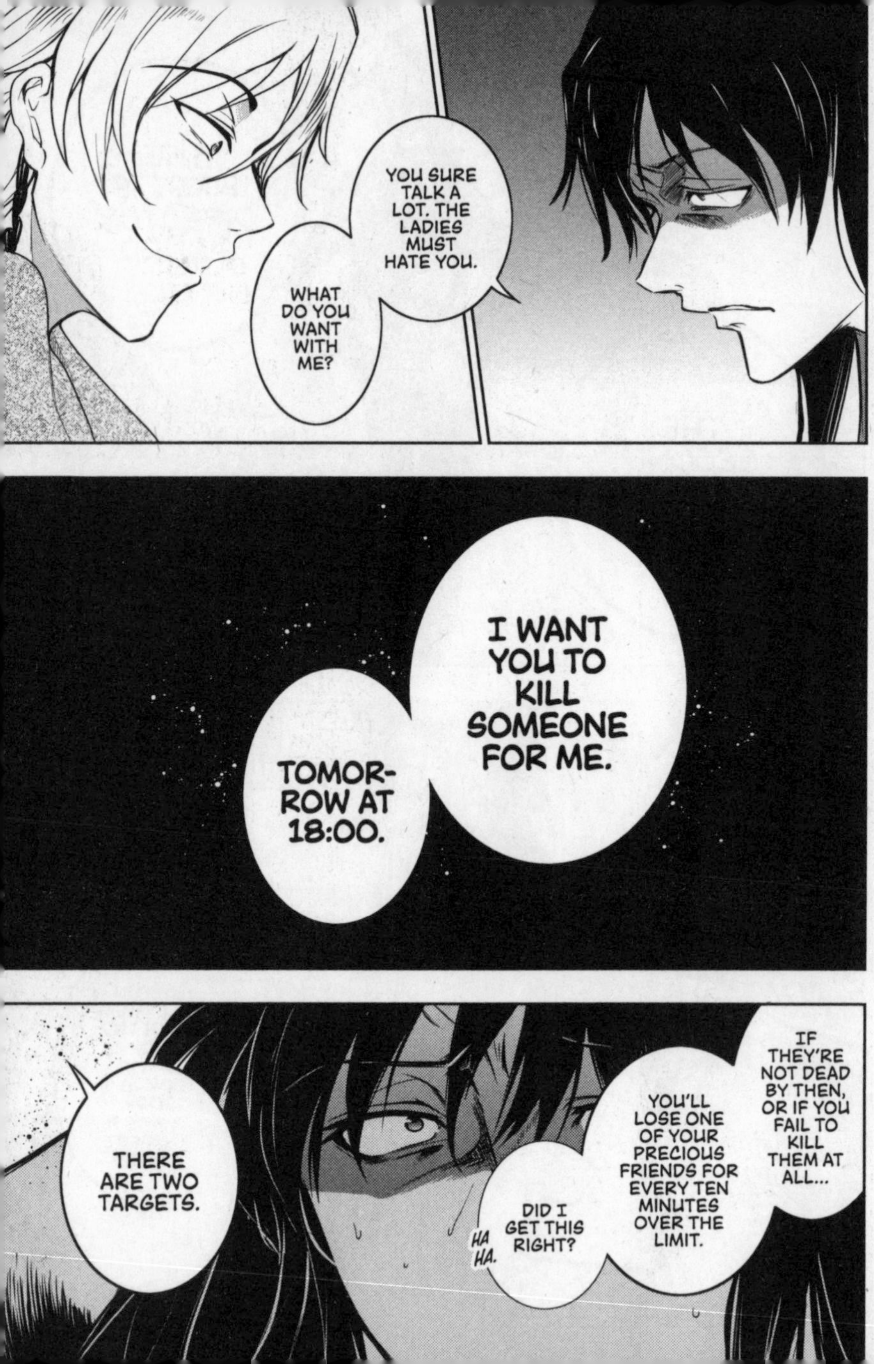
YOU SURE TALK A LOT. THE LADIES MUST HATE YOU.
WHAT DO YOU WANT WITH ME?
I WANT YOU TO KILL SOMEONE FOR ME.
TOMOR-ROW AT 18:00.
IF THEY'RE NOT DEAD BY THEN, OR IF YOU FAIL TO KILL THEM AT ALL...
YOU'LL LOSE ONE OF YOUR PRECIOUS FRIENDS FOR EVERY TEN MINUTES OVER THE LIMIT.
DID I GET THIS RIGHT?
HA HA.
THERE ARE TWO TARGETS.

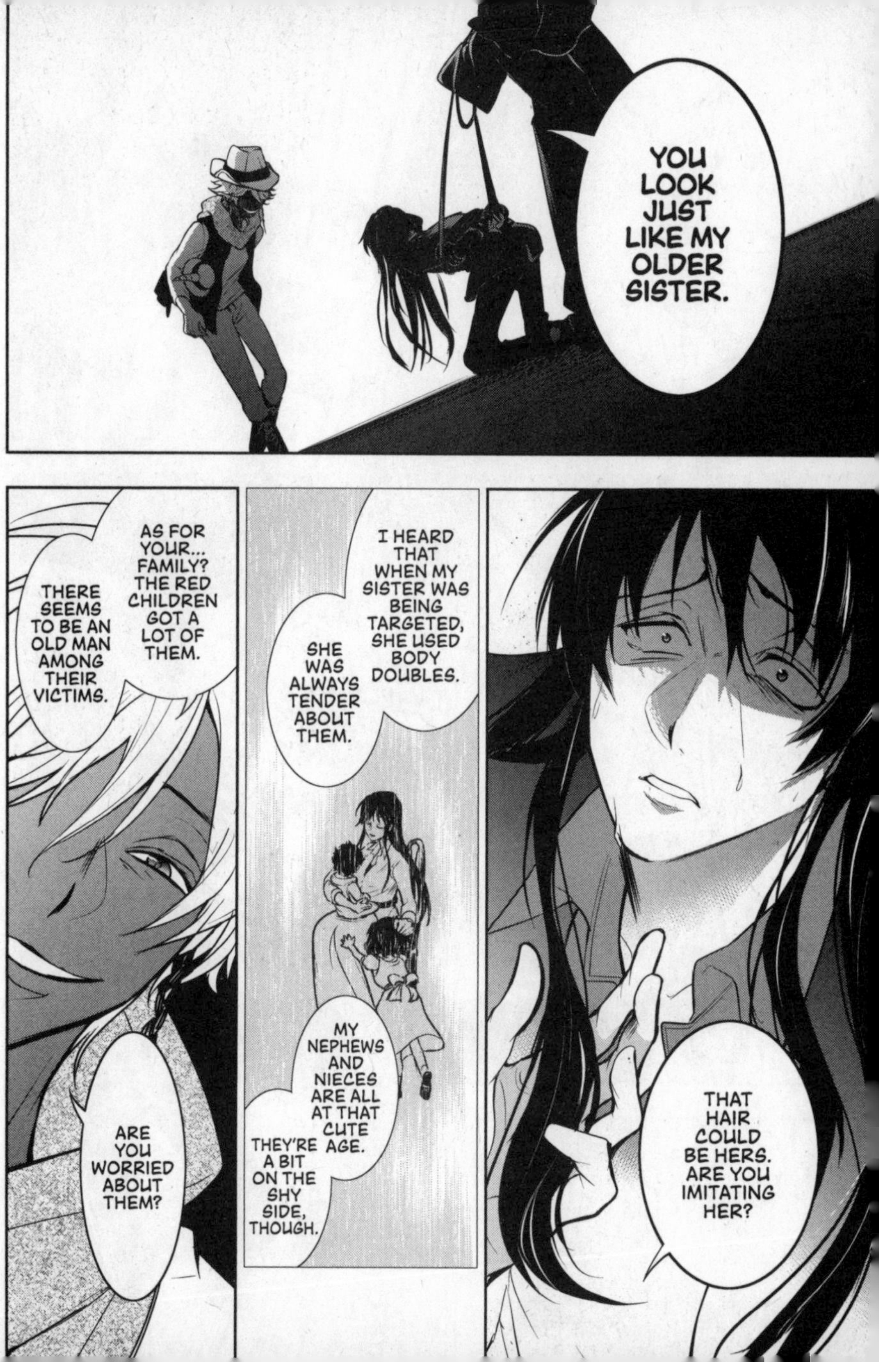
YOU LOOK JUST LIKE MY OLDER SISTER.
THAT HAIR COULD BE HERS. ARE YOU IMITATING HER?
I HEARD THAT WHEN MY SISTER WAS BEING TARGETED, SHE USED BODY DOUBLES.
SHE WAS ALWAYS TENDER ABOUT THEM.
MY NEPHEWS AND NIECES ARE ALL AT THAT CUTE AGE.
THEY'RE A BIT ON THE SHY SIDE, THOUGH.
AS FOR YOUR... FAMILY? THE RED CHILDREN GOT A LOT OF THEM.
THERE SEEMS TO BE AN OLD MAN AMONG THEIR VICTIMS.
ARE YOU WORRIED ABOUT THEM?

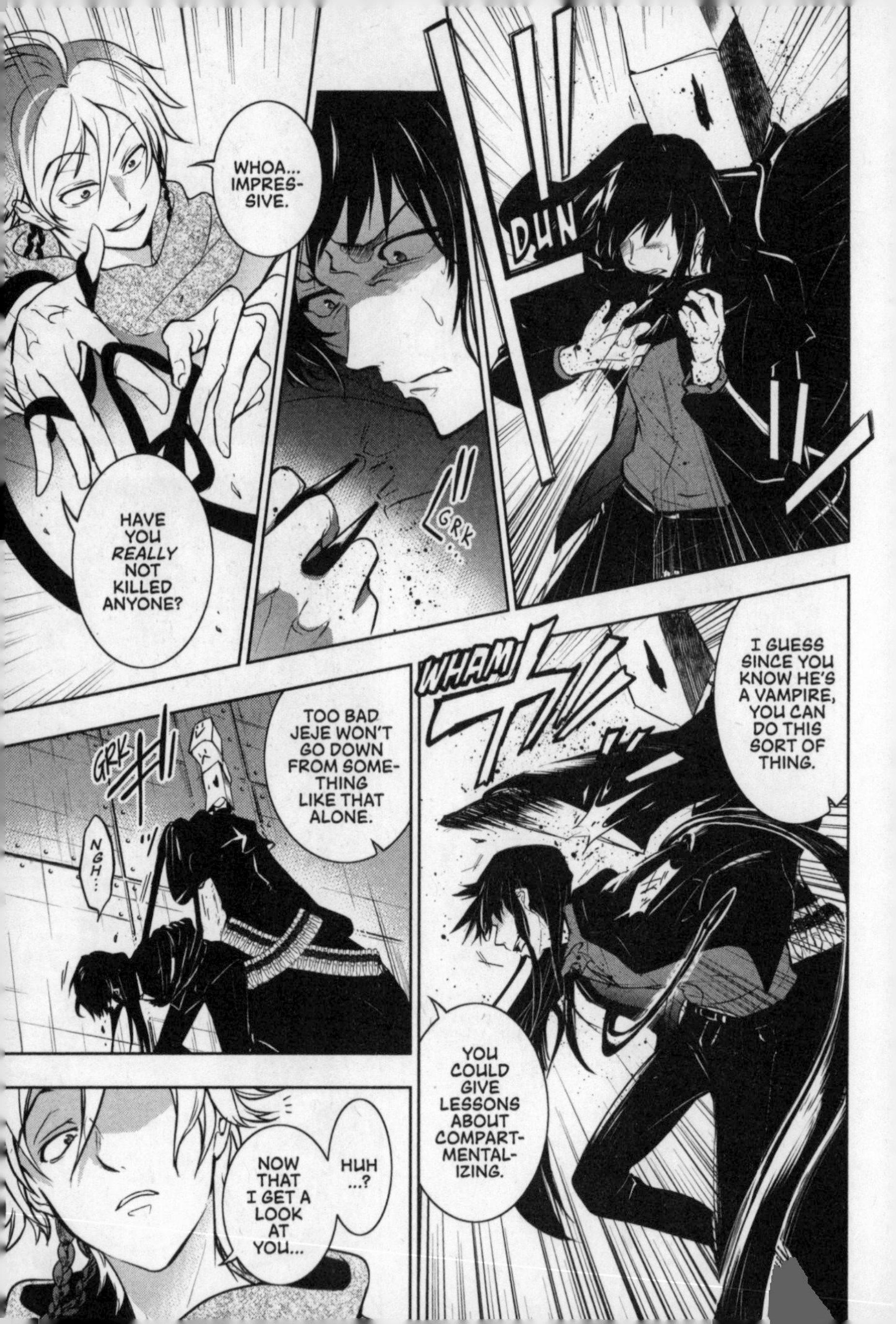
DUN
WHOA... IMPRESSIVE.
GRK...
HAVE YOU *REALLY* NOT KILLED ANYONE?
WHAM
I GUESS SINCE YOU KNOW HE'S A VAMPIRE, YOU CAN DO THIS SORT OF THING.
YOU COULD GIVE LESSONS ABOUT COMPARTMENTALIZING.
TOO BAD JEJE WON'T GO DOWN FROM SOMETHING LIKE THAT ALONE.
GRK
NGH...
HUH ...?
NOW THAT I GET A LOOK AT YOU...

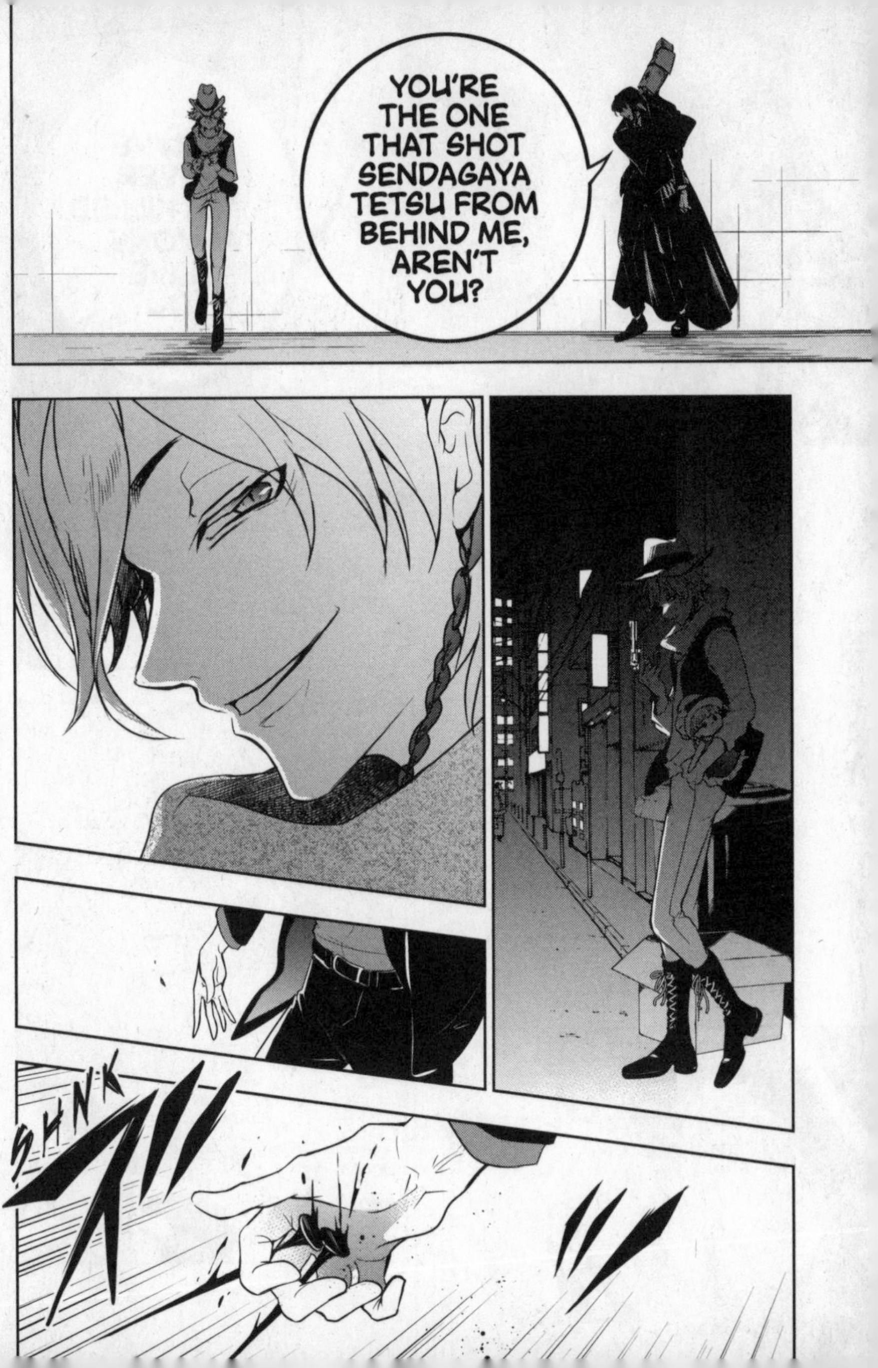
YOU'RE THE ONE THAT SHOT SENDAGAYA TETSU FROM BEHIND ME, AREN'T YOU?
SHNK

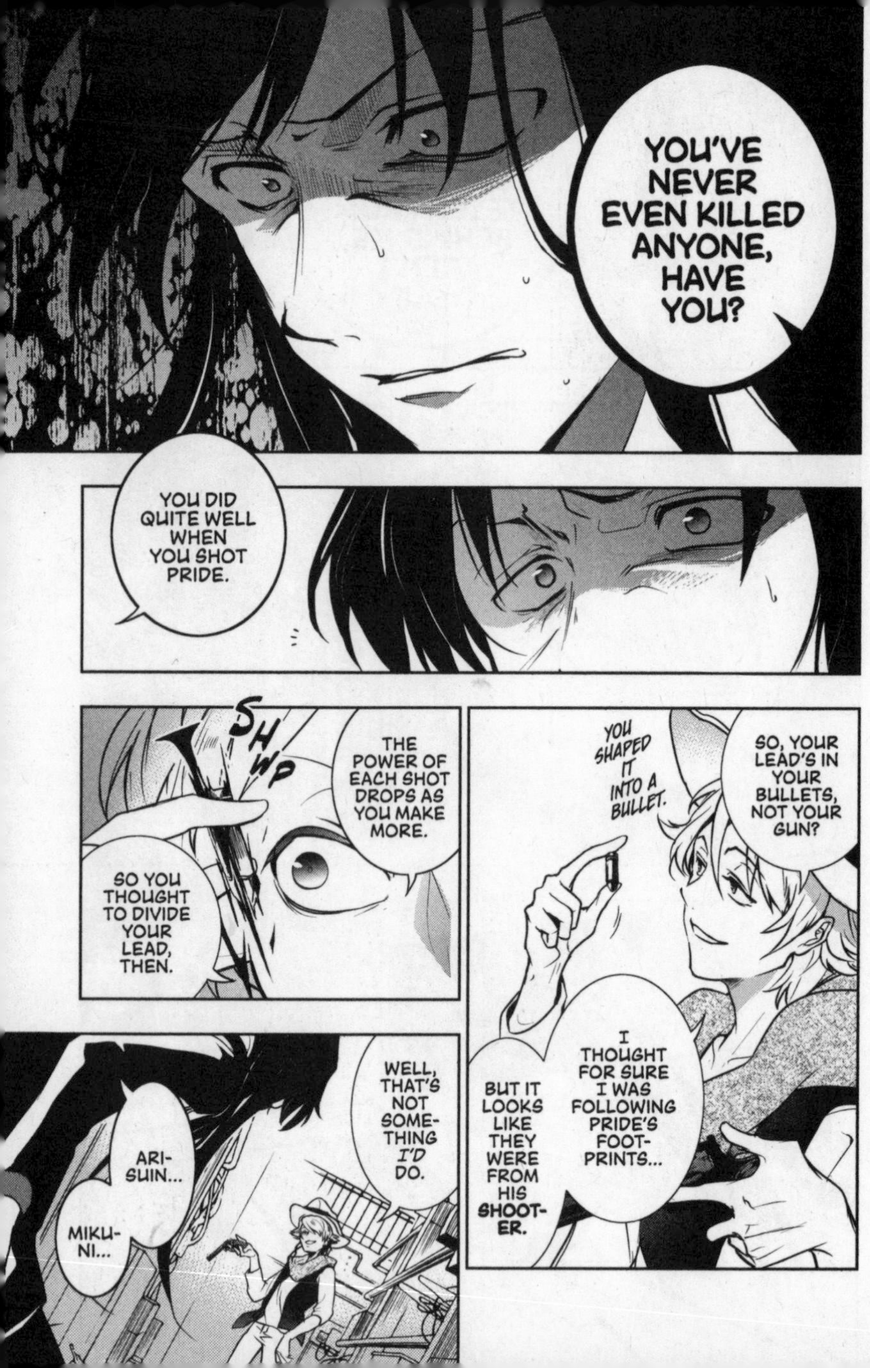
YOU'VE NEVER EVEN KILLED ANYONE, HAVE YOU?
YOU DID QUITE WELL WHEN YOU SHOT PRIDE.
SO, YOUR LEAD'S IN YOUR BULLETS, NOT YOUR GUN?
YOU SHAPED IT INTO A BULLET.
I THOUGHT FOR SURE I WAS FOLLOWING PRIDE'S FOOT-PRINTS...
BUT IT LOOKS LIKE THEY WERE FROM HIS SHOOT-ER.
SHWP
THE POWER OF EACH SHOT DROPS AS YOU MAKE MORE.
SO YOU THOUGHT TO DIVIDE YOUR LEAD, THEN.
WELL, THAT'S NOT SOME-THING *I'D* DO.
ARI-SUIN...
MIKU-NI...

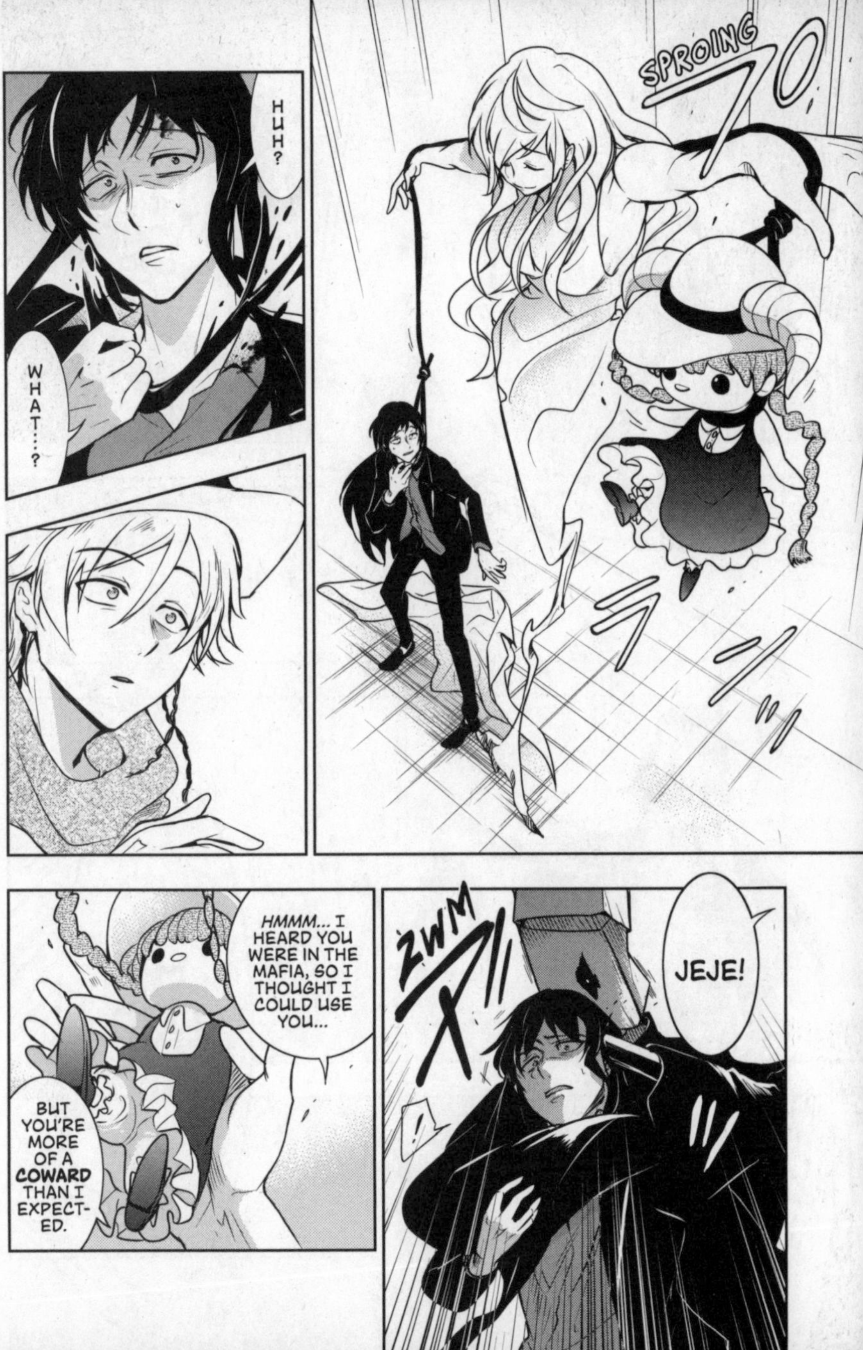
SPROING
HUH?
WHAT...?
JEJE!
ZWM
!
HMMM... I HEARD YOU WERE IN THE MAFIA, SO I THOUGHT I COULD USE YOU...
BUT YOU'RE MORE OF A **COWARD** THAN I EXPECTED.

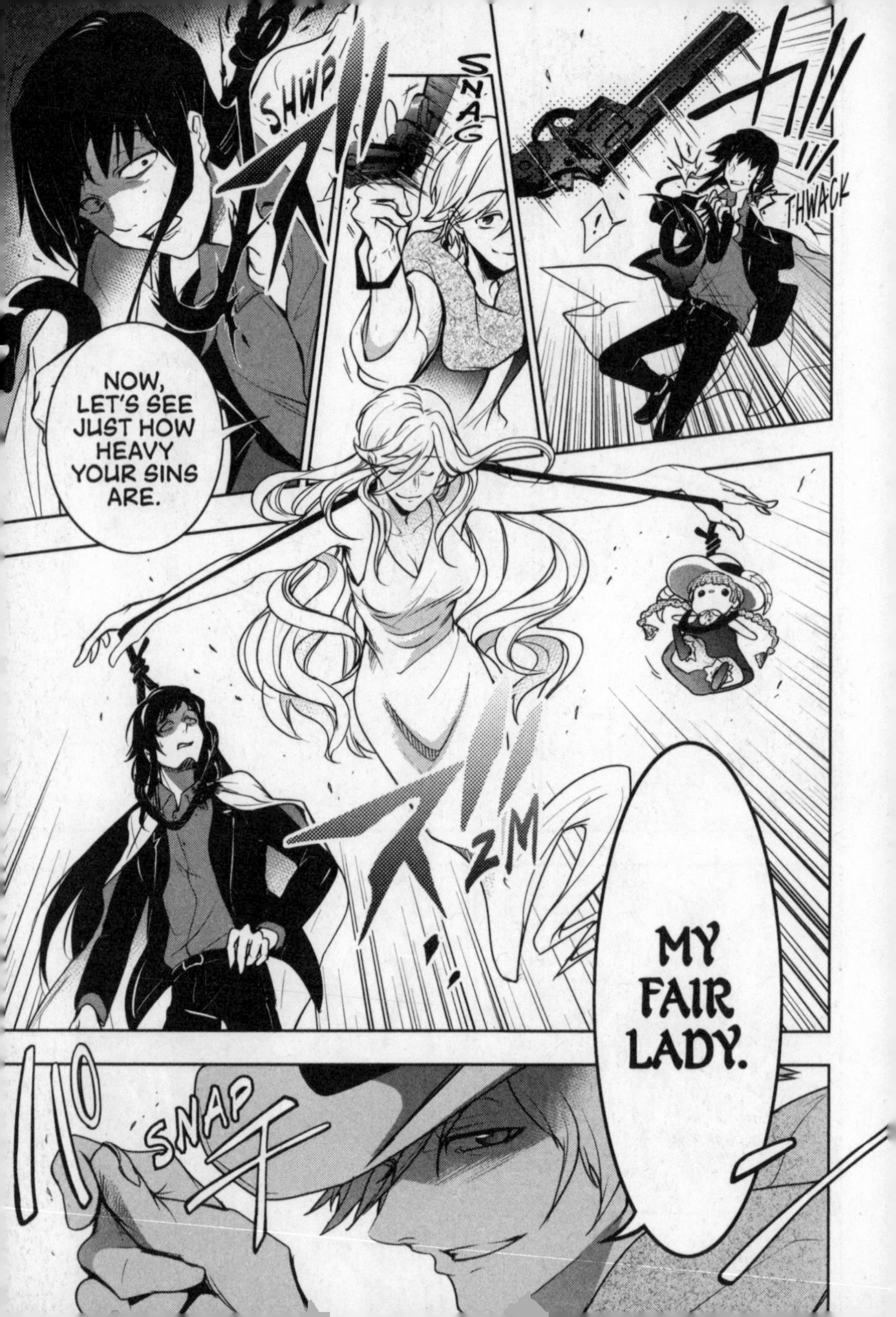
THWACK
SNAG
SHWP
NOW, LET'S SEE JUST HOW HEAVY YOUR SINS ARE.
ZM
MY FAIR LADY.
SNAP

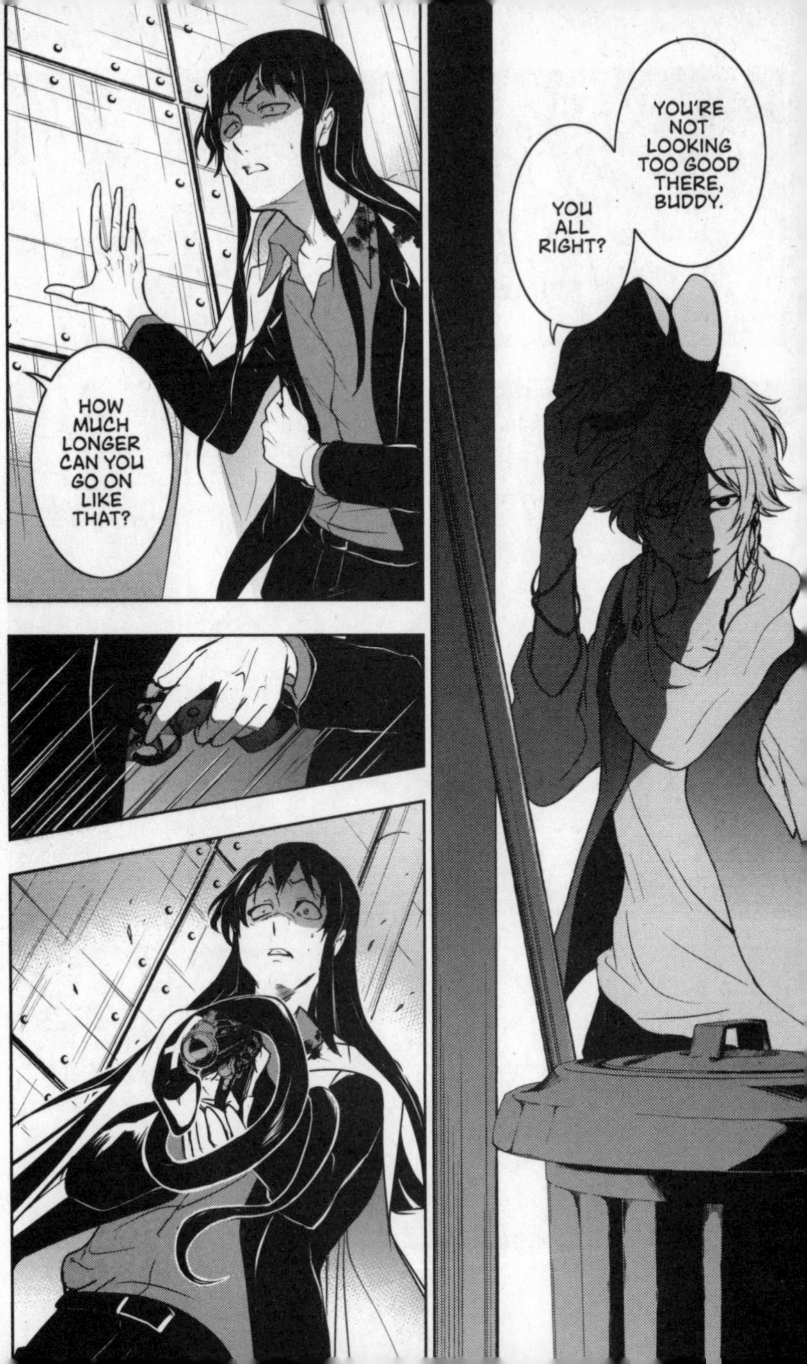
YOU'RE NOT LOOKING TOO GOOD THERE, BUDDY.
YOU ALL RIGHT?
HOW MUCH LONGER CAN YOU GO ON LIKE THAT?

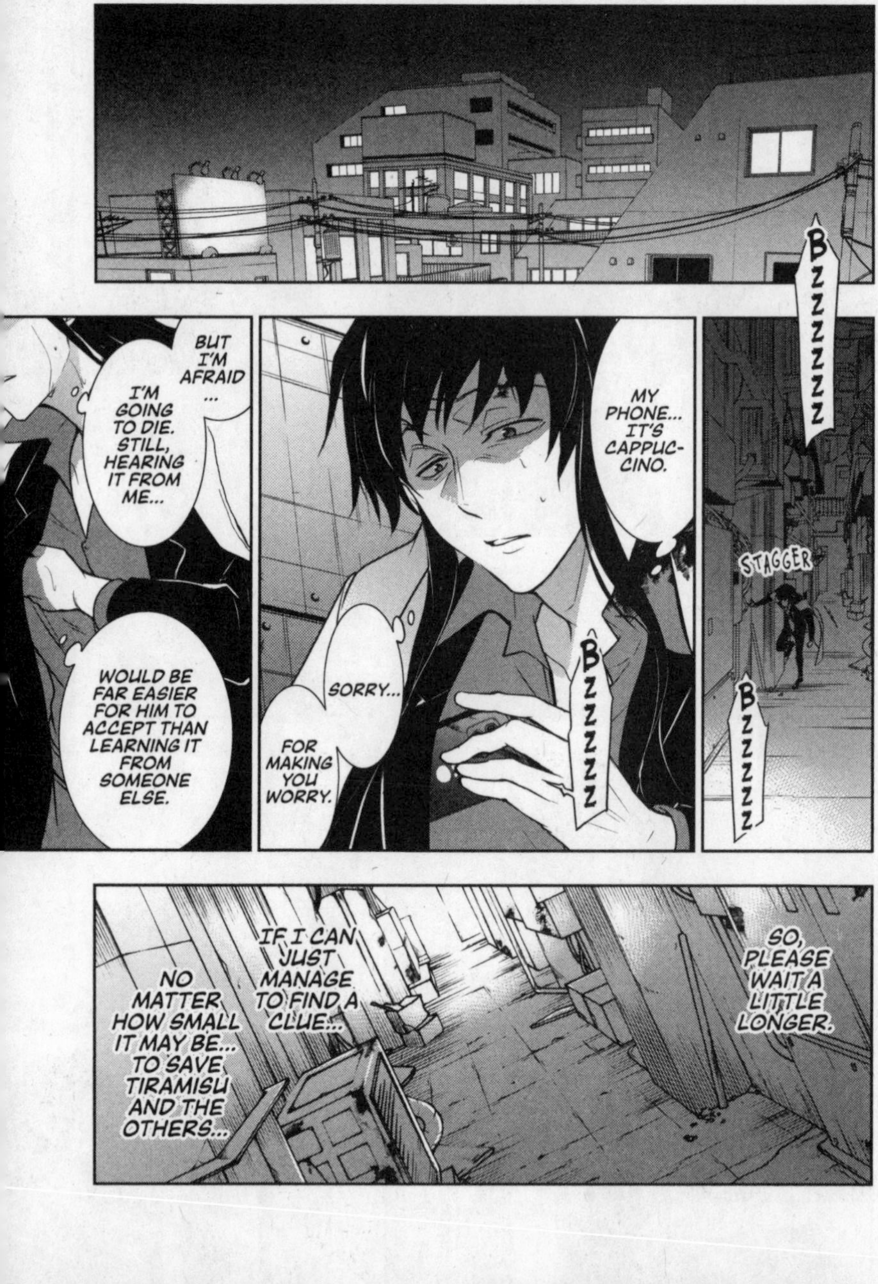
BZZZZZZ
STAGGER
BZZZZZ
MY PHONE... IT'S CAPPUC-CINO.
BZZZZZ
SORRY...
FOR MAKING YOU WORRY.
BUT I'M AFRAID...
I'M GOING TO DIE. STILL, HEARING IT FROM ME...
WOULD BE FAR EASIER FOR HIM TO ACCEPT THAN LEARNING IT FROM SOMEONE ELSE.
SO, PLEASE WAIT A LITTLE LONGER.
IF I CAN JUST MANAGE TO FIND A CLUE...
NO MATTER HOW SMALL IT MAY BE... TO SAVE TIRAMISU AND THE OTHERS...

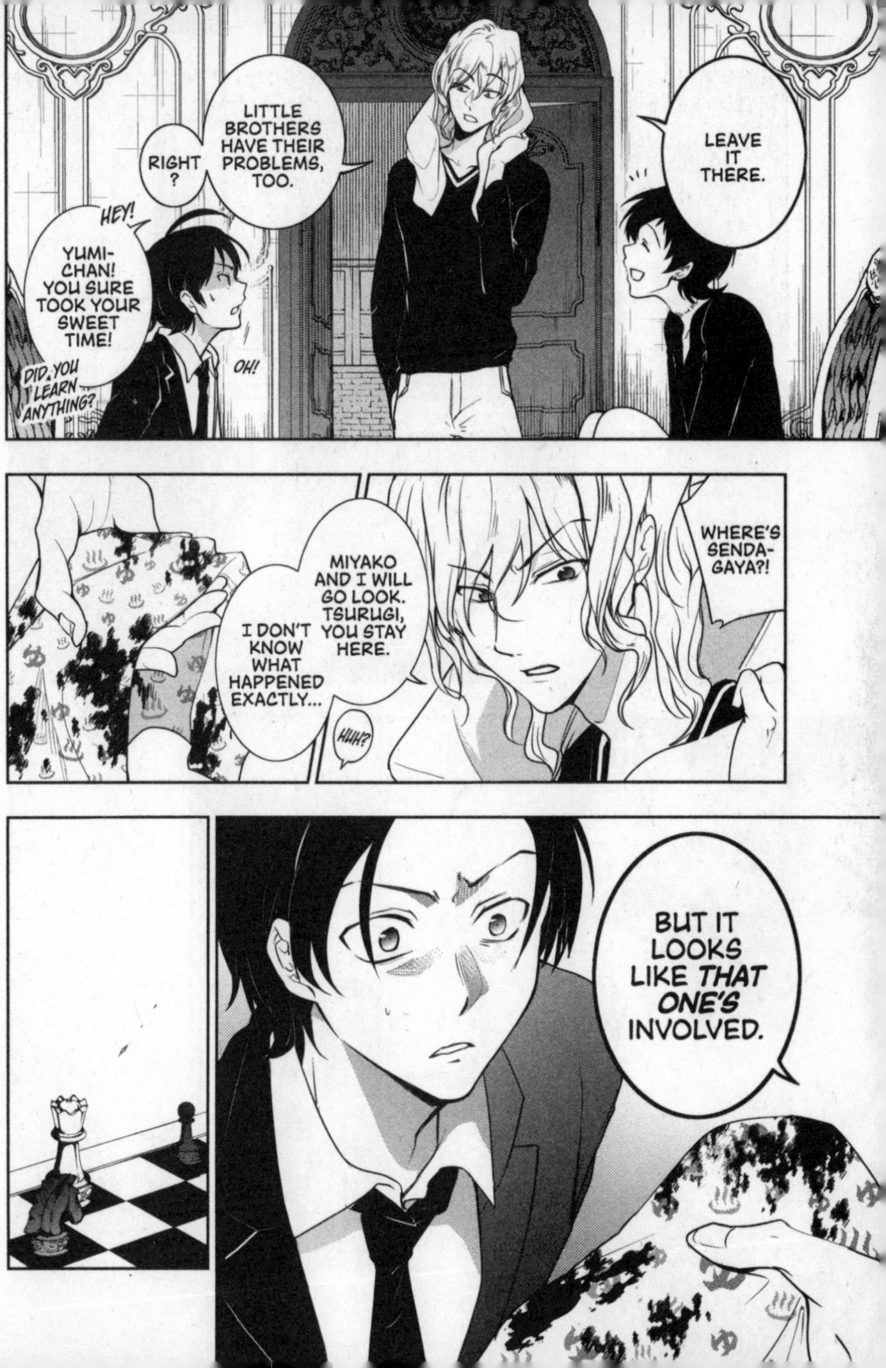
LEAVE IT THERE.
LITTLE BROTHERS HAVE THEIR PROBLEMS, TOO.
RIGHT?
HEY!
YUMI-CHAN! YOU SURE TOOK YOUR SWEET TIME!
OH!
DID YOU LEARN ANYTHING?
WHERE'S SENDA-GAYA?!
MIYAKO AND I WILL GO LOOK. TSURUGI, YOU STAY HERE.
HUH?
I DON'T KNOW WHAT HAPPENED EXACTLY...
BUT IT LOOKS LIKE *THAT ONE'S* INVOLVED.

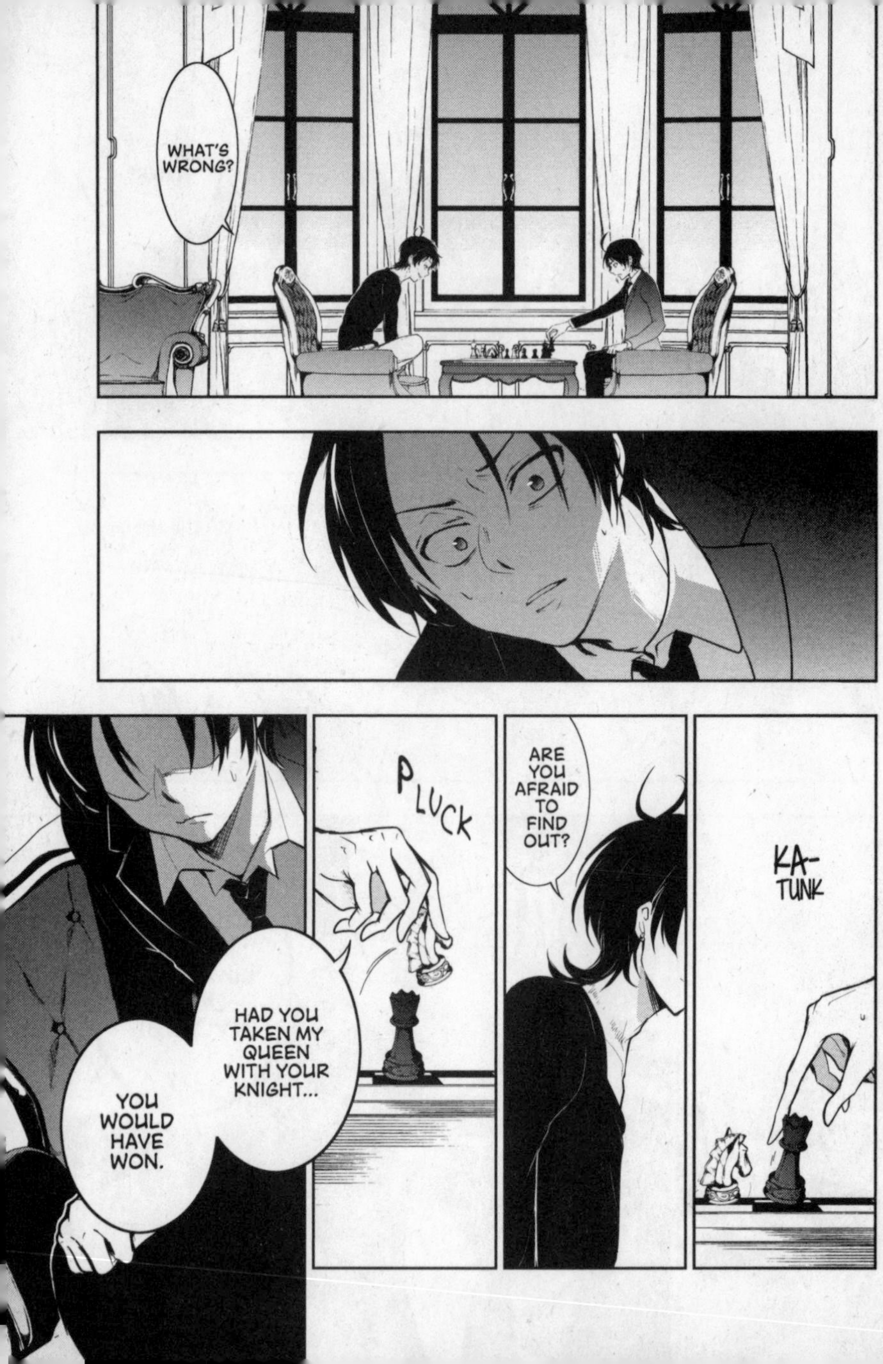
WHAT'S WRONG?
KA-TUNK
ARE YOU AFRAID TO FIND OUT?
PLUCK
HAD YOU TAKEN MY QUEEN WITH YOUR KNIGHT...
YOU WOULD HAVE WON.

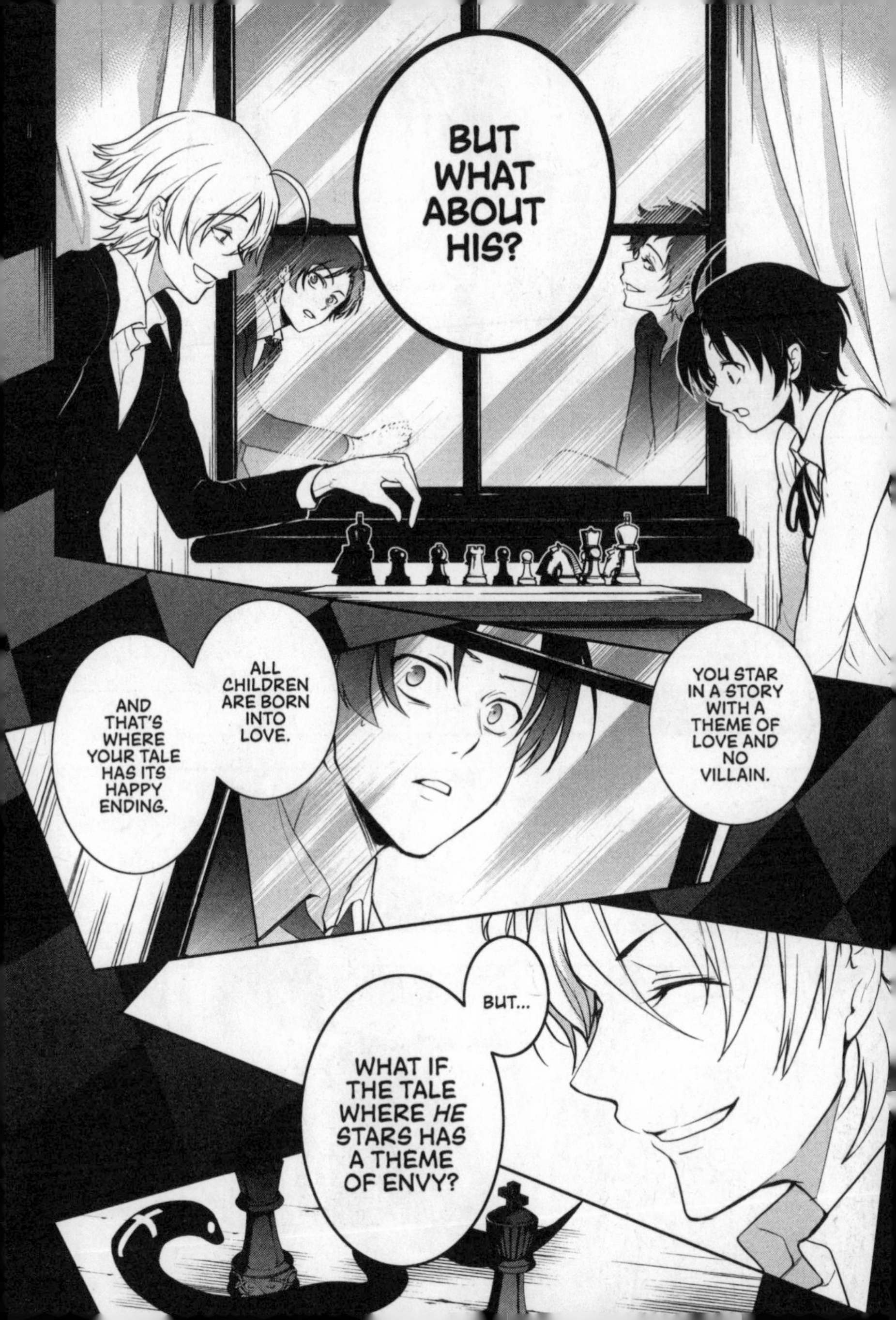
BUT WHAT ABOUT HIS?
YOU STAR IN A STORY WITH A THEME OF LOVE AND NO VILLAIN.
ALL CHILDREN ARE BORN INTO LOVE.
AND THAT'S WHERE YOUR TALE HAS ITS HAPPY ENDING.
BUT...
WHAT IF THE TALE WHERE *HE* STARS HAS A THEME OF ENVY?

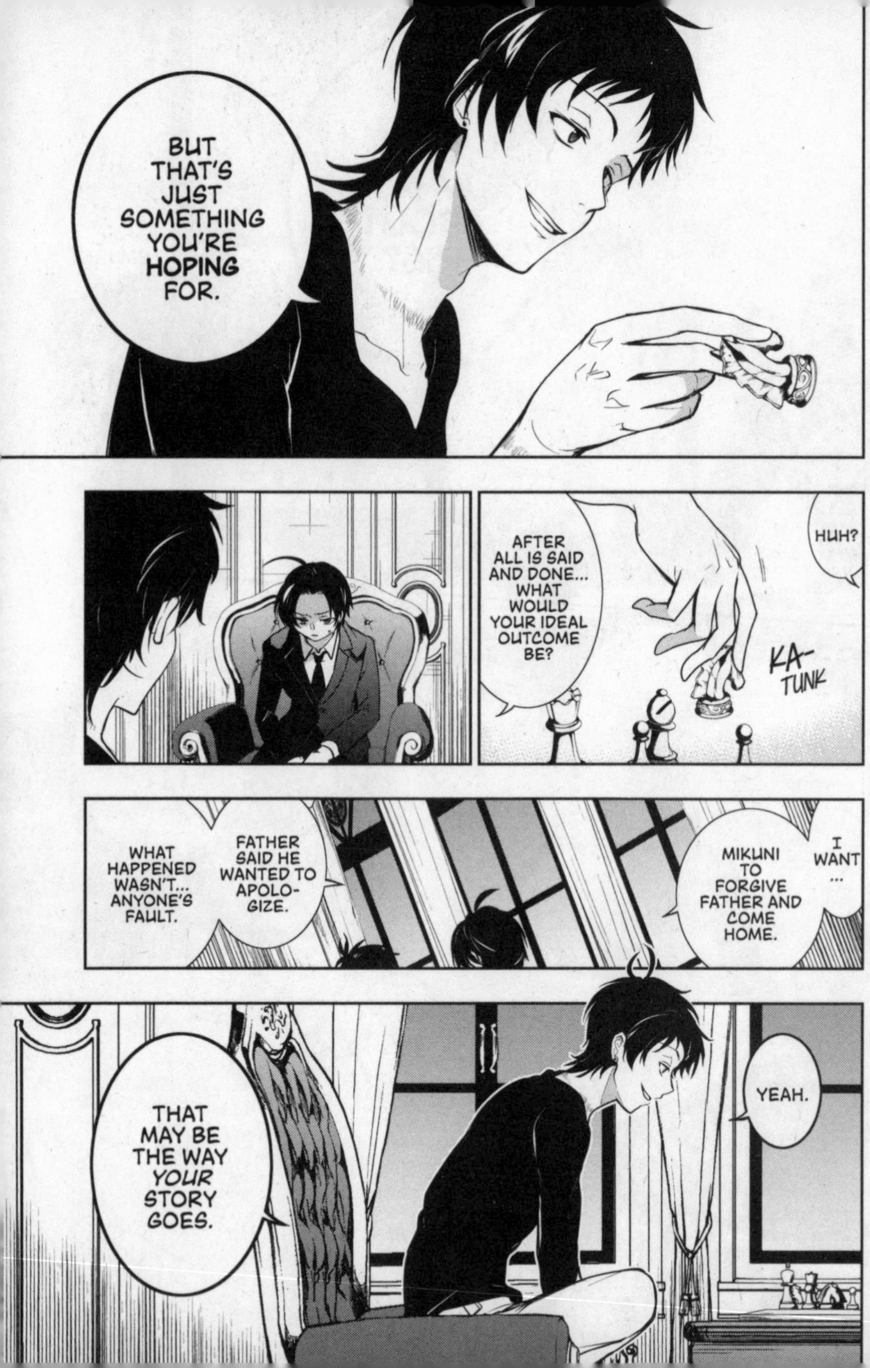
BUT THAT'S JUST SOMETHING YOU'RE HOPING FOR.
HUH?
AFTER ALL IS SAID AND DONE... WHAT WOULD YOUR IDEAL OUTCOME BE?
KA-TUNK
I WANT ...
MIKUNI TO FORGIVE FATHER AND COME HOME.
FATHER SAID HE WANTED TO APOLO-GIZE.
WHAT HAPPENED WASN'T... ANYONE'S FAULT.
YEAH.
THAT MAY BE THE WAY YOUR STORY GOES.

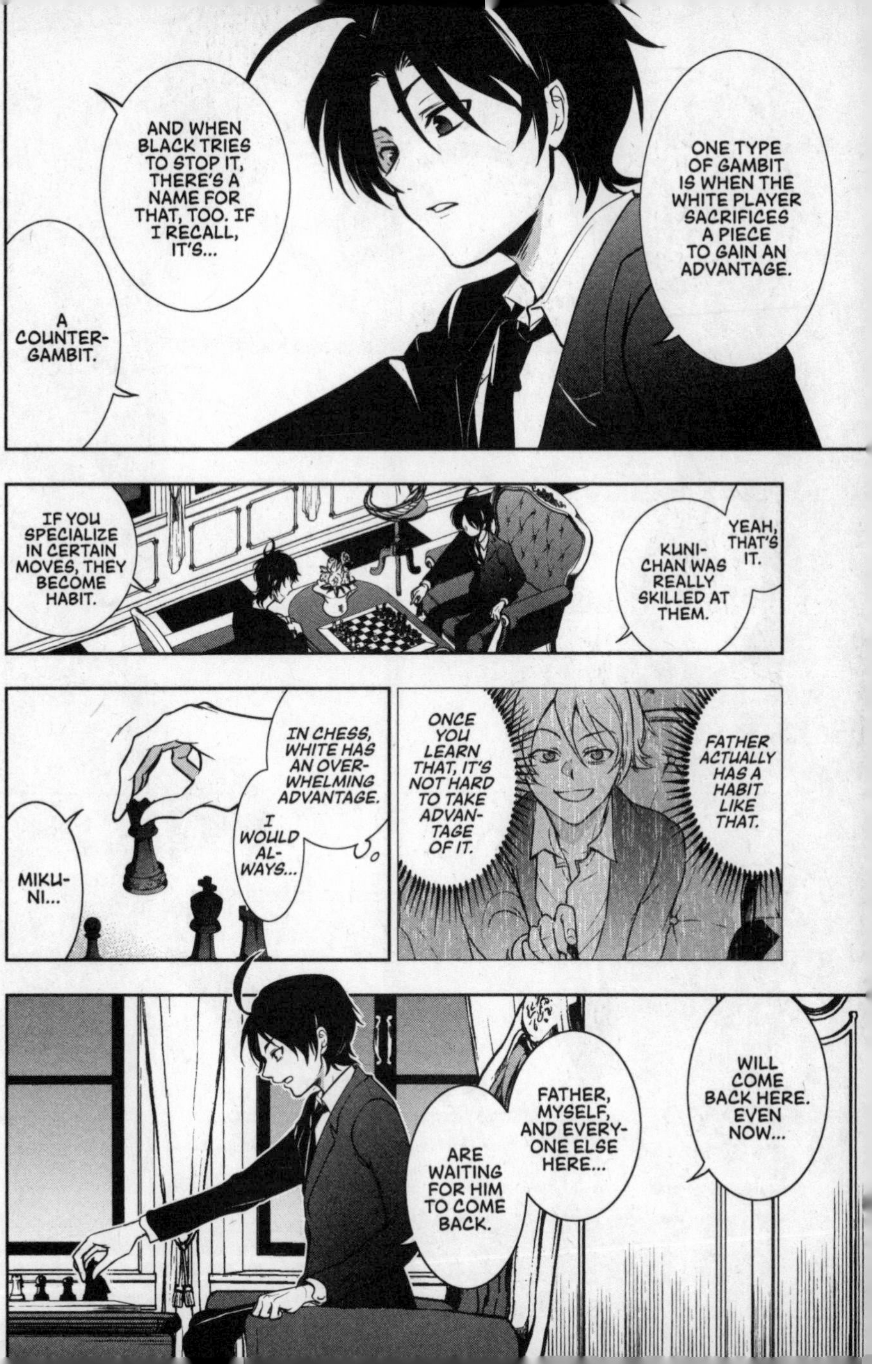
ONE TYPE OF GAMBIT IS WHEN THE WHITE PLAYER SACRIFICES A PIECE TO GAIN AN ADVANTAGE.
AND WHEN BLACK TRIES TO STOP IT, THERE'S A NAME FOR THAT, TOO. IF I RECALL, IT'S...
A COUNTER-GAMBIT.
YEAH, THAT'S IT.
KUNICHAN WAS REALLY SKILLED AT THEM.
IF YOU SPECIALIZE IN CERTAIN MOVES, THEY BECOME HABIT.
FATHER ACTUALLY HAS A HABIT LIKE THAT.
ONCE YOU LEARN THAT, IT'S NOT HARD TO TAKE ADVANTAGE OF IT.
IN CHESS, WHITE HAS AN OVERWHELMING ADVANTAGE.
I WOULD ALWAYS...
MIKUNI...
WILL COME BACK HERE. EVEN NOW...
FATHER, MYSELF, AND EVERYONE ELSE HERE...
ARE WAITING FOR HIM TO COME BACK.

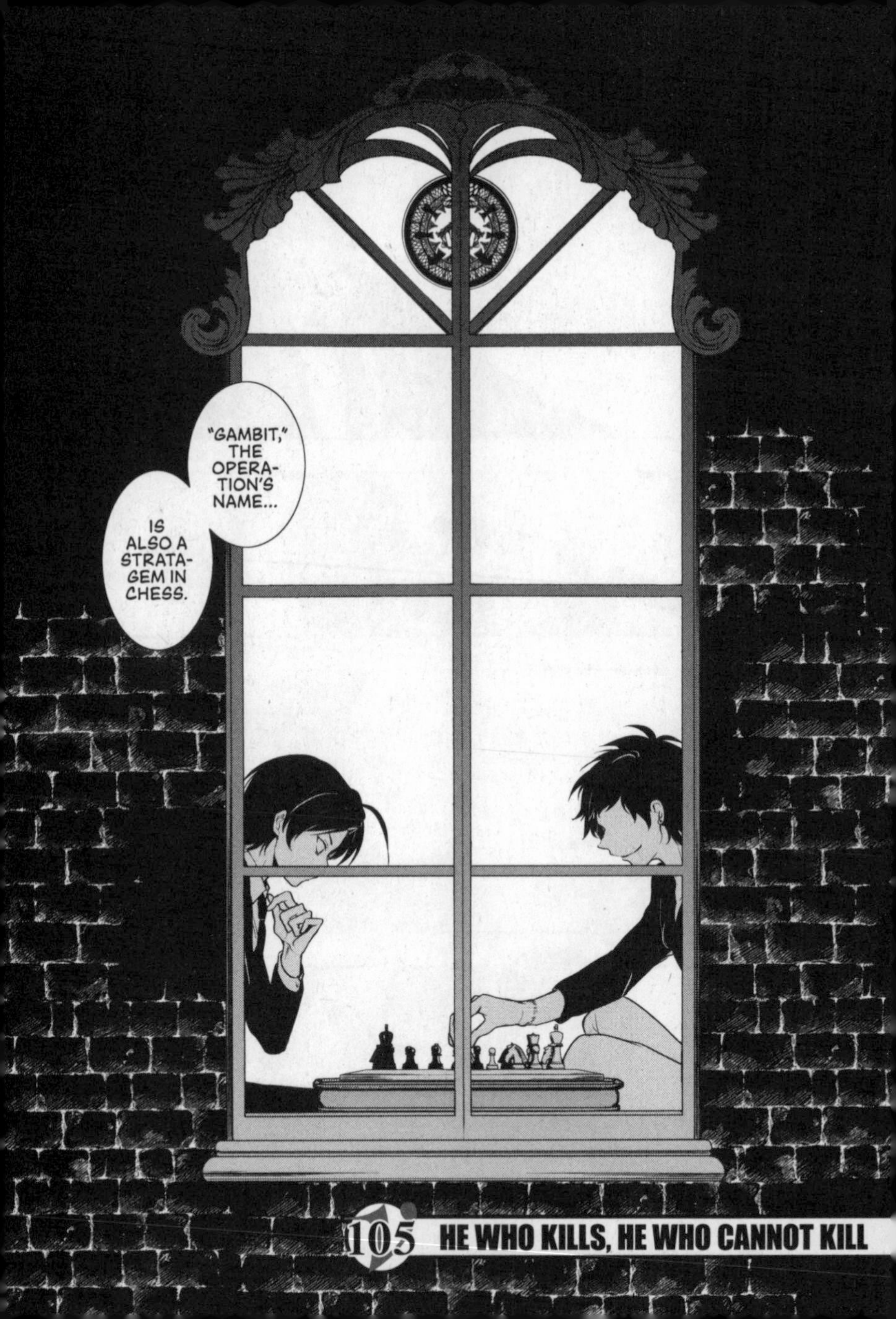
"GAMBIT," THE OPERA-TION'S NAME...
IS ALSO A STRATA-GEM IN CHESS.

105 HE WHO KILLS, HE WHO CANNOT KILL

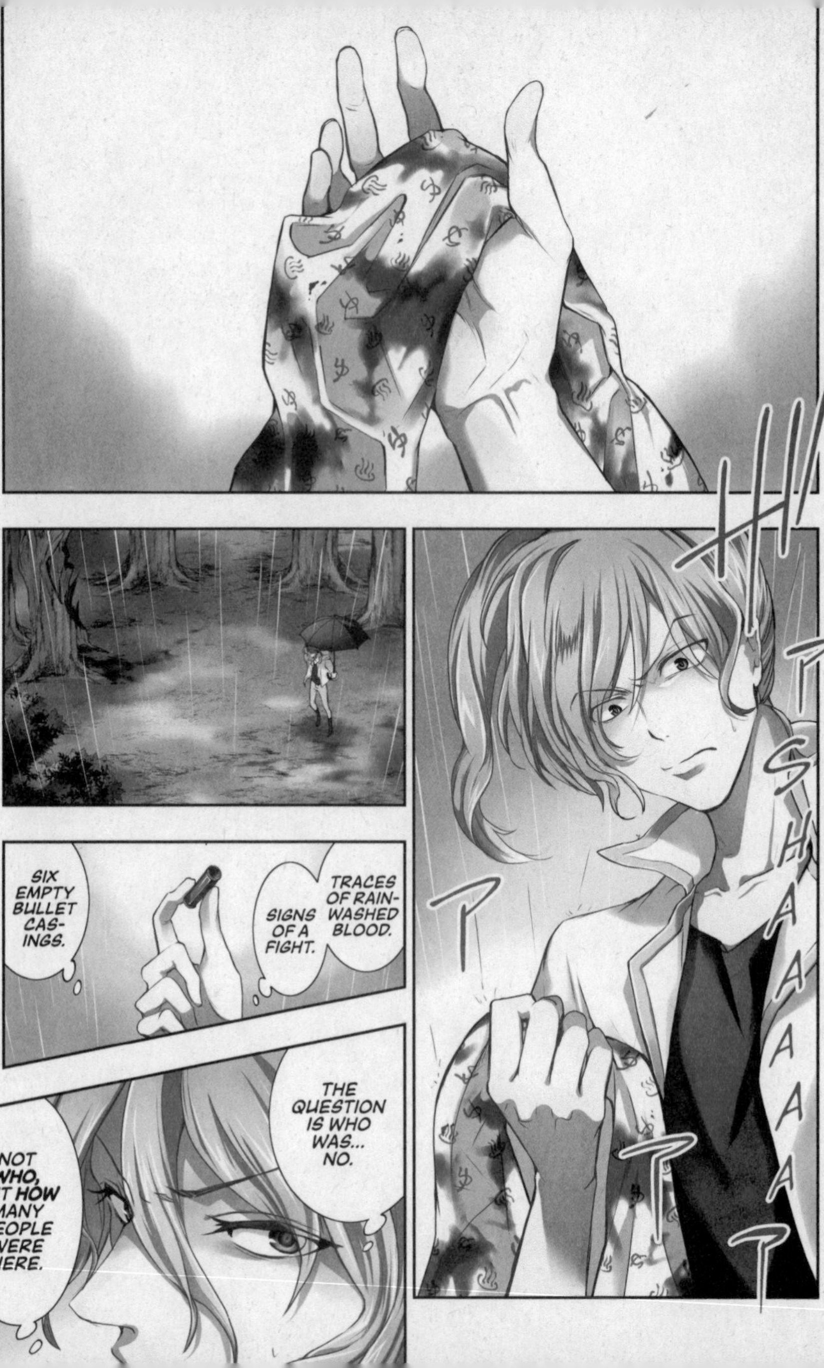
PSHAAAAAT
SIX EMPTY BULLET CASINGS.
TRACES OF RAIN-WASHED BLOOD.
SIGNS OF A FIGHT.
THE QUESTION IS WHO WAS... NO.
NOT **WHO**, BUT **HOW** MANY PEOPLE WERE HERE.

SERVAMP

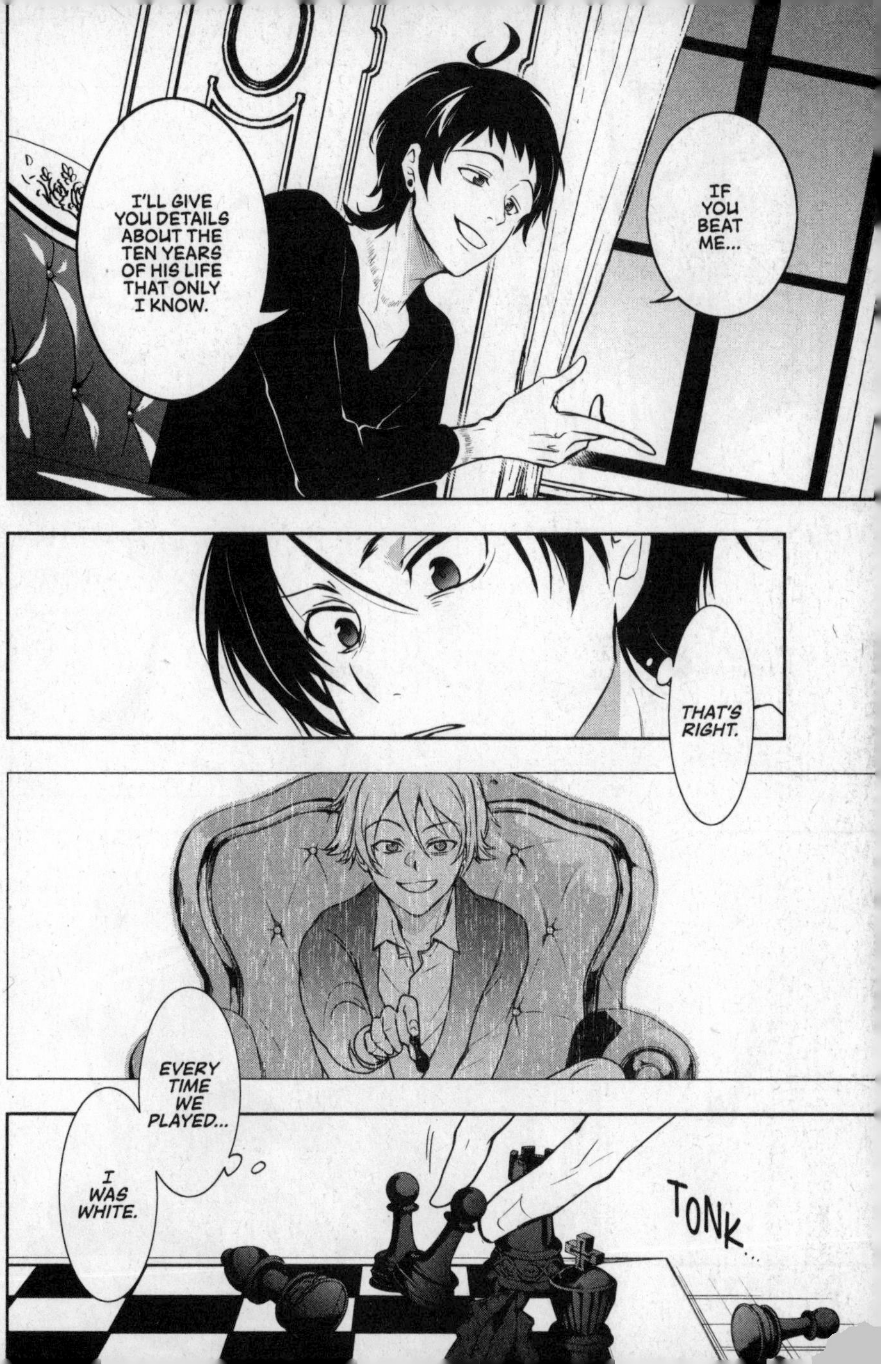
IF YOU BEAT ME...
I'LL GIVE YOU DETAILS ABOUT THE TEN YEARS OF HIS LIFE THAT ONLY I KNOW.
THAT'S RIGHT.
EVERY TIME WE PLAYED...
I WAS WHITE.
TONK...

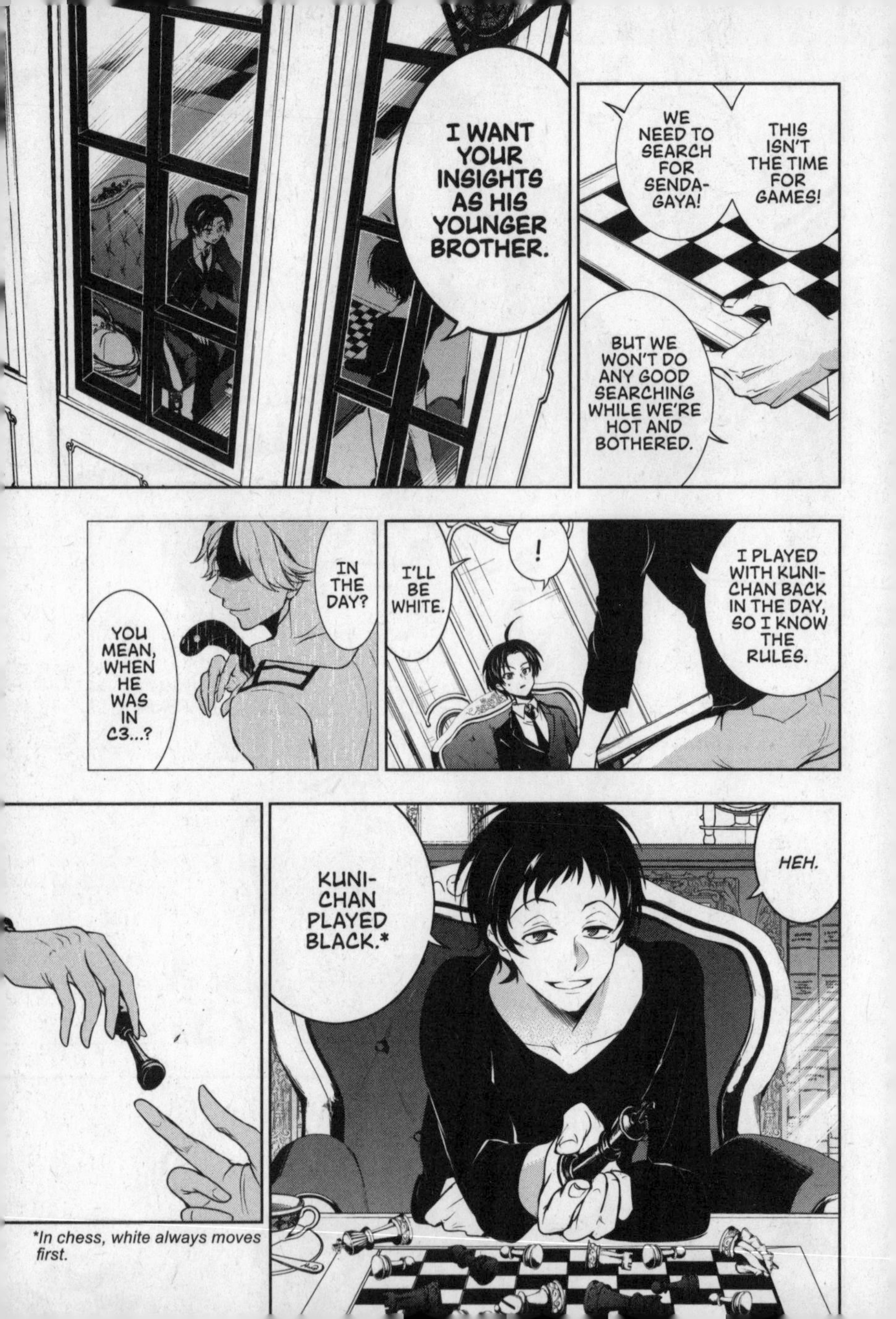
THIS ISN'T THE TIME FOR GAMES!
WE NEED TO SEARCH FOR SENDA-GAYA!
BUT WE WON'T DO ANY GOOD SEARCHING WHILE WE'RE HOT AND BOTHERED.
I WANT YOUR INSIGHTS AS HIS YOUNGER BROTHER.
I PLAYED WITH KUNI-CHAN BACK IN THE DAY, SO I KNOW THE RULES.
!
I'LL BE WHITE.
IN THE DAY?
YOU MEAN, WHEN HE WAS IN C3...?
HEH.
KUNI-CHAN PLAYED BLACK.*

*In chess, white always moves first.

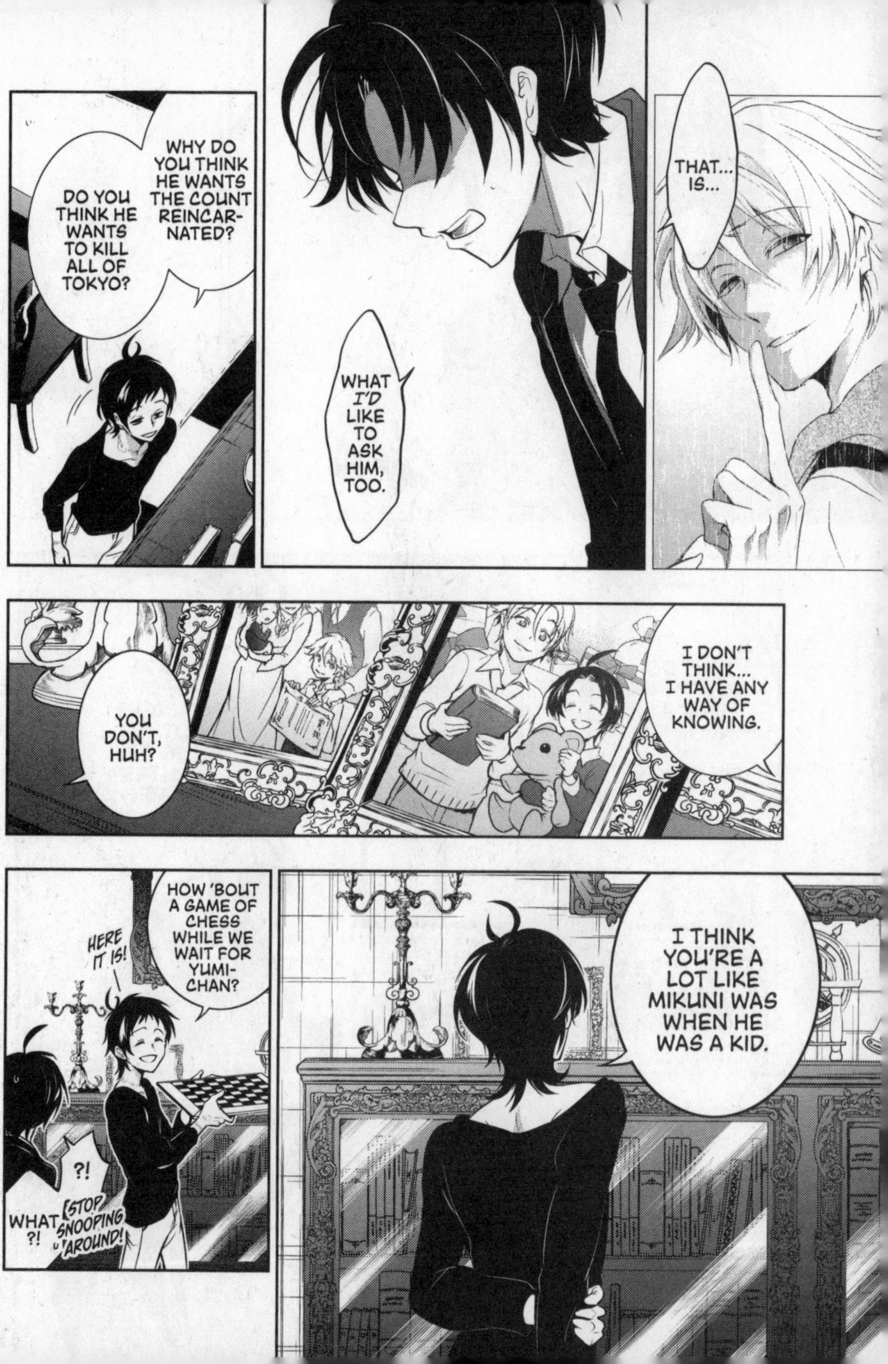
THAT... IS...
WHAT *I'D* LIKE TO ASK HIM, TOO.
WHY DO YOU THINK HE WANTS THE COUNT REINCARNATED?
DO YOU THINK HE WANTS TO KILL ALL OF TOKYO?
I DON'T THINK... I HAVE ANY WAY OF KNOWING.
YOU DON'T, HUH?
I THINK YOU'RE A LOT LIKE MIKUNI WAS WHEN HE WAS A KID.
HOW 'BOUT A GAME OF CHESS WHILE WE WAIT FOR YUMI-CHAN?
HERE IT IS!
?!
STOP SNOOPING AROUND!
WHAT ?!

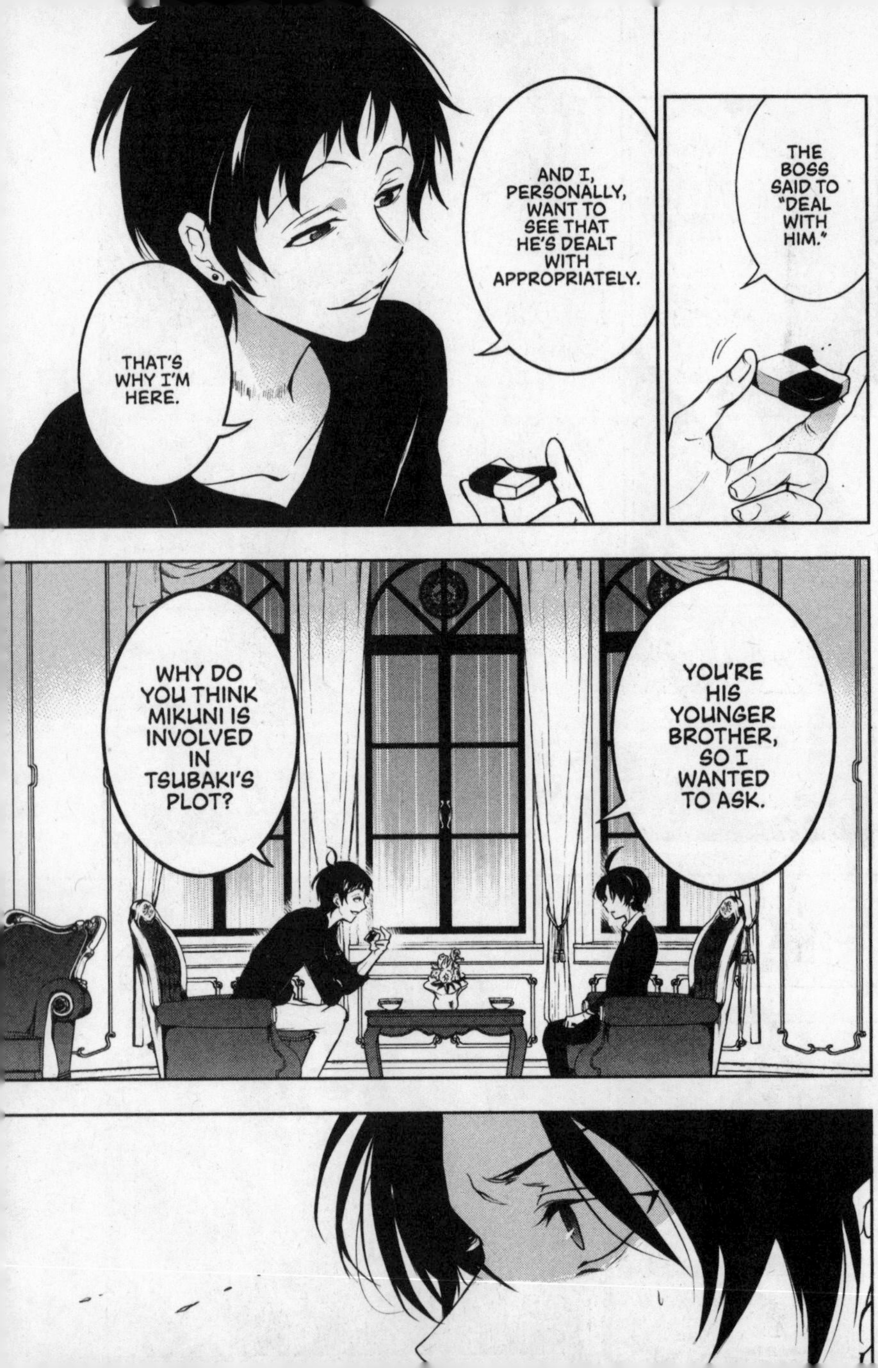
THE BOSS SAID TO "DEAL WITH HIM."
AND I, PERSONALLY, WANT TO SEE THAT HE'S DEALT WITH APPROPRIATELY.
THAT'S WHY I'M HERE.
YOU'RE HIS YOUNGER BROTHER, SO I WANTED TO ASK.
WHY DO YOU THINK MIKUNI IS INVOLVED IN TSUBAKI'S PLOT?

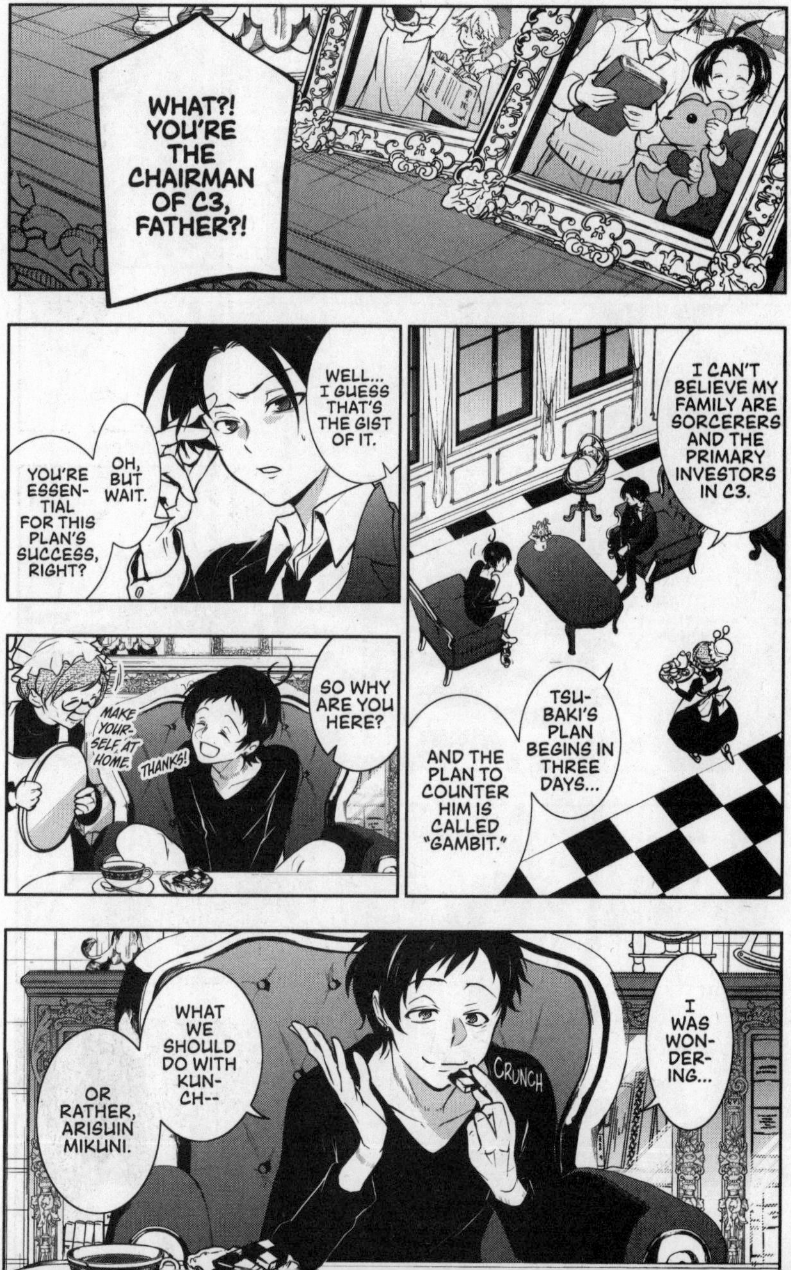
WHAT?! YOU'RE THE CHAIRMAN OF C3, FATHER?!
I CAN'T BELIEVE MY FAMILY ARE SORCERERS AND THE PRIMARY INVESTORS IN C3.
TSUBAKI'S PLAN BEGINS IN THREE DAYS...
AND THE PLAN TO COUNTER HIM IS CALLED "GAMBIT."
WELL... I GUESS THAT'S THE GIST OF IT.
OH, BUT WAIT.
YOU'RE ESSENTIAL FOR THIS PLAN'S SUCCESS, RIGHT?
SO WHY ARE YOU HERE?
MAKE YOURSELF AT HOME.
THANKS!
I WAS WONDERING...
CRUNCH
WHAT WE SHOULD DO WITH KUNCH--
OR RATHER, ARISUIN MIKUNI.

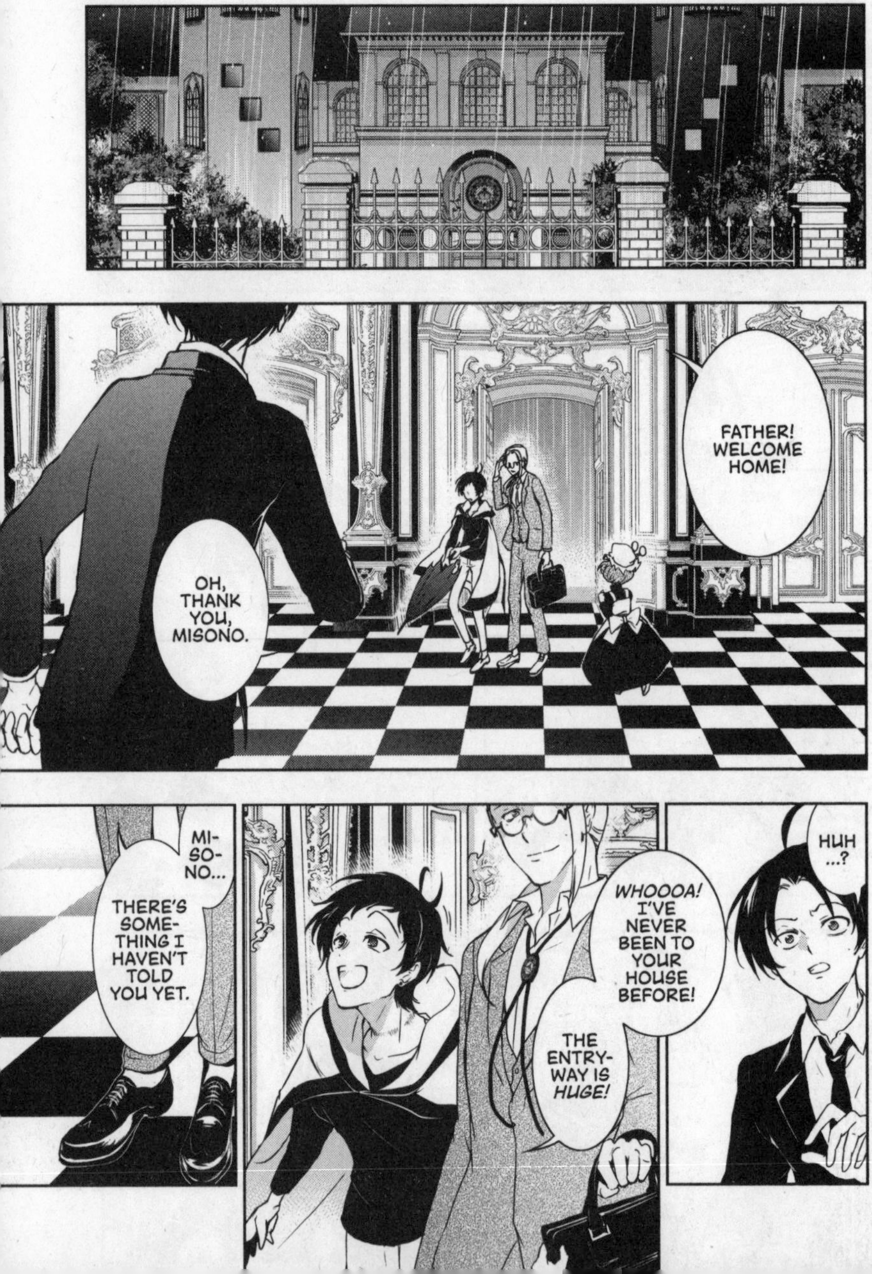
FATHER! WELCOME HOME!
OH, THANK YOU, MISONO.
HUH ...?
WHOOOA! I'VE NEVER BEEN TO YOUR HOUSE BEFORE!
THE ENTRY-WAY IS HUGE!
MI-SO-NO...
THERE'S SOME-THING I HAVEN'T TOLD YOU YET.

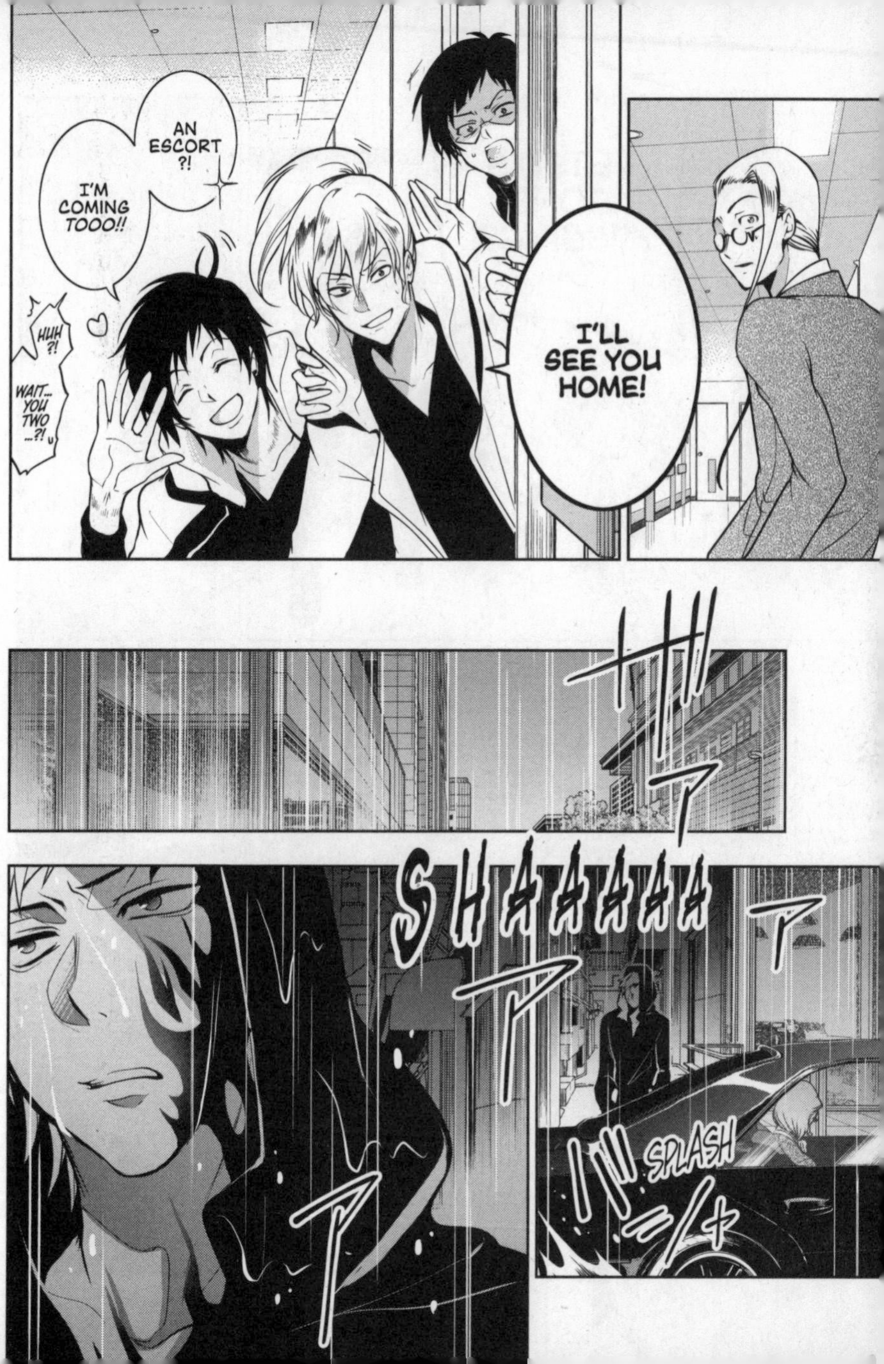
I'LL SEE YOU HOME!
AN ESCORT?!
I'M COMING TOOO!!
HUH?!
WAIT... YOU TWO...?!
SHAAAAAA
SPLASH

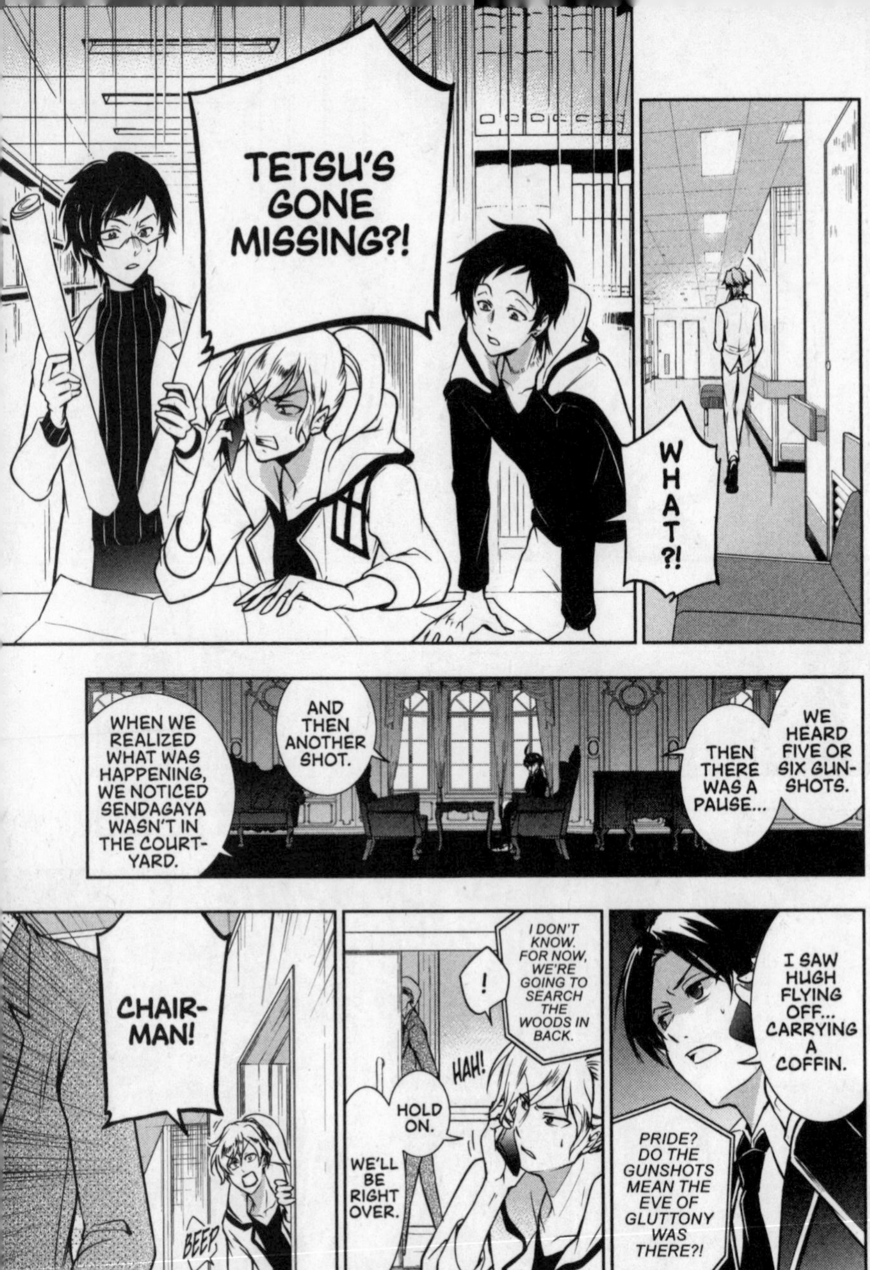
TETSU'S GONE MISSING?!
WHAT?!
WE HEARD FIVE OR SIX GUN-SHOTS.
THEN THERE WAS A PAUSE...
AND THEN ANOTHER SHOT.
WHEN WE REALIZED WHAT WAS HAPPENING, WE NOTICED SENDAGAYA WASN'T IN THE COURT-YARD.
I SAW HUGH FLYING OFF... CARRYING A COFFIN.
PRIDE? DO THE GUNSHOTS MEAN THE EVE OF GLUTTONY WAS THERE?!
I DON'T KNOW. FOR NOW, WE'RE GOING TO SEARCH THE WOODS IN BACK.
!
HAH!
HOLD ON.
WE'LL BE RIGHT OVER.
CHAIR-MAN!
BEEP

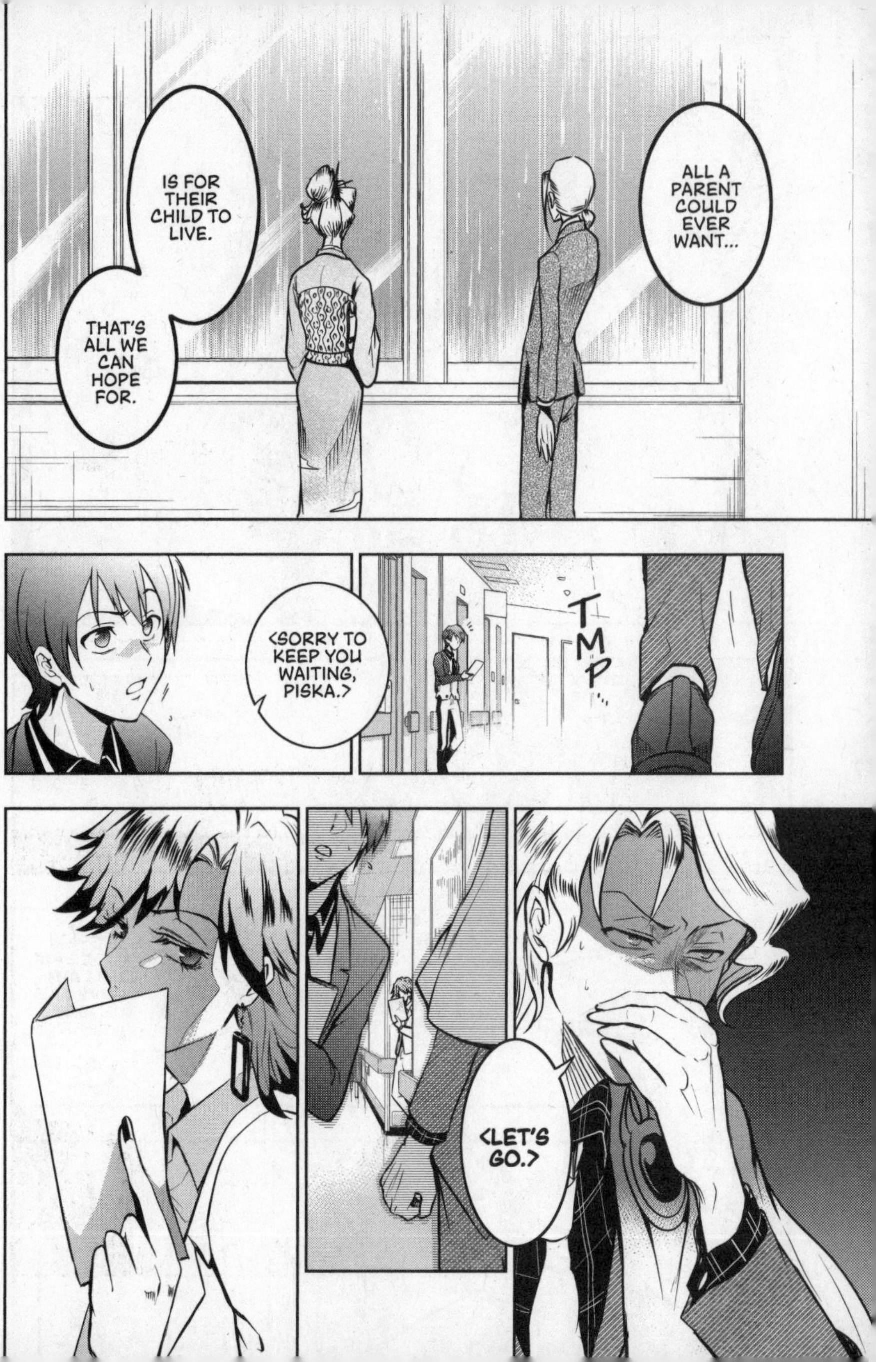
ALL A PARENT COULD EVER WANT...
IS FOR THEIR CHILD TO LIVE.
THAT'S ALL WE CAN HOPE FOR.
TMP...
<SORRY TO KEEP YOU WAITING, PISKA.>
<LET'S GO.>

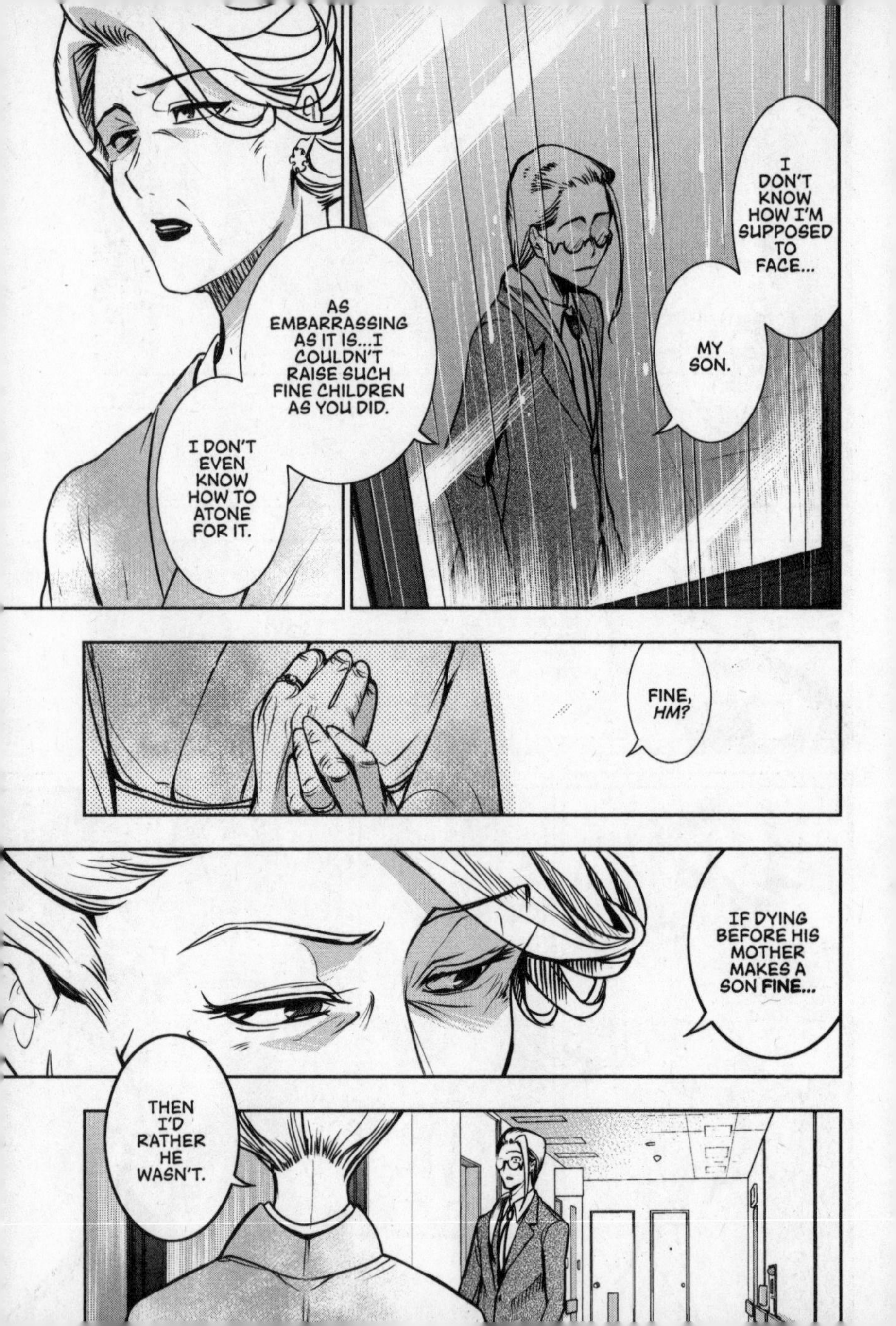
I DON'T KNOW HOW I'M SUPPOSED TO FACE...
MY SON.
AS EMBARRASSING AS IT IS...I COULDN'T RAISE SUCH FINE CHILDREN AS YOU DID.
I DON'T EVEN KNOW HOW TO ATONE FOR IT.
FINE, *HM?*
IF DYING BEFORE HIS MOTHER MAKES A SON **FINE**...
THEN I'D RATHER HE WASN'T.

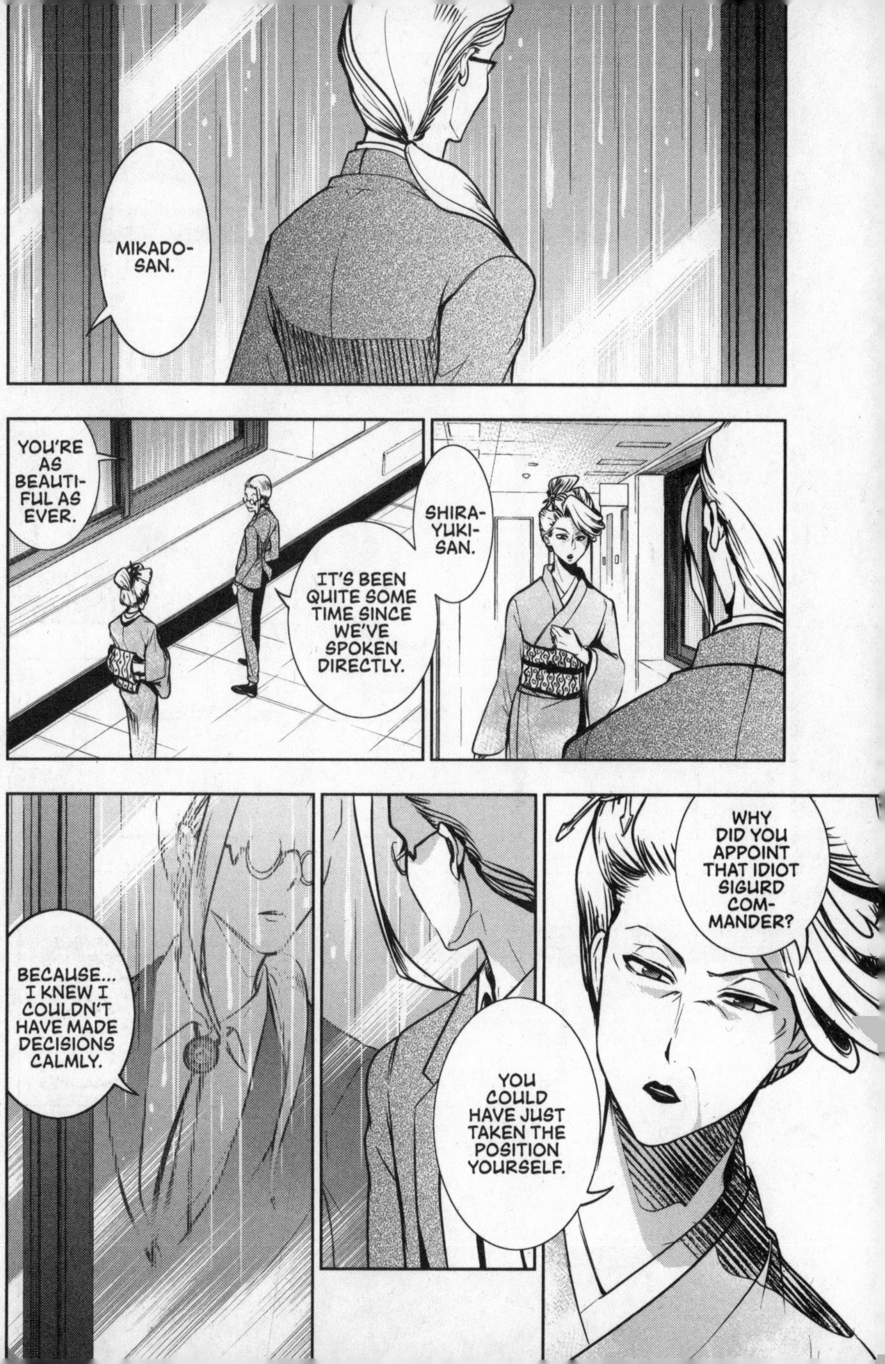
MIKADO-SAN.
SHIRAYUKI-SAN.
IT'S BEEN QUITE SOME TIME SINCE WE'VE SPOKEN DIRECTLY.
YOU'RE AS BEAUTIFUL AS EVER.
WHY DID YOU APPOINT THAT IDIOT SIGURD COMMANDER?
YOU COULD HAVE JUST TAKEN THE POSITION YOURSELF.
BECAUSE... I KNEW I COULDN'T HAVE MADE DECISIONS CALMLY.

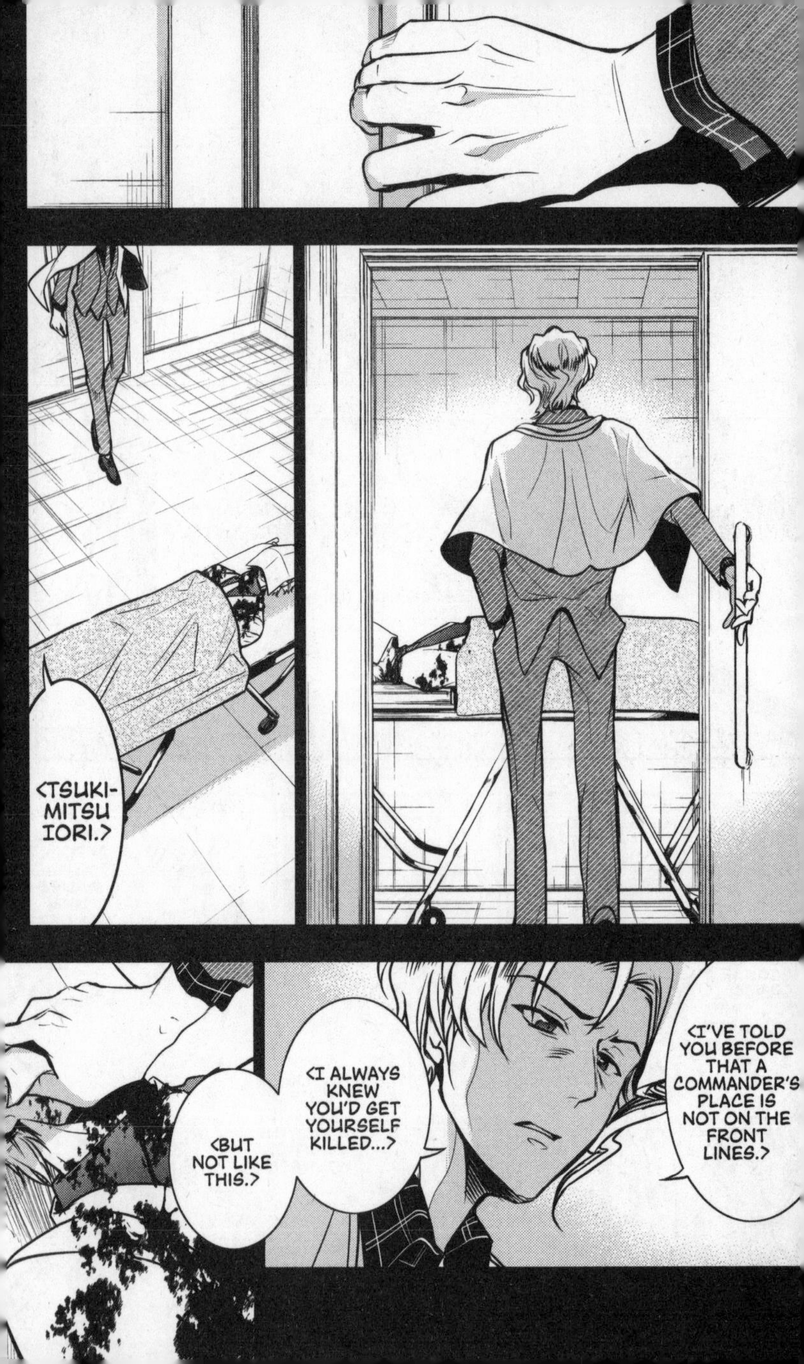
<TSUKIMITSU IORI.>
<I'VE TOLD YOU BEFORE THAT A COMMANDER'S PLACE IS NOT ON THE FRONT LINES.>
<I ALWAYS KNEW YOU'D GET YOURSELF KILLED...>
<BUT NOT LIKE THIS.>

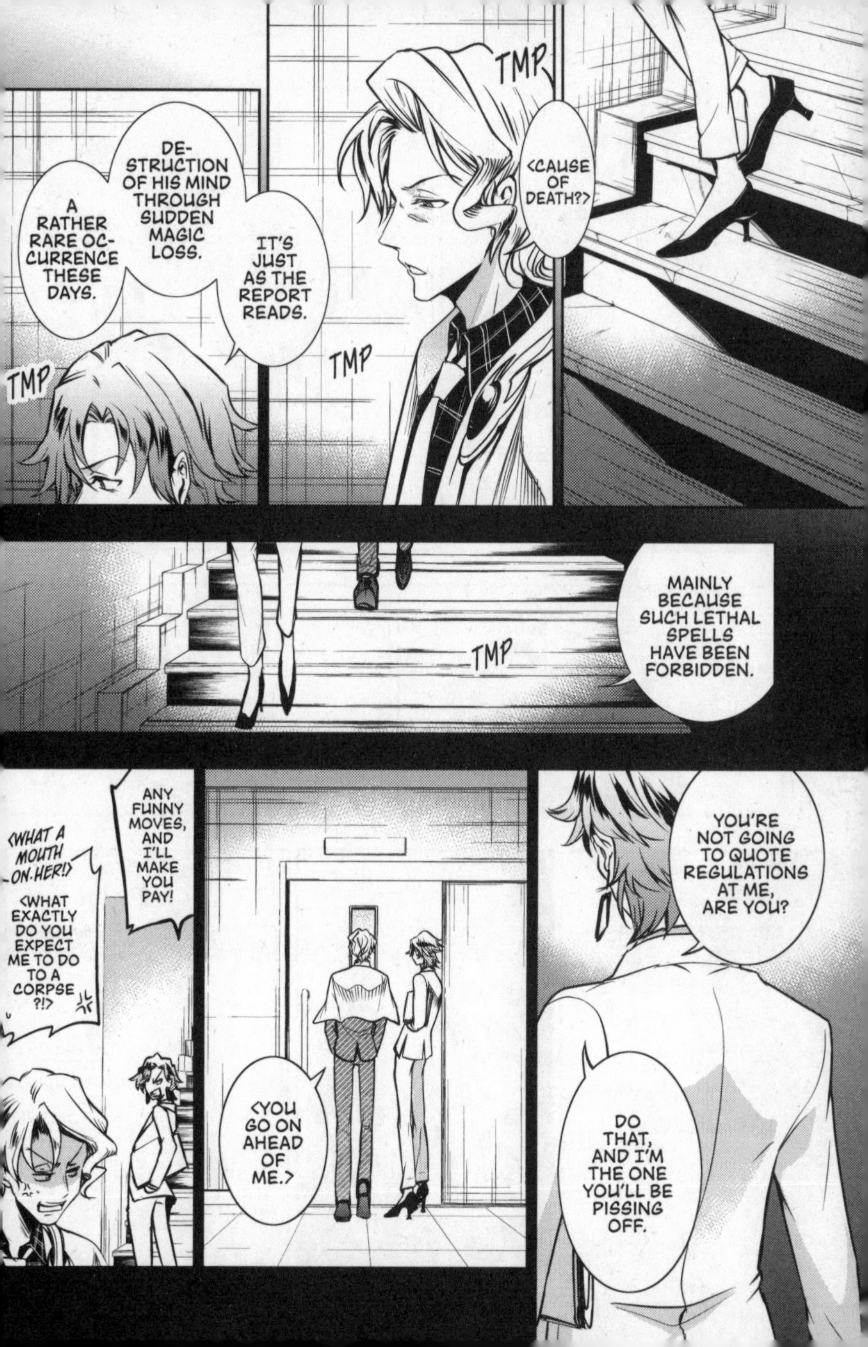
TMP
<CAUSE OF DEATH?>
IT'S JUST AS THE REPORT READS.
DE-STRUCTION OF HIS MIND THROUGH SUDDEN MAGIC LOSS.
A RATHER RARE OC-CURRENCE THESE DAYS.
TMP
TMP
MAINLY BECAUSE SUCH LETHAL SPELLS HAVE BEEN FORBIDDEN.
TMP
YOU'RE NOT GOING TO QUOTE REGULATIONS AT ME, ARE YOU?
DO THAT, AND I'M THE ONE YOU'LL BE PISSING OFF.
<YOU GO ON AHEAD OF ME.>
ANY FUNNY MOVES, AND I'LL MAKE YOU PAY!
<WHAT A MOUTH ON HER!>
<WHAT EXACTLY DO YOU EXPECT ME TO DO TO A CORPSE?!>

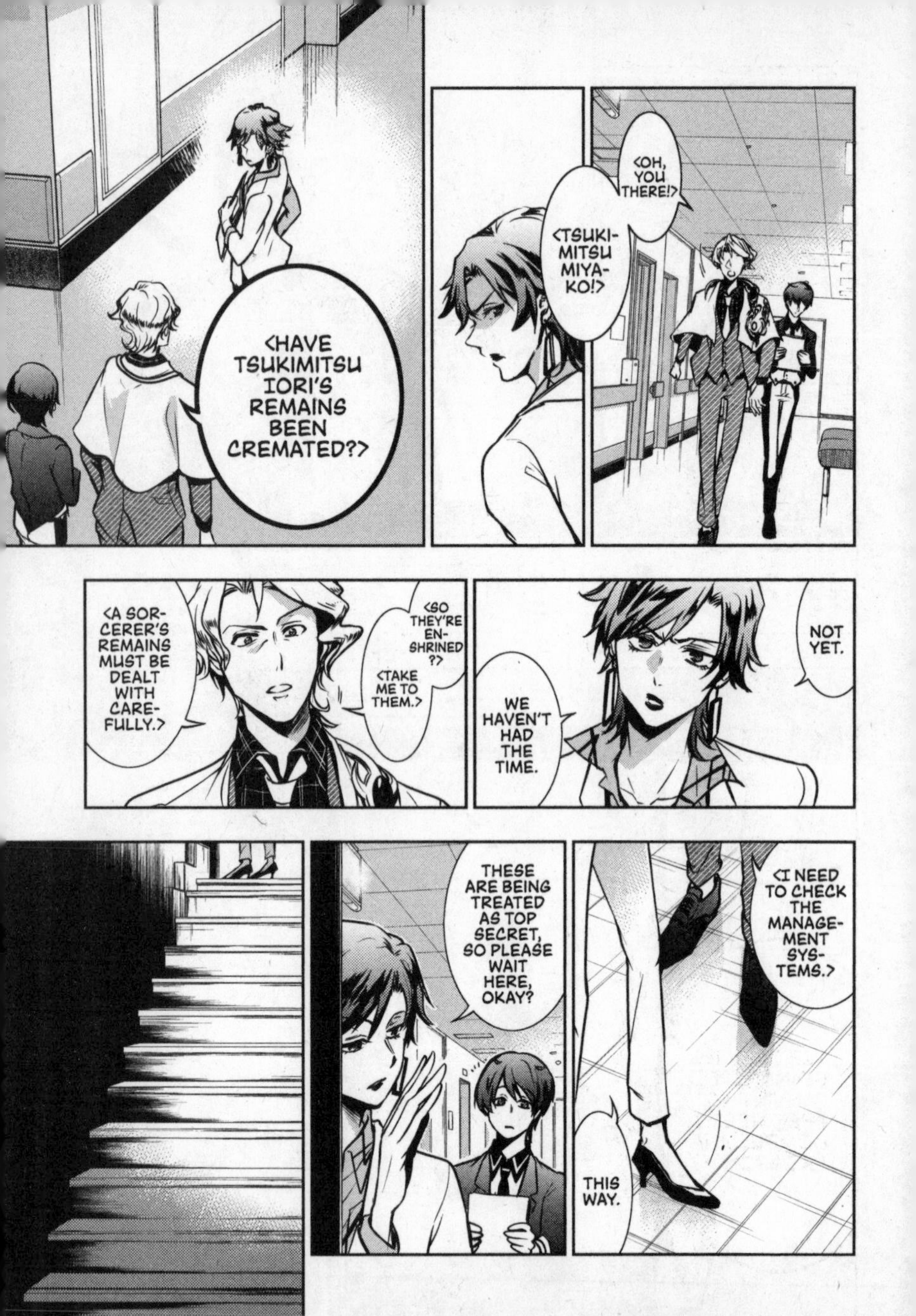
<OH, YOU THERE!>
<TSUKIMITSU MIYAKO!>
<HAVE TSUKIMITSU IORI'S REMAINS BEEN CREMATED?>
NOT YET.
WE HAVEN'T HAD THE TIME.
<SO THEY'RE ENSHRINED?>
<TAKE ME TO THEM.>
<A SORCERER'S REMAINS MUST BE DEALT WITH CAREFULLY.>
<I NEED TO CHECK THE MANAGEMENT SYSTEMS.>
THIS WAY.
THESE ARE BEING TREATED AS TOP SECRET, SO PLEASE WAIT HERE, OKAY?

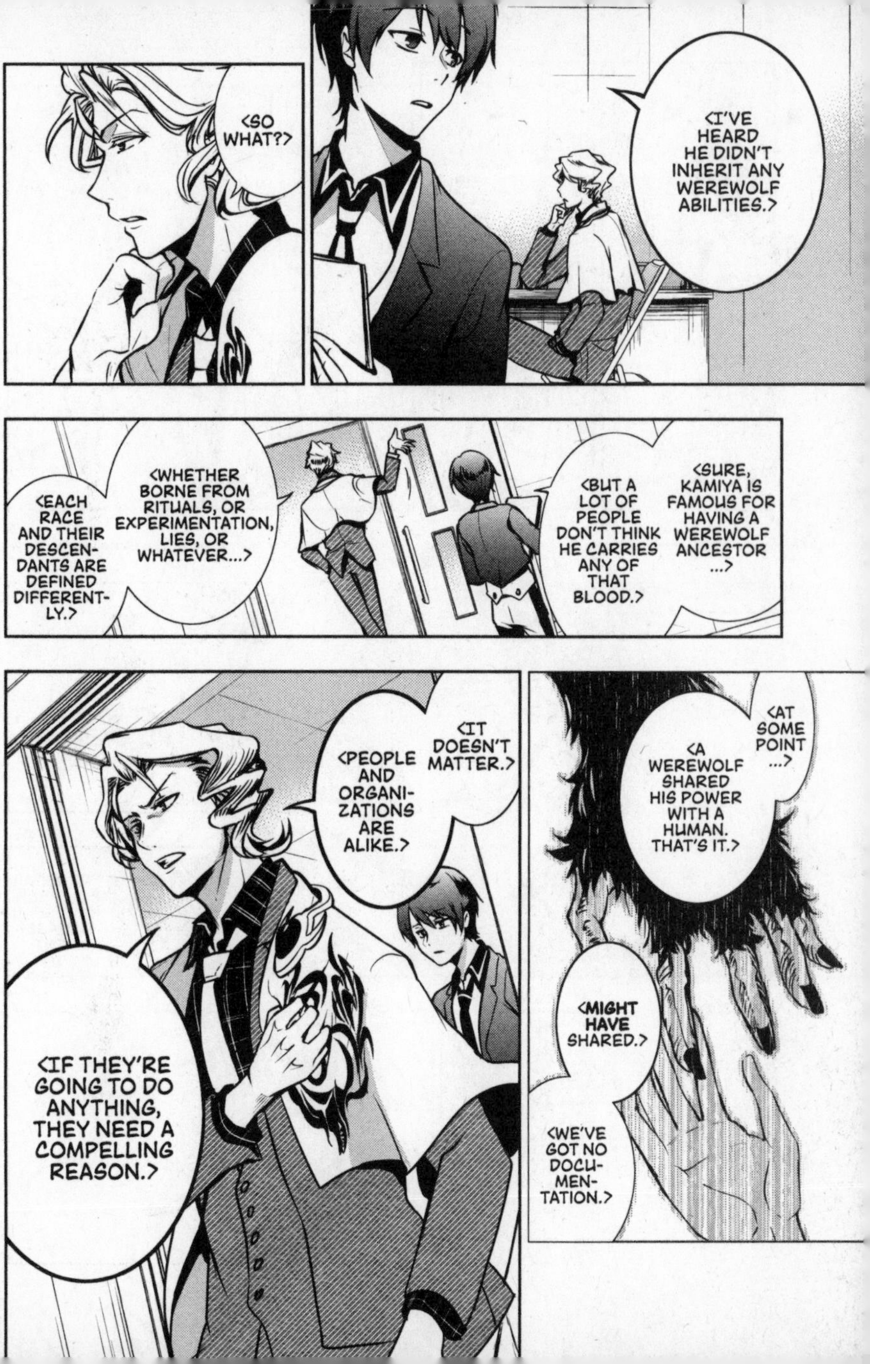
<I'VE HEARD HE DIDN'T INHERIT ANY WEREWOLF ABILITIES.>
<SO WHAT?>
<SURE, KAMIYA IS FAMOUS FOR HAVING A WEREWOLF ANCESTOR ...>
<BUT A LOT OF PEOPLE DON'T THINK HE CARRIES ANY OF THAT BLOOD.>
<WHETHER BORNE FROM RITUALS, OR EXPERIMENTATION, LIES, OR WHATEVER...>
<EACH RACE AND THEIR DESCEN-DANTS ARE DEFINED DIFFERENTLY.>
<AT SOME POINT ...>
<A WEREWOLF SHARED HIS POWER WITH A HUMAN. THAT'S IT.>
<**MIGHT HAVE** SHARED.>
<WE'VE GOT NO DOCU-MEN-TATION.>
<IT DOESN'T MATTER.>
<PEOPLE AND ORGANI-ZATIONS ARE ALIKE.>
<IF THEY'RE GOING TO DO ANYTHING, THEY NEED A COMPELLING REASON.>

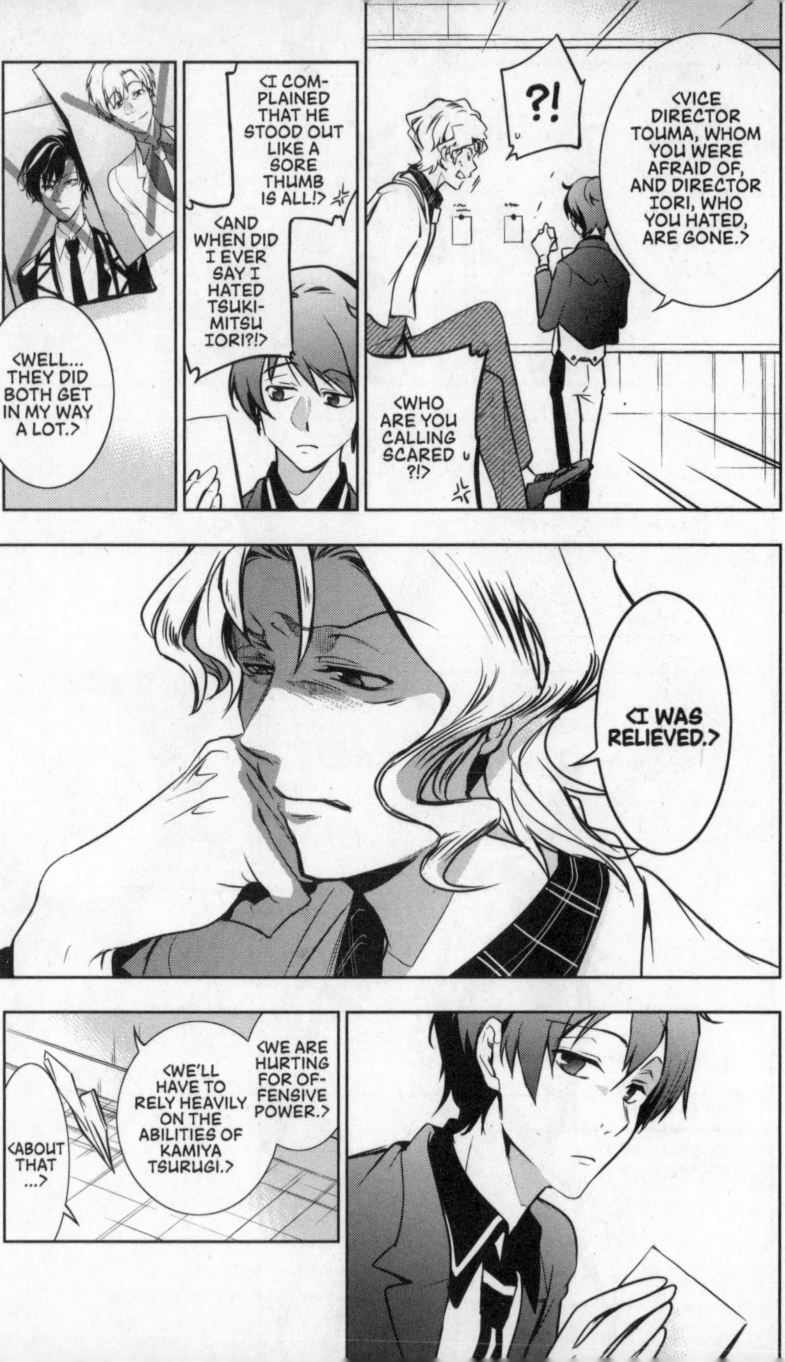
<VICE DIRECTOR TOUMA, WHOM YOU WERE AFRAID OF, AND DIRECTOR IORI, WHO YOU HATED, ARE GONE.>
?!
<WHO ARE YOU CALLING SCARED?!>
<I COMPLAINED THAT HE STOOD OUT LIKE A SORE THUMB IS ALL!>
<AND WHEN DID I EVER SAY I HATED TSUKIMITSU IORI?!>
<WELL... THEY DID BOTH GET IN MY WAY A LOT.>
<I WAS RELIEVED.>
<WE ARE HURTING FOR OFFENSIVE POWER.>
<WE'LL HAVE TO RELY HEAVILY ON THE ABILITIES OF KAMIYA TSURUGI.>
<ABOUT THAT ...>

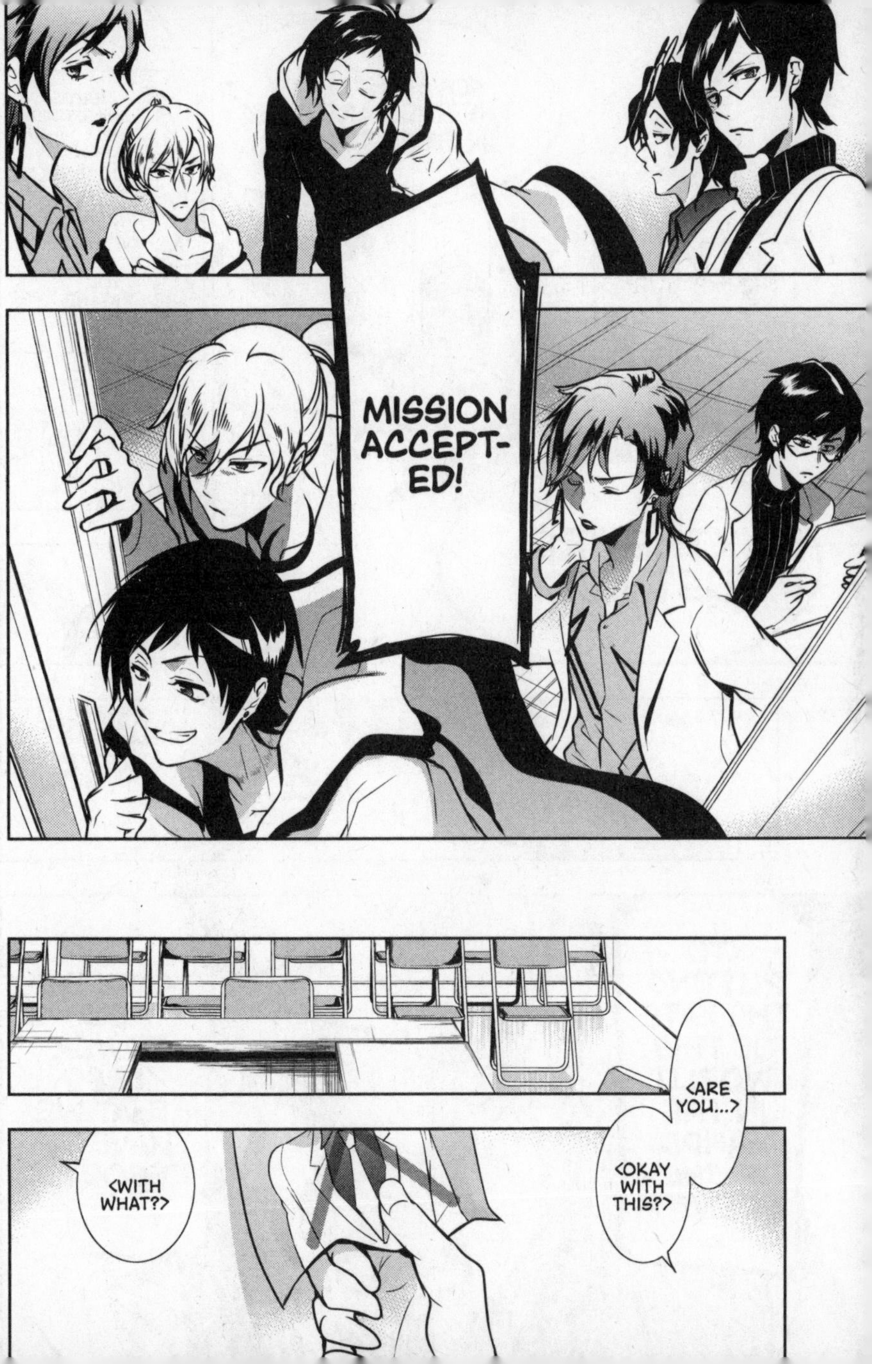
MISSION ACCEPT-ED!
<ARE YOU...>
<OKAY WITH THIS?>
<WITH WHAT?>

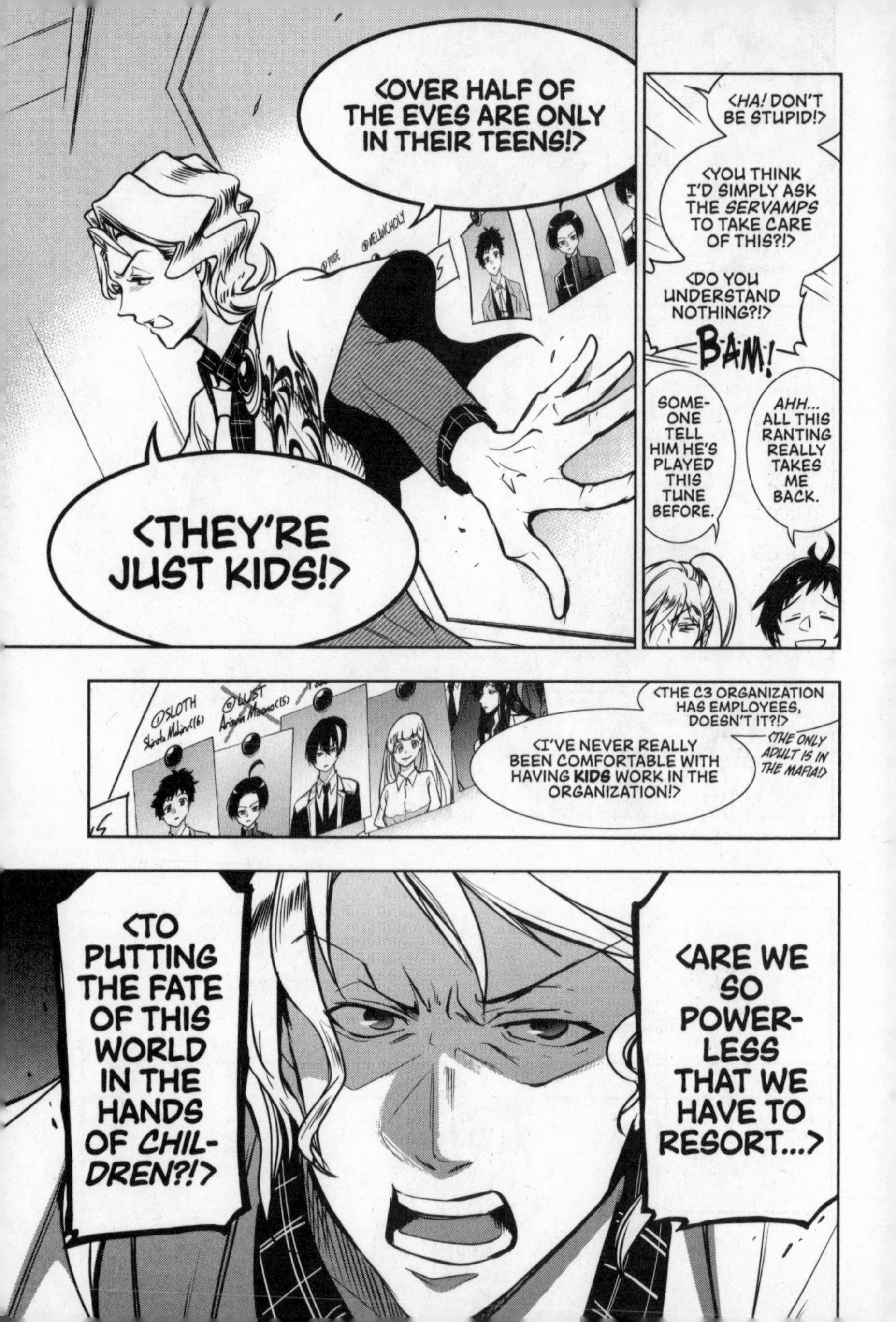
<HA! DON'T BE STUPID!>
<YOU THINK I'D SIMPLY ASK THE *SERVAMPS* TO TAKE CARE OF THIS?!>
<DO YOU UNDERSTAND NOTHING?!>
BAM!
AHH... ALL THIS RANTING REALLY TAKES ME BACK.
SOME-ONE TELL HIM HE'S PLAYED THIS TUNE BEFORE.
<OVER HALF OF THE EVES ARE ONLY IN THEIR TEENS!>
<THEY'RE JUST KIDS!>
<THE C3 ORGANIZATION HAS EMPLOYEES, DOESN'T IT?!>
<THE ONLY ADULT IS IN THE MAFIA!>
<I'VE NEVER REALLY BEEN COMFORTABLE WITH HAVING **KIDS** WORK IN THE ORGANIZATION!>
SLOTH
LUST
<ARE WE SO POWER-LESS THAT WE HAVE TO RESORT...>
<TO PUTTING THE FATE OF THIS WORLD IN THE HANDS OF *CHIL-DREN*?!>

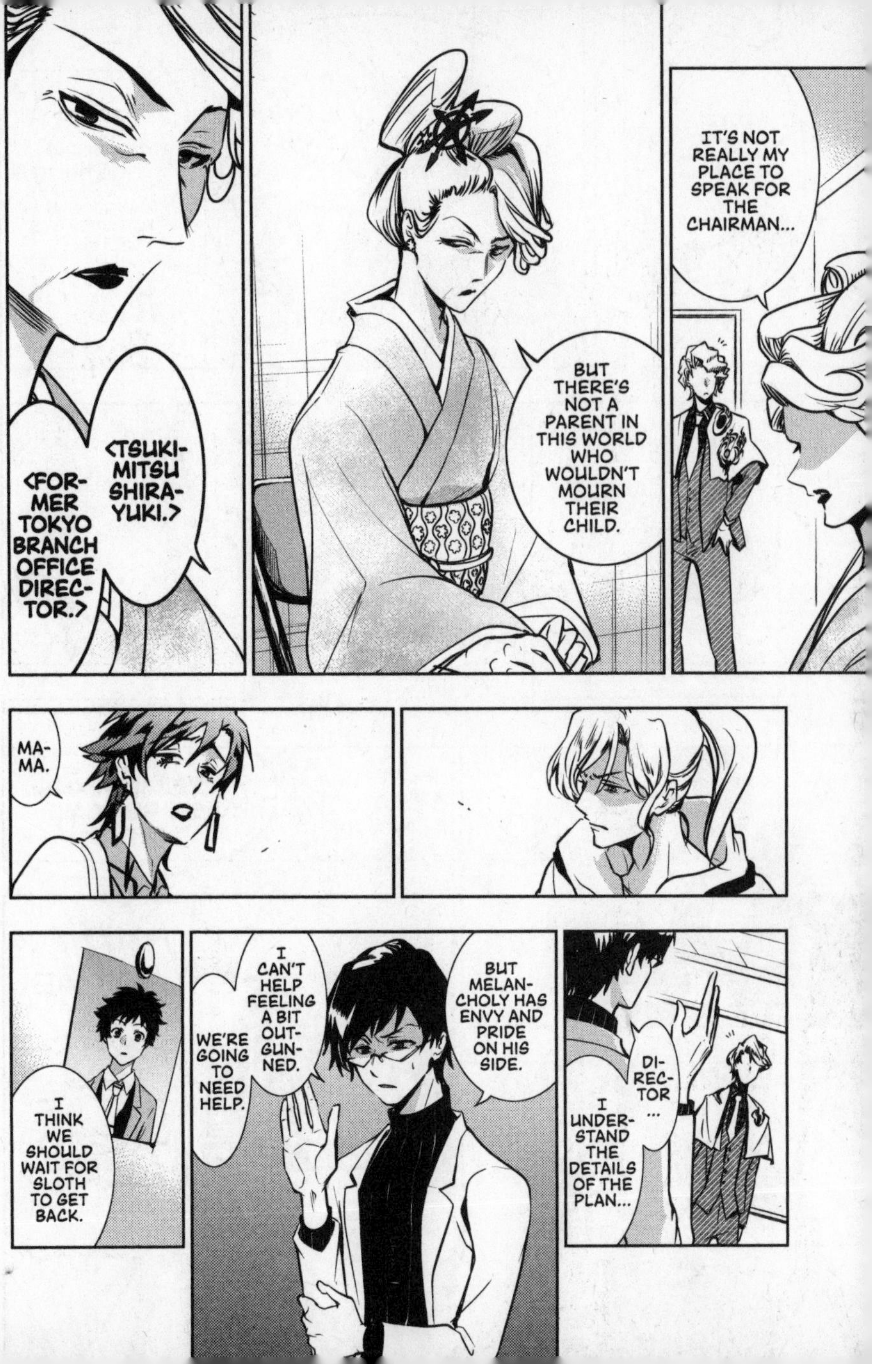
IT'S NOT REALLY MY PLACE TO SPEAK FOR THE CHAIRMAN...
BUT THERE'S NOT A PARENT IN THIS WORLD WHO WOULDN'T MOURN THEIR CHILD.
<TSUKIMITSU SHIRAYUKI.>
<FORMER TOKYO BRANCH OFFICE DIRECTOR.>
MAMA.
DIRECTOR...
I UNDERSTAND THE DETAILS OF THE PLAN...
BUT MELANCHOLY HAS ENVY AND PRIDE ON HIS SIDE.
I CAN'T HELP FEELING A BIT OUTGUNNED.
WE'RE GOING TO NEED HELP.
I THINK WE SHOULD WAIT FOR SLOTH TO GET BACK.

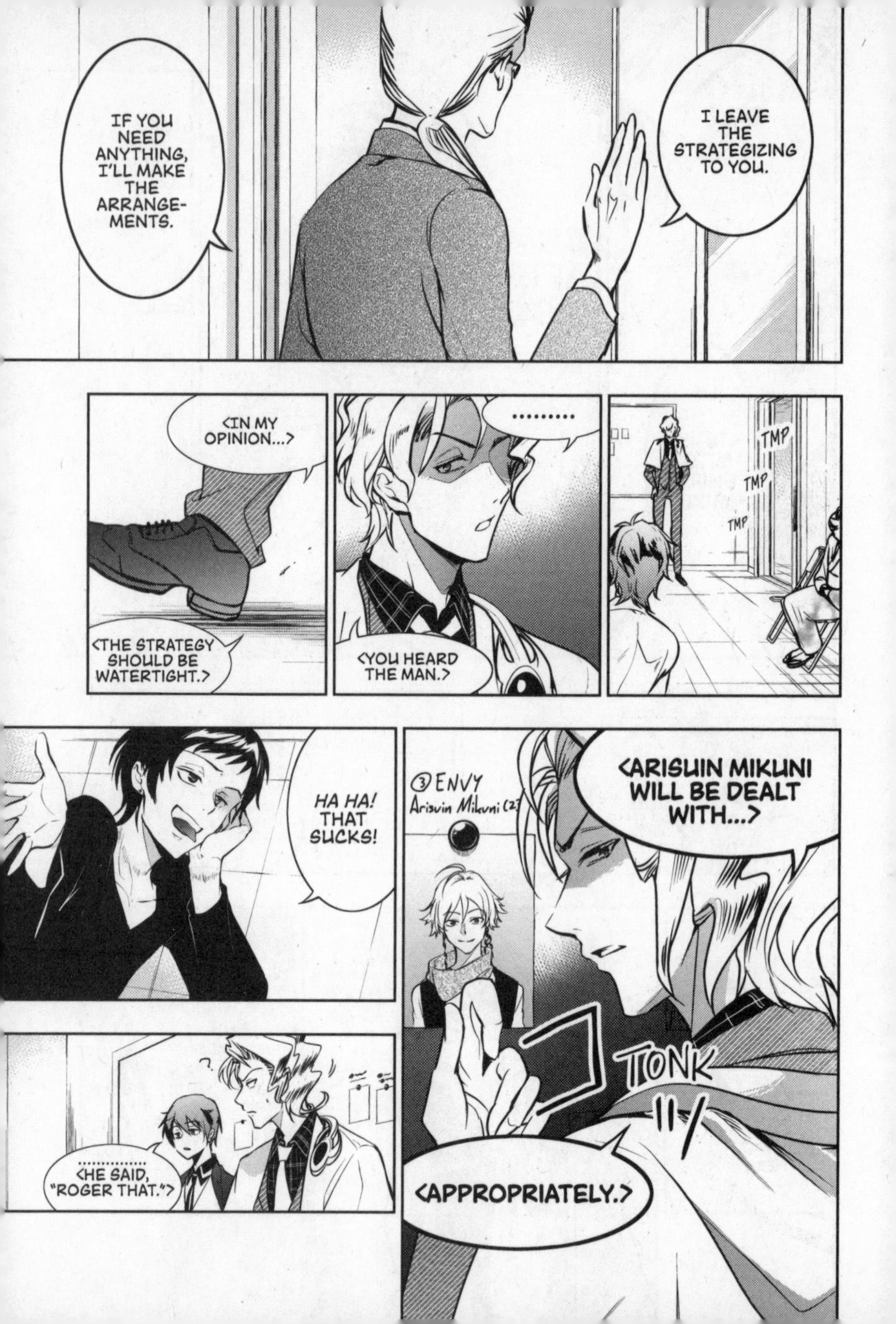
I LEAVE THE STRATEGIZING TO YOU.
IF YOU NEED ANYTHING, I'LL MAKE THE ARRANGE-MENTS.
TMP
TMP
TMP
....
<YOU HEARD THE MAN.>
<IN MY OPINION...>
<THE STRATEGY SHOULD BE WATERTIGHT.>
③ ENVY
Arisuin Mikuni
<ARISUIN MIKUNI WILL BE DEALT WITH...>
TONK
<APPROPRIATELY.>
HA HA! THAT SUCKS!
....
<HE SAID, "ROGER THAT.">

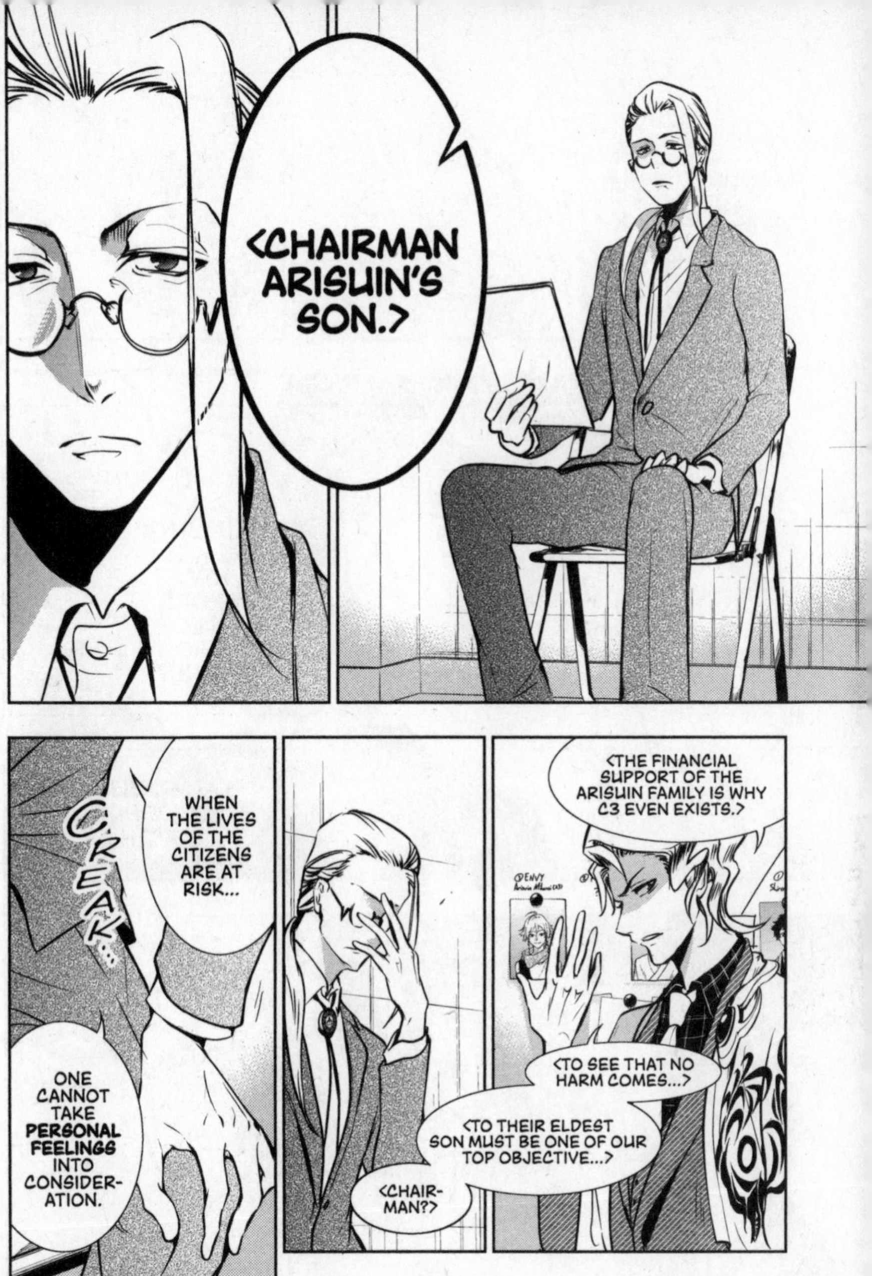
<CHAIRMAN ARISUIN'S SON.>
<THE FINANCIAL SUPPORT OF THE ARISUIN FAMILY IS WHY C3 EVEN EXISTS.>
<TO SEE THAT NO HARM COMES...>
<TO THEIR ELDEST SON MUST BE ONE OF OUR TOP OBJECTIVE...>
<CHAIR-MAN?>
WHEN THE LIVES OF THE CITIZENS ARE AT RISK...
CREAK...
ONE CANNOT TAKE PERSONAL FEELINGS INTO CONSIDER-ATION.

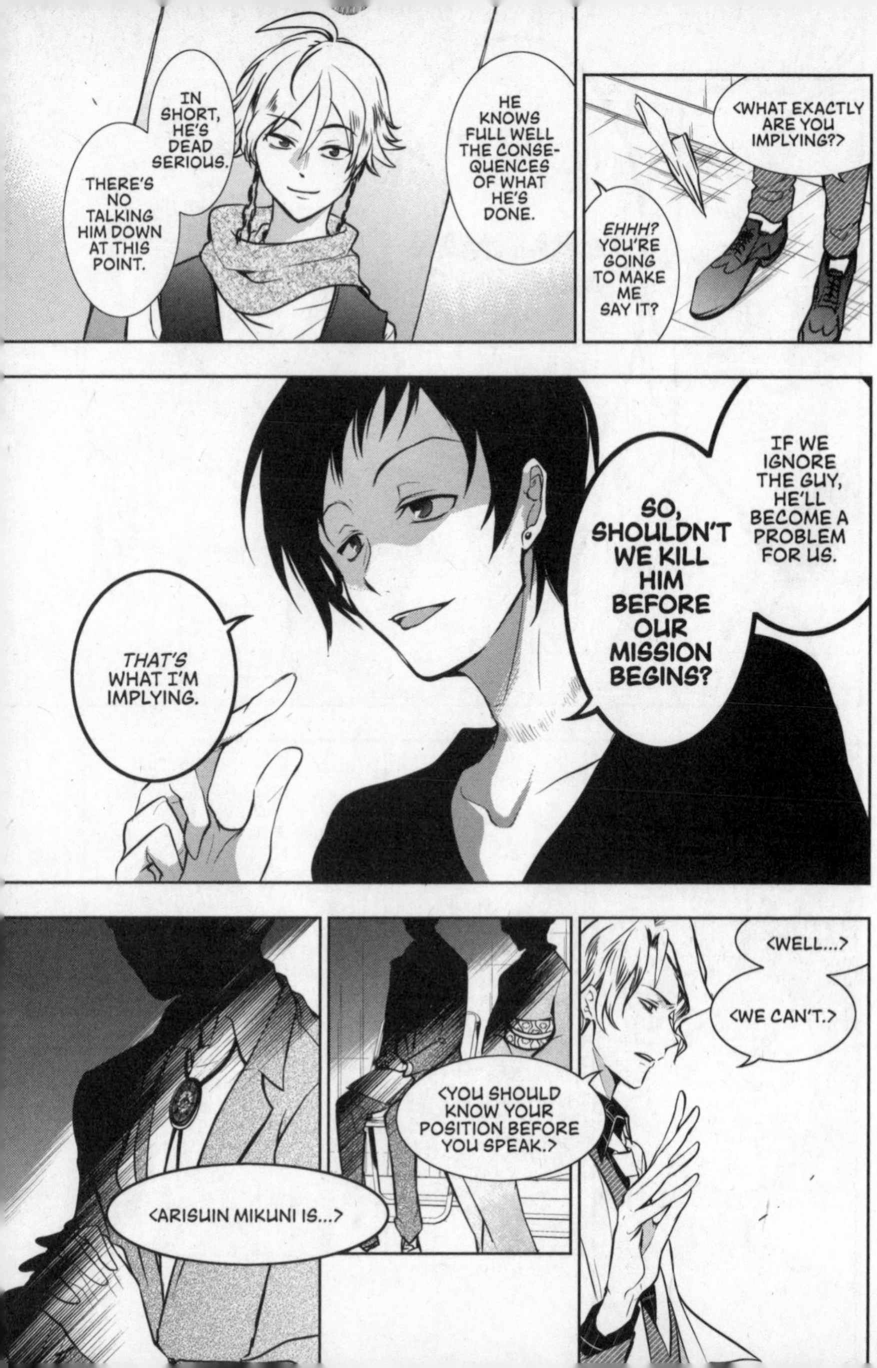
<WHAT EXACTLY ARE YOU IMPLYING?>
EHHH? YOU'RE GOING TO MAKE ME SAY IT?
HE KNOWS FULL WELL THE CONSEQUENCES OF WHAT HE'S DONE.
IN SHORT, HE'S DEAD SERIOUS.
THERE'S NO TALKING HIM DOWN AT THIS POINT.
IF WE IGNORE THE GUY, HE'LL BECOME A PROBLEM FOR US.
SO, SHOULDN'T WE KILL HIM BEFORE OUR MISSION BEGINS?
THAT'S WHAT I'M IMPLYING.
<WELL...>
<WE CAN'T.>
<YOU SHOULD KNOW YOUR POSITION BEFORE YOU SPEAK.>
<ARISUIN MIKUNI IS...>

EHHH? IN THAT CASE, WHY DON'T YOU JUST BUFF ME DIRECTLY?

‹I CAN'T KEEP THIS UP FULL STRENGTH AS YOU'LL BE CONSTANTLY CHANGING POSITION WHILE IN BATTLE.›

‹FURTHERMORE, THE EFFECT IS MUCH HIGHER ON A SNIPER WHO WON'T BE MOVING AT ALL..›

AH. IT'S A SYNCHRONOUS ABILITY.

‹ENHANCEMENT MAGIC!›

‹I CAN INSTANTLY HEIGHTEN THE ABILITIES OF ANY MAGICIAN.›

‹I CAN INCREASE A SNIPER'S PRECISION AND POWER DRAMATICALLY.›

MEEE!

‹DOES ANYONE HAVE ANY QUESTIONS...›

‹ABOUT THE PLAN, OR ANYTHING ELSE?›

WOULDN'T THIS BE THE PERFECT TIME TO TAKE HIM OUT?

WHAT...

SHOULD WE DO ABOUT KUNI--CHA--ER... ARISUIN MIKUNI?

<WELL, OF COURSE HE WILL.>

MELANCHO

THERE'S NO WAY WE'LL HIT HIM. HE'LL DODGE.

<OR SO THEY'LL THINK.>

<THAT'S WHY I'M HERE!>

WHAT ?!

YOU'RE NOTORIOUS FOR NEVER BEING ON THE FRONT LINES!

<THEN WE'LL ATTACK FROM HIS BLIND SPOTS.>

...?!

<A COMMANDER...>

<CANNOT BE TAKEN DOWN AT THE START OF A BATTLE!>

<HE MUST WATCH FROM AFAR AS EVENTS UNFOLD ON THE BATTLEFIELD UNTIL THE END!>

<YOU REALLY DON'T KNOW?!>

<MY SPECIALTY IS...>

SO, WHAT EXACTLY CAN YOU DO, MR. DIRECTOR?

<IN THREE DAYS, ON AUGUST 31ST...>

<WE TAKE OUT TSUBAKI AT THAT SHRINE...>

<AND STOP THIS REINCARNATION RITUAL FROM ROBBING THE LIVES OF MILLIONS OF PEOPLE!>

YOU WANT ME TO FACE OFF WITH THE LITTLE FOXIE~?

<WE DON'T HAVE THE FIREPOWER TO WITH-STAND OUR ENEMY'S QUICK STRIKES.>

<YOU'RE THE ONLY ONE WE CAN TURN TO.>

<AS I STATED EARLIER...>

<KAMIYA TSU-RUGI WILL BE ON THE FRONT LINES OF THIS FIGHT.>

<DUE TO THE FULL MOON, HIS ANCESTRAL WEREWOLF BLOOD SHOULD ACTIVATE.>

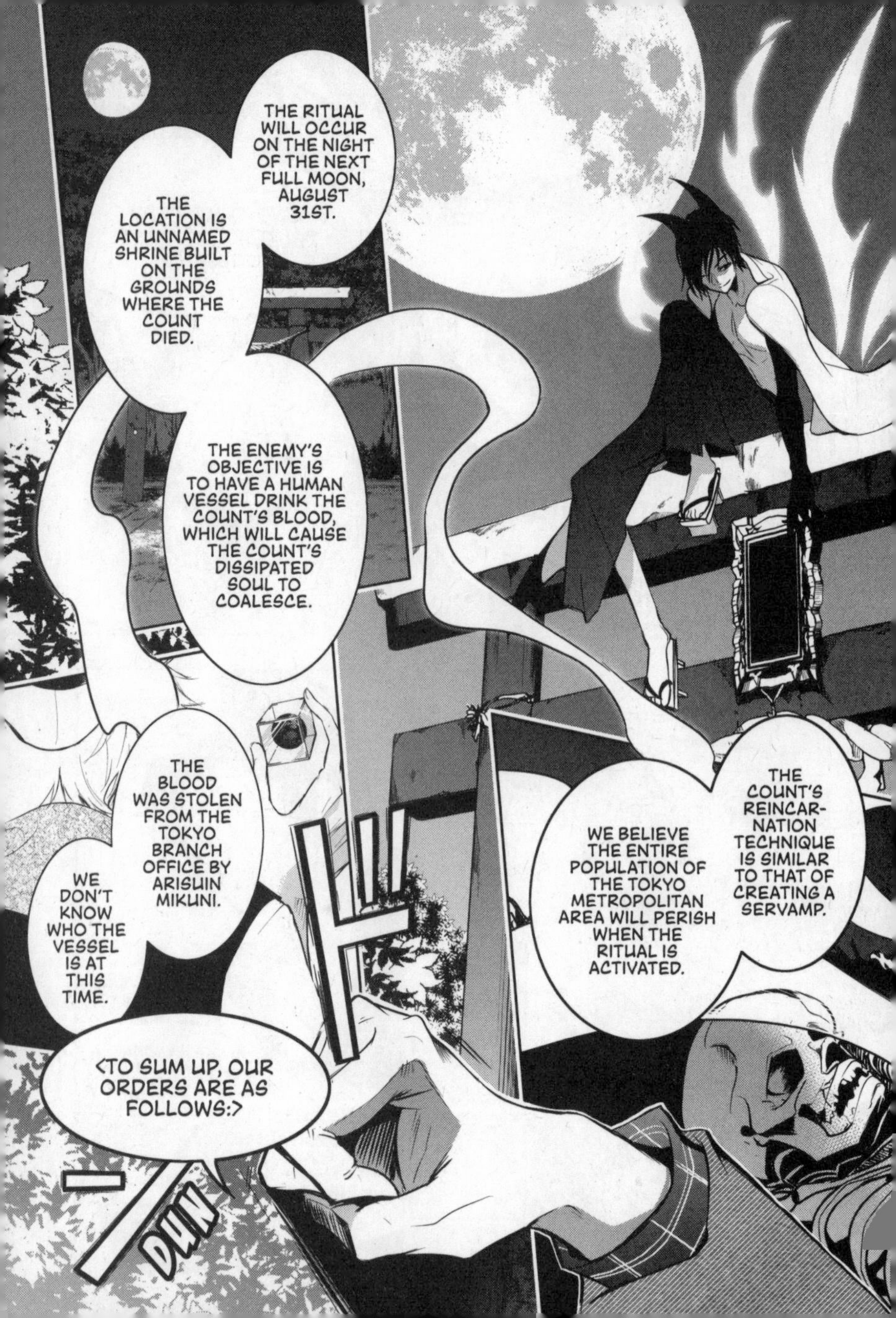

THE RITUAL WILL OCCUR ON THE NIGHT OF THE NEXT FULL MOON, AUGUST 31ST.
THE LOCATION IS AN UNNAMED SHRINE BUILT ON THE GROUNDS WHERE THE COUNT DIED.
THE ENEMY'S OBJECTIVE IS TO HAVE A HUMAN VESSEL DRINK THE COUNT'S BLOOD, WHICH WILL CAUSE THE COUNT'S DISSIPATED SOUL TO COALESCE.
THE COUNT'S REINCARNATION TECHNIQUE IS SIMILAR TO THAT OF CREATING A SERVAMP.
WE BELIEVE THE ENTIRE POPULATION OF THE TOKYO METROPOLITAN AREA WILL PERISH WHEN THE RITUAL IS ACTIVATED.
THE BLOOD WAS STOLEN FROM THE TOKYO BRANCH OFFICE BY ARISUIN MIKUNI.
WE DON'T KNOW WHO THE VESSEL IS AT THIS TIME.
<TO SUM UP, OUR ORDERS ARE AS FOLLOWS:>
DUN

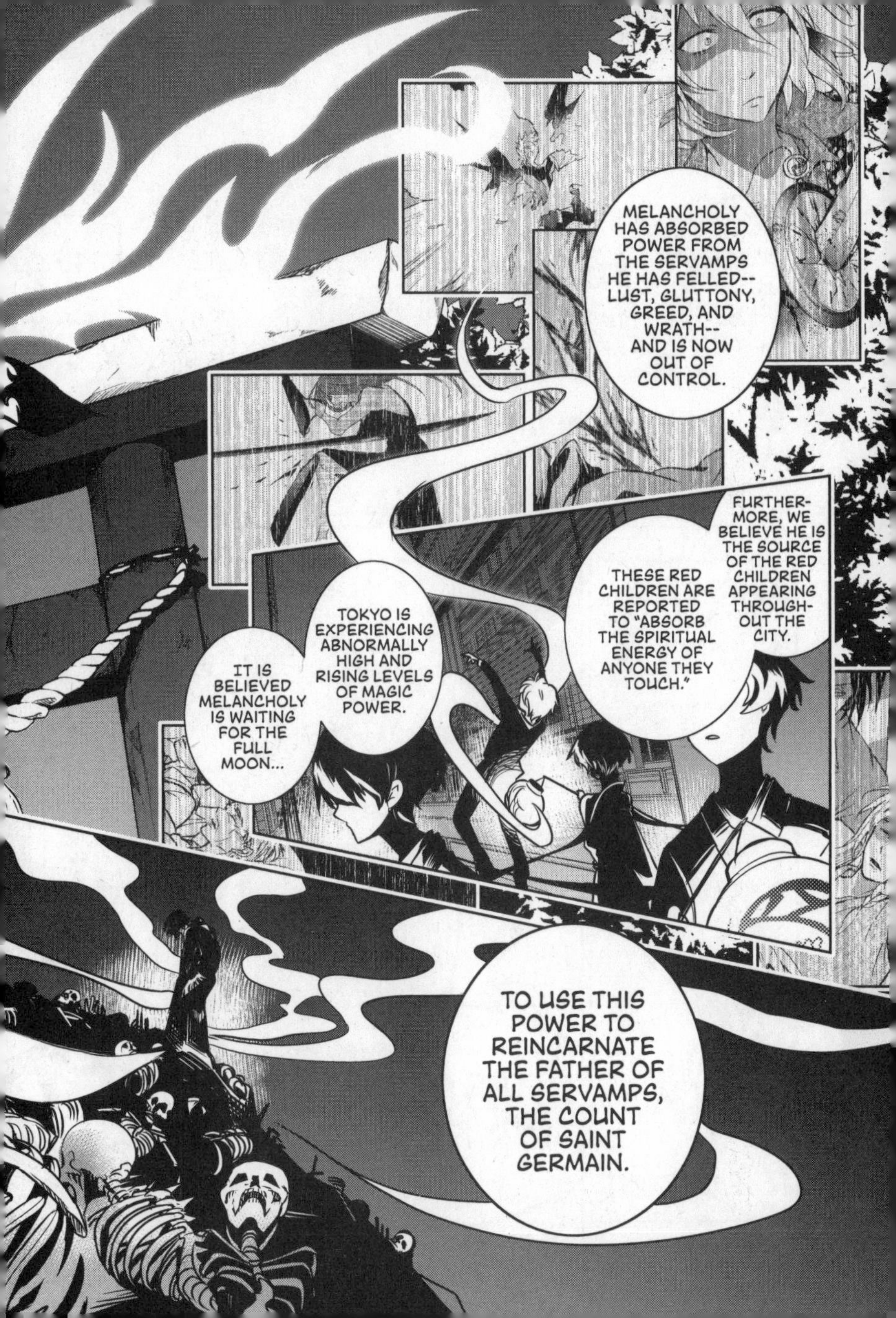
MELANCHOLY HAS ABSORBED POWER FROM THE SERVAMPS HE HAS FELLED--LUST, GLUTTONY, GREED, AND WRATH--AND IS NOW OUT OF CONTROL.
FURTHER-MORE, WE BELIEVE HE IS THE SOURCE OF THE RED CHILDREN APPEARING THROUGH-OUT THE CITY.
THESE RED CHILDREN ARE REPORTED TO "ABSORB THE SPIRITUAL ENERGY OF ANYONE THEY TOUCH."
TOKYO IS EXPERIENCING ABNORMALLY HIGH AND RISING LEVELS OF MAGIC POWER.
IT IS BELIEVED MELANCHOLY IS WAITING FOR THE FULL MOON...
TO USE THIS POWER TO REINCARNATE THE FATHER OF ALL SERVAMPS, THE COUNT OF SAINT GERMAIN.

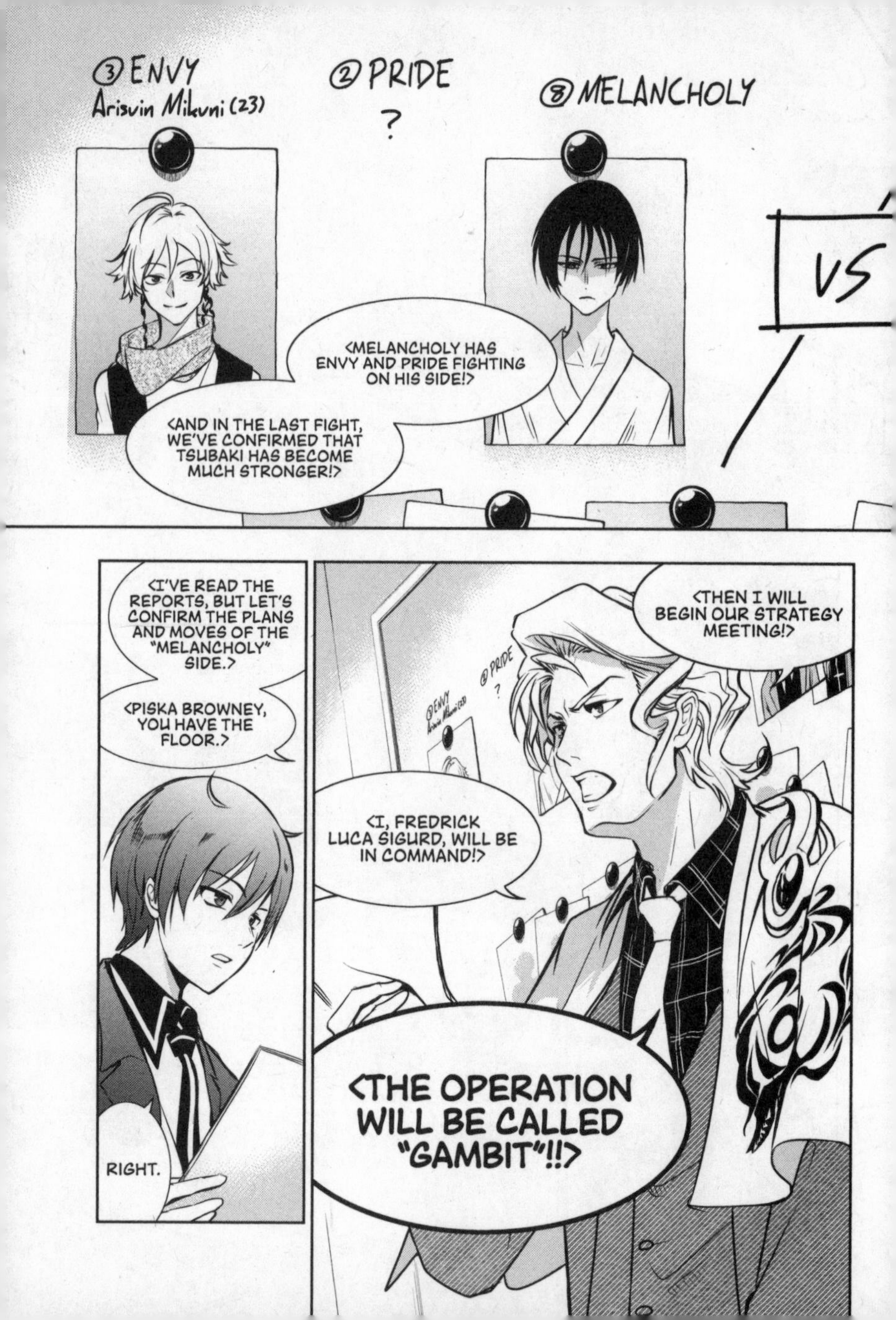
③ ENVY
Arisuin Mikuni (23)
② PRIDE
?
⑧ MELANCHOLY
VS
<MELANCHOLY HAS ENVY AND PRIDE FIGHTING ON HIS SIDE!>
<AND IN THE LAST FIGHT, WE'VE CONFIRMED THAT TSUBAKI HAS BECOME MUCH STRONGER!>
<THEN I WILL BEGIN OUR STRATEGY MEETING!>
<I, FREDRICK LUCA SIGURD, WILL BE IN COMMAND!>
<THE OPERATION WILL BE CALLED "GAMBIT"!!>
<I'VE READ THE REPORTS, BUT LET'S CONFIRM THE PLANS AND MOVES OF THE "MELANCHOLY" SIDE.>
<PISKA BROWNEY, YOU HAVE THE FLOOR.>
RIGHT.

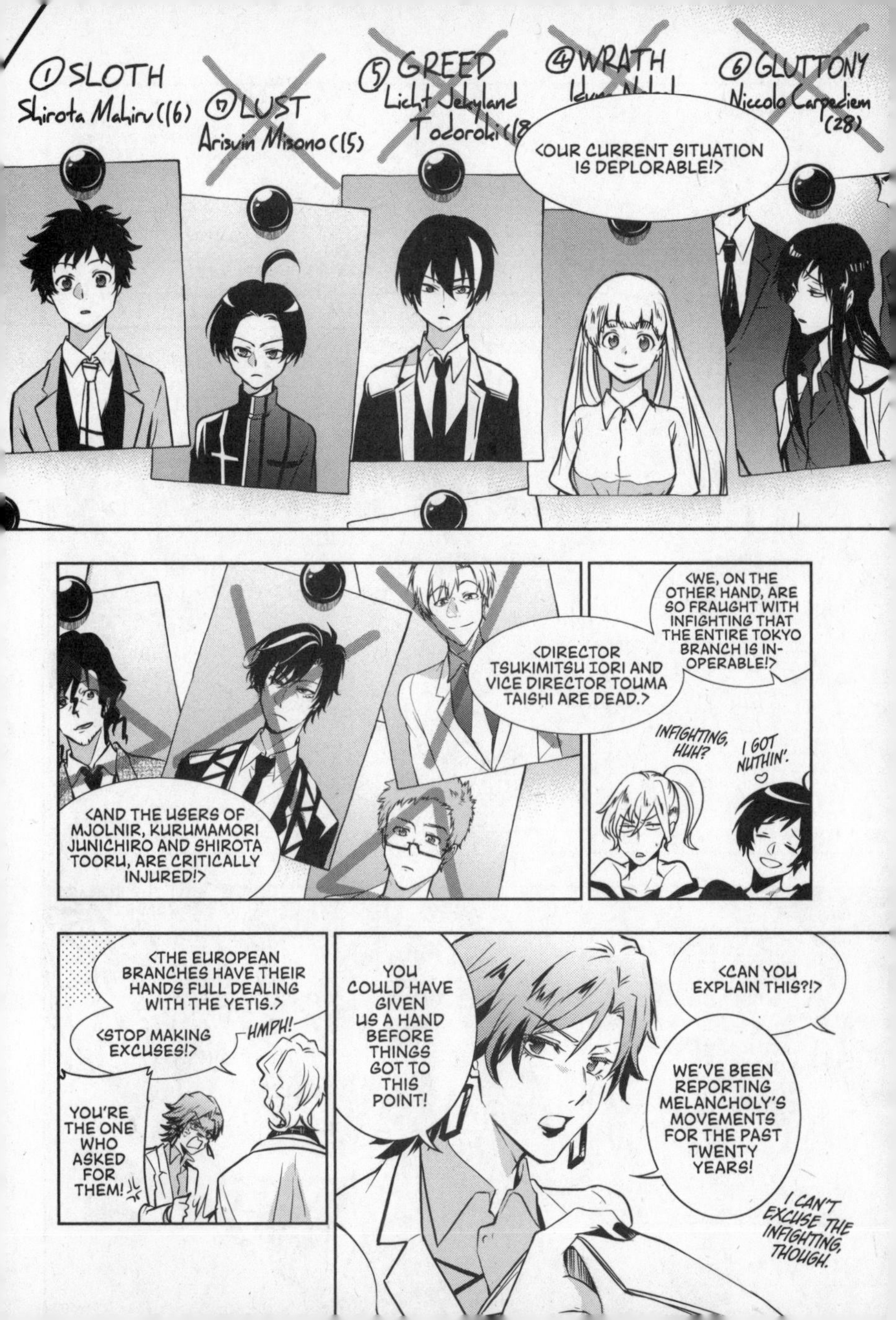

⑥ GLUTTONY
Niccolo Carpediem (28)
④ WRATH
⑤ GREED
Licht Jekyland Todoroki (18
⑦ LUST
Arisuin Misono (15)
① SLOTH
Shirota Mahiru (16)
<OUR CURRENT SITUATION IS DEPLORABLE!>
<WE, ON THE OTHER HAND, ARE SO FRAUGHT WITH INFIGHTING THAT THE ENTIRE TOKYO BRANCH IS IN-OPERABLE!>
INFIGHTING, HUH?
I GOT NUTHIN'.
<DIRECTOR TSUKIMITSU IORI AND VICE DIRECTOR TOUMA TAISHI ARE DEAD.>
<AND THE USERS OF MJOLNIR, KURUMAMORI JUNICHIRO AND SHIROTA TOORU, ARE CRITICALLY INJURED!>
<CAN YOU EXPLAIN THIS?!>
YOU COULD HAVE GIVEN US A HAND BEFORE THINGS GOT TO THIS POINT!
WE'VE BEEN REPORTING MELANCHOLY'S MOVEMENTS FOR THE PAST TWENTY YEARS!
I CAN'T EXCUSE THE INFIGHTING, THOUGH.
<THE EUROPEAN BRANCHES HAVE THEIR HANDS FULL DEALING WITH THE YETIS.>
<STOP MAKING EXCUSES!>
HMPH!
YOU'RE THE ONE WHO ASKED FOR THEM!

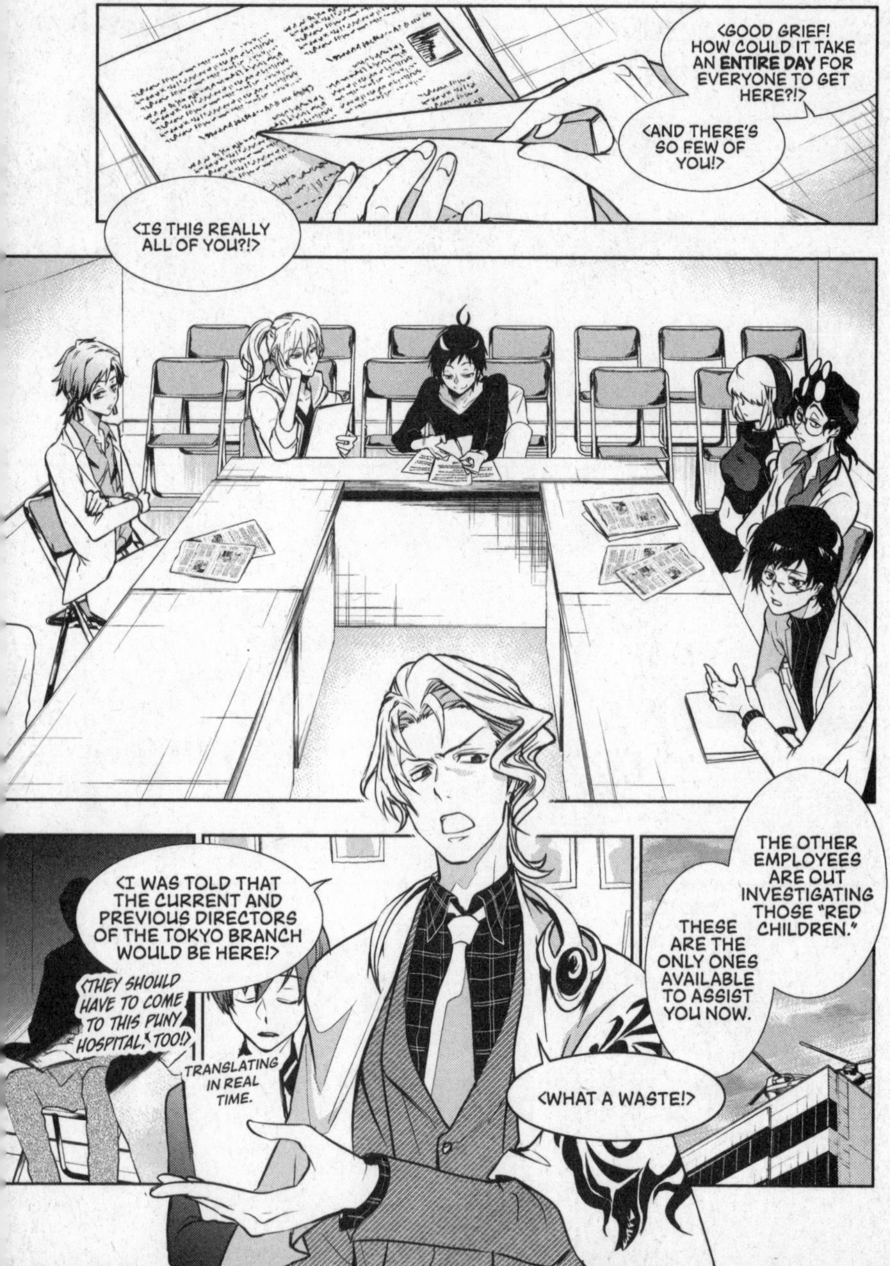
<GOOD GRIEF! HOW COULD IT TAKE AN **ENTIRE DAY** FOR EVERYONE TO GET HERE?!>
<AND THERE'S SO FEW OF YOU!>
<IS THIS REALLY ALL OF YOU?!>
THE OTHER EMPLOYEES ARE OUT INVESTIGATING THOSE "RED CHILDREN."
THESE ARE THE ONLY ONES AVAILABLE TO ASSIST YOU NOW.
<I WAS TOLD THAT THE CURRENT AND PREVIOUS DIRECTORS OF THE TOKYO BRANCH WOULD BE HERE!>
<THEY SHOULD HAVE TO COME TO THIS PUNY HOSPITAL, TOO!>
TRANSLATING IN REAL TIME.
<WHAT A WASTE!>

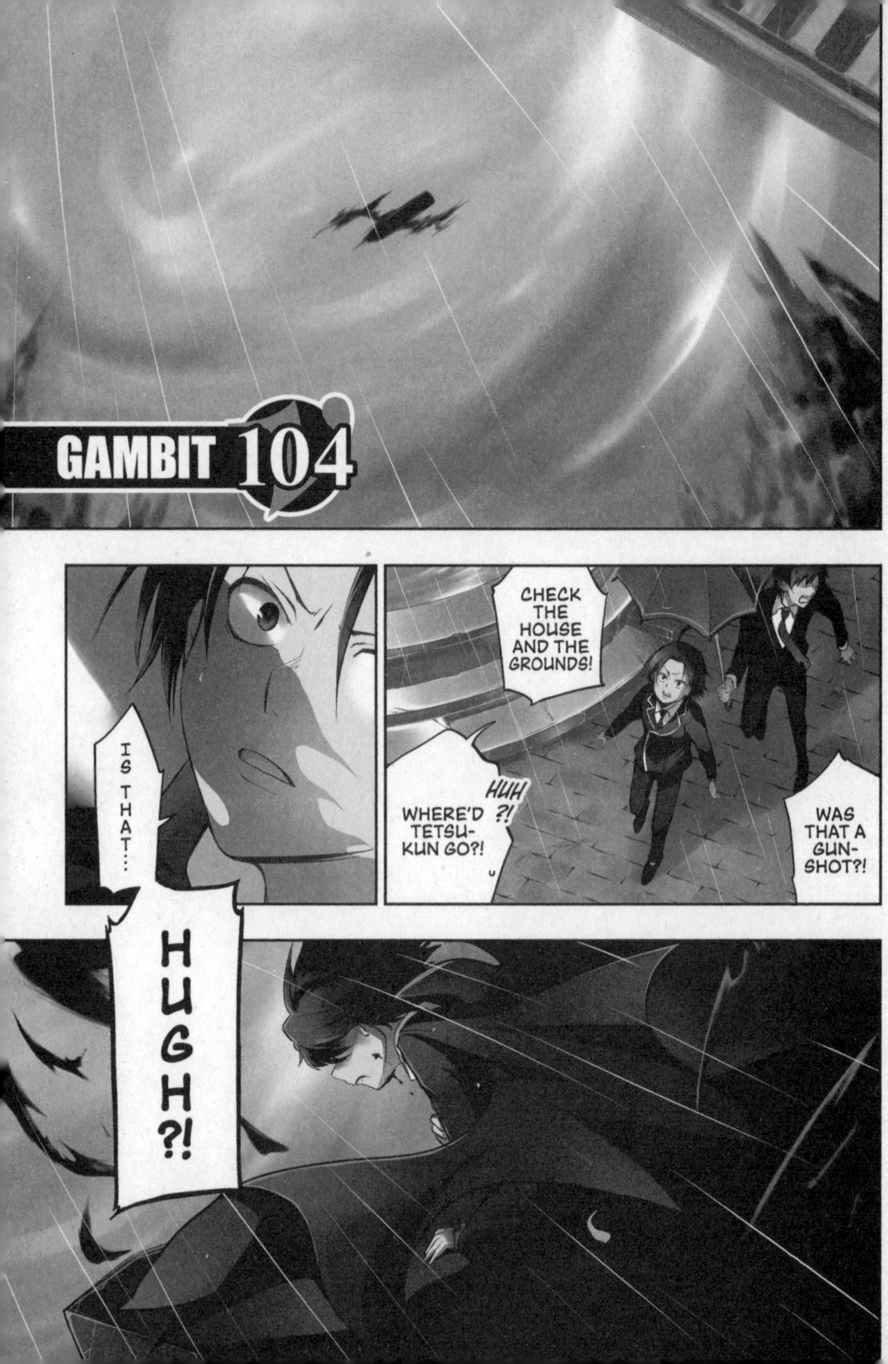
GAMBIT 104
CHECK THE HOUSE AND THE GROUNDS!
WAS THAT A GUN-SHOT?!
HUH ?!
WHERE'D TETSU-KUN GO?!
IS THAT...
HUGH?!

SERVAMP

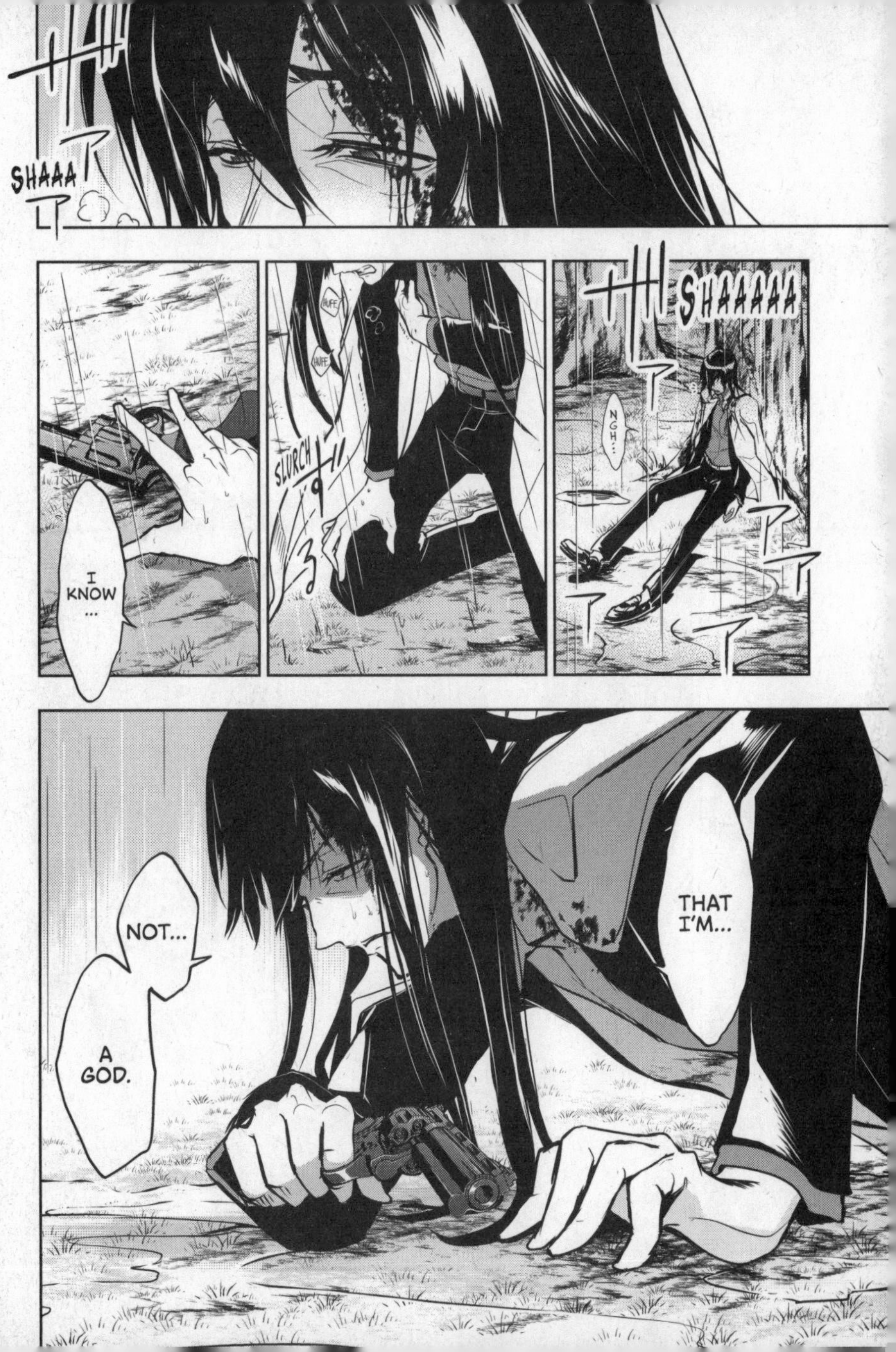
SHAAA
SHAAAAA
NGH...
HUFF
HUFF
SLURCH
I KNOW...
THAT I'M...
NOT...
A GOD.

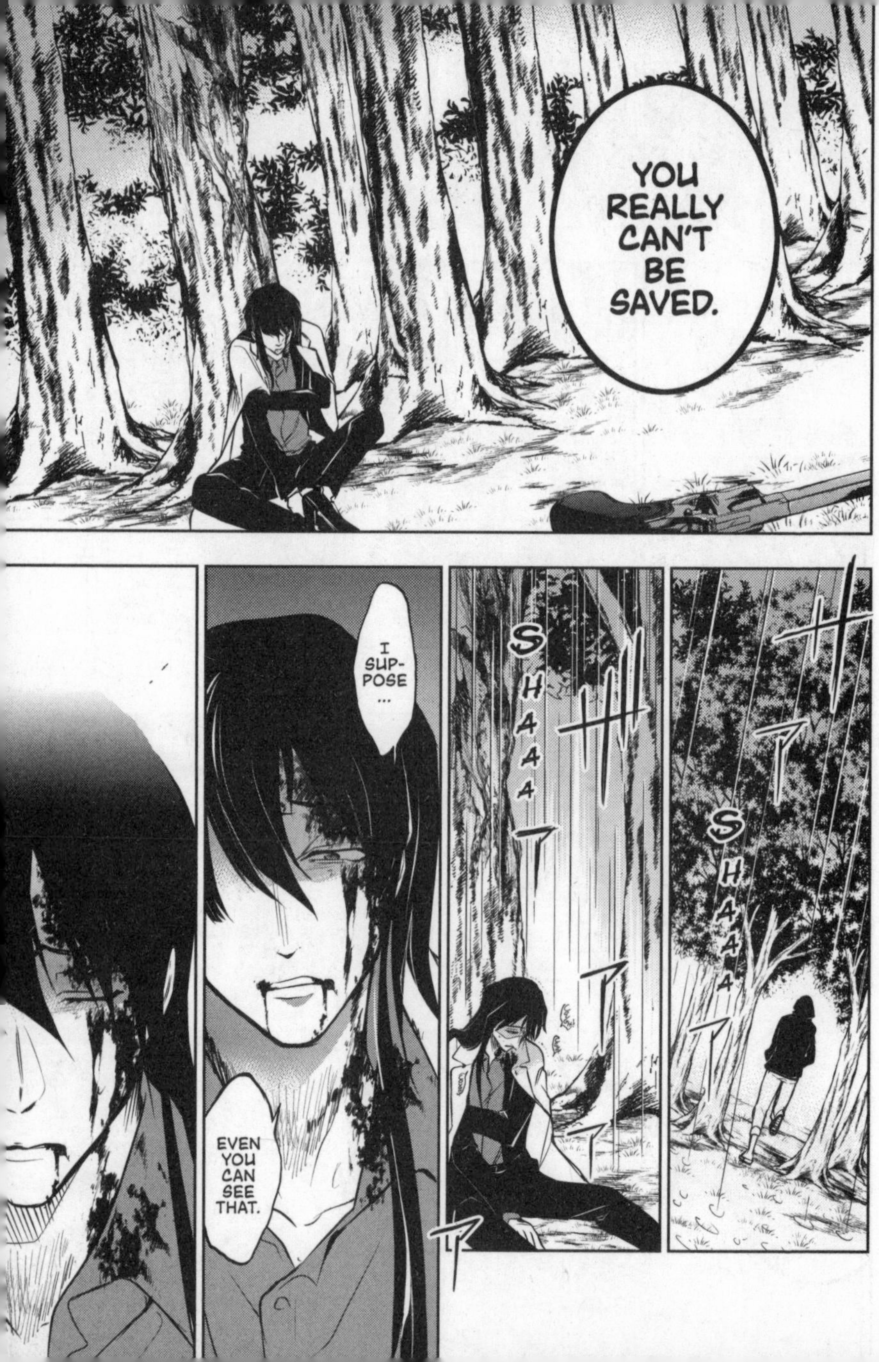
YOU REALLY CAN'T BE SAVED.
SHAAAA
SHAAAA
I SUP-POSE...
EVEN YOU CAN SEE THAT.

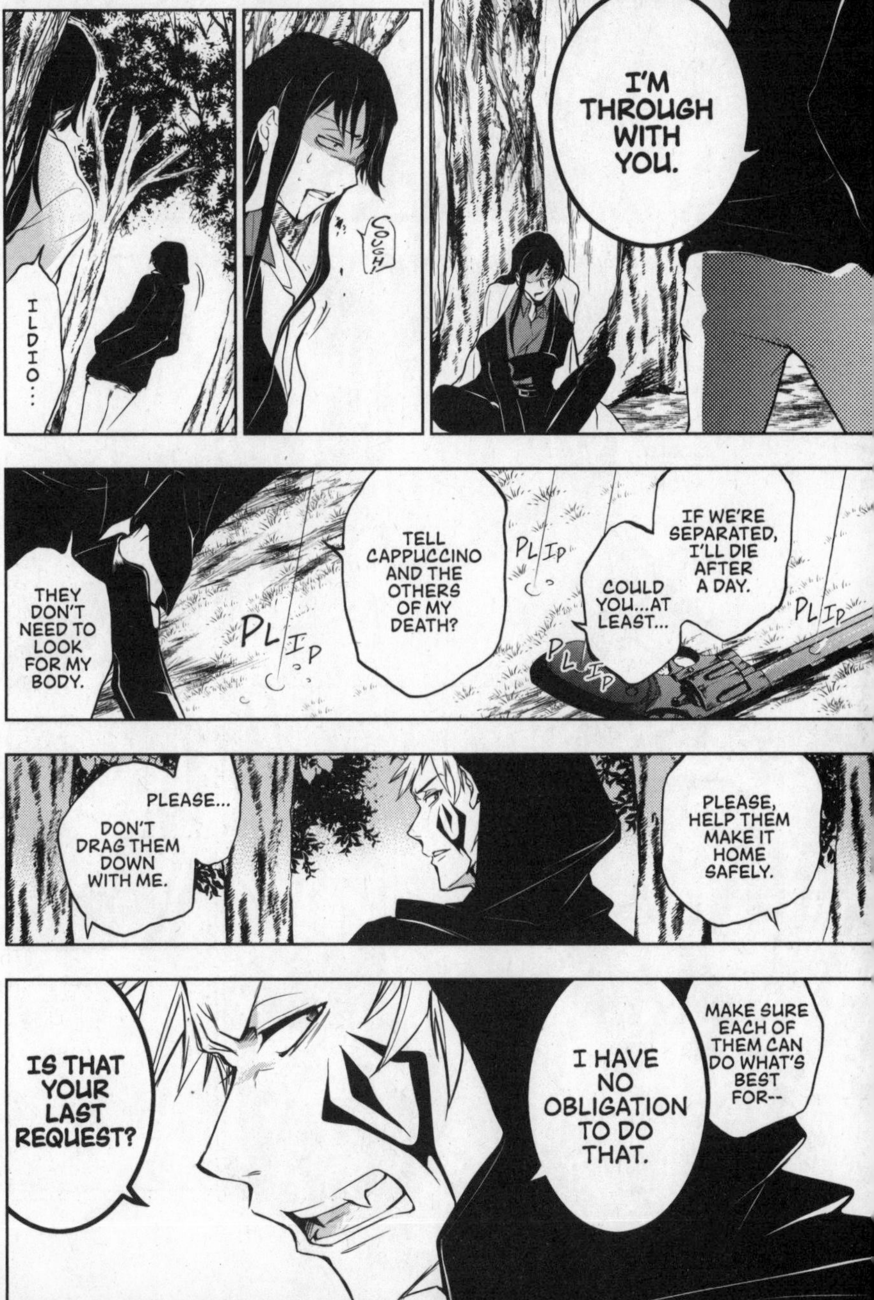
I'M THROUGH WITH YOU.
COUGH!
ILDIO...
IF WE'RE SEPARATED, I'LL DIE AFTER A DAY. COULD YOU...AT LEAST...
PLIP
PLIP
PLIP
TELL CAPPUCCINO AND THE OTHERS OF MY DEATH?
PLIP
THEY DON'T NEED TO LOOK FOR MY BODY.
PLEASE, HELP THEM MAKE IT HOME SAFELY.
PLEASE... DON'T DRAG THEM DOWN WITH ME.
MAKE SURE EACH OF THEM CAN DO WHAT'S BEST FOR--
I HAVE NO OBLIGATION TO DO THAT.
IS THAT YOUR LAST REQUEST?

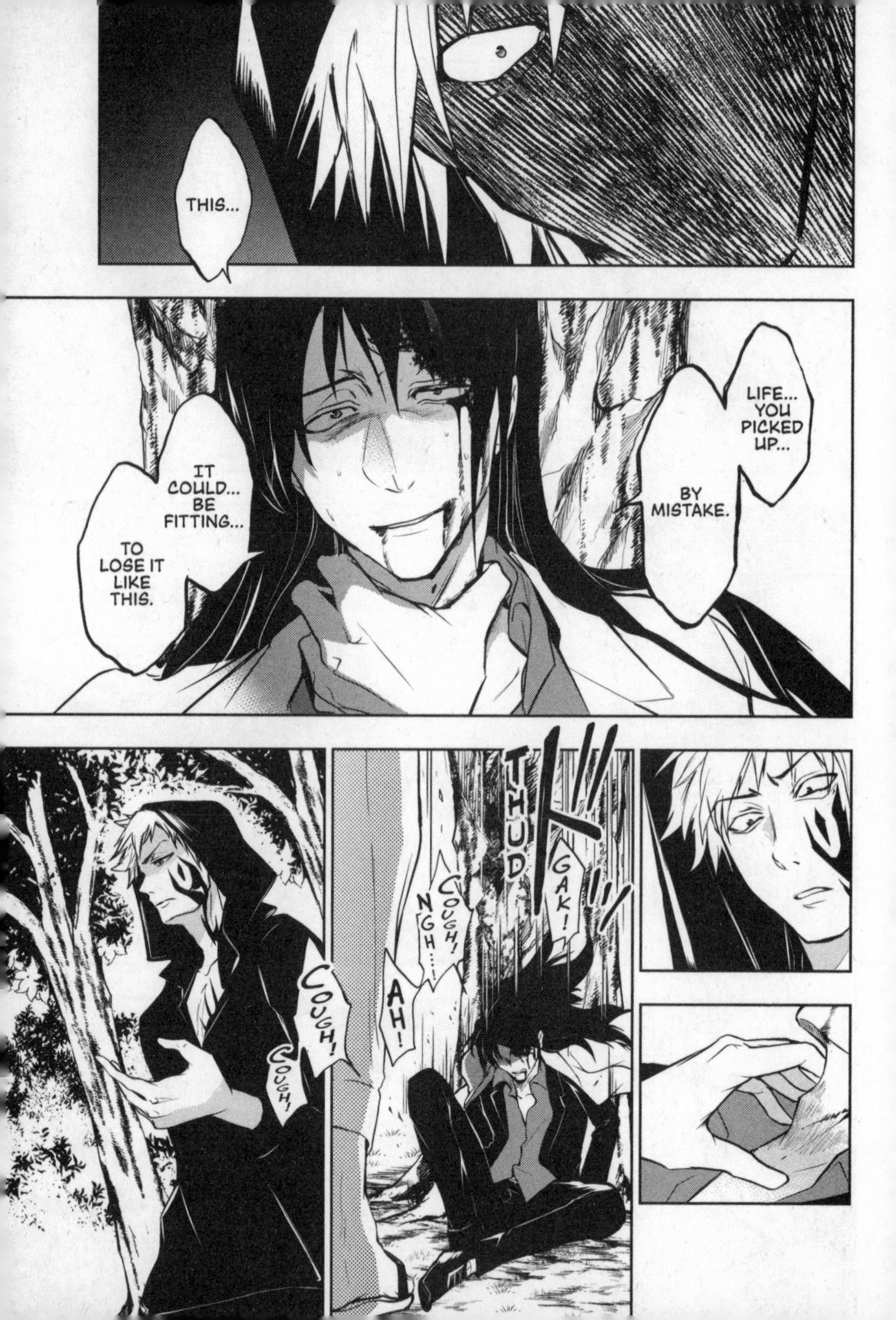
THIS...
LIFE... YOU PICKED UP...
BY MISTAKE.
IT COULD... BE FITTING...
TO LOSE IT LIKE THIS.
THUD
GAK!
COUGH!
NGH...!
AH!
COUGH!
COUGH!

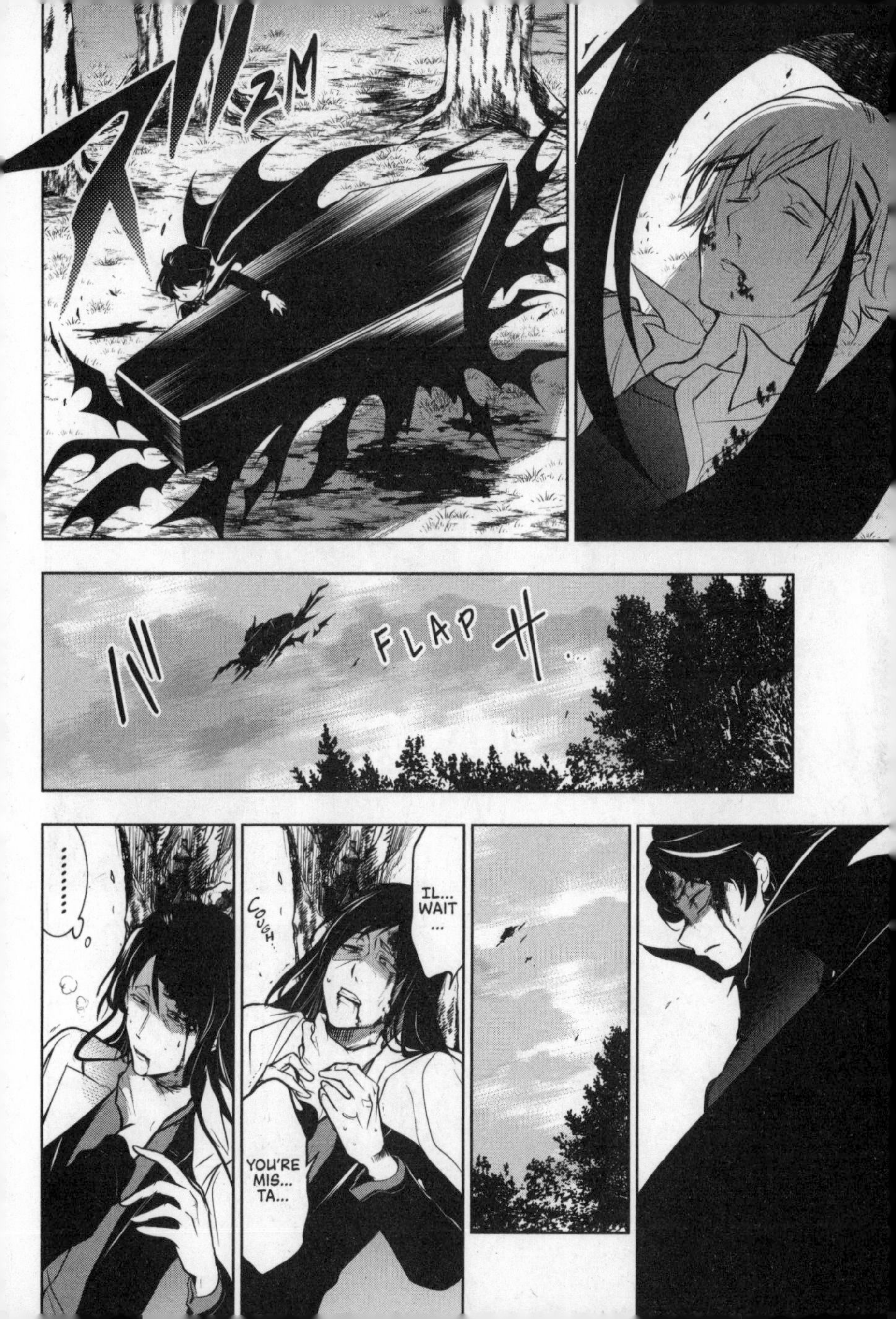
ZM
FLAP
IL... WAIT ...
COUGH...
YOU'RE MIS... TA...
......

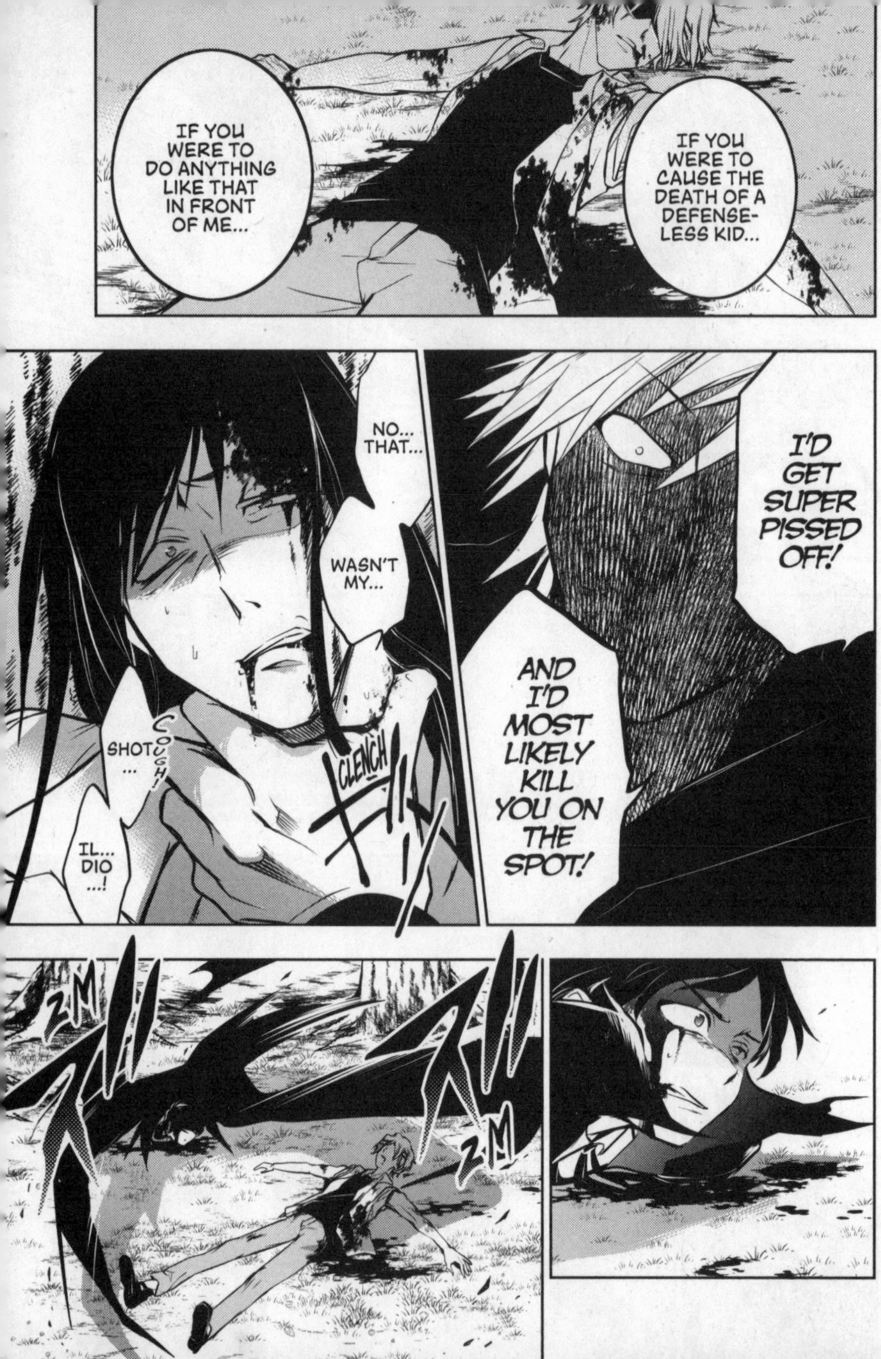
IF YOU WERE TO CAUSE THE DEATH OF A DEFENSE-LESS KID...
IF YOU WERE TO DO ANYTHING LIKE THAT IN FRONT OF ME...
I'D GET SUPER PISSED OFF!
AND I'D MOST LIKELY KILL YOU ON THE SPOT!
NO... THAT...
WASN'T MY...
CLENCH
SHOT...
COUGH!
IL... DIO ...!
ZM
ZM

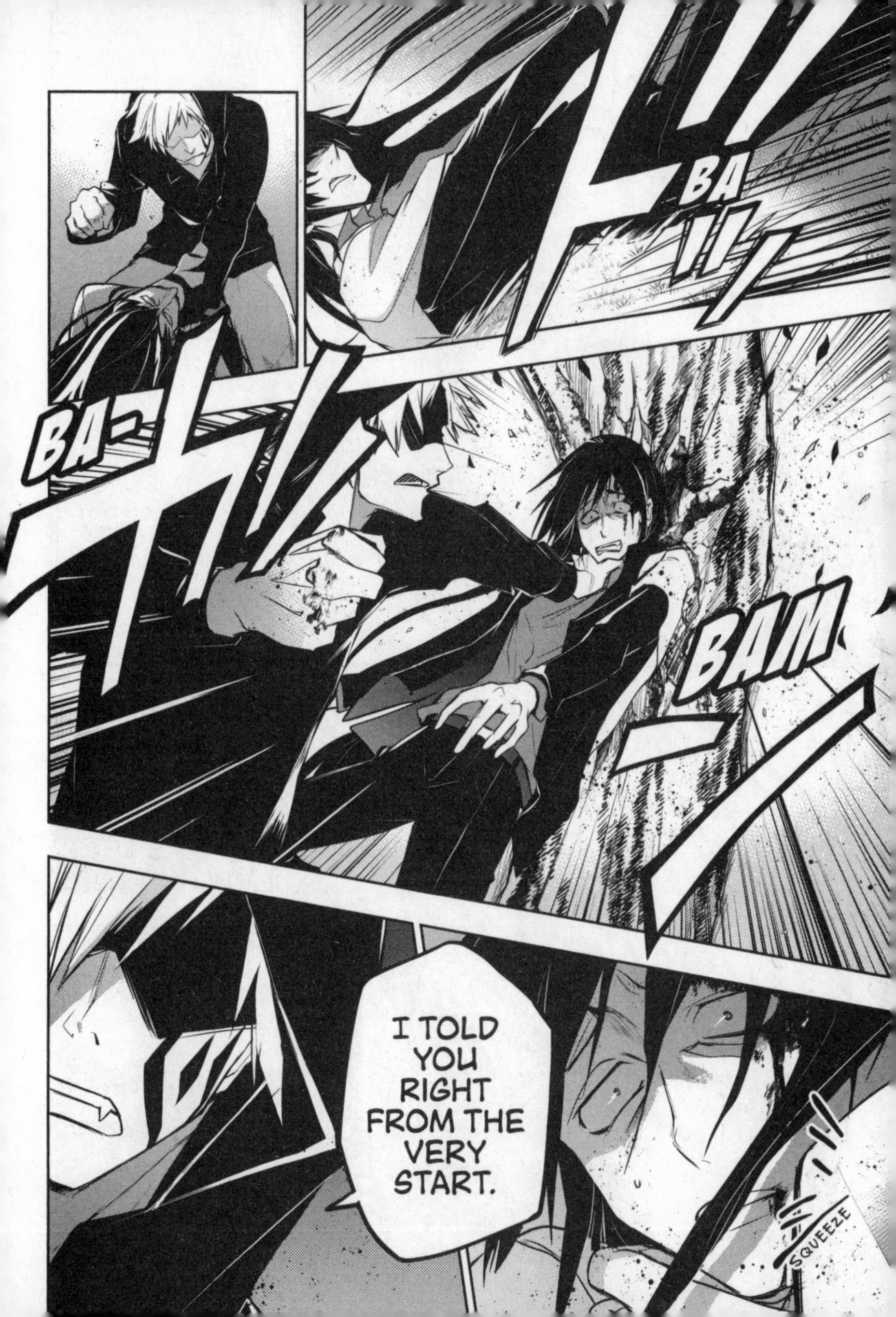
BA
BA-
BAM
I TOLD YOU RIGHT FROM THE VERY START.
SQUEEZE

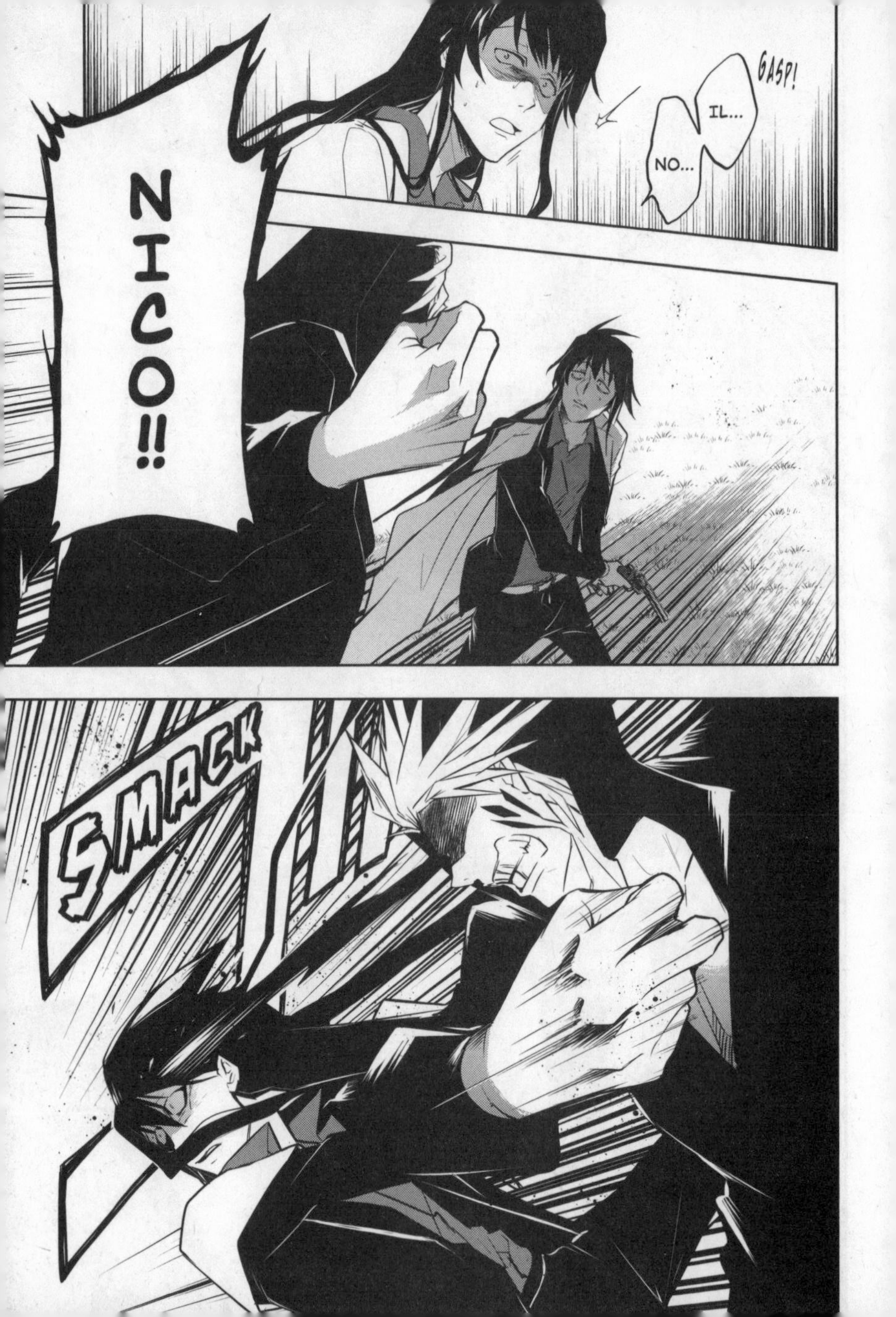
GASP!
IL... NO...
NICO!!
SMACK

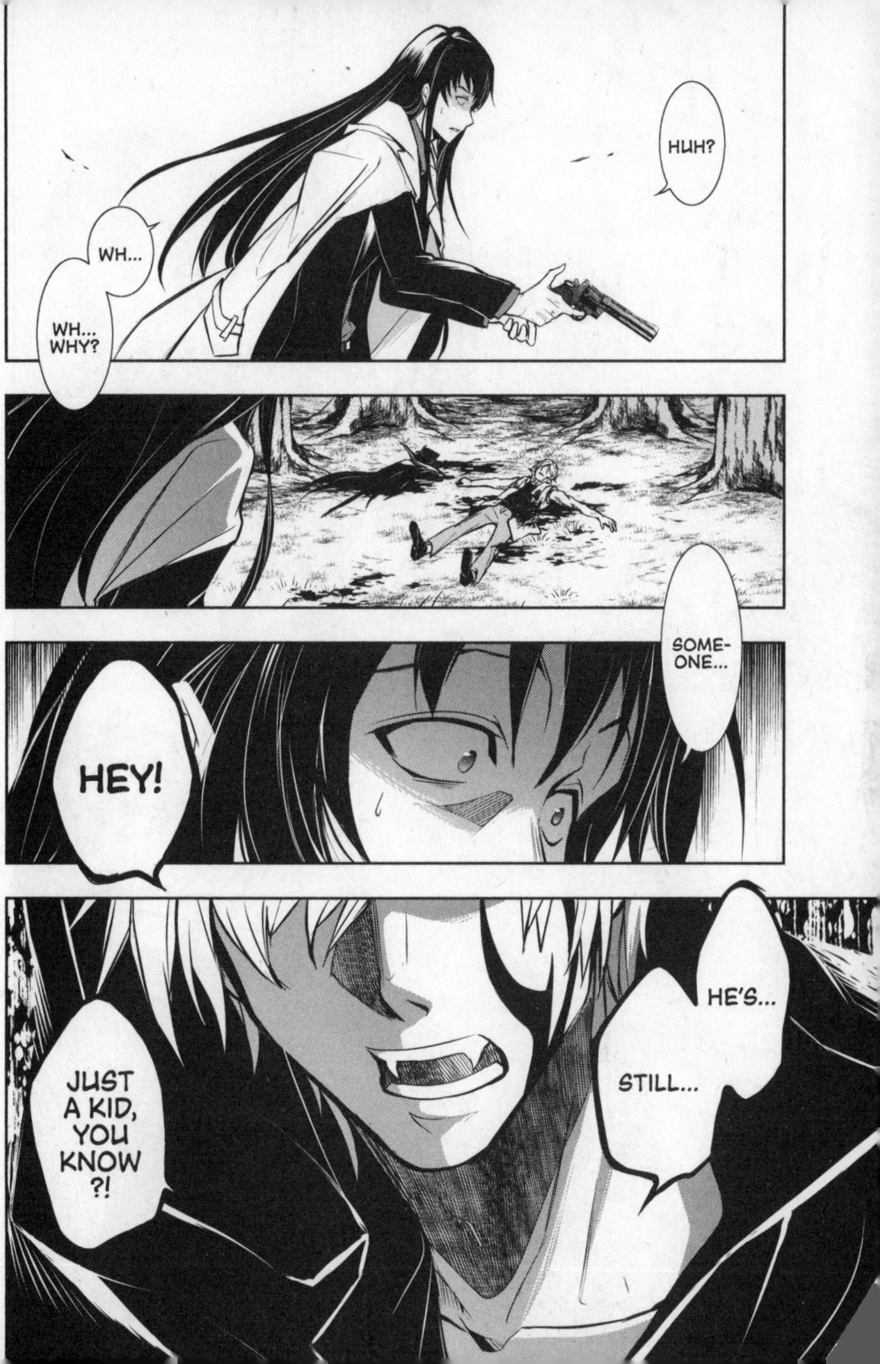
HUH?
WH...
WH... WHY?
SOME-ONE...
HEY!
HE'S...
STILL...
JUST A KID, YOU KNOW?!

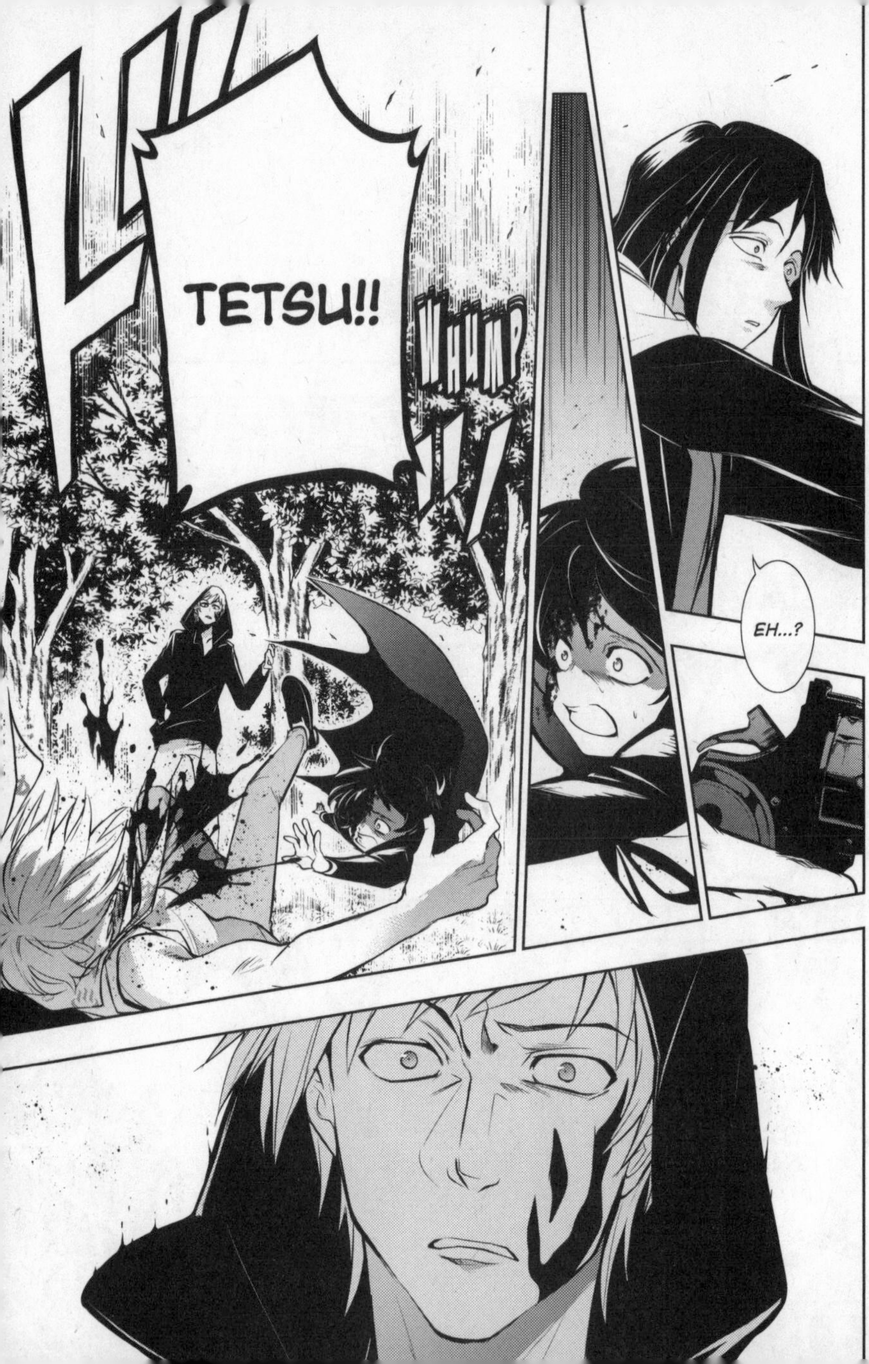
EH...?
TETSU!!
WHUMP

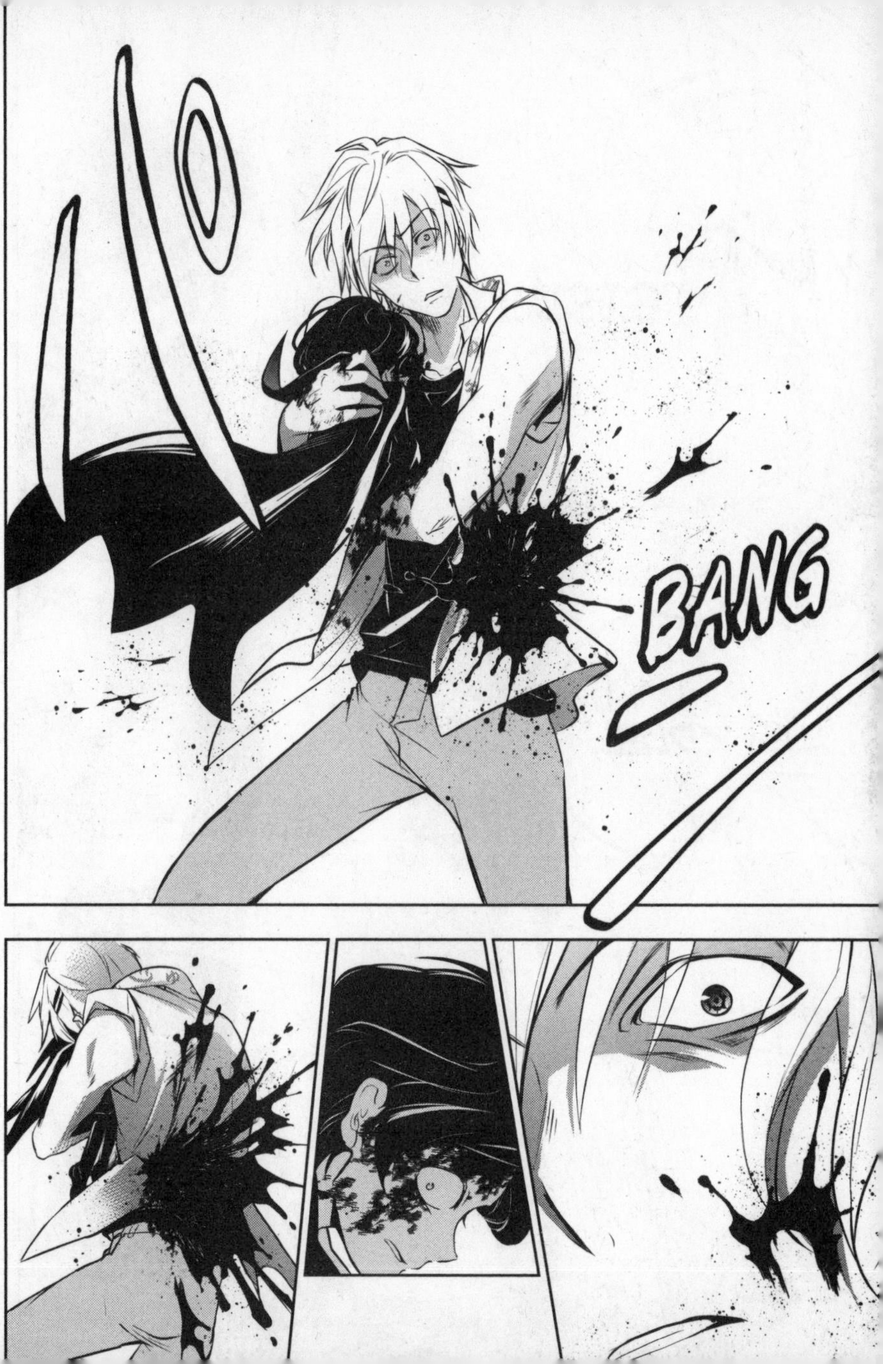
BANG

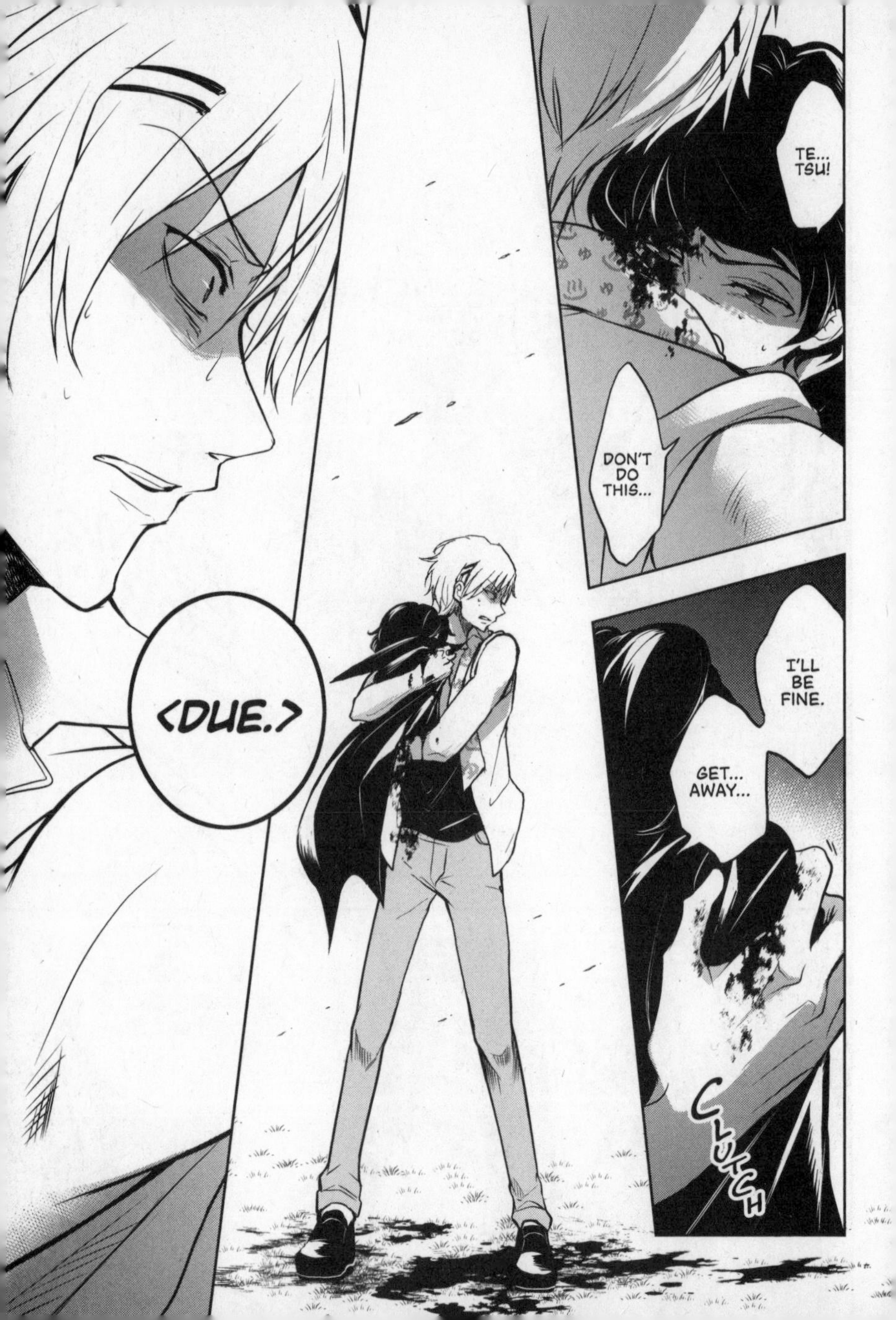
TE... TSU!
DON'T DO THIS...
I'LL BE FINE.
GET... AWAY...
CLUTCH
<DUE.>

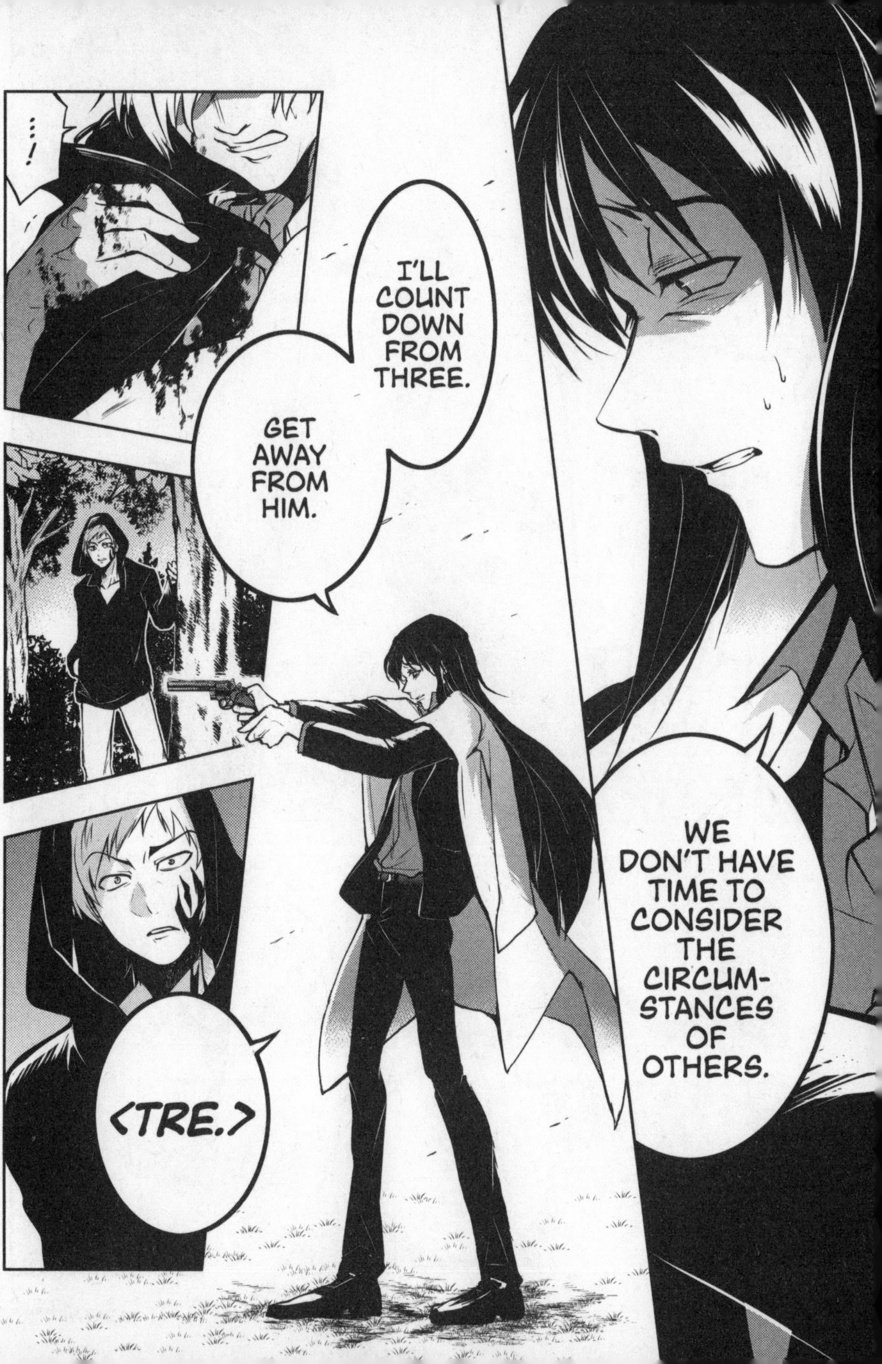
I'LL COUNT DOWN FROM THREE.
GET AWAY FROM HIM.
...!
WE DON'T HAVE TIME TO CONSIDER THE CIRCUMSTANCES OF OTHERS.
<TRE.>

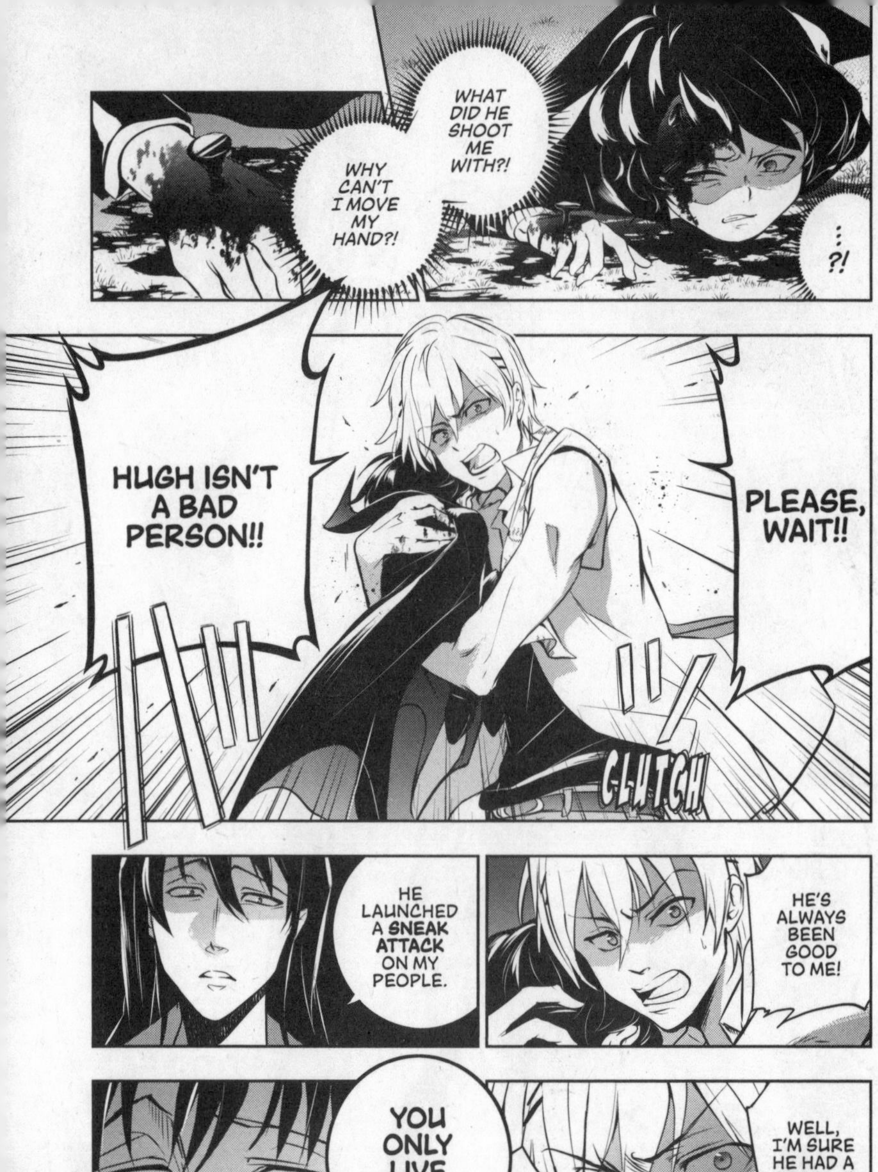
...?!
WHAT DID HE SHOOT ME WITH?!
WHY CAN'T I MOVE MY HAND?!
PLEASE, WAIT!!
CLUTCH
HUGH ISN'T A BAD PERSON!!
HE'S ALWAYS BEEN GOOD TO ME!
HE LAUNCHED A SNEAK ATTACK ON MY PEOPLE.
WELL, I'M SURE HE HAD A REASON!
SO--
YOU ONLY LIVE ONCE.

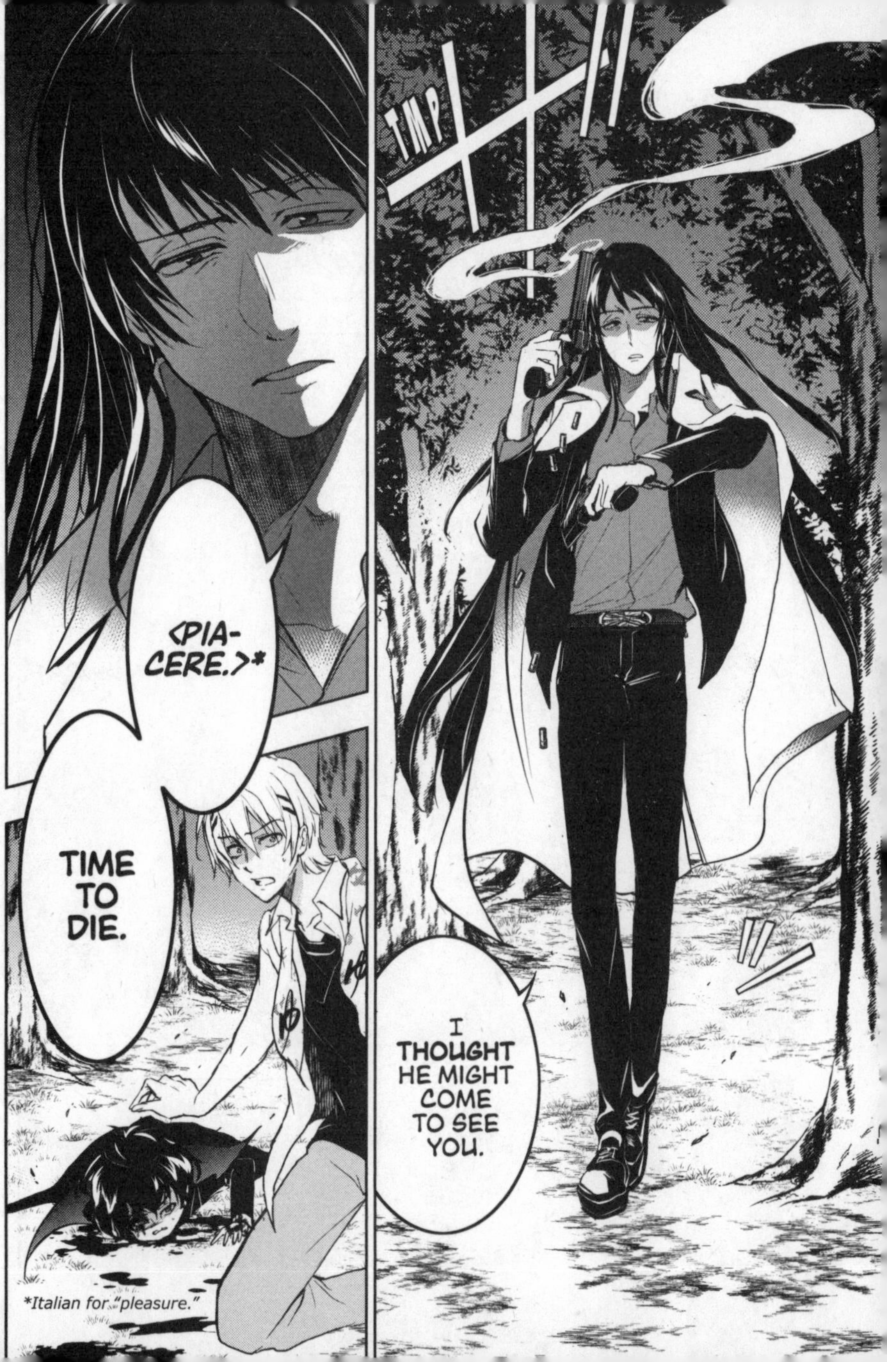
TMP
I THOUGHT HE MIGHT COME TO SEE YOU.
<PIA-CERE.>*
TIME TO DIE.
*Italian for "pleasure."

103 ISOLATED PAWN

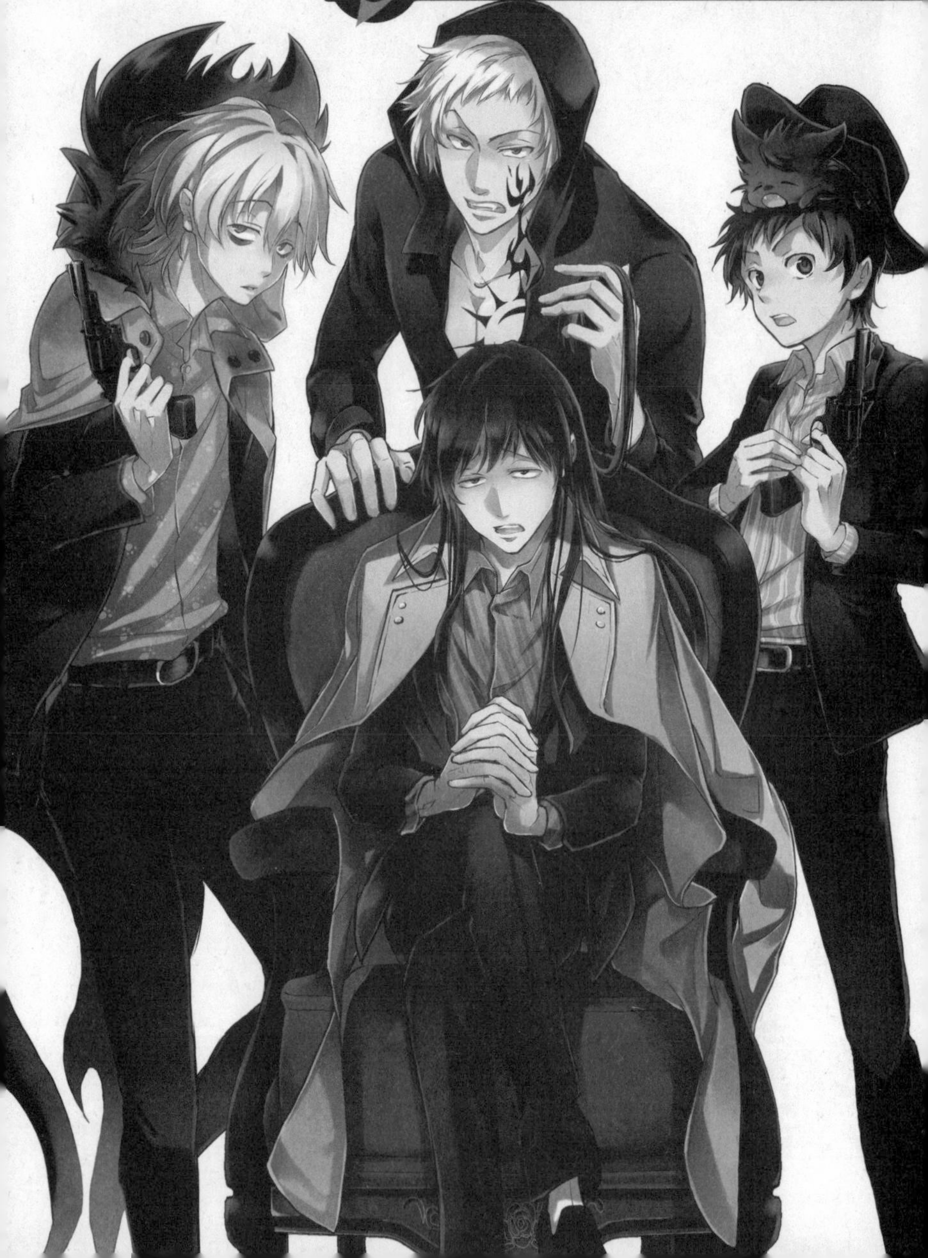

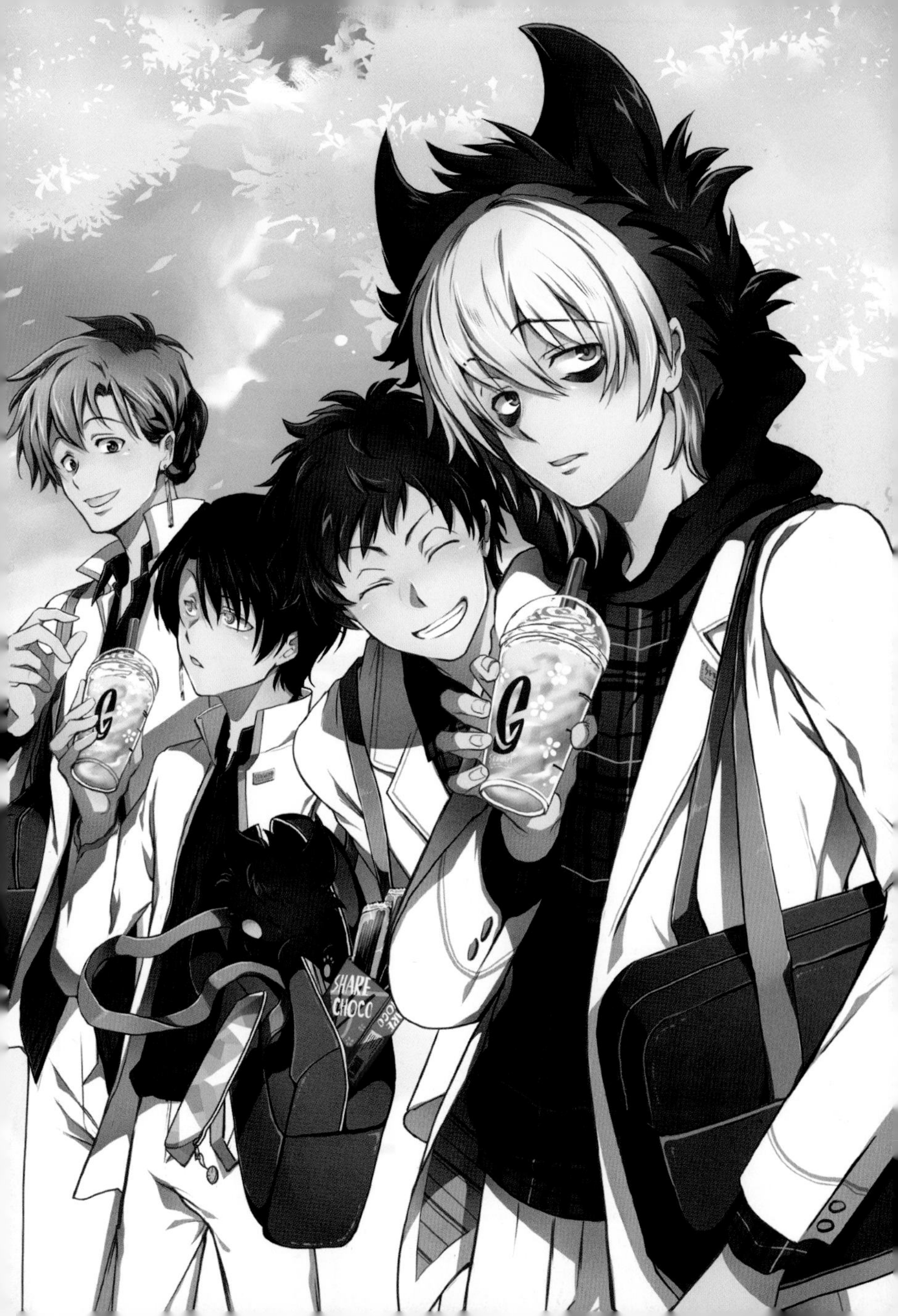
SHARE CHOCO

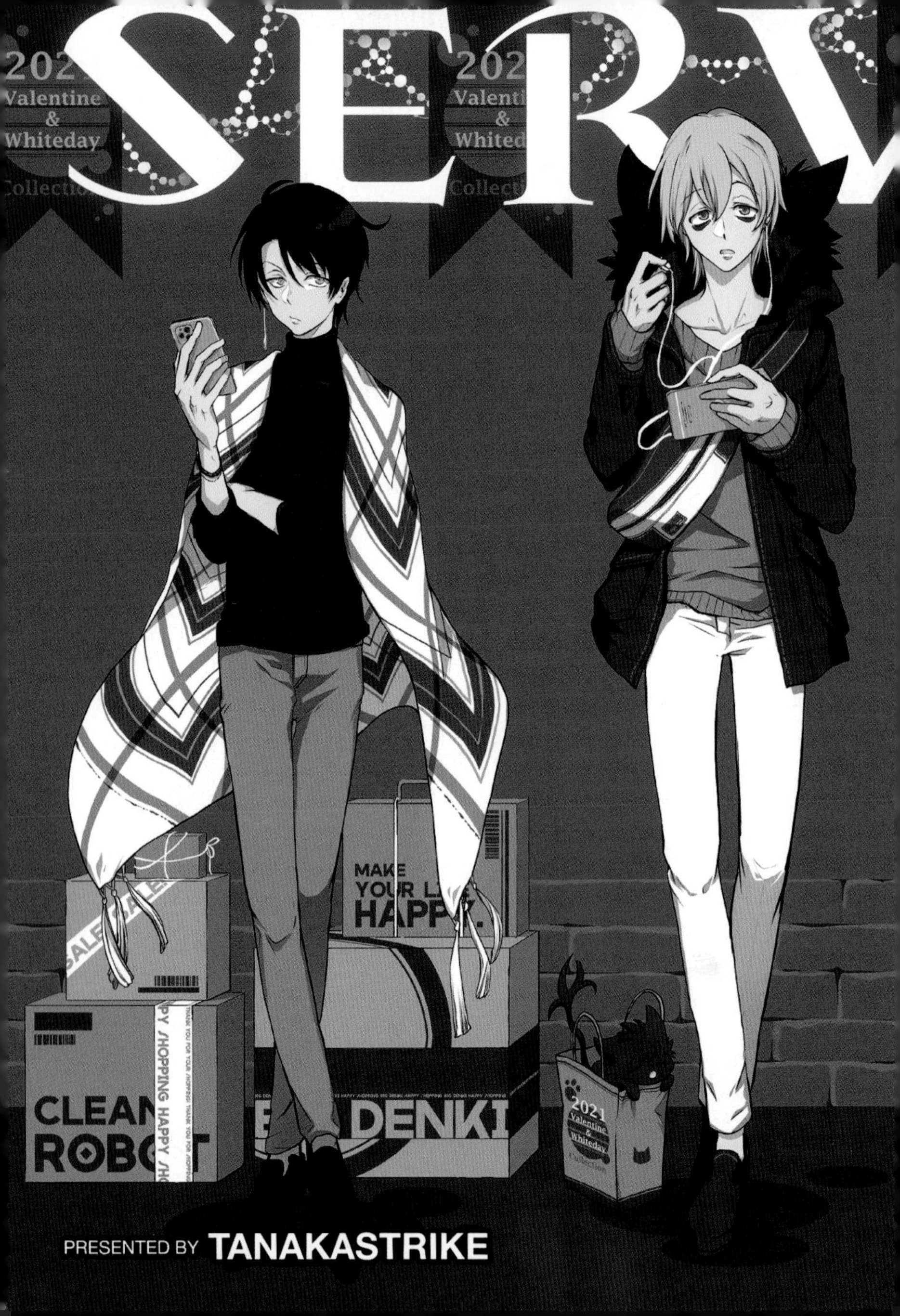
SERW
2021 Valentine & Whiteday Collection
MAKE YOUR LIFE HAPPY.
SALE SALE
THANK YOU FOR YOUR SHOPPING
HAPPY SHOPPING
CLEAN ROBOT
DENKI
2021 Valentine & Whiteday Collection
PRESENTED BY TANAKASTRIKE

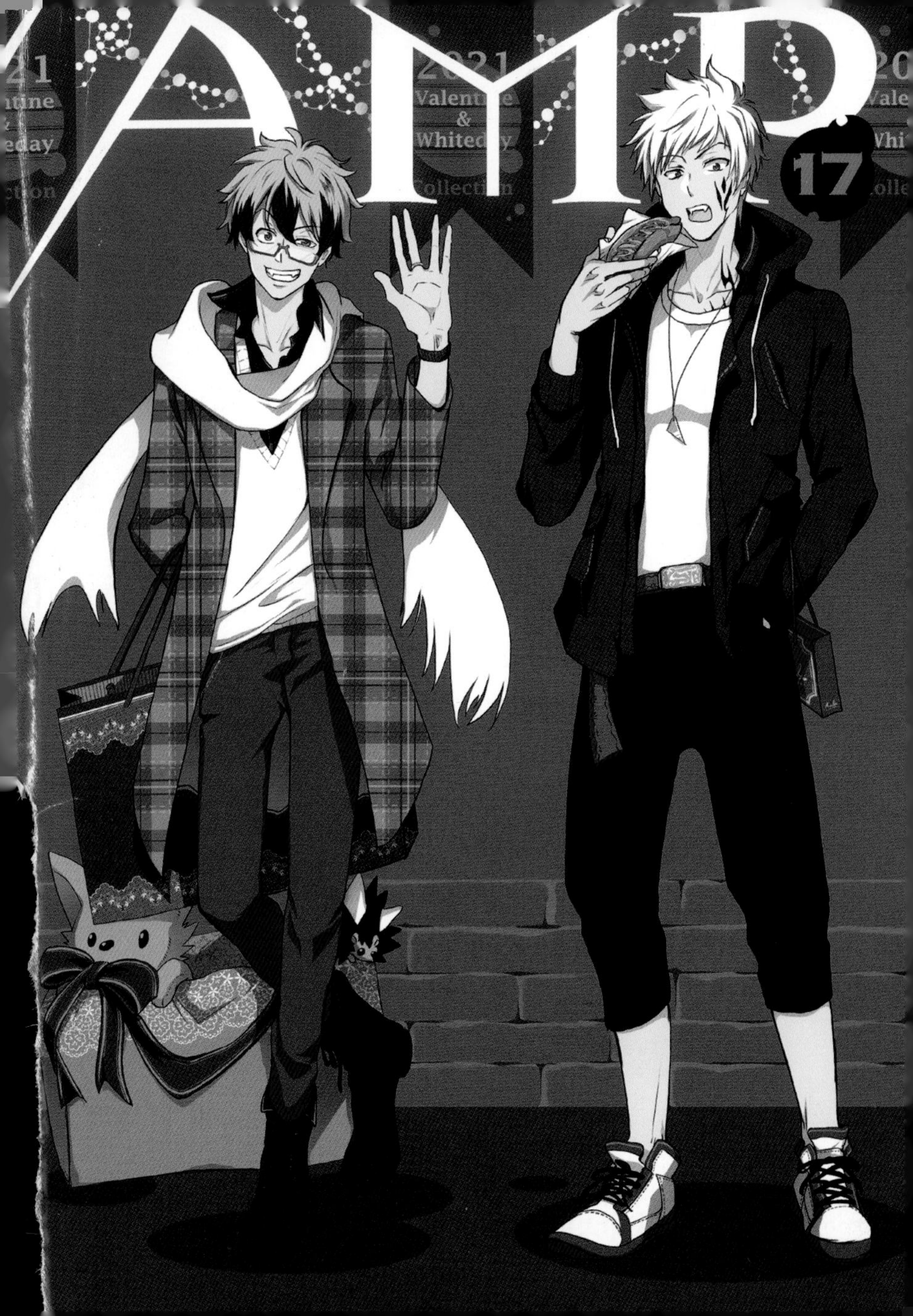
AMP
2021
Valentine
&
Whiteday
Collection
17

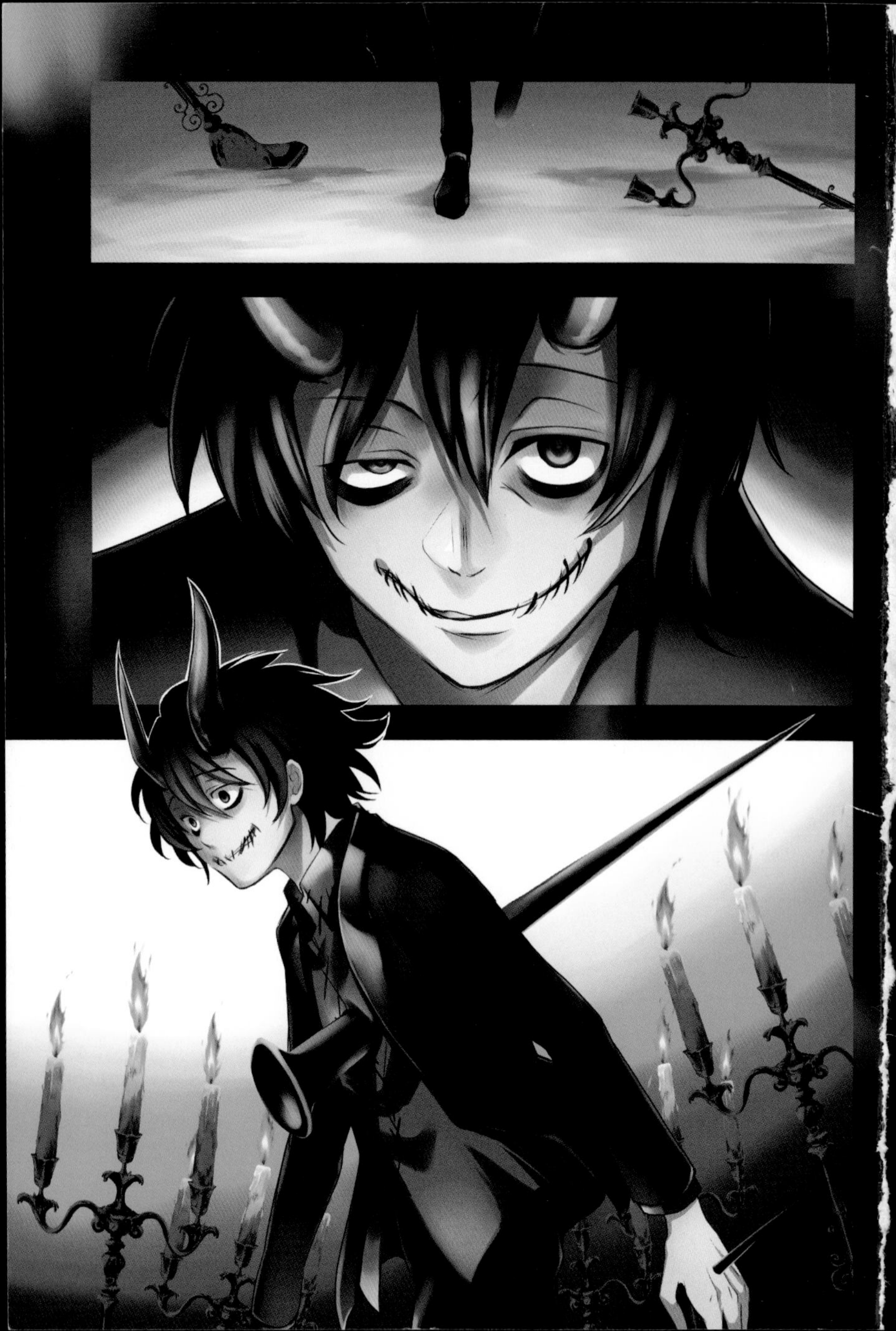